THE CLOSER

T0348676

THE CLOSER

A Novel

JASON SMITH

$|$ N, $|$ O₂ $|$ N,
CANADA

*Publisher's note: This book is a work of fiction. Names, characters, places and
incidents are either the product of the author's imagination or are used
fictitiously, and any resemblance to actual persons living or dead
is entirely coincidental.*

Library and Archives Canada Cataloguing in Publication

Title: The closer : a novel / Jason Smith.

Names: Smith, Jason (Novelist), author.

Identifiers: Canadiana 20220265941 | ISBN 9781989689417 (softcover)

Classification: LCC PS8637.M5632 C56 2022 | DDC C813/.6—dc23

Printed and bound in Canada on 100% recycled paper.

Now Or Never Publishing
901, 163 Street
Surrey, British Columbia
Canada V4A 9T8

nonpublishing.com
Fighting Words.

We gratefully acknowledge the support of the Canada Council for the Arts
and the British Columbia Arts Council for our publishing program.

For Anthony
Thanks for teaching me about baseball.

THE OFFSEASON

Casey rolled over, groped through the pile of clothing by the side of his bed for his phone, and got the thing to read the time by tapping its only button. It was only 5:53—an ungodly hour—yet there was somebody violently knocking on his front door, shouting for him to open up. He couldn't think of anyone who would be calling at this hour, not having had many visitors since he'd got out of the clinic and moved back to the city. Even his immediate family had been giving him the cold shoulder of late. He sat up and rubbed his eyes. Could it be somebody from *back then* calling about some debt he'd forgotten to repay? That seemed unlikely. As far as Casey knew, he was all squared up.

Nowadays, Casey was living on the level. When he'd got out of the clinic, his uncle Morris—who he'd always thought of as a lowlife creep—reached out, wanting to help Casey get back on his feet. Uncle Morris pulled a few strings at the private security firm he worked for and landed Casey his position as a night guard in a downtown condo building. There wasn't much to complain about: the work was relatively easy, paid better than minimum, and allowed him to mostly avoid contact with people who might know who he was.

The millions of dollars he'd received from the Cheesesteaks once upon a time were now long gone. Most of it had gone straight up his nose, and the rest spent on hookers and his beloved yellow Ferrari. Then there were the legal fees for the DUI last October. He'd totaled the car by wrapping it around a lightpost, nearly killed a pedestrian, and was now essentially penniless.

Unfortunately for Casey, October's incident had returned him to the public eye. The twattersphere had erupted in content relating to his near-death experience. His mugshot was posted all over the web, along with several cellphone photos taken by bystanders. It was such a big deal that it was common for people to recognize Casey in the street and hail him, usually by flipping him the bird or yelling that he ought to go die in a ditch. He couldn't leave his house in broad daylight without getting into some sort of altercation.

Casey was only too happy to work the night shift, when the people coming and going were usually too drunk to take much notice of him. An added perk was he could get away with doing nothing, which was about all he felt capable of at this moment. Mostly, he just fucked around on his phone, but occasionally he'd get up and walk around on 'patrol'. This was just an excuse for him to slip out to the rarely used guest parking lot and smoke a joint before wandering the hallways and pretending to look for signs of trouble.

Often, the only sounds he heard on patrol were his own footsteps. There was the occasional television, muffled by one of the heavy wooden doors. Sometimes he'd press his ear up against one and listen to whatever was pumping through the speakers on the other side. He'd catch snippets of the *Antiques Roadshow,* some nature program, and, occasionally, the heavy moaning and slapping of hardcore pornography.

On his days off, Casey only rarely left his apartment. It was a dingy one-bedroom in a lo-rise building. None of the surfaces were what could be called level or square. The floors and ceilings were so warped by age and moisture that they had started to sag in the middle, lending the rooms and corridors the feeling of a funhouse. A single lamp and his laptop's screen served as the room's only sources of light outside the dim grey haze that managed to seep through the cheap, plastic window coverings.

He spent most of his free time just sitting there on his living room couch, surfing the internet. He wasn't doing anything of much import: hitting the bong, tracking down old television shows he used to like as a kid, watching porn, and playing video games. He'd do all that until his eyeballs felt like they might just fall out of his head if he didn't stop right then and there. Then he'd stand up and amble over to the bedroom, hoping to get a few hours shuteye before he had to get up and go back to work.

Burying his head beneath his pillow wasn't enough to block out the knocking, especially now that his downstairs neighbours joined the fray. They pounded their ceiling with a broomhandle, screaming for him to *shut the fuck up!* The knocking showed no sign of stopping, so Casey got up, stumbled down the hall, leaned against the door, and peered through the fisheye lens of the viewer. There stood a short old man in a very fine suit beside a much younger and taller man combing back his hair before donning a chauffeur's hat.

"Whaddya want?" yelled Casey through the door, reaching for the bat he kept leaning in the corner for such occasions.

"We were just in the neighbourhood and thought we'd drop by," said the short man in what sounded like a British accent. "I've got a proposal I think you might be interested in."

"I'm not looking to buy anything," shouted Casey.

"That's good, because we aren't selling anything. Now would you please open the door? It seems we're causing a bit of a disturbance, yelling like this."

"How'd you get in?"

"An old lady let us in."

"Her name?"

"I didn't think to ask."

Casey chewed on his lip as he thought it over, then unlocked the deadbolt and opened the door to peek out, pulling the chain taut. The man on the other side was quick and slid his foot between the door and the jamb. "We'd just like to have the opportunity to speak with you for a few minutes if you don't mind, then we'll be on our merry way. May we come inside?"

"Are you Mormons or Jehovah's Witnesses or something?" said Casey, glancing down at the short man's foot and passing the bat from his left hand to his right so his guest could see it. "Or do I owe you money?"

"Heavens no!" said the man, looking perplexed. "Whatever made you think that?"

"No reason," said Casey as he unchained the door and swung it open. "Come in and take a seat. I'll give you ten minutes before I call the cops."

The two men stepped inside and crept over the carpet of dirty laundry and paper plates and unfinished dinners, plodding along until they had reached the living room. Casey made room on his armchair for his guest by sweeping away a pile of napkins that appeared absolutely *hardened*.

"Sit," Casey said, pointing to the chair with the bat, "and get to the part where you tell me who the fuck you are."

The short man inspected the seat before taking it and attempted to get comfortable before responding to Casey's demand. "My name is Don. Don Billingsley."

"Is that name supposed to mean anything to me?"

Don held up one finger, reached into his blazer, and pulled out his business card, which read:

DON BILLINGSLEY
PRESIDENT OF BASEBALL OPERATIONS AND GENERAL MANAGER
TORONTO BLUE BIRDS

"What's all this about, Mr. Billingsley?"

"My friends call me Don. Please, take a seat," said Don, gesturing towards Casey's soiled couch. Without exactly knowing why he was following this tiny man's instructions, Casey sat down and reached for the ashtray on the nearby end-table. He sparked up a half-finished joint that had been resting on its lip using one of the many lighters scattered around his apartment.

"I'm going to tell you right now that if this is about me playing baseball, I ain't interested."

"Come now, how can you not be interested?"

Casey shrugged. "I've retired."

"My boy, you haven't retired. You're barely twenty-four! You're in your prime."

"Well, it sure was nice of you to come down here, Mr…"

"Billingsley."

"Mr. Billingsley. I mean, you could've timed it better, but it's nice of you to come down all the same. The thing is, I'm just not that interested. All I've ever gotten out of baseball is a headache."

"And a few million dollars," said the chauffeur, rolling his eyes.

"Remind me of your name again," said Casey, pointing the bat at the chauffeur.

"His name's Tom," said Don, casting a severe glance at his companion. "And if he values his position, that's the last we'll be hearing from Tom today."

"It's alright," said Casey, exhaling a hit. "I mean, he's got a point. At one time I was a millionaire, but there ain't any millions anymore."

"Well, you know the cliché, 'if at first you don't succeed,' etcetera, etcetera."

There was a moment of silence as Casey ghosted a hit, letting a tongue of smoke slip between his lips before pulling it back in through his nostrils. If Don was perturbed by Casey's smoking, he showed no sign.

"Point of my saying that," Casey said, coughing and placing the joint on the ashtray, "is that I've had my fill, both of money and baseball. Neither did the trick, you know what I mean?"

"My boy, I'm afraid it's you who didn't do the trick."

"Yeah? Well, maybe, but then why are you coming here wearing a swanky suit and flashing me your card? Do you normally pay people house calls?"

"You know perfectly well why I'm here."

"Yeah, but it's starting to become a real mystery why you and your lackey over here are still hanging around after I've already given you my firm answer."

"What answer was that?"

"I'm pretty sure I told you to fuck off."

"I must admit I'm rather confused. Here I am offering you a lifeline and you're throwing it back? Tut tut. Don't be foolish."

"I already told you: I've retired. I'm done. I was probably no good in the first place and now, believe me, I'm definitely no good."

"The numbers say otherwise," said Don, pulling a fat brown envelope from his breast pocket and placing it down on the cluttered coffee table. "I see value—at the right price, of course."

"Oh yeah? Where's it at? Nobody else seems to see any."

"If everybody else saw your value, I wouldn't be here. I've been burned too many times over the years getting into bidding wars. For me it's all the better if nobody else wants you. What I like is that the numbers say you can catch the ball."

"So can practically anyone else."

"I'm going to level with you," said Don. "I've got particular reasons for wanting a player who won't miss baseballs and I've been shopping around for one since the end of October. I have a number of pitchers who require... let's just call it 'special attention'. You have you heard of Phil Reardon, haven't you? Surely you have."

"Phil Reardon?" asked Casey, trying to recall. "The name rings a bell. Should I have heard of him?"

"No, no, it makes no difference, no difference at all. None at all!" said Don, smiling. "But you're starting to sound like you're interested."

"I'm not, but now that you've dropped his name, maybe you wouldn't mind explaining who this Phil Reardon is."

Don let out a sigh. "Oh, he's just my problem child. A great pitcher. A *great* pitcher, but he's a little... what's the word? High maintenance. He likes things done his way. The kind way of putting it is that he's a real believer in gamesmanship. I've also got a need for someone who can handle the knuckleball."

"I've never caught a knuckleballer in my life!"

"The numbers suggest that you might have what it takes. You know how many passed balls you've allowed over the past two seasons?"

"Not off the top of my head."

"Three. Three! Remarkable, considering you were allegedly coked out of your head most of the time. Wouldn't you agree?"

"So what? You're going to bring me in just to catch those two starters?"

"Reardon isn't a starter. He's the team's closer. The other one? We'll see how the chips fall."

"Wait, so you'd be bringing me in just to catch the closer?"

"I have got the other project in mind, but you would mostly be working with Reardon."

"You must be out of your fucking mind, pal. I've never heard of a closer with a personal catcher."

"There's a first time for everything," said Don. "In this case, he's worth it."

"How the fuck can he be worth that?"

"Because there's nothing more valuable than a sure thing, and that's what I've got in Phil Reardon. Well?"

"Why didn't you call my agent?"

"My boy, you don't even *have* an agent, remember? I phoned Liam, and he said you told him to get lost months ago."

Casey was silent.

"Well?"

"Not interested. I've got too much going on to go and fuck it up now."

Don threw up his hands. "But you don't even know the terms!"

"Not interested."

Don stood up and looked around the room. His gaze finally reconnected with Casey's and he said, "Well, I should've known after entering your little... abode. I'm clearly barking up the wrong tree. Let me be the first to say that it really looks like you've got your shit together, Casey. Far be it from me to mess it up with a golden ticket."

"What? You think I care about money? I don't care about money. I've been rich and found that it makes no difference to me either way. It all ends up the same."

"Yes, yes, of course! Money is worthless! Money is the root of all evil. Silly me, for thinking you would be better off playing ball for my club then skulking about in here feeling sorry for yourself. Now, I'm afraid you've aroused my curiosity. How many people have you entertained in this lovely little hovel of yours?"

"If you're going to insult me, you can get the fuck out," said Casey, pointing towards the door with the bat. "I want you out of here right fucking now, or I swear to God I'll call the cops."

"Listen," said Don, reaching out and placing his hand on Casey's shoulder.

"Don't fucking touch me!" shouted Casey, shoving the hand away.

"Listen," said Don again, this time holding his hands out in front of him. "What I'm offering isn't just a contract. In fact, the best part isn't even money."

"What could you possibly offer me besides money, you vulture?"

"Redemption," said Don. "Redemption in the eyes of the game. Or, at least, redemption in the eyes of those that matter to the game."

"Why the hell would I want that?"

"Because the game has this way of taking care of its own. Suppose you come back now that you're clean and sober and you give it your all. If you can prove that you belong, that you're willing to learn, then maybe—later on—all your troubles work themselves out. Things have a way of falling into place. Past transgressions can be forgiven."

"And then what?"

"I'll let you fill in the blank," said Don as he typed something into his phone. "Anyhow, you have my offer. It's a minor league deal, but if you make the team it becomes a one-year Big League contract, guaranteed. The door's open if you want to step through it. And I should say, that if I were you, as soon as we're out of sight, I'd make a phone call to my former agent and tell him we've got a contract to sign."

"Listen, Mr…"

"Billingsley."

"Mr. Billingsley. Don't you know that everyone hates my guts?"

"That's all in your head," said Don, standing up and walking to the door. "But there is one more thing I should mention before I go."

"What's that?"

"Part of your—let's call them duties—part of your duties would be to keep an eye on our troublesome friend. You could do that for me, couldn't you?"

"Is that in the contract?"

Don had to laugh as his brooklands green Rolls Royce pulled away from Casey's building. The boy thought Don would care that the internet hated him, but Don couldn't have cared less. As far as the Blue Birds' President was concerned, likeability was the new market inefficiency, and he was in the perfect position to capitalize on it. Many of his peers griped about the meddling of ownership in player acquisition. There was a reticence on the part of the owners to take on any sort of character risk due to the times being such that the smallest of personal foibles were liable to be dragged out into the open for the mob to hack to pieces. Meanwhile, Don had just picked up a first-round talent—with years of control—for the Big League minimum, just because the kid had some makeup issues for which he had received treatment.

The Blue Birds' President set about answering the emails remaining in his inbox. He had managed to get quite a bit of work done while making his pitch to Casey, so he was able to finish with his communications before he reached the next stop on what was a jam-packed morning itinerary.

Steele's condo was out in the West End, not far from Don's place. It was the penthouse of a factory loft and featured floor-to-ceiling, single-panel windows where the old, lead-lined ones used to be. There were hardly any interior walls, and the few it had were exposed brick or white-primed Sheetrock. All the furniture was either black or red. The floors were made of rugged yellow hardwood, partially covered with shag carpet and a variety of animal skins.

Don was sitting on an Italian leather sofa checking his messages while Steele stood behind the kitchen island pouring a glass of water he proceeded to drink with abandon. He was still wearing his running gear on account of Don having ambushed him at the front door.

"To what do I owe the pleasure?" asked Steele as he refilled the glass.

"I was in the neighbourhood and thought I'd stop in. I don't live too far from here."

"Where you at?"

"Oh, just a little northeast—St. Clair and Bathurst. The Commodore."

"I've been up that way. Nice digs."

"I do alright."

"Me too. It does seem strange, though, don't it?"

"What exactly?"

"That here you are, Don Billingsley, showing up at my door just after eight in the morning. I never knew you made house calls."

"I thought I'd try out a new approach. Consider this the new, friendlier Don Billingsley."

"I like the sound of it, way better than what I've heard some people been callin' you."

"You'd be better off not reading the news. It's full of nonsense."

"Who said I read it in the news?" said Steele, walking over and sitting in the chair opposite Don. "Who's got time for that shit? Social media, that's where the pulse is at. But let's cut the chit-chat. We both know why you're here, so let's just get on with it and talk business."

"I've spoken with Larry up in corporate and he said the big boys upstairs are willing to increase my budget so we can up the offer by another year to bring it to four."

Eddie looked down at his glass. "And how much money does that take us to."

"The offer I'd hypothetically be putting on the table is four years for eighty-eight-point-five million."

"Now, did you just say eighty-eight-point-five million?"

"Yes."

"Eighty-eight million," said Steele, whistling. "Them's a lot of zeroes."

"Let's not forget that half million. I think we can all agree it's a fairly ample offer."

"Well, you see, that's just the issue," said Steele, setting the glass down on the coffee table, "because we don't all agree. You see, my agent thinks that when I hit the market at the end of this season, I'll be worth a hell of a lot more than that."

"So he's told me."

"Has he told you the number?"

"He said four hundred million."

"Four. Hundred. Million. Dollars. My word! That is a hell of a lot of money, ain't it? I might even be able to move my ass out of this dump if I get that sort of payday, and, with the way things are headed, I will probably have to."

"Sadly, that may be the case. Corporate would never approve that much."

"They might if I have another monster season like this last one, and you can bet your sweet, fat ass that's just what I plan to do. I'll make it so they think they've gotta sign me or else they'll wind up losing revenue. Suppose I go and win that Silver Slammer again this year, what's it gonna look like if they let me walk? Pretty fuckin' ugly if you ask me."

Don cleared his throat. "You may not find the market as hospitable as you expect."

"Why, because you're going to hit me with a qualifying offer? You see, it's all been explained to me, Mr. Billingsley."

"You have to understand, the team's objectives come first. Let me assure you that from a front office's perspective that lost draft pick is a serious deterrent."

"Only if you're a smalltime, nickel-and-dime club like this here Blue Birds organization. You think your qualifying offer's gonna stop the Sams or Rebels from getting better? Naw, somehow, I don't think it will be much of an issue. I'm young, haven't had many injuries, have a track record, and a player like me doesn't come around too often. I'll be damned if I can't do no better than eighty-eight."

"Eighty-eight and a half." Don looked around. "Well, maybe at the end of the season we'll be able to put together a better deal."

"Maybe we can and maybe we can't, but if you're expecting a discount it's better to pony up now than later. You see, four hundred million is where the bidding starts. But shit, it doesn't matter anyway, since you probably won't be the one getting me to put pen to paper, even if I do re-sign. You know what I'm saying?"

"I'm afraid I don't. Why on earth wouldn't I be the one to do that?"

"The way I understand it, the fans around here—and the media—they're all sick of you. How long have you been on the job? Five years?"

"Six."

Steele sucked his teeth. "Damn! That is a long time, isn't it, Mr. Billingsley? And you've upped payroll, what, like fifty million?"

"Somewhere around that number. But really, we were just keeping up with inflation."

Steele's lips shrunk to a line. "You see that there? That there's called an excuse. I wonder what sort of excuse would get me off the hook if I was doing my job as poorly as you've been doing yours. I could go around telling people I'd been playing hurt, or my dog died, or some other such bullshit. Do you think anyone would give a fuck? *Hell* no."

"You certainly are in bad spirits, Eddie. Perhaps I caught you at a bad time? We should continue these discussions later. This has been a good ice-breaker."

"There won't be another time. Let me let you in on a little secret, Mr. Billingsley: I don't like it here in Toronto. Don't get me wrong, the city is alright. It's the team I can't stand. It would be one thing if we just lost all the time, but the truth is we ain't even good enough to suck. We're just mediocre and never get no better or no worse. No matter what tricks you go and pull out of your hat in the offseason, we still end up the same."

"If you've got some solution at hand for me, Eddie, I'm all ears."

"Fuck if I know what you should do with the clusterfuck you've created here, but I can sure as shit tell you what you've gone and done wrong. You see, what you've gone and done is taken a prize stallion," said Steele, indicating himself, "hitched him up with twenty-five mules, and called it a team. It's like a bad joke."

"I didn't realize your eight wins were such a meaningful contribution."

"That's just it—they weren't. That's the problem, dig? I should've been the MVP last year, but because our team was garbage, I hardly got any votes."

"I can see this is getting personal," said Don, typing something into his phone and standing up. "Perhaps I should go."

"Let me assure you, Mr. Billingsley, this is the furthest thing from personal. It's strictly business, baby."

"If it's strictly business then what has all this been about? All this stallion nonsense! I know that agent of yours has filled your head with that four hundred million number, but what I'm offering you is a solid deal and guaranteed money. You play as well as you've played up until now and you could be looking at hitting the market at the youthful age of thirty-one. Maybe then you'll looking at four hundred million. That's where salaries are headed, but we aren't there yet."

"Look," said Steele, "you're right. It'd be smart to get some decent cash now and then earn a beefier contract later. Hell, maybe I really would get four hundred million four years from now. Who knows? But suppose that somewhere in the next four years I go and break my leg, or rip up my shoulder, or any of the various other things that can happen to a body out there on the diamond. Then I'm looking at your eighty-eight and a half and I'm spitting on it. It's all been explained to me, see. I've got three things going for me right now: I'm under thirty, I'm good, and I haven't been hurt. I know for a fact I'd get way more than that out there on the open market, so when you offer me eighty-eight and a half million, it's a lowball offer. Frankly, it's an insulting offer because Riley just got that and he's coming off a season where he was one of the worst pitchers in the Big Leagues."

"That's pitching. It's a different market entirely."

"Now, I know y'all value things differently up there in your front office, but you know what that says to me? That says to me that you think I'm worth the same amount as Ben fucking Riley. And that? That feels like a slap in the face."

"Be reasonable. This is guaranteed money, Eddie. A lot of it, I might add."

"But see, the issue is the cabbage can only take you so far. I mean, let's be honest here: who *needs* four hundred million dollars? I've already got a sweet ride and a swag condo and all the clothes and food I could want, I bought my momma a property out near Cooperstown, so I know she's all set up for when I get into the hall. Don't got children, wasn't planning on having any. What the fuck does a man like me need four hundred million dollars for?"

"Heavens, I don't know. Amusements?"

"Do I look like I'm the sort of brother who's into *amusements*? I want that four hundred million so the people have something to talk about. They can go on and on about how I've gone and got myself paid. When people see me out in the street, I want them to say, 'There goes Eddie Steele: four hundred million dollar man.' The other thing I want them to say is, 'There goes Eddie Steele: Globe Series champion.' I'm not playing for no charity and I'm not playing to lose, so don't blame me if the Sams offer me the chance to win and the opportunity to get paid while I'm doing it. Don't be mad. It's strictly business, baby. I thought that's what you was all about."

The tires of the plane squealed as they made high-speed contact with the runway. The jolt of the fuselage woke Casey up with a start from his seat, 13E, where he sat wedged between two rather obese men in golf shirts, whose sweat-stained armpits made the recycled air rank. As the plane approached the terminal,

Casey rifled through the duotang in which he'd been carrying his travel documents. Along with the ticket, his passport, and a travel itinerary, there was a manual he'd been forwarded a few days after he had signed the contract. There was a list of the suggested travel items, a list of things he should avoid carrying over the border (cocaine had been noted in bold), and a sheet of paper with the hotel's contact information. Whoever compiled this document had felt obliged to include *ROOMMATE: PHILLIP REARDON.*

In truth, Casey had not even bothered to read the thing before his departure, and now that he was seated here in 13E, perusing it while waiting for the seatbelt light to turn off, he began to wonder if he made the wrong decision in coming here. He looked back down at the page and read the name to himself again and again, as if by lingering over these four syllables he might discover some clue as to his own fate. There came a strange gasping sound and then the bing of the seatbelt light. Now the pilot's voice crackled over the intercom system and informed the passengers that it was safe to unfasten their belts and stand up. He hoped they had a pleasant flight, and that they would all fly with the airline again in the near future.

The siren over the baggage claim briefly droned and a few seconds later bags started sliding onto the conveyer belt. Casey was relieved his bag was one of the first down the chute, but this small pleasure quickly dissipated when he approached the line for customs. They'd screened him before he boarded the aircraft, but a number of bomb attacks that had taken place in Europe over the past few weeks had caused the Department of Homeland Security to double down on their screening procedures and perform a second interview upon arrival. Before Casey could utter a word to the bored looking man in the kevlar vest, a gentleman wearing a navy airport uniform and powder blue vinyl gloves materialized, grabbed hold of Casey's elbow, and instructed him to come along. He was led through a door that provided access to areas restricted to *Airport Staff Only*, a privilege Casey suspected he was better off without.

Where they were now was hard to say, but Casey knew that they had to be somewhere deep in the bowels of the terminal on account of the total absence of natural light. The man in blue led Casey first down one hallway and then another, until finally the labyrinth emptied out into a large room. Here, a number of glass enclosures stood vacant, their interiors dark except for the one whose open maw Casey was compelled to enter. Somehow, all his equipment had already been conveyed here, and in the middle of the booth they had a large table on which another man in blue was busy unloading all of Casey's gear. The notes of the man in blue's voice were muted by the walls.

They wanted to know if he'd brought any narcotics with him and they were very thorough in their examination. The man on the other side of the table swept each of Casey's possessions with one of those wands used to detect explosives. Each time he was finished with an object he would rip the swab off the wand and put it into the machine, which deliberated for a few moments before deciding to turn on the green light to indicate the object was clear. There was, of course, a red light that would indicate a positive and Casey watched in horror each time they inserted the sample pad, even though he knew he was clean. Next, they took his belongings out and examined them for any contraband. The whole time this was happening, a man in full tactical regalia stood in the corner of the enclosure with a semi-automatic rifle pointed directly at the back of Casey's head. It was a relief when they finally left him to repack his things.

The airport taxi Casey got into happened to be a Crown Vic with a yellow leather interior. The front windows were already rolled down, so Casey asked the driver if he was waiting for somebody, or if he was taking fares. The driver explained that he had been waiting for one for the past twenty minutes and was finished waiting, so Casey got into the car.

"Where did you wanna go, man?"

Casey explained that he had a room reserved at the Holiday Inn Express in Dunedin.

The man mulled over this information a moment, adjusting his rearview mirror. His eyes met Casey's in the reflection. "You with the team?"

"Yes."

"Man, you should have said so," said the driver as he started the car.

They were now accelerating onto the freeway entrance ramp and the engine noise was ferocious. Its pitch climbed and lowered with the driver's frequent gear changes. They flew with bowel-melting speed across the Courtney Campbell Causeway, the driver shooting the Crown Vic through the very smallest of gaps in the weekday evening traffic while Casey clenched his teeth and gripped the assist handle for dear life. The world outside was nothing but a smeared neon blur. Casey glanced at the speedometer and immediately regretted it, seeing the hand on the dial nudging just past the bar that read one hundred and ten. There was a jolt as the car hit a bump in the pavement and a feeling of weightlessness that seemed to last forever as Casey watched the beaded rosary hanging from the rearview mirror float sideways. The car came down hard on the pavement, its whole suspension whining with the effort of keeping the thing from bottoming out.

The one hope that kept Casey from jumping out onto the causeway right then and there was that the driver might slow down when they entered Dunedin proper, which he did, but not by much. He approached each corner at impossible speed, flicking out the tail of the car as he rounded them, leaving the vehicle in a moment of wobbly indecision before straightening into its new direction. The bright green sign of the Holiday Inn rose over the black silhouettes of rooftops against the Day-Glo sky. Soon they were swinging into its drive, tires screeching from the heavy braking. Casey nearly face-planted into the passenger seat as the car came to a stop. A bellboy walked up to the Crown Vic and shouted, "Andres!" as he fist-bumped the driver through the open window.

Andres turned around with a smile and said, "That will be forty-five."

By the time Casey wandered over to the curbside ashtray and started vomiting into it, the bellboy had already taken his bags out of the trunk. He asked, "Would you like me to take these upstairs for you?"

Before Casey could reply, he was interrupted by the driver, who called to him, saying, "Hey, kid!"

Casey turned around.

"Do Andres a favour. If you see that good for nothing sonofabitch Reardon, tell him he still owes Andres four hundred dollars for the last time."

"What?" said Casey, but Andres had already put his foot down and was as good as gone. The roar of the Crown Vic receded into the distance until no sound remained but the squawking of the gulls, the laughing of people walking by on the sidewalk, and the distant waves crashing on the beach.

The elevator doors opened with a chime and Casey's nostrils were hit with pungent stink of high-grade marijuana, which only intensified as he progressed down the hallway toward his room, number 313. It took him a few tries with the cardkey to get the thing unlocked and even then, it opened but reluctantly. At his feet he discovered the source of his difficulty: a towel had been wedged into the gap between the carpet and door. "Get in and seal it, dipshit," he was greeted as he stepped inside. He complied with this direction, almost instinctively kicking the towel firmly into the gap to keep the smoke from escaping.

Turning around, he discovered a fog hazed the room's atmosphere, pierced through with brilliant aqua light emanating from the pool in the courtyard below. A man was lying on one of the beds, his face briefly illuminated by the lighter he was using to corner the bowl of a clear glass bong. The hit became so milky it turned green, then disappeared when he pulled the choke and sucked it all in. Neither of them said anything for some time. The man on the bed just lay there and stared at Casey as if expecting the new arrival to make some sort of proclamation.

"Aren't you worried about the smoke alarm?" was all Casey could think to say.

"I've already thought of that," croaked the figure as he let the hit slowly trickle from his nostrils. He pointed at the ceiling, where over the white disk of the smoke alarm was a sandwich bag sealed with duct tape. "What? You think I'm fuckin' brain-dead or something?"

Casey stepped further into the room and set his bag down near the desk. Now that he was closer to his interlocutor, Casey could make out the bulk of his features. He was struck by how much this man stereotypically resembled a pirate or a lumberjack. He had to be at least seven feet tall, but had none of that slenderness one usually sees in absurdly tall people. Nature and effort had instead crudely hammered him into the shape of a bodybuilder. Casey could be forgiven for thinking this guy might be on steroids. Jagged, white teeth flashed from behind the man's bushy, black beard and the shaved dome of his head gleamed in the weak orange glow of the bedside lamp.

"Well?" asked the man, as he let out the rest of the hit.

"I didn't—I didn't mean anything by it."

"Relax, kid. I'm just fuckin' with ya."

"You must be Reardon."

"Go ahead and take a seat," said Reardon, gesturing towards what Casey supposed was his own bed. "Tell me why I would give a shit what a burnt-out little fucker like you thinks about me?"

"I'm sor—"

"Jesus, and there you go apologizing again after I've gone and insulted you. To your face! People are going to think you're a pussy. I mean, I'm just busting your balls and all, but fuck. You'd think you'd never had a roommate before."

Casey didn't say anything. He just took the bong that was offered to him. The hit brewed cleanly, the smoke pure and cold from the ice that clinked in the tube. "Maybe. I really don't remember," he said as he handed the piece back to Reardon.

"You don't, eh?" said Reardon. "Must've been all that blow."

"Oh," said Casey, "so you heard about that."

"Of course I heard about it. It was in the papers, wasn't it? You oughta know there ain't nothing that moves slow in this game, 'specially not the gossip. Course, I make it my business to know that sorta thing. After all, information's pretty valuable shit. I mean, that's the mind game of baseball isn't it? If I know your secrets and you don't know mine, who has the power? Who's more likely to come out on top?"

"You think you've got the goods on me then?"

"You and every other motherfucker."

"What would you do to get me out?"

"I'd throw you three pitches straight down broadway and let you get yourself out," said Reardon, rooting around in a tin of Kodiak wintergreen. "Last I heard, your swing was so busted after that eighty-gamer, the Cheesesteaks outrighted you after getting one look. Don't look so fucking surprised, I told yas news travels quick. That was almost three months ago, October the eighth, I believe."

"You sure seem to think you know a lot about me," said Casey.

"Unlike you, I've learned to take any edge I can get," said Reardon. "I'll bet you didn't even think to look me up before you flew your ass down here."

"It just slipped my mind, I guess."

"Of course it did," said Reardon, packing tobacco into his lip. "I mean, you do know why they put you with me—don't you?"

"I'm supposed to be catching you."

"Bingo. Figured you'd wanna know a thing or two about the only thing you're here to do and the only person you're here to do it for. Make no mistake: without me you're nothin' but camp fodder. A warm body—that's all you are. They've got seven other guys comin'. They're just like you, they've been sold the same song and dance. The only edge you've got on anyone else is that you're roomin' with me and that's just because nobody else will."

"But you're so charming."

"Keep chirping. Note that I ain't the one sitting on a crestin' bubble, now am I? You know, I was thinkin' of maybe helping you out some, but not if you want to go on and act like you know me like that."

"Sorry, I didn't mean anything by it."

"And there you go apologizing again. Jesus, don't you never fuckin' learn?"

"I guess not."

"Shit. I should probably quit giving you such a hard time. It's like drowning a puppy, I just ain't got the heart for it," said Reardon, extending his massive hand. "The name's Phil, by the way."

"I know," said Casey, taking Reardon's hand. "Casey."

"Thought we oughta be formally introduced."

Casey watched as Reardon took another impressive hit from the bong.

"Before you said you could help me?"

"Forget it. I was talking nonsense."

"Come on."

"Well, if you're sure."

"I'll take any help I can get."

"It's like I said," said Reardon, leaning in close and resting his elbows on his knees. "I've got the goods on everybody. I gather information and I exploit it."

"What good is that?"

"If you'd ever played in the Bigs before, you'd understand. It's not like down in the minors where you can get a long way just based on what some dicks in tracksuits think about the size of your biceps. Up in the Show? It's a whole different game entirely. Up here you've gotta do your homework. You have to be willing to do anything you can to grab an edge, or the riptide will take you out so fast ain't nobody will ever hear of your ass again. It's Darwinism out there, survival of the fittest, eat or be eaten, and you're talking to the great white shark."

"So you're going to give me pointers."

"Something like that."

Casey thought this over a moment. "But you said that you wanted nothing to do with me."

"I don't, but all the same, I could certainly be pretty fuckin' useful to you," said Reardon. "Especially if, say, I were the fella who made the call on who's the second catcher on the roster." Then, spotting Casey roll his eyes, "What? You don't believe me?"

"Not really."

Reardon smiled. "Either way, I've got a lot to give you and you don't have much to offer in return."

"Well, I guess there's no fucking deal to be made then, now is there?"

"Unless," said Reardon. He spat into a plastic cup that until now had remained on the end table. He leaned in closer, and in a hushed tone said, "Say I *were* to help you make the team, maybe there's something even a little cokehead like you could offer me."

"Yeah? And what's that?"

"Your total and unwavering loyalty. Don't smirk! I'm being serious. Not much to ask considering whatever happens to me is bound to happen to you. I get traded? You get traded. I get cut? You get cut. Get it? So long as ya do what you're told, everything oughta turn out great for the both of us."

"I'm not going to blow you, man."

"You ain't gotta," said Reardon, backhanding Casey's knee. "Not unless you wanna. But that wasn't what I had in mind. I won't need you to drink no Kool-Aid, neither. I've just gotta know we're on the same page, being battery mates and all. I can't have nobody fuckin' my shit up, understand? I need someone I can trust."

"What makes you think you can trust me?" asked Casey.

"I don't know," said Reardon. "Certainly doesn't make much sense to go and trust your shit to some addict—no offense—but I like the look of ya. I like the cut of your gib. It helps you're from my hometown, makes me feel like I know yas already. Trust me, so long you stick with old Reardon, we'll both end up rich. My right arm here will take us all the way to the bank. So what do you say? Are we humming the same tune or what?" Reardon extended his hand as if to shake.

"You're one paranoid son of a bitch, you know that?" said Casey, reaching forward and allowing his hand to be swallowed by Reardon's once again.

"One can never be too careful. And if you think I'm crazy, just wait 'til you get a load of the rest of these nuts. But you're a little peculiar yourself, ain't ya?"

"How do you figure?" asked Casey.

"It's just that I heard you was a bad apple—a regular hellion—and here you are as fresh as a goddamned daisy."

"You think I'm innocent?"

"Not at all, kid. Not at all! I've looked up your dossier—and all I'm going to say about that is: *nice*. But, no offense, sitting here looking at you, you seem like you're what my moms would call *such a sweet young man*. By which, of course, she'd mean a totally naïve, helpless wimp."

"The doctors told me cocaine was having a strong effect on my personality."

"I'll fucking say. I know what you mean, though. The funny stuff has a way of giving ya a little edge. Say, maybe you should think about picking it back up."

"Fuck that, man. That's how I got myself into this mess in the first place."

"See, that's where you're wrong," said Reardon, picking up the bong and brewing himself another hit. "Where you've got yourself is on a fast track to the Big Leagues. You shouldn't knock it."

Even here in the Sunshine State, January managed to ration the stuff to a mere handful of hours, so that Casey had yet to see daylight since he'd arrived in Dunedin. Every morning he rode the team "shuttle"—a white GMC Savana piloted by one of the team trainers—to the Robbie Attick training centre, in darkness. He spent the daylight hours inside running a daily circuit of activities approved by AC.

AC, or Alvin Chan, was the head trainer and served as the primary liaison between Casey and the team. He was not impressed with Casey's overall conditioning, which, admittedly, had deterio-rated since he had been dismissed by the Cheesesteaks. The job behind the security desk—where he regularly scarfed a half dozen donuts—hadn't served him very well, either. His body had turned to dough in the absence of real physical activity, and AC was charged with transfiguring it back into rock.

AC had Casey flip tires, lift weights, spin, do plyometrics, perform sit-ups while hanging upside down, work the battle ropes, do more squats than Casey thought possible, flip more tires, throw medicine balls, and run, run, run until Casey's mus-cles burned so bad he thought he couldn't take it anymore. But the head trainer had methods with which to milk the last drop of strength from Casey's body. He always insisted on just one more rep, on just one more lap, and once that lap was finished: howabout just one more? Afterwards, AC would watch from behind a clipboard as Casey consumed his evening meal with a fistful of supplements for dessert, all of which he washed down with filtered water. By the time Casey climbed back into the shut-tle at the end of the day, it would already be dark. Even now, many weeks later, the only landmarks Casey could have identi-fied were the lit-up signs that dotted the lawns and boulevards of Dunedin.

At night, he'd find the room he supposedly shared with Reardon empty. Closing the door behind him, Casey would stagger over to his bed and flop himself down. He was so exhausted his sleep was no longer troubled by dreams. The moment between when he closed his eyes and woke up ceased to exist, so that one day cut seamlessly to the next. He'd wake with a start to the ringing of a phone. On the other end of the line would be AC telling Casey that he planned to be there, at the Holiday Inn Express, in thirty minutes. Then Casey would get up and repeat the whole process again.

When he wasn't weight training or working on his cardio, Casey could be found in one of the batting cages where Joe Fremont, the team's Minor League Hitting Instructor, watched Casey take swings. He was constantly making adjustments to how Casey stood in the box and where he held his hands, citing all sorts of reasons why this or that modification would prove useful, none of which Casey particularly understood. After the debrief, Joe would lead Casey to the film room and they'd watch tape while Joe broke down everything that was going wrong. "The flow of motion is broken here," Joe would say, freezing the frame and tapping on the display to indicate Casey's hands, "You're not letting your lower body do the work, you're trying to punch the ball instead of hit it."

At other times, AC would lead him down a series of corridors to a room with a bunch of men sitting around the table who said things he didn't understand. Their words—spoken in thick, truly American drawl—might as well have been spoken in an entirely different language for all the content that made it through to Casey. He could tell this was all very important, and he could tell that they expected him to somehow translate it all into action, but how he was going to do that remained beyond his understanding.

This didn't trouble him because most of the time he was too tired to think. His body was reduced to its function as machinery, its only purpose to repeat given motions until it physically couldn't anymore, until all his muscles were so ragged that even the slightest movement became a Herculean labour. Despite this sensation of weakness and exhaustion, there was a noticeable increase in strength, in how much he could take, and in this he found at least some encouragement. When he picked up the bat, it no longer felt like some foreign object, but as if it was simply meant to be there. He still whiffed a lot, but when he did make contact the hard crack of wood against leather echoed off the walls so loud it sent his hair standing on end. Swinging off the tee, he'd begun to put a regular charge into the ball and in the film room he witnessed the gradual improvement of his swing as it fell more and more into a recognizable sequence.

One of the team's scouts had made a habit of watching Casey as he took his licks in the cage. He never said anything, the scout, he just sat there in his corduroy suit, fanning himself with a white straw fedora as he chewed seeds and spat the husks into a cup.

Casey was, of course, flattered at first, but after around a week these visits began to feel uncomfortable. He could feel the man's gaze bearing down on him, oppressing the little ability Casey possessed with its malice, until all the phases of Casey's swing broke down and he was back to flailing the bat around helplessly.

One day, Casey looked up from the towel he was using to wipe his face after batting practice, only to meet the gaze of his persecutor. The man beckoned him over with the wave of a hand. Casey looked over to AC for guidance, but the trainer merely shrugged his shoulders. "Hi," said Casey, walking over and extending his hand to the stranger. "My name's Casey."

"I know who you are," said the man with a New York accent. "The question is, do you know who I am?"

"No, but I'm sure you're very important."

"What makes you so sure?"

Casey didn't know what to say.

"I'll tell you something. If this were the Dandies or the Sams, then I might be somebody. As things stand, I'm just the lowly manager of these sad sack Toronto Blue Birds."

"You're Lou," said Casey.

"Yeah? And you're quick to the draw. You know, you're pretty brutal with the bat there, kid."

"I'm working on it."

"Well, if you want my advice, you'd be better off if you quit working at it. Any bonehead can see you've got no idea what you're doing up there. What makes you think you can be a professional hitter?"

"They told me they needed me for my defense."

"Don't get me wrong, you can drive the ball when you luck into hitting it, but you don't seem to be none too lucky. Otherwise, you wouldn't have ended up with this joke of an organization. Just tell me something. How's your arm?"

"Feels good."

"I meant is it anything special?"

"I guess not."

"Can you steal?"

"Not really."

"Can you run?"

"I've always been slow."

"You can say that again. What are you good for?"

"Apparently I can catch."

Lou's face screwed up. "What? You're a wise guy now?"

"No—"

"I'm going to level with you, kid," said Lou, spitting more husks. "I don't like you. I don't like what you stand for, and the first chance I get I'm going to ship your ass out of here. Maybe then they'll go out and get me someone who can play, instead of some burnt out loser who's only good for shoving wads of coke in the old schnoz."

"Cocaine doesn't come in wads," said Casey.

"Forgetaboutit!" hollered Lou, turning his back to Casey and waving a dismissive hand as he walked towards the door. "Let me know if you ever learn to play ball."

"Don't you think you oughta at least give me a chance?" Casey called after him.

"Chance? You've already had your chance, shithead," said Lou before slamming the door shut behind him.

Like the sun, Casey hadn't seen Reardon since that first evening. Not one of the items on the pitcher's side of the room had been disturbed: the barrel-sized containers of supplements still sat in the same place against the wall, his nail clippers still sat on the edge of his nightstand exactly where he had left them, and even though Casey found his own bed luxuriously re-made every morning, Reardon's bed was always made-up in the same tight, military fashion.

Not that there were many objects to be disturbed. Casey had observed that his roommate had a peculiar lack of personal belongings. Even on the evening of Casey's arrival, Reardon's side of the room had shown no signs of either clothes or a suit-case, nor any of those good luck charms that players usually carried around with them. Other than the supplements and nail clippers, Reardon had left behind a mason jar filled with carefully arranged dental stimulators and a foldable straightrazor.

There were a few traces suggesting Reardon had at least visited the room while Casey was absent. One evening, Casey had come home to a rancid smell and discovered a full cup's worth of chewed tobacco dumped in the garbage. On another occasion there had been a bayonette-style knife left unsheathed on the dresser next to the television. A third time, he found weed dust on the cover of the hotel room's guide booklet. Until now, these had been the only signs suggesting that Casey was not the room's sole occupant. He assumed Reardon had given the whole thing up and forgotten about their ridiculous deal.

It was thus understandable when, returning home from his interview with Lou and flicking on the light, Casey was shocked to find Reardon lying on the room's until recently unoccupied bed, smoking the bong. It was just like the last time Casey had seen him. He was even wearing the same black t-shirt and jeans.

"Jesus!"

"Relax, kid. It's just me."

"You scared the shit out of me. Who the hell sits around in the dark like that?"

Reardon shrugged. "I can't stand the light from those halogen bulbs. They give me a headache. Now do old Reardon a favour and turn that shit off and I'll turn on this lamp. That's it. Jesus. Look at you, acting like you've gone and seen a goddamned ghost."

"I just wasn't expecting you to be lying here in the dark like that, that's all. Where the hell have you been anyway? I haven't seen you in like a month."

"I've been in and out," said Reardon. "Had to get away for a few days here and there. You know the score: things to do, people to see. What am I supposed to do? Sit around in this shitty room and jerk off like some agoraphobic shmuck? No, friend, I leave that to you."

"But where'd you sleep?"

"I've got a tent in the back of the car, but most nights I just slept here," said Reardon, offering Casey the bong. "You were just too far gone into fuckin' dreamland to have noticed. Granted, a hurricane probably could've rolled through here and you'd've been none the fuckin' wiser. I even tried putting my balls in your mouth to see if you'd wake up."

"You what?"

"Relax, brother. I'm just fucking with you. I consider myself a gentleman," said Reardon, spitting into his cup. "I heard you've been doing well for yourself. Hell, you're already looking better than that fat sack of crap that wandered in here a few weeks ago."

"Not according to Lou just now."

"Oh, so you met Lou. How's the old buzzard doing?"

Casey said nothing for a moment. "What have you been doing all this time?"

"Like I said, I've just been doing my thing. It's nothing you need to worry yourself over. The official story, if anybody asks, is that I spent a few days on a fishing charter out there in the gulf."

"Yeah? And what's the real story?" asked Casey.

Instead of answering, Reardon reached for the bong and brewed himself another hit.

"Aw, come on."

"Alright. If you've gotta know, I was up in Pensacola racing stock cars."

"That's all? Then why are you acting so cagey about it?"

"Because I'd rather the team didn't find out."

"Why not?"

"They don't like it when I drive. They say it's too much of an injury risk. My agent's not a huge fan of it either. Says it will negatively impact future contract negotiations and—let's be honest—it probably will."

"Then why are you still doing it?"

"Because fuck it, I'm still going to get paid. What's a couple of hundred thousand here and there when I'll be making a clean twenty million per?"

"What makes you so sure they'll give you that?"

"Because they're desperate, and desperate people will do almost anything. Take this past offseason, for example. The

Maroons signed that hack Ben Riley for seventeen million per annum. And if there's someone out there willing to give that bum seventeen million just because he can give them six innings every now and then, somebody's gotta be willing to pay the real deal a nice even twenty per."

"That's a hell of a lot of money."

"Sure is. But the free agent market's gone plum crazy. And with the new CBA being negotiated, I'm hoping they won't be able to slap me with their damned qualifying offer, neither. So long as I stay healthy, I'm looking at a hell of a lot of cash. And don't worry, I won't forget my friends."

"Is that what we are?"

"Sure. Why not?"

"In that case, there's probably something I should've told you."

"Oh yeah? What's that, pal?"

"When Don offered me the contract, he kinda implied that part of my job was to spy on you."

"He would. And what did you tell him?"

"I said I would."

"Excellent," said Reardon.

"You sure don't seem too worried about it."

"Why would I be worried? It's all just a game we play."

"I don't think he knows that it's a game."

"Of course he does. He's always wrapped up in his big schemes and his five-year plans. His head's so caught up in that general manager game that he can't hardly see what's going on right in front of him. It's adorable really. He takes everything so seriously, thinks he's got it all under control. I mean, somebody's gotta keep the guy on his toes. Keep him honest."

"Is that why you buttered the floor of the locker room shower last spring?"

"Aha! You finally looked me up, eh? Well, alls I'm gonna say about that particular episode is that—funny as it may have been—it couldn't never be conclusively linked to yours truly. But say I did do it? I'd still be doing the poor sons of bitches a favour. Accidents happen and you've gotta plan accordingly."

"I read that some guy broke his arm," said Casey. "He was out four months."

"It's not like there aren't worse things that could happen to a person. You know, whatever wrongs I may perpetrate down here amongst the plebs, it's sure as shit ain't no worse than what Don's up to in his ivory tower."

"You mean putting together a baseball team?"

"Oh, is that all he's doing?" said Reardon. "Don't go thinking his game's so innocent. I mean, hell, you've seen how cold-blooded these assholes can be. You think he wouldn't cheat or steal if he thought it would do the smallest thing to help him save his own neck? No, brother, he'd tear your whole life apart, move you all the way across the continent, and strand you in the middle of buttfuck nowhere if he thought it would help the team steal another tick for the old doublya column. Not out of any loyalty to the team, mind you. He'd do it purely for his own self-aggrandizement. He'd do it to you just the same way he's done it a thousand times before."

"When you put it that way—"

"What other way is there to put it? In the end, all you or I are to these bastards is commodity, something that can be bought and sold. And until you make good on their investment, they don't give a fuck about your rights or your privacy. They'll even hire a talentless dipshit to snitch on ya. I mean how do you think he got a shmuck like you to come down here and live with a sociopath who puts butter all over the shower floor?"

"I'll be honest and say that I didn't need much convincing."

"And don't think he didn't know it."

The two sat there smoking and not saying much.

"Where'd ya get that," said Casey eventually, pointing to a scar on Reardon's elbow.

"What, you mean this?"

"Yeah," said Casey, "I've seen it before."

"Are you tellin' me you don't know what this is? Hell, it seems everybody in my line of work's got one nowadays. This here's my Tommy John scar."

"You mean the elbow surgery?"

"That's right. My body's no different than a car: if everywhere I drive, I go and really take her to the limit, sooner or later something's gonna go bust. You're just driving along, minding your own business, and *wham*—your tire pops. Well, this motherfucker right here's just where they replaced my popped tire. You know anything about Tommy John?"

"Not really," said Casey in what he thought was a sarcastic tone.

"Jesus, kid. You know, that's what makes you kinda alright. You're willing to step up and admit you don't know nothin' about what anyone oughta feel ashamed for not knowing. It's all real simple: you've got this ligament in your elbow, the UCL, and it can snap if you're too rough with it. For some lucky fuckers, they can be throwing hard heat their whole careers and never have it go on 'em. In my case, I managed to bust three. I guess I've finally found the right fit."

"What makes you so sure this one won't snap?"

"Well, the thing is that the first two times I had the surgery they went about it in the old way. This last time I went to see Dr. Abrams, and he says that my career's probably over. You get what I'm saying? This son of a bitch sat across the table from me and told me just like that."

"What did you do?"

"I told him he was full of shit and that I wanted to get myself a second opinion. He starts telling me nothing can be done, and that's when I get really angry. I started shouting and getting up in the doc's face and telling him there had better be something he could do. He looked just like a frightened puppy the way he sank back into his chair. After I've been letting him have it for a while he finally relents and says, well, maybe there is something they can do for me after all.

"He shows me on a tablet a picture of this red, cord-looking thing and I ask him what the hell I'm looking at and he tells me it's this prototype they've been developing—a new, synthetic, UCL. They grow it in a lab, living tissue coating some cable. I told him to sign me up.

"But doc says it ain't that easy, that this thing's still in the prototype stages. It ain't even, strictly speaking, FDA approved yet. There's a possibility that it wouldn't take and then I'd be up shit-creek, but good. But if it works, he says, it won't never break down. That I'll be able to throw as hard as I want with no fear of it tearin' on me again."

"How do you know it won't snap anyway?"

"I don't, but that didn't stop me the other three times, now did it? You can't go worrying about that shit. You just gotta go out there and pitch, and if a tire pops—it pops. Nowadays alls you do is go under the knife and rehab from the surgery and away you go. Part wears out? Just go and replace it. That's just the way it is."

"I guess so. You said that the one you've got now is a prototype."

"Yeah."

"How'd they get them before?"

"They harvested them from cadavers."

For a few moments the only sound was the bubbling of the water in the bong's beaker.

"What about you, kid?" asked Reardon, withholding the smoke. "You got any battle scars?"

"Just this," said Casey, lifting his shirt and pointing to the spot where they'd taken his appendix out.

"That's it? An appendix scar?"

"Can't ever remember having another scar. To be honest with you, I can't even really remember being injured."

"Bullshit! There ain't no such thing as a professional athlete who ain't never been injured. Hell, midway through August we're all playing hurt."

"I mean, sure I've rolled an ankle or twisted a wrist, but I've never dealt with anything too serious, not even back when I played football."

"Maybe that's why you don't remember. Too many concussions."

"Plenty of the other guys would come off to the sidelines and ask me about seeing stars, but I can honestly tell you that I never did. Never broke a bone or anything. Then again, the football thing didn't last long."

"Oh yeah? Why's that?"

"I guess I didn't have the temperament for it. I mostly just did it because the football coach followed me around for a week begging me to join. Everyone thought I was some superstar athlete or something. Let's just say he wasn't nearly as aggressive when I didn't bother to sign up the next year."

"Well ain't that just the piss of the beer," said Reardon, letting out another bong hit. "Here a dipshit like you ain't never been injured and ol' Reardon here can't seem to avoid the old junk heap. You know, I almost quit after the third time."

"Good thing you didn't."

"I thought about it," said Reardon. "Had a coupla rough years after the most recent surgery. Ligament didn't take as fast as everybody hoped it would and one day I woke up and I was twenty-nine years old. In what was supposed to have been the prime of my career I was playing for Joliet out in the Frontier League. I wound up playing for them for two years. Almost made me quit."

"Why didn't you?"

"Because when you think about it, what else was I gonna do? It's not like I had any skills other than throwing a ball really hard. Besides, once the new ligament took, I was throwing harder than I did when I was twenty. Back then I threw ninety-seven, ninety-eight no problem. Now I was hitting one-oh-three, one-oh-four. Thing was, I couldn't hit the broad side of a barn door. Once my command came back, I had these Frontier League hacks falling over themselves tryin'a get at it. One day, old Donny boy shows up and offers me a two-year deal."

"You don't seem too thrilled about it," said Casey.

"What's there to be thrilled about? The bastard's getting himself a piece of the prime rib at the cost of ground beef."

"Could be worse," said Casey. "You could still be over there in the Frontier League. I could still be sitting behind that security desk or in prison. Most people would look at you and say to themselves that at least you get to play a game for a living, while they've gotta get up and go to work at jobs they hate."

"What's that? Some humility bullshit they taught you in rehab?"

"People would say you ought to count yourself among the lucky ones."

"They would say that, wouldn't they? They probably think I spend my time walking through fucking flowered meadows and shit, picking daisies at my leisure. But isn't it the case that we all end up playing games for a living?"

"No, man, I really don't see how that's the case."

"Are you serious? Sometimes it seems to me that games are our species' only damn occupation, and it's understandable because—let's face it—we humans are hardwired for competition. Probably 'cause our knuckle-dragging ancestors had to be competitive, for mates, for property, to not end up with their head smashed in. Brother, they could only dream of the kind of comfort and security you and I experience every day. We're living that dream, and now that we're here there's more than enough food to go round, police stalking our streets keeping the old public in line, cars and trucks and planes that ferry us wherever the fuck we need to go, and now that we've got all that there's no real need for competition no more. Problem is, the craving's still in there. When we don't get to experience the real thing, we go and make it up for ourselves. We've gone and made up all sorts of little games we compel people to compete in and we call the result a job or a career."

"So what? You think paramedics and teachers are playing a game?"

"Sure. Just the same as how a lawyer's lawyering is just an elaborate word game, or stock broking's just a bunch of number crunching and social manipulation. Hell, even those pimply-faced kids flipping burgers at McDonalds are playing a game. It's just a really fuckin' stupid one."

"Come off it, man."

"It's true that none of the games we play are very much fun, even baseball. I mean, look at you. What's your day like? You're bustin' your ass from dawn 'til dusk in order to get that dough-boy body of yours into game shape. Tell me, is that fun? Months from now, in September, when we're maybe out of the hunt and you're still fighting for a job—will that be your idea of a good time?"

"I guess not," said Casey.

"Well it oughta be," said Reardon, smiling. "Because that's what this game's all about. Kill or be killed. Eat or be eaten. It's the same old drumbeat. In the end someone's getting swallowed up and better you than me."

"That's very reassuring."

"Well it's the truth, isn't it? It's like this: when I get the call out of the bullpen, I've got no idea who I'm gonna face. The man standing down there in the box could be a superstar like Husam Pereyra, or some greenhorn scrub fresh outta buttfuck-nowheresville, and in the end it doesn't matter, because if they ring me up that counts against me and my record and if I keep fuckin' up every time I step out there, well sooner or later they're gonna stop callin' on me and, fast as that, it's hasta la vista. Same goes for the guy down there in the box. I could be the last opponent that hitter will ever face in the Big Leagues. This at-bat might result in his fuckin' ruina-tion. And I've got only one thing on my mind when I'm standing up there, that I'm gonna rattle the little son of a bitch. I'm gonna shake him so good that hopefully he don't never recover. Nothing makes me happier than when I see some-one's got sent down after coming up against me. No, nothing's better than that."

"The way you were just spouting off, I thought you would have hated all that."

"I do, but what's it matter? You could go anywhere and end up doing anything, and you might be able to fool yourself for a while, but one day you'll wake up and realize that you're still playing the same game you was before and the only thing that's any different is the props."

"You don't even believe that. And even if you did, it'd still be bullshit."

"It ain't bullshit," said Reardon, spitting into his cup. "I've fuckin' lived it. Anyone who comes up against me is getting torn to pieces. That's my mentality and that's how you gotta think. Like it or not, every hit you make, every positive thing you do for us, is a negative thing done *against* some other fucker. In my experience, there are two ways to deal with this reality: either tolerate it, or revel in it. You sure as shit won't be changing it."

Things were different after Reardon took up residence in the room. Before, Casey could step in and within minutes be face down in his pillow, sawing some serious logs. Now that his roommate had returned, Casey was nightly subjected to Reardon's idea of small talk, which was to bombard his conversation partner with as many of Reardon's opinions and ideas as time and patience would permit. Whenever Casey would contrdadict his roommate during these long rants with some fact or observation, Reardon had some explanation ready at hand that— at least to his own mind—appeared to smooth over the issue in its entirety.

He had other strange habits, too. For one thing, Casey never caught him sleeping. When Casey went to bed, Reardon would be sitting up reading some repair manual and hitting the bong. In the morning, Casey would wake up to find Reardon in the same spot: still reading, still hitting the bong. He even set his phone's alarm to three in the morning just to see if he could catch Reardon dozing, but when it woke Casey up, there was Reardon, reading his manual and brewing himself a hit.

"Jesus, don't you ever sleep?" Casey asked, sitting up and rubbing his eyes.

"Not if I can help it," Reardon replied, blowing smoke in Casey's face.

The hours of daylight began to stretch out again as the end of January approached, so when Casey took the shuttle in the morning he was able to catch a brief glimpse of the orange-pink airbrushed sunrise before being ushered off into the confines of the training centre.

One day he found himself standing on the the sidewalk out front, admiring the last touch of sun against the horizon, when his attention was broken by a black Volkswagen Golf squealing to a stop in front of him. It had flame decals along the side and gold rims. A pair of red dice hung from the mirror.

"Need a lift?" asked Reardon through the open window.

Casey looked around and found the white shuttle van nowhere in sight.

"I would, but what if AC comes looking for me?"

"What? Don't you got a phone?"

Casey pulled his phone from his pocket and examined it. He figured AC's number had to be in there somewhere, so he walked around to the other side of the car and got in.

The interior of Reardon's Golf was almost entirely stripped out. The plastic moulding, the carpet, almost all the creature comforts had been removed for the sake of—what? Performance? The thing had to be nearly forty years old. Casey dropped his duffle into the cavity where a back seat must once have been. He figured it had probably been torn out so the car could accommodate Reardon's oversized frame.

"Nice wheels."

"This? This here's just my beater. I've got the real thing parked back at Pearson," said Reardon, putting the car into first gear. "I call it *The Beast.*"

And they were off, the hand on the speedometer steadily climbing past thirty, to forty, to fifty. Reardon weaved through gaps in the traffic even narrower than that lunatic cabbie had driven through. He drummed on the steering wheel, nodding his head to the Swedish uber-technical death metal he had blaring through the speakers—the car's one legitimate frill. The cabin rattled almost as loudly as Casey's teeth, giving him the impression that the whole thing might disintegrate at any moment.

By the time they reached their room, Casey was so exhausted that he dropped onto his bed and fell asleep with his clothes on. When he woke up, Reardon was there slipping another plug of dip into his mouth.

"How long was I asleep," asked Casey, rubbing his eyes.

"A few hours," said Reardon, opening his straight razor and examining the blade. "Time to shave the old dome."

Casey lay there staring at the ceiling, listening to the *schnick-schnick* of the razor against Reardon's scalp, and got lost in a daydream of what it might be like if Reardon ever slipped while shaving his head. He concluded that the son of a bitch would probably just come out and try to shoot the shit like nothing happened while blood spurted from a severed artery. When Reardon finally emerged from the bathroom safe and sound, Casey sat up on his elbow and said, "I thought you said you had no marketable skills."

"Yeah? I don't."

"You sure can drive like a maniac."

"There's folks out there even faster than me. Like that fuck-face Andres who dropped you off when you first got here, and the only way he gets paid to drive is by driving useless rich fucks such as yourself to and from the old aeroport."

"It's still a marketable skill. And what about all those repair manuals you've always got your nose in? Is that just leisure reading?"

"Your alternatives to being a millionaire ballplayer are being a grease monkey or a taxi driver."

"At least then you could have a clean conscience, since you seem so worried about it."

"I couldn't never have no clean conscience," said Reardon, sitting down on his bed and resting his elbows on his knees. "But even say I could. Say back when I was with Joliet—when I hardly had a dime to my name—I woke one morning and decided to go work on cars, because that's what I love to do and it pays better. Sure, maybe at first I would've loved it. Working with my hands all day, wearing a monkey suit—the whole shebang!"

"Why not? That's what everyone's trying to do, aren't they? Everyone says they want to do what they love."

"Well, the thing is, one day—maybe years later, maybe decades—you might wake up and realize that, after all this time, whatever made you love your job in the first place, that special spark that brought you so much fuckin' happiness, is long gone. What was once delicious as shit? Now it's just ashes being funneled down yer yap. For one reason or another it ain't satisfying no more, but that don't matter 'cause now you depend on it. That's how you get by in this world from here on out."

"Whatever, man," said Casey, rolling onto his back.

Reardon opened his weed jar and extracted a nug to put in his grinder. "You wanna know the real reason I never quit playin' ball?"

"Sure. Enlighten me."

"Because while I see through all this bullshit, when I step onto the mound it doesn't matter. The fans are chanting my name, clapping, rooting me on, hoping just the same as I do that I up and end the career of whichever poor fucker's had the misfortune of stepping into that batter's box. When I throw that ball, they all go quiet and wait to see what the umpire has to say, and when he punches the air the whole place goes nuts because we won and I made it happen. In that moment, all the shit I've seen and know goes out the window and I'm on top of the whole fuckin' world and I think to myself: let's rock and roll again, baby. Let's rock and roll again. It's nice to lose yourself in it. It's a nifty little trick. You can almost fool yourself into thinking you're still in love with the game."

"And you're not?"

"We've all been suckers at some point. Sure, even when I was touring around the Frontier League, I still believed in that 'for the love of the game' bullshit. But seeing the things I've seen, I can't believe in that no more than I can believe in the damned tooth fairy. I spent two years out there, two years of mean, hard living where sometimes I didn't know if I'd come back from a road trip evicted or not. Go through two years in the old Frontier and come back and preach to me. You do that sort of thing long enough and you start asking questions. You start wonderin' if any of this shit actually means anything. Does it matter if you can throw the ball really fast and set records that may never be broken? Does it matter if you win the Globe Series, or get yourself inducted into the Hall, or obtain some other sort of prestige?

Does any of that shit matter once you know you're just part of the circus? After you've gone down that rabbit hole, I'm afraid there ain't no turnin' back. You see the thing for what it is: just another means of survival."

"So for you this is just a paycheque."

"Isn't it the same for you? Would you be here if it weren't for the five-hundred-thousand smackers being deposited into your bank account over the course of the next eight months? Yeah fucking right. There ain't no shame in it. At some point we've all gotta learn that this is just another kind of business. The rules out there still apply in here. There ain't no escaping it."

Don looked on as Paul Kim fitted a pair of goggles over Casey's head. This was the last piece of a full ensemble; Casey wore a lycra bodysuit fitted with two hundred and eighty-six sensors. A bat was placed in his hands, its surface dotted with sticky white circular patches, each of which centred by a square black iris where all its gadgetry was stored. Lights flooded the batter's boxes and home plate, which were situated in real dirt. Terry Lerman—the hitting coach—and Joe Fremont sat at a desk watching a large display monitor. On it was projected a flattened version of what Casey was seeing, several graphs, and a virtual Casey as he stood there in the batter's box, looking around at the suddenly materialized Uncle Sam Stadium and its over fifty-four thousand fans.

"What do you think?" asked Paul.

"This is amazing!"

To put it bluntly, the technology was sublime. It had come a long way since Don had started out as a fresh Harvard Economics grad, crunching numbers for the ballclub. He had been part of the first wave of advanced metrics that swept through Big League front offices in the 2000s. He had managed to keep his skills current during the age of algorithmic projection while serving as the head of scouting—but this? This he only understood schematically, as a collection of systems that came together into *this,* his vision for the future of the game.

The idea had occurred to him his first week on the job as the team's General Manager. Don had been travelling with the squad on their first west coast swing under his tenure, and was enjoying breakfast in the hotel's restaurant when something on the television caught his eye. It was tuned to ABC7 news and they were running a story on the Stanford football team's use of virtual reality to gain a competitive edge. Don had watched in awe as the team's quarterback put on VR goggles and the screen cut to what he was supposedly seeing—which was his own offensive line and some other college's defense. Don hungrily read the closed captioning as the head coach explained that the team used the tech to practice by recreating the tendencies of opposing defenses.

Two hours later Don was in an Uber being ferried down Palm Drive with the golden mosaic of the Memorial Church filling the windshield's vista. His mind had been running through fantastic imaginings: an immersive baseball environment in which players played out a million scenarios, perfected their decision making, and turned into something *else.* Don imagined the near limitless advantage his team might reap if they only managed to be the first pigs to the trough on this new technology in what had, since the *Dollarball* era, become a technological arms race. Information and technology were being weaponized around the league, and getting this would be like securing a nuke.

The car dropped him off at the apex of the oval. He was anxious not to be late and kept glancing at his phone—which he was also using to navigate—with agony because there was only one minute separating his arrival time and their scheduled meeting. He marched past the bookstore, the post office, and the library until he arrived at an outdoor pavilion with the sign reading *Coupa Café*. At one of the tables was the man Don recognized from the broadcast as the head coach. He was drinking from a bottle of water sporting the words *Stanford Football.*

"You must be Brock Lancaster," said Don in a near pant, extending his hand. "Thank you for taking the time to meet with me."

"And you must be Don Billingsley."

"The same."

"You want coffee?" asked Lancaster.

"I thought you'd never ask."

They stood in line for some time. While their coffees were being made, the two men made small talk—about Don's flight, about the weather (every day was the same here in Silicon Valley), about Lancaster's kids. Finally, the coffees were delivered. Don paid for both in cash and the barista made a displeased face when he saw the size of the tip. Then they took their beverages to a near-by table and sat down. Lancaster took a sip and said, "So, Mr. Billingsley, what brings you all the way to California?"

"I'm just here circumstantially," said Don, affecting detachment. "I travel with the team and they're playing in Oakland. Which of course means I am staying in San Francisco where this morning while eating breakfast I saw a news segment about your football team."

"The one about VR?"

"Correct."

"And?"

"And," said Don, "I want to know if it works."

"Why don't you come and see for yourself?"

"It's about reps," said Lancaster as he and Don marched down a corridor leading to the Cardinal locker room. "While practice is obviously important, there's only so much physical practice we can do before it begins to have a negative impact on in-game performance. That's where the VR comes in. We can surpass the physical limitations of our players by increasing the number of mental repetitions. Our athletes spend as many as three hours a day rehearsing various in-game scenarios, so that they're ready when they're confronted with those scenarios on the field."

"How do you determine which scenarios merit repeating?"

"We let the data tell us that," said Lancaster, opening a door for Don to walk through.

Inside the room stood two glass cubes, each containing a player in a VR headset plugged into a sculpted white column. Above the cube was a monitor on which a first-person camera swiveled this way and that, surveying the offensive and defensive lines of two inversely coloured teams.

"Is that what he's seeing?"

"Yes," said Lancaster. "Except he feels like he's in it, at least visually. He also hears everything on the field."

"Both teams are wearing Stanford uniforms."

"We have to use our own players to model various formations and audibles that we expect our opponents to use."

"I see," said Don. "It's like some sort of immersive video."

"Guess you could call it that. We just call it VR. Sounds better than IV, you know what I mean?"

"And you say it works."

"You're in the sports business. You ought to know as well as anyone that you take any edge."

Don left the campus extremely disappointed. The technology was too rudimentary to be of any real use, and yet he had to admit that there was something there, some protean form of a truly revolutionary idea. It was on this hunch that, while restructuring the staffing of the team's front office that fall, Don hired seventeen programmers to man the new R&D department.

In the short-term, the R&D department was tasked with the development of information tools to allow coaches and players to make better on-field decisions, facilitating quick access to scouting reports, heat maps, and the like through easy-to-use software, but Don had also intended that they have a second, somewhat secret purpose, which was to continue developing VR technology. His first hire had been Paul Kim, an employee of the startup supplying Stanford with its VR technology. Don had found out that Kim, a pivotal figure in their startup's success, was disgruntled with the direction it was headed. He'd offered Kim a ridiculous amount of money, a huge research budget, and was thus able to lure him away. Kim knew coming in that his job was to realize Don's vision: a system where a hitter could take reps against a digital copy of a specific pitcher as many times as they desired. A pitcher could practice certain pitches against the virtual doppelgangers of major league hitters to uncover holes in their opponents' swings and develop pitching strategies tailored to each batter. The simulation would have to be close enough to the real thing—making similar mistakes, making similar adjustments—so that it wasn't just some sort of video game, where everything happened perfectly. You couldn't have your players getting overly habituated to perfect scenarios because the game wasn't perfect, and it never would be.

When the StatMan system was rolled out league-wide three years later, Don knew he had found the missing piece of the puzzle. The data this glorious system collected was far more powerful than the endless succession of algorithms and stat-line extensions that had preceded them. What had before been invisible was now laid out for anyone with a computer to see. A new frontier had been opened for exploration, and anyone who saw its potential could strike it rich.

The raw biometric and physics data available through StatMan was staggering and Don saw its potential immediately. He was almost giddy over the next few weeks as he watched the system spew out a whole range of beautiful data points, measuring things that Don had for so long thought would always be unmeasurable and others he had never even thought to measure. Paul Kim and his team went to work mining it for anything of use.

It was around this time that Don began to wonder how detailed a picture the system could paint. Could they, for example, track the kinetic chain of a batter or a pitcher? Could it map the route an outfielder took on a fly ball and measure its efficiency? As Kim and his team discovered, it could do a whole lot more than that. Don felt greatly emboldened by the system's advent. With it, they could not only monitor the performance of players around the league—as he was sure his rivals were already doing—but, with time, develop virtual models for his conceptualized VR system. He took the idea directly to the board.

At the meeting, several members were hesitant to invest money in a project that appeared to be doomed from the start. Peter Nickelbrook was vocal in expressing his doubts, pointing out that it would require a small army of experienced VR programmers and designers to bring this technology to life, if it was even possible.

"This is the stuff of science fiction. We're not in Silicon Valley here. We're not in the technology business. We're in the business of selling stadium tickets, merchandise, television contracts, and ad time."

"And putting together a winning ball club."

"To our shareholders, that's a secondary concern."

"When you have fifty-three thousand asses in the seats every night because of how many runs we're scoring, I hope you'll be humble enough to agree with me that it should be our primary concern," Don responded.

Nickelbrook rolled his eyes.

Even with Nickelbrook's opposition, the board cleared a shoestring budget for VR development. Don was given the money to hire twenty of the forty programmers and designers he had asked for. Of course, almost all the teams had done a wave of hirings at that time, presumably with machinations of their own on how to best take advantage of the new landscape created by StatMan. He had to assume that at least one other team had come up with the same idea, so it was a source of constant anxiety that someone might beat him to the punch and perfect the thing first. He found some solace in media reports that his team had by far the largest programming staff in the league and that there had been quotes from rival executives referring to the number of programmers on the Birds as "excessive."

Was it excessive now that he had Weapon X in his hands and was about to unload it on the unsuspecting baseball universe? A weapon which—if it worked as expected—would turn this young man—who the rest of the league had written off as a lost cause—into the all-star the various scouting bureaus had once predicted he would be.

It was a queer feeling, wearing all this stuff down here in some concrete chamber in the bowels of the training centre. The temperature was cool, the air damp and musty, and yet a sea of people writhed and shrieked and booed as he looked around, bewildered. The sun beat down overhead, causing the air to ripple with heat that wasn't there. Out on the mound was the pitcher, his face entirely featureless. His skin looked like pink rubber stretched over whatever it was underneath.

"Jesus," said Casey. "What the fuck is that?"

"That's BP Barry," said Paul's voice.

"Why doesn't he have a fucking face?"

"Because he isn't a person," said Paul. "He's a simulation. He's a model we made. He represents what we consider to be an ideal BP pitcher. He throws accurately, he varies speed, and he does what he's told. Say hi, Barry."

The thing on the mound waved.

"See?"

Casey gripped the bat. "It's going to pitch?"

"That's right."

"What am I supposed to do?"

"Hit."

The boy looked frankly ridiculous standing there, flailing at pitches that didn't, strictly speaking, exist. Lerman and Fremont shook their heads as they watched the monitor. Casey didn't look much better from their perspective, swinging right through what should have been very hittable pitches.

Don opened the app on his phone so he could follow the action in real time. It was a messy swing. Loopy. This wasn't a surprise. Everyone knew that rebuilding it was a work in progress, but there was always the nagging question of how long it was going to take.

"What's the software telling you?" called Don.

"It's recommending an adjustment."

Lerman got up slowly from his folding chair and hobbled over to the dirt circle. "Get in your stance," he said, and the boy complied. He repositioned Casey's hands until a female computer voice said, "Lock."

Next the hitting coach tapped Casey on his front knee and told him to bring it about two inches forward.

"Lock."

"Why does it keep saying that?" asked Casey.

"The software is designed to help you repeat your motions. It will support you by letting you know when you aren't aligned properly. It can also make suggestions on how you can improve the efficiency of your swing," said Don.

Or at least that was what it was supposed to do. There was no point in telling the boy that he was the guinea pig for this new system. It was important that he believe in its efficacy for the training to do its work.

After you spent enough time in this virtual environment, you eventually began seeing the imperfections. For example, even though the stands were loaded with tens of thousands of screaming fans, there were only twenty-or-so individuals who kept recurring in different seats repeating the same gestures. There was also this faceless thing on the mound that kept throwing stuff Casey couldn't put the bat on. Sometimes BP Barry would throw a pitch inside, and instead of the sensation of air rushing to fill the vacant space left in the wake of the ball, Casey felt nothing. The flags were waving up on the lip of the stadium, but there was no wind. His arms were bare, but he could feel the body suit compressing his flesh. He hadn't even broken a sweat, even though he could feel his wet hair clinging to his scalp.

"That's enough," said Don.

"Say goodbye, Barry," said Paul, and the faceless thing on the mound waved collegially before vanishing into thin air.

Fuck you, Barry, thought Casey, still catching his breath.

He took off the headset and looked around the room. Everybody was packing up and moving on. Only Paul remained to collect the equipment.

SPRING TRAINING

By the beginning of February, there were manifest signs of Spring Training's imminent arrival. Almost everybody associated with the team was in town, and though some of the players had opted for condo rentals with their families over in Clearwater Beach, the majority of Casey's new teammates were now residing at the hotel on the Birds' dime. The steady trickle of players had pushed all the families and octogenarians out. By the end of the month, the team had taken over the entire third floor.

Now that camp was approaching, Reardon was a permanent fixture in the hotel room. He spent his evenings stretched out on his bed with his nose in some repair manual or else some other boring, overly practical text. Sometimes Casey would amuse himself by watching Reardon from across the room as his eyes darted first left, then right, then back again in a steady, unbroken rhythm, soaking up the information contained in those lines the same way Casey used to soak up lines of coke from toilet lids with rolled up twenty-dollar bills. Sometimes he would would turn on the TV and crank up the volume to see if Reardon would notice, but he never did. He just keep on reading, only pausing to lick the tip of his finger and turn the page.

At other times, the closer would shut the book violently and throw it onto the nightstand. Then he'd sit up, turn toward Casey, and just start talking about whatever thought happened to have made the mistake of wandering into his head. During these diatribes, Casey would drift in and out of the "conversation" and allow his thoughts to be carried away in some other direction. At other times, try as he might, he couldn't help but become an active participant, and they'd spend hours just shooting the shit.

Reardon was awful curious about Casey's time with the Cheesesteaks, back when, as far as the closer understood, the coke and hookers had been plentiful. However, Casey could never seem to satisfy him with his recollections. "Don't you know how to tell a goddamned story?" Reardon would ask after being regaled. "When you get to the part where the truth is kind of boring, you're supposed to just make shit up."

When Casey called it a night, Reardon was even polite enough to leave the room and wander off to do whatever Reardonish things he did while everyone else was asleep or at work. Whenever Casey questioned Reardon about his sleep habits, the closer maintained he never slept more than four hours a night.

"On account of my condition."

What condition that could be, Casey never was able to puzzle out. All he knew was that, by the time he woke up, Reardon would already be wide awake, brewing a cup of coffee in the room's miniature coffeemaker, and reading the local paper dropped outside their door that morning.

For his part, Casey was usually too drunk with sleep to engage in any conversation, let alone any reading. Instead, he'd mechanically slug back a mug of black coffee while staring down at the hotel pool. From this vantage he could see past the pool to the parking lot, which might as well have been paved with gold for all the money sitting on it. There were LaFerraris, Mercedes S-Classes, BMW M models, a neon green Lamborghini Huracán, more Porsches than Casey cared to count, and many top-trimmed pick-ups. Against the backdrop of these exquisite automobiles, Reardon's beat-up old Volkswagen, with its flame decals and hood scoop, was conspicuous and, frankly, absurd—a teenager's beater amongst all these dignified examples of taste arranged around it in orderly rows. The thing was an eyesore.

Since that first drive home it had somehow been understood between the two men that Casey could catch a ride with Reardon, so long as he was ready before 09:00, and since then Casey had yet to miss the boat. It was thus a very unfortunate discovery when, on the morning that pitchers and catchers were expected to report to camp, his body woke up independently of his alarm, his phone display already reading 09:30.

He skipped the shower along with the continental breakfast and had to run in order to catch the last of the morning shuttles. As he approached the Safari, he could hear chatter inside the vehicle. Those inside must have heard him approaching, because when he arrived at the van's side door their discussion halted abruptly. In the back sat two men identical in every detail, even down to their clothing. In fact, the only way they could be told apart were their shoes: one wore a pair of purple New Balance while the other sported the same model in lime green.

After Casey had climbed aboard and fastened himself in, the two men resumed whatever conversation they'd been having prior to his arrival. They spoke a thick, nasally French that Casey recognized as Québecois.

One of them leaned forward and tapped Casey on the shoulder. "You are the one. Casey, right?"

"That's what they call me," said Casey, turning around. "How'd you know."

"Hoho, how could I forget? Your face was in all the papers, no? You're the one who drived their auto into the pole. Yes?"

"That seems to be my claim to fame," Casey sighed, trying to rub the sleep from his eyes.

"Is it true you were se poudrer le nez behind ze wheel?" asked the other twin, with a wink.

"I don't really remember. Probably? It's all hazy."

"Sounds like yes to me," said the same twin to his brother.

"Probably off the tits of some hooker, eh?" said the first twin, backhanding Casey's shoulder.

"I've been instructed not to discuss it."

"And who is going to tell about it? Huh? Look at us: do we look as if we give the two of the fucks? The shit—how you say?—it happen."

"Well thanks for the vote of confidence, I guess."

"Eh! Do not mention it! By the way, we have not introduced ourselves. Forgive our bad manners, mon ami. I am Patrice and this is Felix."

"Nice to meet you," said Casey, extending his hand. "When did you get in?"

"We arrived last night. And You?"

"I've been down here since December."

Neither man seemed surprised by this revelation; they merely exchanged glances.

"Is it true that you are staying with Phillipe?" said Felix, leaning forward and lowering his voice.

"Yeah. Why are you whispering about it?"

"You never know who could be listening," said Patrice, nodding his head up towards the driver's seat.

Casey had turned to face them and now had to glance over his shoulder to get a look at the driver sitting stiff as a board and staring straight ahead.

"Who? Him? Are you guys off your rockers or something? Why would he want to spy on us?"

"Someone who is after the—how you say?—*information*. Your roommate, por example."

"He wouldn't do that."

The twins looked at each other dubiously. "What, are you his girlfriend? Have you not read the stories in the paper?"

"I've heard the stories, all right. Don't get me wrong, I thought he was a nut when I first met him, too, but since then he's been nothing but nice to me. He seems alright."

"He's not so bad right now, eh? But… this Reardon? This Reardon is like un animal sauvage. He will make you think there is no harm, and then? Then he will strike."

"I'll be sure to keep a look out."

"Hoho, you do not believe moi? You will see, mon ami. Il est un bête. Mark Patrice's words: do not trust him."

"Is it true you are the one who will catch him?" asked Felix.

"Seems to be a major consideration in whether or not I end up sticking around."

"You must be pretty good, no?"

"I can catch a ball, I guess."

"You will have to. The words on the internet is that the fans, they don't like you. They say you can't hit."

"I can't."

"Who gives a shit? Me, I get the lefties out. My brother? He likes the righties. We all fill a need, and not everybody needs to be this superstar. If you can catch Phillipe? To these people that is worth something, no?"

"At least he better hope so, eh?"

Everywhere Casey looked he saw the game's superstars, past and present. They lined the dugouts, bleachers, tunnels, and the parking lot out front of TH Park. They'd been drawn here once again to bask in the glare of this heatless March sunlight, completing the seasonal migration they had made every year of their adult lives. The movements of the old-timers were slow and leisurely, like lizards just emerging from their burrows after a long winter's hibernation. Some of them were here on official business, either as members of a Big League front office, or wearing press badges. Others were just lounging in their Hawaiian shirts, chumming it up and taking selfies with any fans who might recognize them.

Members of the press drifted over to the bullpen, where Casey now got into a crouch behind one of the plates. The face of the man on the mound was as recognizable to Casey as any; it was burned into his memory from hanging on his bedroom wall for most of his childhood. *Chet Hardy*, the old Smith and Wesson himself, was digging at the clay with his cleat, just like Casey had seen him do a million times on television and on trips to the ballpark. It was a trademark gesture, the way he'd stand up there staring down the batter and hoofing the earth, just like a bull before it makes its charge. Casey used to get shivers watching Chet. Back then, the gesture radiated immense and unquestionable power.

Now that Casey was crouched here behind the plate, he could see that the years had robbed this ritual of much of its original intensity. Hardy's arms and legs had grown thinner in inverse proportion to the growth of his now impressive potbelly, his skin sunbaked and wrinkled, and his Adam's apple so distended he now resembled a plucked goose as he reared back for the first pitch. Casey prayed not to drop the ball.

The ironically nicknamed Big John Henderson was standing just a few feet away with the radar gun pointed at the plate. When the pitch, a fastball, sailed over the dish and into Casey's mitt, it left the five-time all-star shaking his head at the dugout. "Seventy-nine," he shouted. Hardy spit a brown wad of tobacco into the dirt, muttering to himself as he caught the ball and got set again, pausing until his hand had found its grip. In came the next pitch, another limp fastball that barely made a sound as it hit the pocket of Casey's mitt. Again, the results were less than impressive:

"Eighty-one."

It's true that Hardy's fastball had lost a few klicks over the years. When he'd arrived in the league, his four-seamer had topped out at around 92-93, and he could mow guys down with just his fastball. Now there were journalists and bloggers and armchair general managers publicly questioning if he'd be able to get Big League hitters out at all this year, or if the sixteen million owed to him was a sunk cost.

Not that he'd given them any reason to doubt him. Even with all those horses escaping the old engine, Hardy had found a way to keep his ERA close to that 3.50 mark it had been hovering around for the past ten seasons. For Casey, there was no forgetting Hardy's heroics in the big ULDS elimination game fifteen years ago with the Monks, when he'd pitched the no-hitter and got the W to upset a Red Birds team that had led the UL in wins and had been heavily favoured to win it all.

Former Sams outfielder, John Smelt, was standing by the bleachers, dusting something off the shoulder of his navy pin-stripe suit while a man holding a camera counted down on his fingers to rolling. By the time the cameraman got to one, Smelt was fully composed: shoulders square, smiling with brilliant white teeth for the people at home as he held a microphone up to the frowning mug of Lou, who had just finished chewing out the team's starting left fielder, Dominic Hernandez, for taking it easy during wind sprints that morning and was flushed red like a tomato from the exertion.

"John Smelt here from BLB Network and we've got the Blue Birds skipper Lou Caputo joining us from here at the Blue Birds training facility in Dunedin, Florida. He's taken some time out of his busy schedule to talk to us about his ball club. Thanks for speaking with us, Lou."

"No need to thank me—it's what I'm paid for."

"I guess that's a big part of it."

"Some days it feels like the only part."

"I'm sure it does, especially since this is the just the first day of Spring Training. Now, I know a few of these guys have been down here all winter, getting ready for the season—"

"Let's not overstate the situation. Only two fellas have been down here all winter: one of 'em's a nutcase and the other's plain desperate."

"What I was getting to," said Smelt, managing to maintain his television smile, "is that a lot of people at home probably think you mostly sit on the bench and make calls out to the bullpen, but you and I both know that as the manager you've got your fingers in a whole mess of pies. In fact, you probably have just about the clearest idea of what's going on with the team as anybody. Even though camp has only recently started, I was hoping you could give the folks at home some insight into what you're seeing in this team so far."

"I'm going to level with you, Smelty," said Lou, taking off his hat and running his fingers over his bald crown. "That's the longest damned question that anybody's ever had the nerve to ask me. Do you really want to know what I think of this here baseball team after the first few days of camp?"

"Well, that's my job," said Smelt, turning to the camera and flashing a smile.

Lou drummed his fingers on the equipment rack as he contemplated his response.

"Do you really want to know?"

"If I didn't, why would I be asking?"

Lou spat some seed husks on the floor and looked out onto the field. "You know what I see when I look at this here team? I see a bunch of talented deadbeats. The problem is that not a one of them believes in anything that could be thought of as a team concept. With these goons it's just me, me, me, me all the time. Whether we win or lose—what's any of that matter? So long as they can look at the box-score at the end of the night and say, *Well, I did my job*, that's good enough for them."

"I think what you're trying to say is the team needs to come together if they're going to be competitive."

"No, Smelty. What I'm standing here saying to you is that— barring a miracle—this team's as good as dead in the water."

"Would you care to elaborate?"

"Let's look at the facts here: I've got a full-blooded narcissist at the keystone, who's more concerned with marketing sports drinks than he is about contributing to a winning atmosphere; I've got a couple of uppity frogs in the bullpen more worried about getting strippers' phone numbers than preparing for their next appearance; I've got a fifteen million dollar pitcher who couldn't hit the broad side of a barn; a closer who is an undiagnosed psychopath but—believe me—the diagnosis is forthcoming; I've players here in camp who oughta be serving time in state penitentiaries, not getting served invitations to a Big League Spring Training; and Old Man Time himself up there tossing eighty mile-per-hour meatballs even my dead mother— God rest her soul—couldn't make no juicier. I'll tell you something, this team could maybe do something if they all managed to stop sniffing their own farts long enough to take a look at themselves and figure their shit out, but that's got about as much chance of happening as hell has of freezing over. The way things are shaping up, we could end up last in the division."

"That doesn't exactly sound like a ringing endorsement of your squad or the front office."

Tubs, the team's bench coach, stepped in, pushing Lou aside. "I think what the boss here is trying to say, is we've got a long way to go until opening day and we plan on using this time to whip these here boys into shape. Ain't that right, Lou?"

"That's one way of pinning a bow on this donkey's ass of a situation."

"As you can see," said Smelt, all smiles again for the camera as Tubs dragged Lou out of frame, "longtime Toronto bench boss Lou's still candid as ever. Back to you guys at the studio."

"What in the hell's the matter with you?" said Tubs once he was sure Smelt was out of earshot. "You tryin' to get your crack-er-ass fired or somethin'?"

"Why not? Better now than later, when they can hang this season around my neck."

"Here we go again," said Tubs, rubbing his forehead.

"I mean, why stick around? So they can parade me through the streets and the masses can flog me to death for being saddled with this collection of human waste?"

"Tell me somethin'. If you want to be done with it so badly, why don't you just up and quit?"

"If I quit, who'd keep this bunch of freaks from murderin' one another?"

"I would," said Tubs flatly. "You ain't the only one who can manage a baseball club. You might not even be the best person for the job. You know Don's gonna be awful sore once he sees that there interview."

"I wouldn't worry too much about that prick. If he were going to fire me, he'd have done it back in October, when it might have bought him a little credibility. Now that we've made it to camp he'll just wait until it looks like this team is ready to go off the goddamned rails and only then will he offer my head up to the fans, hoping buy himself a few more weeks."

"Yeah? Well, I don't think too many teams will be looking for a manager that goes and squawks to the media about how bad a job the front office has done before the season's even started."

"Who said I'd be looking to join a team anyway?" said Lou, tossing a handful of seeds into his mouth.

"So that's how it is," said Tubs, turning his head slightly to examine Lou's expression.

Neither man said anything for some time. As the position players gathered behind the cage for batting practice, Lou stepped to the bottom of the steps and checked the clipboard. There, at the very bottom of the page, was Casey's name.

"How long do you suppose we'll be expected to humour this kid?" asked Lou.

Tubs looked down at the name Lou was pointing at and said, "Quite some time, I'd expect. You and I both know what he's here for."

"See, that's where you're wrong, because I *don't* understand what this son of a bitch is doing here. I'd understand seeing this kid's name here on the Spring Training roster if he could play, but I've seen this kid in the cage and I'm telling you this guy would have a hard time competing in A-ball, let alone the Big Leagues."

"The eggheads at the top figure he might have enough value with the glove that it don't matter whether or not he can hit, so long as we don't gotta rely on him to be an everyday player," said Tubs. "Course, that's assuming that by accident or incident he don't somehow, over the course of the season, become an every-day player out of necessity, now don't it?"

"Over my dead body!"

Tubs regarded Lou through his coke-bottle glasses. "It may come to that. Rumour has it the big man asked for this punk by name."

It was now Lou's turn to regard Tubs. "Is that so?" he asked, leaning down and spitting seed husks onto the dirt. "Reardon requested this son of a bitch?"

Tubs nodded.

"And since when do players get a say in roster decisions?"

"It's just a rumour—something a little birdy told me," said Tubs, returning his gaze to the field.

It was the morning of the first practice. So far, through the team meetings, the warm-up drills, and the bullpen sessions, Casey hadn't felt overmatched. He was able to keep up with everybody during the work-out and was even in better shape now than some of the veterans like Chet or Ramirez, who were noticeably winded by what Casey now considered to be mild exertion.

During the morning bullpen session, he caught everything Hardy could throw at him. Of course, Hardy wasn't exactly making catching the ball difficult. It didn't seem to matter what Casey threw down, or where he put his glove, Hardy hit the target. He painted both corners with fastballs, sliders, and change-ups so accurate Casey barely had to do any job at all.

Twenty minutes after the bullpen session, Casey was scheduled to join the rest of the position players at Field 3 for batting practice. By the time he arrived, the first batter was already warming up.

Casey stood at the far end of the cage, watching the first guy take his hacks. This was Cruz, the right fielder, who was now thirty-two, but still considered to be one of the game's premier contact hitters. He was peppering balls all over the field: to right, to left, centre, along the baselines, and over the fence. His swing was one, smooth, predictable motion—a quick, rotational stroke that allowed him to get his bat through the strikezone in a hurry. By the time Cruz stepped out of the batter's box, any confidence Casey had accrued that morning was completely and utterly crushed. He was nowhere near this good. It didn't matter how much he practiced; he'd probably never look like that out there.

He wasn't allowed to dwell on this thought for long, because his shoulder was jostled into the fence by the next man up as the batter rounded the barrier and stepped out onto the diamond. He gripped his bat in his armpit, squeezed his hands into a pair of batting gloves, and looked back over his shoulder, muttering, "Watch it, rookie."

Nobody had their names on the back of their jerseys yet, but Casey knew by the piped number one this must be the second baseman, Eddie Steele.

Steele was short for a ballplayer, standing a mere five-foot nine, but what he lacked in height he more than made up for in the breadth of his shoulders. His cleats were custom made and the same Royal Blue as the Birds' Uniform, except down towards the sole where a deep purple bled from the fabric to the rubber, punctuated by day-glo green spikes composed of some space-age material. His gloves were the same colour as the spikes. He blew a pink bubble as he prepared to take his hacks.

Steele's stance looked awkward, his feet spread open toward the pitcher and his chest almost parallel to the rubber, like he'd just opened some door and was on the verge of stepping inside. In the media lab later that afternoon, Reardon would slow it down and Casey could see the whole sequence unfold frame by frame. Casey watched Steele's front foot lift off, and arc back to the middle of the batter's box into something resembling a traditional batting stance. Casey's gaze kept flipping from the foot to the ball, foot to the ball, as one approached the earth and the other approached the plate, and then the white blip was gone, the foot was down and—

Pop.

Everyone's heads turned to follow the trajectory of the ball as it shot out towards right field, slicing, slicing, and finally glancing off the distant foul-pole. By the time those in attendance returned their attention to the batter's box, Steele was already back into his stance, acting like nothing had happened, ready for the next pitch. He proceeded to crush everything that the pitching coach could throw at him.

And those two weren't alone. To Casey's surprise, almost every position player here at the Big League camp was an excellent hitter. Player after player stepped to the plate and proceeded to knock the cover off the ball.

The crowd around the batting cage swelled when the pitchers began to trickle in from a meeting at one of the backfields. Reardon and the Aucoin twins leaned against the fence, laughing about something, while the team's number three starter, Amuro, and his translator watched from the bench. The rest huddled on the other side of the chainlink, whispering their observations.

Casey was slow to take the bat when his name was finally called and even slower walking out to the batter's box. He squeezed his sweaty hands into his batting gloves and velcroed them up tight. His sweeping, questioning gaze was met by the hard eyes of his appraisers, who stood motionless in the various poses of disrespect and apathy that always accompany the entrance of the outsider, the upstart, or the guy who probably shouldn't be here. Casey knew there was only one question on their minds, and that was: could he, or couldn't he? As he stepped into the box and dug in his spikes, he knew definitively that he could not.

Casey skipped the shower, changing straight into his street clothes and attempting to slip out before anybody noticed. Just as he put his hand on the clubhouse door, someone said, "Hold up."

He turned around and found Steele with his arms folded across his chest. Casey looked around the clubhouse and saw that most of the eyes were pointed in his direction. He returned his gaze to Steele, who was inserting a pink tab of bubble gum and awaiting Casey's response.

"Yeah?" Casey said, finally.

"Weren't you supposed to be some big deal or somethin'?"

"If I was, this is the first I've heard of it."

"You hear that?" said Steele, turning to the rest of the players. "He says it's the first he's heard of it. That's strange, you know, because I've sure as hell heard of you."

Casey cleared his throat. "Really?"

"Sure I have! You were that guy who got drafted first overall and spent all your damned bonus on blow and hoodrats. Ain't that right?"

Casey's mind raced through rapidfire fantasies of escape. He daydreamed of mounds of coke on a dark black table, surrounded by a harem of the finest offerings the Clearwater meat-market had to offer, no expenses spared.

"I said, ain't that right?"

"I guess so," said Casey, shaking it off.

"You guess so?" said Steele, sucking his teeth. "Motherfucker, let me tell you something: you don't belong here."

"I'm jus—"

"*I'm just.* You're just what?"

"I'm just trying to make the team."

"Man, you ought to just quit now and save yourself the embarrassment. You won't survive this first week, let alone make the team out of camp. I mean, who the hell are you tryin' to fool?"

"Too bad you ain't the one who gets to make the decisions, Ed," said Reardon.

"If it ain't the famous Phil Reardon," said Steele. "Shoulda known. Whenever something doesn't smell right it's a sure sign that your big, dumb ass can't be too far away."

"Alls I'm saying is you don't got no crystal ball—a hell of a lot can happen between now and the end of Spring Training."

"You don't say. Well maybe I don't got no crystal ball, but I can spot a scrub from a mile away. This punk right here? He's a scrub. We all just saw him crash and burn harder than the goddamned Hindenburg."

"Well since you're so sure, why don't we make a little wager?"

Steele looked first at Casey, then back to Reardon. "How much we talking?"

"Say," said Reardon, spitting into his cup. "That there's a mighty fine watch. Mont Blanc, ain't it?"

"What do you got to bet against it?"

"If I lose, you get my wheels."

Steele sucked his teeth. "What would I want with that pile of shit?"

"I don't know," said Reardon. "Sell it if you want to."

"Fuck that. I probably couldn't find nobody to take that junk off my hands for free."

"What's the matter? Scared you'll lose?"

Tubs was over by the coffee machine and had stopped mixing creamer into his mug when he heard the commotion and decided to intervene. "What in the hell are you two on about?"

"They are about to engage in a bet," offered Patrice.

"You fuckin' narc," said Reardon.

"Thought so and no: they ain't. You know the rules, Reardon. There ain't no betting in the clubhouse. It's bad enough you fleeced Davis for as much as you did."

Reardon's face was the picture of surprise. "I never fleeced Davis."

"Sure you didn't. I bet you didn't hustle Bryant, neither."

"Well I may have bested him at a few honest games of cards from time to time. What of it?"

"Point being that you and those like you are the reason we've got the damned rule in the first place. Now quit stirring the damned pot and hit the showers so we can all go home."

The players grumbled as they turned their backs and began to disrobe, tossing their dirty apparel into the caddies for Rahim to wash and have ready for tomorrow. That is, everyone except Casey, who now made his way to the parking lot, where he stood next to Reardon's car so long that security came by to make sure he wasn't a *disturbed person.*

In truth, Casey hardly noticed the time pass because he was so engrossed with his cocaine fantasies. All he would need is one good score, just enough to get him through training camp. He could be disciplined. He could stretch it out—keep it down to a bump a day. No, he couldn't fall back into old bad habits. Nonsense, he didn't have to go the full monty with sobriety. He could just pick himself up an eight-ball and stretch it out by keeping it to just a bump, just when he really needed it. Maybe he still knew somebody down in the Tampa Bay area who could hook him up.

"Yeesh, you fucking reek," said Reardon once the two men were in the car. "Did you not shower or something?"

"I guess I forgot."

"Yeah? Well do us both a favour and don't forget before you get into my fucking car next time."

Reardon spent most of the drive back to the Holiday Inn Express blasting a Steppenwolf album at full volume. Casey sat in the passenger seat with his forehead pressed against the window, staring out at the signs and palms as they whipped by. His ruminations alternated between replaying this afternoon's events and his cocaine fantasy.

"Don't put your face on the glass, would ya? You're gonna grease it all up."

"Today was bad, wasn't it?" asked Casey as he sat up. "I'm fucked, aren't I?"

"I ain't gonna sugarcoat it for ya, kid. You were pretty fucking awful out there." Reardon kept his eyes on the road as he blindly spat a wad of used tobacco into his cup. "But, you know, the swing's coming around. Sooner or later it'll click and you'll be laughing."

"Yeah? It sure doesn't feel that way."

"You've gotta trust the process. Put your head down, do the work, and sooner or later it'll turn around. I ain't saying you'll be a superstar, but you'll quit embarssin' yourself out there."

"Fantastic."

"Games are comin' up quick. Lemme ask you something. When you step into that batter's box, what exactly are you aiming to do?"

"Put the bat on the ball, what else?"

"You mean you're planning on just going up there and swinging at anything, hoping you'll make contact?"

"Pretty much."

"Jesus. Hitting ain't like batting practice. Even the fans know that you can't just go waltzing into the box without a plan and expect to be able to put your bat to a baseball. What them Cheesesteaks saw in you to go and take you first overall I won't never understand."

"You and me both."

"I didn't mean nothing by it," said Reardon. "It's just everybody knows you've gotta have a plan. I mean, how are you s'posed to hit something when you don't even know what you're lookin' for?"

"How am I supposed to know what to look for?"

"That's simple enough. Alls you gotta do is think about where, ideally, you'd want the pitch to wind up."

"Right down the middle of the plate would be nice."

"Yeah? Well the way you're swingin' the bat right now, it don't seem like you can hit those pitches either." Reardon sucked his teeth. "Even the worst pitcher in the Bigs don't serve it up like that for you unless they make a mistake. They all work the corners, work back and forth, just the same as you and I do when we're trying to get the other guys out. What you've gotta do is pick part of the strike zone and wait until the ball winds up there and then you just let 'er rip. Would you rather have the ball come in below or above your waist?"

"Below, I guess."

"Well then there you go."

Casey didn't appear to know what he meant.

"You're a low-ball hitter," said Reardon, swatting Casey's skepticism away like a fly. "Can't say I'm surprised, what with you being a lefty and all. Now that you know you're a low-ball hitter, all you've gotta do is look for pitches in the lower half and let all the high stuff pass on by. Sooner or later you'll get your pitch, and then you can let 'er rip. Because nobody thinks you can hit, they'll be throwing you nothing but heat, so sooner or later you'll get hold of something."

"And how the hell am I supposed to know if it's coming in low or not?"

Reardon shrugged. "How am I supposed to know? Some things can't be told—they've gotta be experienced. Just keep in mind that you want that low pitch and your body will figure it out."

"And what if I never figure it out?"

"Then I guess you're shit out of luck. Don't worry about it; it's not like you're here to hit anyway. All you oughta care about is making sure I look good every time I step onto that mound, because between you and me, that's the only thing that's gonna get you to the Big Leagues."

The plate Casey had taken from the caddy was still warm in his hands as he approached a buffet tray of greasy, artificial-looking eggs, when all of a sudden he heard: "I wouldn't if I were you, mon ami."

Casey turned around to find Patrice and Felix standing behind him.

"Have you not read the dietary plan?" asked Felix.

"No, I've just been eating whatever's put in front of me."

"Not me either," said Patrice, stepping in front of Casey and loading his own plate with three of the eggs from the warming tray. "You only live once, no?"

"This is true," Felix said as he slid a couple onto his own plate. "Go on, we will not—how you say?—rat you out."

"Well thanks, I guess," said Casey.

"Do not mention it, eh? How have you been enjoying camp so far?"

"It's been just fine. I'm just trying to stay out of everyone's way. You know, be useful and all that."

"Ah, that is a good attitude to have, mon ami. While myself and Patrice, we appreciate your effort, the same cannot be said for everyone. No?"

"I'm aware that not everyone likes me."

"Oui, and some, they dislike you more than others," said Patrice.

"Some, they may be looking for ways to get rid of you."

"Yeah? Like who?"

"Word around is that this Eddie, he has been complaining about you to the people up on the top."

"Is that so?"

"This is the rumour," said Felix. "Watch your back. Steele? He is just as dangerous as this Reardon. No? I would steer clear from him if I were you."

"I'll keep that in mind," said Casey, spooning some home fries onto his plate.

"May I suggest," said Patrice with a concerned glance at Casey's plate, "some salade de fruits?"

The stuff about Steele having it in for him sounded ridiculous to Casey, who tried to write it off as Patrice and Felix fucking with him. All the same, he went to great lengths to avoid Steele over the next few days. It helped that the second baseman was preoccupied with all the attention the media was shoveling on him. He could hardly take two steps without being stopped by some reporter for an interview. Then there were the constant demands for autographs from fans and profiteers alike. Steele would spend twenty minutes walking along a length of oustretched hands, signing all sorts of merch: baseballs, hats, jerseys, shoes, baseball cards, autograph albums.

The worst Casey had to deal with were the reporters, their questions different phrasings of the same query, *How can you justify being here?*

He didn't have an answer for them. Casey knew he had no place being in a Big League training camp, so he stuck to the stock answer that had been provided him in the pre-camp package and rehearsed in the mirror every night: "I'm just happy the Blue Birds have given me this opportunity.

The suits Don had been wearing all winter simply would not do as the makings of a wardrobe for Spring Training, not with all these rub-a-dub types like Lou hanging about, making one stand out like a sore thumb. One had to properly accessorize if one was to leave the right impression—that one was both the boss and at the same time not completely out of touch with the task at hand. Here Don certainly looked the part, wearing a pair of creased khakis, a tucked-in, blue cotton polo emblazoned with the team logo, and on his wrist the platinum Rolex he had procured at a police auction. He sipped from a paper coffee cup as he watched the hand glide from one second to the next. Where did the time go? At least with his old Patek Philippe there was always that little pause where you felt like you might be able to hold on to a second, but there was no fooling with this—the time just melted away. No matter how well one organized its use, it was always escaping through the cracks.

His eyes were hidden behind a pair of Ray Ban aviators, which reflected the gleam of the Florida sun as he looked up to see the players spill from the dugout tunnel. It was little comfort that Spring Training meant nothing, not when the team was playing this badly a week and a half in. Nothing seemed to be going right. Chet had looked like the tired old man he probably was, and Amuro couldn't keep his knuckleball in the strikezone. The twins had both been sidelined for the next week with identical hamstring strains Don suspected of being totally bogus, the outfield regulars were a combined three-for-fifteen, and the team had only scored five runs in ten games. The only silver lining was that Steele and Reardon were as dominant as expected. They looked like they could start the season tomorrow.

The press was already after blood. The widely publicized interview between Smelt and Lou had fanned the flames of a PR war Don was deep in the process of losing. Tedd Chair had gone on the corporate radio station the previous evening and blasted the front office's offseason as being laden with half-measures and missed opportunities. "But let's not blame the corporation for holding firm to the purse strings," Chair had opined to his listeners. "After all, they added more than fifty million to the payroll over the past few years, and what do they have to show for it? Third and fourth place finishes and the lowest attendance in decades."

Tedd had, of course, been spot-on in his assessment. Nobody had held a gun to Don's head and forced him to do anything. There were countless opportunities and paths he could have pursued, but he and those he had surrounded himself with had chosen this one. Of course, members of the press had the advantage of hindsight, and those very same people, Tedd Chair included, had been lauding those same decisions when they first were made. It was just bad luck that none of them had turned out. That was baseball.

Don felt his phone buzz in his pocket and fished it out. It was Harry Ruben of the Monuments. He'd been after Don to move one—or both—of the Aucoin twins all offseason, making a bunch of lowball offers designed to prey on Don's desperation and Don *was* desperate. Ruben had whittled him down and whittled him down, and they had almost gotten to the point where Don thought he could make a deal for an BLB-ready third baseman who was, at present, blocked by the Monuments' incumbent Johnny Luvello. He had sent a text to Harry that morning to ask if he could still count on the deal taking place after the twins came off the IL and his response now was, "We'll see." With that deal scuttled, it seemed like Don was stuck.

There was, of course, the nuclear option. Out at short stood Manny "The Thing" Singh, the team's top prospect. The media had been howling for him to make the team all winter. He had slashed an impressive .332/.450/.477 and stolen forty-seven bases the previous year in the International League. He was just the player to complement this old, increasingly ineffective roster, but Don didn't want him to make the team out of camp because it meant Singh would achieve super-two status. If he turned out to be the player everyone in the front office hoped he would be, the arbitration numbers alone could become cost prohibitive in the relatively near future. If they wanted to keep him from achieving super-two, Singh had to play in Buffalo until June.

The way their present starting shortstop, Fletcher, had played so far made it increasingly difficult to hold off members of his own front office, who pointed out that it didn't matter if they had an extra year of control if they all lost their jobs at the end of the season. Don had to concede that they had a point, but had so far been steadfast in his resistance to Singh's call-up. All the same, he harboured doubt.

Casey knew Singh from back in his National Junior days. Not well, since Singh had joined the team near the end of Casey's time as a junior, and by then he was already spending most of his free time doing coke. From what little contact they had, the one thing Casey remembered was that Singh never stopped moving. He was always bouncing up and down on his feet when out on the field and his bat was always wiggling when he was in the box. Even on the team bus or on the rare occasion they flew in an airplane, the kid bounced continuously up and down in his seat.

Here he was sitting down at Casey's table and he still hadn't stopped moving.

"Hey, buddy! Long time no see, except on the front page, huh?"

It took Casey a moment to recognize him. "Hey, Manny," he said. "What are you doing here?"

"I am the number seven prospect in all of baseball. Where have you been, brother?"

"Congratulations."

"Thanks, man. It doesn't seem to help me much though. The powers that be say I'm not ready yet. They'd rather keep trotting out that dinosaur every night and hope for the best," said Singh, nodding toward Fletcher. "Whatever they've gotta tell the media to create some doubt that what they're really doing is trying to put the screws in me. You know what I'm saying?"

"No," said Casey.

"I'm saying they're trying to get between me and my money. You feel me?"

"Sure," said Casey.

"And what're you doing here? I heard they got you on a minor league deal."

"Yeah, but I've been promised a spot on the team, so I guess it's a Big League deal."

"They gave *you* a Big League deal? After the shit you pulled?"

"They needed a backup catcher."

Singh gave Casey a sly look. "Yo, is it true what they've been saying about you?"

"I don't know. What have they been saying?"

Singh lowered his voice and leaned in. "That you're here to catch that crazy fool Reardon."

"That's what they've told me."

"Then you better watch your back, brother."

"Why's that?"

"Because that dude is straight loco," said Singh, digging into the somewhat flavourless lunch provided by the nutrition and development department.

The days were long, longer even than the ones Casey had been ticking off the calendar since December, with endless drills and meetings and practices and side-sessions and more meetings. Everything was happening so fast that had Reardon not turned to Casey and asked if he was ready, Casey might have never guessed.

"Ready for what?"

Reardon smiled and spat into his cup. "You mean you forgot?"

"Forgot what?"

"You're in today's lineup, dipshit."

It was an abnormally cold day for Central Florida at this time of year. Most of the players had taken the field in their cold weather gear: turtlenecks, double-eared helmets, and earmuffs. A few even wore royal blue balaclavas. The bitching had started almost the moment the players had began trickling in. The regulars wanted to be swapped out of the lineup for so-and-so. Meanwhile, the tenured backups begged not to be swapped in, so they could rest this or that injury.

"I gotta rest it up for the regular season," Chandler had said to Lou that morning. "You want me good and ready for opening day, right?"

"What in the hell is there to get ready for? How's sitting on your ass going to help you get ready for the regular season?"

"I'm a little banged up right now."

"Sure, you and everyone else in this goddamned locker room. Do you think I can't see what's going on around here? It's forty degrees out there and I've got a room full of players that don't want to play."

"I'm telling you that something isn't right with my body, Lou. I can feel it."

"Speak to Frank."

"He doesn't think there's anything wrong with me, but I don't think he's right. If you'd just give me the day off, I'd really appreciate it."

"I'll take Frank's word for it. You play the first three innings, or is three innings too many for a delicate snowflake?"

Chandler shook his head. "I can't believe you think I'm making this up."

"Let's get one thing straight right now," said Lou, poking the air. "I never said a thing about thinking you're lying, but this ain't a goddamned radio station request show. I write the lineup card the way I think it oughta be and we stick to it, end of story. Now maybe you're banged up and maybe you ain't. I don't know. What I do know is that if my trainer and the team's doctors say you can play, you can play. Now get the hell out of my office and suit up."

It was crap like that—people wanting to get out of their responsibilities—that stuck in Lou's craw the worst. He'd played at Exhibition Stadium in April and he'd played at Greenway in the last days of October and had the good sense to just be thankful for the God-given opportunity to play. Here these losers didn't want to be out there if it got a little nippy.

Tubs sat on the other side of Lou's desk with his hat resting on his knee and said, "Don't you think you were a little hard on the guy?"

"I'm sorry, next time I'll be careful not to crush any of our little flowers. You know he's the third guy this mornin' that's come in here begging for the day off. You think Mel Zipkin would take a day off when he could help it? No. The only way you'd get him off that field is in a stretcher or a goddamned body bag. And do you know why?"

"Because he was lucky?"

Lou spat seed husks into his cup. "Because he just wanted to play. Believe me, none of the mediocrities in there would play hurt because they're too busy worrying about their hair or their next contract."

"I hate to be the one to say this, Lou, but he's right. It's just a preseason game. Besides, what if he ain't lying and he really is hurt?"

"Then I guess it will be one hell of a character-building experience, won't it?"

The players' attitudes hadn't improved much since they'd taken the field. Cruz had ordered six space heaters on same-day delivery which were now plugged into a power bar running under the bench. Lou had nearly tripped over one of the damned things and broke his neck entering the dugout, so he kicked it down the stairs into the tunnel, where it lay smouldering a few minutes before stadium personnel quietly came and cleaned it up. By now all the heaters had been removed save one in the middle of the dugout where a group of veterans stood with their hands spread before them.

Lou had to admit it was cold. Sitting on the bench, his knees stiffened to the point where he wasn't sure if he could even stand, so instead of testing them out, he had the batboy run down to the clubhouse to get him a cup of coffee and a fresh bag of seeds.

The home team's regulars took the field in their cold weather gear. Lou looked at the lineup card and saw he had that snot-nosed punk batting ninth. He let out a groan. This had gone far enough. Hadn't two weeks of anemic swings in the cage proven that this piece of human excrement couldn't play? Lou felt like he must be taking crazy pills or something.

At least the kid's defense was something to write home about. The way he was able to handle Amuro's knuckleball was one thing of which Lou—a former catcher—stood in envy. The kid had lied about his arm, too. On more than one occasion during the intrasquad matchups he came up throwing before he'd hardly caught the baseball, drilling it right at the bag and into the webbing of the shortstop's mitt for the tag. Casey was clocked going pop-to-pop in a blistering 1.6 seconds, which put him in the ninety-ninth percententile of Big League catchers, meaning the best. But what did any of that matter when he didn't know how to frame pitches, call a game, or hit a baseball to save his life? Yet there was his name again, right at the bottom of the card.

This wasn't of Lou's choosing. The decision had come all the way from the top. After Lou had benched Casey for the eleventh game in a row, Don had come down and knocked on Lou's door.

"What are you waiting for?" Lou had shouted.

When he finally looked up from an advance scouting report on the Robins, Don was sitting on the opposite side of Lou's desk, typing something into his phone.

Lou took off his glasses and rubbed his eyes. "Haven't seen you around here in a while."

"I haven't needed to come down in a while," said Don, sliding his phone into the pocket of his Khakis. "But I was following the game on my phone and I noticed you benched him again."

"Who? Estavez? I played him just last night."

"I'm talking about Casey."

"Casey? Why would I play that schmuck?"

"Well, we've got him in camp. He's on a Big League contract. Don't you think you should be giving him a look?"

"I look at him plenty."

"That's not what I meant."

"With all due respect, Mr. Billingsley, don't you think this has gone on long enough?"

"How can it have gone on too long when Spring Training isn't over yet? I mean, that's what Spring Training's for, isn't it? To see what we've got."

"Ideally, Spring Training would be about getting your Globe Series contenders ready for the regular season. But as things stand, Spring Training is about getting some of the younger guys experience against Big League competition. One thing it ain't about is trotting out felons and acting like they're goddamned ballplayers."

"You sure do seem prejudiced against him."

"That's because I *am* prejudiced against him. I've got about five guys I'd rather have on the team and you're making me play him, even though you know as well as I do it's a waste of time. The kid can't hit. And if he can't hit, he can't play. It's as simple as that."

"Then teach him."

"Teach him? What in the fuck are you talking about?" asked Lou, taking a handful of seeds and tossing them into his mouth. "You know where this kid is at right now? He's at ground level.

Not even that, he's in the basement. He's got no swing, he can't see the ball, and he looks like he's never held a bat a day in his life. I tell ya, when he takes batting practice, it's like watching my three-year-old grandson tryin' to hit off a tee. I mean, it's adorable and everything, but I wouldn't put money on it striking fear into the hearts of our opponents. To make matters worse, the son of a bitch is dumber than a box of goddamned Junior Mints. And you want me to teach him? Well I can't teach him, and I'll pay you big money to find me somebody who can. Men spend their whole lives learning how to hit a ball and seventy percent of the time the best ones still can't do it. What makes you think this ingrate can learn it when he's starting from scratch at the age of twenty-four? I know he went first overall and everything, but he ain't so young no more."

"I've got my reasons."

"Don't think I don't know what this is really about. It's that son of a bitch Reardon again! Can't you see he's playing you?"

"I would like to remind you that I'm still the one in charge."

"Yeah? Then why don't you act like it and let Reardon know where he can shove his demands?"

"He's our best player. It's in our best interest to keep him happy."

"See, that's where you're wrong, Mr. Billingsley. I work with these guys day-in-day-out, and I can tell you for a fact that Eddie Steele's our best player," said Lou, spitting seed husks into a cup. "Reardon's just another relief pitcher on a roll."

"He's good for marketing. The fans eat it up."

"Fanfare's about all that scrub is any good for. I mean, he's a great player—I'll give you that—but in the end he's just a late-inning reliever who's got a maple leaf stamped on his passport where the eagle oughta be. You can't rely on that. Besides, he ain't re-signing here. As soon as October's through, he's going to the highest bidder. At least that's what he goes around telling anyone not wearing a press badge. Hell, he'll probably wind up in Boston or New York for twenty million, so unless you've got twenty million per annum in extra payroll just lying around, for-getaboutit."

"This isn't just about Reardon," said Don, typing into his phone. "We've also got Takazawa to consider. Do you know how many runs he gave up on wild pitches and passed balls alone last season? How many quality pitches—not even borderline—went for balls? The answer is too many. Casey's defense and blocking are off the charts, and you know it. You also know that defense is the most valuable contribution a catcher can provide. I mean, you weren't exactly much to look at in the batter's box yourself."

"Yeah, but I wasn't any degenerate, neither."

"He's made some mistakes."

"One hell of a booboo, if you ask me. Now, I know even before you open your mouth you're going to try to paint it as some sob story, but I'm telling you right now that won't fly with me. I don't feel sorry at all for that little son of a bitch. In fact, I wish they'd thrown the book at him like they would anybody else. He could've killed somebody."

"Everybody deserves a second chance."

"Yeah, but not many second chances get handed out, now do they? What makes this criminal so special?"

"As far as I'm concerned, the only thing that matters is that Casey can catch a ball really well," said Don. "And that's all anyone should care about until I say otherwise."

"With all due respect, this ain't really your decision to make. You get to play your little games up there in the front office, but down here in the clubhouse—down here on the field—I'm the one calling the shots. Do you know why? Because when things go wrong down here, I'm the one who's held accountable. "

"Your neck isn't the only one on the line," said Don nonchalantly.

"Maybe, but we both know the first head that's gonna roll as soon as things start going south."

"Please—"

"And do you wanna know somethin'? It ain't my management that's gotten us into this mess. You're the one who brought this bunch of self-centred turds together. Not a-one of them can lead us where we wanna go."

"Sometimes," said Don, brushing something off his pantleg, "I wonder what the hell you think I'm paying you for."

"I know you don't understand this because you've never played the game, Billingsley, but it can't be me who leads them. I mean, let's be real about this thing: I'm an old man with two bum knees who sits on a bench, writes lineup cards, and tells base runners when to steal and when to wait. You think these guys are gonna listen to me? Keep dreamin'. If anyone's gonna step up and lead these nutjobs, it's gonna havta be one of them."

"That sounds like an excuse. You know how I feel about excuses."

"You can feel however the hell you want about it. Say I'm making excuses, say I'm not—I don't give a rat's ass. It is what it is. You know, if you fired me now, you'd almost be doing me a favour. You'd be putting me out of my goddamned misery, is what you'd be doing. You might even feel pretty good about it after. But that won't happen, will it? No. As long as you've got me to point yer finger at, you can keep lying to yourself about who's really responsible for this train wreck." Lou slammed his hand on his desk. A moment of tense silence ensued before he reached up and loosened the collar of his uniform. "It don't matter. Sooner or later, you'll find out the team you've assembled is nothing but a steaming pile of busted garbage. Sure, they're talented, but none of them play according to a team concept. They're all nothin' but a bunch of degenerates, has bins, and never wuzzes."

Despite Lou's protests, there was Casey at the end of the bench, rolling his bat between his palms and staring out at the field. In the end, Lou figured he might as well give the boss what he asked for. What did it matter to him? Maybe once Don had seen the kid play some more, he'd decide he didn't want the lowlife on his team after all. What made this kid so special? He wasn't more than a dime-a-dozen rat.

Lou was wrenched from his thoughts by the realization that the rat's eyes were meeting his. He quickly looked away and spat conspicuously onto the floor before grabbing a tablet from one of the cubbyholes behind him. He swiped through the data until he found the scouting report on the other team's starter, not that it would be of much use in this Spring Training game. Everybody knew what to expect this early on: a lot of straight heat with a few changeups and curves mixed in to keep the Bird batters honest. Lou put the tablet back into its cubby, stood up with difficulty, and managed to climb the stairs to the top of the dugout, where Tubs was already positioned.

"Fine day for baseball, ain't it?" said Lou.

"Quit moanin'. Everybody done told you it was cold."

"You know something, Tubs? You're right! We'd best just forfeit and head back to the hotel."

"Don't say that too loud or you'll give the boys all sorts of ideas."

"You and I played in worse than this a hundred times over."

"Maybe we did, but it don't change the way things stand now. What're you up here for anyway? I was starting to think your plan was to spend all Spring Training with your ass planted on the bench."

"If I sat down for any longer my knees were threatening lock up. I'd rather not have to be wheeled out after the game, thank you very much."

"That ain't the reason."

"If you've gotta know, every time I look over at the moron sitting at the other end of the bench, I feel the urge to walk down there and choke him to death. Is that a good enough reason?"

Tubs sucked his teeth. "What you got against him anyway?"

"I'd tell you," said Lou, tossing a fistful of seeds into his mouth, "but it'd take me the whole damned afternoon and I've got a game to manage here."

Pittsburgh's starter was a regular beanpole, some schlep they'd fished out of Sidney, Nebraska named Jared Langston. From the dugout he looked nearly as tall as Reardon, but lacked the breadth. His arms were abnormally long, hanging almost to his calf when he stood at ease. StatMan systems in the minor leagues had clocked his average fastball velocity at 97 MPH. His secondary offering was a curveball with an average break depth of fourteen inches. He used it as his strikeout pitch.

He didn't seem too intimidating from here in the dugout. He had this old-timey delivery with an exaggerated leg kick that went up and over his head before coming back down as he fired the ball, which was hardly even a white blip against the background of the sideline wall.

Hernandez was leading off and the first pitch was a fastball that just clipped the outside corner at the letters. Hernandez wanted no part of it and let it pass for a strike. Langston followed it up with another fastball, this time inside at the knees for strike two. Hernandez took one foot out of the box and looked in towards the bench where Tubs was clapping his hands together, a sign that he should protect the plate. Hernandez hoofed at the dirt until he felt dug in and readied himself for the third pitch. Langston set into his windup and fired. From the dugout, Casey watched the ball come in nice and level, looking like it would shoot right through the heart of the strike zone. Hernandez couldn't resist and took a big hack, but it was a changeup and he swung through it so hard that he lost his grip on the bat, which went flying towards the home dugout and sent the opposing team's players and coaches ducking for cover. The umpire pumped his fist to signal the strikeout and Hernandez was forced to take the long walk back to the bench shaking his head.

And Langston was just getting started. The Blue Birds could do nothing but watch as he cruised through the first inning. He had them swinging at everything, needing only twelve pitches to notch three consecutive strikeouts.

Looking around at the other players, it struck Casey that not one of them seemed at all fazed by their failure. They just kept working their tobacco, their seeds, or their chewing gum. Least concerned of all was Lou, who stood at the top of the stairs spitting husks onto the grass.

None of this mattered to them. After all, most of them knew exactly where they would be by the time camp broke. Casey couldn't shake the feeling he was playing for his life, even with all the guarantees.

Four of them stood on the mound, gloves and hands raised to cover their mouths. Casey and Amuro stood listening to Tim Glickey while Saito translated.

"Now, on absolutely no account are you two to throw anything but the knuckleball. I don't care if the bases are loaded. Hell, I don't care if Jesus hisself come on down and tells you to throw the fastball, the only pitch I wanna see is that floater. I wanna see it dip and duck all over the place. You hear?"

Amuro had to wait for Saito to finish translating before he could respond with a simple nod.

"And you," said Glickey, turning toward Casey, "don't fuck up."

"I'll try not to, asshole," Casey mumbled as Glickey marched back to the dugout.

Saito scrambled off the field and Casey took the long walk back to the plate, where the umpire was standing in a heavy suit jacket and a pair of mitts.

"Hurry it up," said the umpire. "The sooner we get this over with the better."

Casey got into his crouch and put down the sign for the knuckleball, to which Amuro, sixty-feet-six-inches away on the mound, gave a nod of affirmation and got set. Casey rested the lip of his mitt on the dirt and watched as Amuro rocked back and fired the ball, his fingers pushing it straight ahead. A balloon on a string, the ball made its slow approach, bobbing first one way and then another, until it was the size of a bowling ball. Casey lifted his glove out of the dirt and kept tracking the pitch as it took one last break down, under the swinging bat of the Swashbucklers' shortstop, Paredes.

"Strike."

Casey looked down into the glove and there it was, the ball, a big smear of red clay forming a bright checkmark on its white hide. Amuro wouldn't use this, so Casey had to trade for one with the umpire. When he turned his head, he found the umpire had already fished one from one of his gigantic ballbags and held it next to his head. Casey pivoted around to look at the umpire, whose face was hidden behind his mask.

"Hurry up," repeated the ump. "The way you're movin' we're all liable to freeze to death out here."

And they were off. Casey stuck to the game plan and called for nothing but the knuckleball. So far, it had totally neutralized Pittsburgh's hitters, who didn't know what to make of it. They were either lunging across the plate to get late-breaking pitches on the outer half, or else swinging out of their shoes at pitches that looked like they were right in the danger zone but wound up near their ankles. It was all Casey could do to keep the ball in front of him. By leaping this way and that he was somehow able to smother the errant pitches. He was so busy in the first that even in this cold, beads of sweat began to trickle down his forehead.

Amuro came back out for the bottom of the second inning and continued to mow down the Swashbucklers' hitters by striking out the side. Only one ball had managed to get past Casey, but it was a third strike that kicked off his left shoe and went all the way to the backstop. Casey stood up, tore off his mask, and ran for the ball, which he barehanded and fired to first. Thankfully, the batter wasn't very quick, and Casey's strong throw was just in time to beat the runner. He didn't make the same mistake when Amuro punched out the final hitter of the second inning on a pitch that broke out of the zone just off the end of the bat. This time he laid out, got a hold of it, and was able to sidestep the runner and fire the ball cleanly to first, where Thompson's open mitt was waiting. Thompson held up the ball for the umpire, who punched the runner out.

While the Birds' defense jogged back to the dugout, Tubs and Lou stood at the bottom of the steps, pointing to the field and whispering to one another. The veterans made a bee-line for the space heater, around which the regulars who had been lucky enough to have the day off were already arranged as if around a campfire: crouching with their palms out to soak in as much of the warmth as they could. Casey walked past and started taking off his pads to get ready to bat.

He was scheduled to hit second in the third, but was secretly hoping it wouldn't get that far, that maybe Lou would pull the plug. Casey knew with the way the guy on the mound was pitching he didn't have much of a chance, and hoped to be spared the embarrassment. Someone might come over, tap him on the shoulder, say *that'll do,* and tell him to head on back to the safety of the dugout. He hoped it even as he was walking towards the box. He looked back to the dugout, but no help was on the way—Lou just stood there with his arms folded across his chest, chewing his seeds, spitting out the husks, and talking to Tubs. *Man*, thought Casey, as he stepped into the box, *what I wouldn't do for a bump.*

It started to spit at some point during the bottom half of the second, and now the rain was coming down in a steady drizzle. Water beaded on the plastic shell of his helmet and came streaming down in rivulets, dripping steadily off the bill. The pitcher was out there on the mound, the moist rosin bag in his hand. Casey got set, digging in his spikes, and lifted his bat so that his hands were almost at his ear, the bat's end wagging back and forth in his loose grip. White veins of doubt writhed across his consciousness like lightning on a plain. *Just see the ball and hit the ball*, he told himself as Langston fired in the first pitch. Casey watched the arm come up and over like the blade of a wind-turbine and release the ball. It strobed in and out of Casey's field of vision and before he knew it, he was swinging as hard as he could, his eyes closed and his mind hoping for the best. The bat zoomed through the zone so fast it nearly spun him around and he opened his eyes to find that he had come up empty, the first pitch changeup having fooled him.

A man wearing a poncho and a hat with an umbrella fastened to it kept shouting, "Get off the field, ya bum!" as Casey stepped back into the box, kicked his spikes into the dirt, and waited for the next pitch. This time everything happened just the way it had before, with Langston getting set, the windmill, the ball leaving his hand and zooming towards the plate, but

Casey saw it better—way better. No longer a white blip, the ball exploded in size. He tracked it almost all the way to the plate with his eyes, but for some reason closed them at the last second, just before the moment in which he made contact. He knew he'd gotten a piece of it it on account of the heavy wooden crack and the pain shooting through his hands into his wrists—a fistful of bees. He opened his eyes and was getting ready to leave the box when there came the umpire's strike call. Casey looked back at the catcher, who wiggled his glove, showing the ball was safe and secure, a foul tip.

Now Casey was down 0-2 and knew that he'd really blown it on that second pitch. *Stupid*, he thought to himself. *You've got to see the ball and hit it, dummy,* came a familiar voice. He stared down at the barrel of his bat like he was checking it for imperfections, breathed in deep, and then stepped back into the batter's box and got set again. The rain was really coming down now and Casey could see the grounds crew gathering around the roll-up tarps, getting ready to lay them out over the playing surface.

Langston came set, repeated his delivery, and there wasn't even a blip. The ball just plum disappeared, leaving Casey standing there dumbfounded as the umpire pumped his fist for strike three.

When Casey came back to the dugout, everything was pretty much the same as when he left it: the skipper and his bench coach were still mumbling to each other; the starters all crowded along the bench in their jackets and toques worshipping the space heater; Chet was pointing and saying something to Ordoñez, whose bloodshot, yellow eyes were trying to make sense of the chaos out there; Thompson leaning out over the fence and spitting dark brown phlegm onto the grass. Nobody so much as raised their heads to acknowledge Casey as he put his equipment away and walked past them to the end of the bench where he picked up his chest guard and slung it over his shoulders.

Casey was about to return to the field for what was to be his last inning when a sudden gust of wind blew back the fronds of the palm trees beyond the outfield fence like dandelions. The rain picked up, causing puddles to form in the grass and making play impossible. The groundskeeper signaled to his crew to roll out the tarps and they ran across the field, their collars held up with one hand while dragging the unfurling tarp with the other. The clouds grew darker by the minute and a flash of lightning cracked the sky, causing the fans to head for the exits. The home plate and first base umpires, who had taken shelter in the Toronto dugout, held their hands out in the rain and shook their heads gravely.

They got on the phone with the umpires in the home team's dugout and it was decided they would have to telephone New York to get permission to call it. Golfball-sized raindrops fell from the sky and pelted the surface of the white tarps.

"I think we're to call it," said the crew chief, as he hung up the phone.

"You won't hear me complaining," said Lou, spitting husks onto the floor and walking towards the tunnel. "See you boys tomorrow."

And that was the ballgame.

By the time they had showered, changed, attended their post-game meetings, and driven back to the Holiday Inn Express it was nearly eight o'clock. All Casey wanted to do was hit the sack, but Reardon kept insisting on taking him out to eat. "You've gotta try it, man, this place is the best in town. We'll smoke a doob and hit the road. There's no saying no on account of it being my treat."

This supposedly amazing place turned out to be nothing but a Waffle House over in Treasure Island. It was already swarming with drunk tourists, the college types that stretch Spring Break into Spring Month, and teenaged townies out with their friends getting milkshakes. A few guys looked like truckers, but where were their trucks? Heads turned and gazes followed the ballplayers as they were led to a booth.

"Whaddya think?" asked Reardon, stretching his arms over the back of his seat.

"I don't know what to say. You brought me to a Waffle House."

"Anything you want," said Reardon, slapping his menu, "by God, you've got it. It's your day, kid. We're celebrating."

"What the fuck is there to celebrate?"

"Your failure. What else?"

"Fuck off."

"If you wanna know the truth, you've been looking like a beat dog ever since the game was called. It was starting to get mighty stale."

Casey combed his hair back with his fingers. "Today I lived out my worst nightmare."

"That's your worst nightmare? Shit, that wasn't even so bad. At least you were able to make contact with the ball and that guy was filthy. The problem is you're putting too much pressure on yourself, dipshit. You ain't here to swing the bat, remember?"

"How could I forget when you won't quit reminding me?"

"I'll quit reminding ya when I see you haven't let it slip. You're going to be a little bitch about this, aren't you? I can already see it. You struck out one time—big deal!"

"I struck out looking on three pitches."

"If you ask me, it's more embarrassing to go down swinging. Strike out looking and at least when you walk back to the dugout you can act like you got beat on a close call. When you strike out swinging, then everybody knows you just plain got fooled. Trust me: at this point you don't wanna go up there looking to swing because, brother, your odds of hitting the ball are pretty much nil."

"Thanks for your support."

"I mean, I've seen amputees with sweeter strokes."

"I appreciate it."

They were interrupted by the waitress coming to take their order. "Hello, darlins, what can I get for you?"

Casey looked over at Reardon for some sort of cue. "I haven't really looked at the menu yet."

She looked perplexed, "Then what you bin doin' this whole time?"

"He's a little slow," said Reardon.

"I'll have the cheeseburger," said Casey, picking the first thing he recognized.

"Make it double," said Reardon and then to Casey as she was walking away: "Say, maybe I can help you out."

"What're you going to do, stick a needle in my ass?"

"Hadn't considered that," said Reardon. "No matter, it wouldn't do you much good anyway. You gotta know how to hit in the first place before that stuff could be of use."

"Fuck off. What would you know about it?"

"I'd be willing to wager a hell of a lot more than you do, fuckface. If you were smart you'd do whatever I tell ya. I'll take you where you wanna go. I'm good like that."

"That's not what I heard. Everybody keeps saying that if I knew what was good for me, I'd steer clear of you."

"Who's everybody?"

Casey shrugged. "Everybody."

"Think yer smart, eh? You know, I was gonna treat you here, but now you can go fuck yourself."

"But the prices are so outrageous. Whatever will I do?"

Reardon leaned forward. "You know what? Maybe I do like to stir the pot every now and again. What of it? It keeps things interesting. Besides, it's not like I've ever fucked you over any. In fact, I've done nothing but stick my neck out for ya since you stepped foot off that plane."

"It's just that I don't think there's much anybody can do for me. I mean, you saw me out there today—it's hopeless."

The waitress came back, "Sorry, sugar," she said to Reardon. "I just about plum forgot to get your drink orders. Did you boys want anything?"

"We'll take a couple of waters."

"I'd like a Coke," said Casey.

"You know what your problem is?" said Reardon as the waitress walked away. "Your problem is that you worry too much and you give up too easy. You're a pussy, Casey. News flash: this is just one shitty day among the many you'll have in your relatively short, mediocre career. Look on the bright side—at least nobody was there to see you crash and burn. That won't be the case during the regular season."

The waitress eventually returned with the waters, the Coke, and the hamburgers, and the ballplayers dug in, with Reardon pontificating the whole time, even with food in his mouth. Casey was halfway through his burger when Reardon nodded over Casey's shoulder and said, "Now what in the fuck is this shit?"

Casey turned to see what Reardon was gesturing towards. Five men were standing by the jukebox, staring at them. Two of the men were wearing army fatigues even though they were clearly not military personnel. One was even pounding his fist into his open hand, as if he were some greaser looking for a fight at the milkbar. Casey now realized "I'm Proud to Be an American" was pumping through the restaurant's speaker system and the group of men standing next to the juke box were singing along, saluting in all directions.

"Do you think this boyband wants to start something?" said Reardon.

The waitress came just as Casey was going to respond. She looked distressed.

"Just ignore them, sugar. They've just had too much. I'll go on and ask them to leave."

"Those guys are tanked, lady. You sure it's a good idea to go over there and say you're throwing them out? I can handle them right quick."

"Naw, shug. Them boys are in here all the time. I went to high school with a few of them. They'll be cooperative, you'll see."

Casey and Reardon watched as she sauntered over and said something. The men laughed, and the biggest one, clearly the drunkest of the bunch, yelled, "You tell them Canadian sons of bitches that this here's a free country and that if they don't like it, they can git."

The waitress walked back to the table shaking her head. "I don't know what's gotten into them boys," she said, casting a glance over her shoulder.

The manager, a balding, middle-aged fellow, appeared from the back to try to talk some sense into them, but soon found himself surrounded by the laughing posse, and beat a hasty retreat.

"I think Fred's gonna have to call the cops," said the waitress, watching the manager try to wrangle the drunks. "This happens from time to time."

The song started up again.

"What good are the pigs gonna do?" asked Reardon, standing up. "I'm not putting up with any more of this shit."

"Don't!"

But it was too late. Reardon had already dropped a couple hundreds on the table and was lumbering towards the juke box.

"What's he planning on doing?" asked the waitress, her voice trembling.

"I don't know," said Casey, wiping his mouth with a napkin. "I'll bet nothing good."

"Well you've gotta git over there and stop him. We cain't have no fighting in here. This ain't that sort of place."

Casey threw the napkin down on the table and stood up. By the time he reached Reardon, the closer already had the plug from the jukebox dangling from his fist. The man who'd just been leading the drunken sing-along had fallen to the ground and now shrunk against the face of the machine, wiping some leaking spittle from his mouth with the back of his hand. Reardon held the lapel of the man's flak jacket in his other hand.

"Now you can explain why in the fuck you were singing that."

"Because we're in America?" offered one of the man's friends. "Jesus, man, he didn't mean anything by it."

"If he didn't mean nothing by it, then why was he staring us down while he was singing it? Why'd he start yelling about Canadian sons of bitches?"

"I didn't mean nothin' by it."

"Of course you didn't, and you certainly wouldn't have been trying to start a fuckin' brawl with a coupla foreign nationals, now would ya?"

"N-no."

"Just celebrating freedom in the good old U- S-of-A, eh?"

The man looked towards his friends, who were nodding vigorously. "Y-y-yes."

"Good. What do you think, Casey. Is this piece of shit talking real smart or what?"

"We should go," said Casey.

"Why? The party's just getting started," said Reardon, turning to his captive, a big smile on his face. "Ain't it, Jimbo?"

"S-s-sorry."

"Please," said their waitress from a few feet behind. "Leave 'em alone. Them boys is just drunk."

"He's sorry," said the man's friend. "I swear he didn't mean nothin'."

"He shouldn't be sorry!" said Reardon, releasing the lapel and slapping the man on the shoulder. "After all, I'm probably the biggest fan of freedom there is. There ain't nothing better than a big, old helping of freedom if you ask me. But the problem is, Jimbo, as I stand here looking at you, I don't see no freedom." Reardon leaned close, baring his teeth. "Do you know what I see? I see a drunk, ignorant piece of shit who's gone and tried to start a fight with the wrong motherfucker—a pussy who's backing down now on account of having figured out he's about to get his ass beat. Wouldn't you agree?"

Casey leaned in and whispered, "Jesus, Reardon, let's just get out of here. They look like they might be calling the cops."

"Who gives a fuck?"

"I think people are recording this," said Casey, glancing around the restaurant. People were leaning over the seats of their booths with their phones out, camera lenses gleaming in the artificial light.

"Lemme ask you something, Jimbo," said Reardon, poking the man in the chest. "What, exactly, does the word freedom mean?"

"I guess—I guess it means you can do whatever you want."

"Well, you see, that's only half of it. The second half of it is accepting the consequences of whatever choices you've made. Like, suppose a racist, ignorant, bigoted piece of shit tries to start a fight with a couple of canucks of his own free will, doesn't it follow that he must then accept the ass-kicking as a consequence of *them* exercising *their* own free will? Or is that not what you mean when you say the word freedom?"

The man sat there for some time, the horrified look on his face unchanged.

"Well?"

"I-I don't know."

"Well then," said Reardon, leaning in even closer so that his nose almost touched his victim's, "how the hell can you know that you're free? You don't even know the meaning of the word. Don't you worry, though. Reardon's here to learn ya."

Faces pressed against the windows of the Waffle House as Casey and Reardon walked to the Beast and got inside. Casey had hardly engaged the buckle on his seatbelt before the acceleration forced him back into his seat.

"You know, you really didn't have to do that," he shouted over the engine noise and wind tearing through the cabin. "They were just drunk."

"What's it matter whether they were drunk or not? It's all the same. In the end, that guy's an asshole."

"I didn't know you were so fucking culturally sensitive."

"I'm not," said Reardon, spitting into his cup and putting it back in the holder. "I just wanted that son of a bitch to know that he's nothing but a caged rat—just like everyone else."

"You sure showed him."

"No. You see, that's the problem. That drunk sonofabitch is probably still back there cramming burgers down his gullet with his buddies, spewing a bunch of nonsense and thinking he's free. People are quick to forget their own cowardice."

By the time Casey and Reardon arrived at the training centre the next morning, members of the media had already swarmed the locker room door with their cell phones ready to record anything. The battery mates were immediately spotted by press corps and soon found themselves surrounded by recording devices. The reporters asked questions, but it was impossible to make sense of it because the reporters were all talking at once. It was a relief when they were finally muted by the clack of the locker room door.

"What the fuck did you do this time?" said Steele, stepping away from the mirror in his locker.

"I—" began Casey.

"Not you, dipshit. I'm talking to this big motherfucker right here."

"You're just jealous, admit it," said Reardon, inserting a fresh plug of chew into his lip. "It's not my fault they find me so interesting. At least I've got the decency not to go giving it any of my fucking time. If the shoe were on the other foot, you'd be more than obliged to bend over and let them take turns licking your asshole."

"That's not what I hear them good ol' boys out there are aiming to do."

"I'll deal with them once all the facts are out," said Reardon. "Although I've gotta say, it's kinda sweet how you're trying to look out for me."

"Speaking of looking," interrupted Tubs. "Don's been in here looking for you. Says he's got some questions."

"He's probably finally grown a sack and is ready to suspend your ass," added Steele.

"Wanna bet?"

"I'd feel bad taking your money," said Steele. "Y'all better hurry along now. Don's been looking awful angry all mornin'. You better not keep him waiting."

"He knows where to find me," said Reardon, spitting into his cup. "He don't need you to be his errand boy."

"Reardon. My office. Now," said Lou, who'd come out just to deliver this instruction. "Bring that snotnosed punk with yas."

The ambience in Lou's office reminded Casey of his grade school principal's. There were the two authority figures—Lou and Don—one standing with his arms folded over his chest and the other sitting at the desk with his hands on top, looking first at Casey, then to Reardon, then back to Casey.

"Well?" Don asked.

"Well, what?" said Reardon.

"Would you mind explaining to me what happened last night that led to me waking up to a PR nightmare this morning?"

"I couldn't say what you're talking about. You're gonna have to be more specific."

"Don't try to play dumb with us, you no good sonofabitch," said Lou, stepping forward and poking his finger in Reardon's direction. "You know damned well what's going on."

"So yous twos have gone and pulled me in here just because somebody's bitching on social media about me telling off some drunk redneck?"

"We don't exactly need all this bad press at the moment."

"First of all" said Reardon, leaning forward and resting his gigantic arms on the desk, "there ain't no such thing as bad press. Second of all, this ain't bad press."

"What world is this guy living in? That's what I want to know!"

Don held up his finger to signal for silence as he scrolled through his phone. "*'Someone oughta put a price on that traitor Reardon's head. If he hates America so much he can get out.'* That was someone calling themselves TimmyTee93."

"At least those dickwads last night were familiar with my nationality," said Reardon.

"*'Why haven't they arrested this walking blowhole yet? Another celebrity gets away with what anybody else might get time for #NoJusticeInAmerica'*—that was supersleuth77."

"What do you want me to say? He isn't wrong."

"*'If I saw that son of a bitch Reardon in the street, you can bet I'd put a few holes in him.'*"

"Who said that?"

"The state's chief justice," said Don, putting down his phone. "This is no joke, Phillip."

"Well so far you've given me the opinions of a fucking KKK member, some dipshit conspiracy theorist, and an Alzheimer's patient. Can you get to the part about telling me exactly who gives a shit what any of these nuts have to say?"

"The chief justice ain't no goddamn' Alzheimer's patient," shouted Lou.

"The son of a bitch just threatened to murder me over social media. Don't think I won't be bringing charges."

"Hold it," said Don, raising his hand. "Let's all calm down. Listen, Phillip—whether or not you respect these people, you've still pissed them off."

"So what if I did?" said Reardon, spitting into his cup. "So what if they think I'm a villain?"

"There have been threats on your life, you lunatic," said Lou.

"Yeah, by the chief justice! You and I know it's just a bunch of empty fuckin' talk. Eventually they'll forget all about it just like they forget everything else. It'll just be another factoid, a useless piece of datum that don't mean a damned thing to nobody. How am I supposed to take any of it seriously when it comes straight from the mentally ill? Besides, all our fans love it, guaranteed. Just search it on your little device there and find out for yourself."

"No doubt the fans are loving it," conceded Don.

"Then what's the problem?"

"The problem is the league sure doesn't love it. They've notified us of their intention to hold a suspension hearing. The commissioner himself is flying in from Arizona. I've heard he's still holding a grudge over what happened last time."

"How many games?"

"Three."

"I'm fine with that."

"Yeah?" said Lou, throwing a handful of seeds into his mouth. "Well who says we're fine with it?"

"They've offered to reduce it to one game if you agree to apologize, in an acceptably public manner, to the person or persons you assaulted last night at the Waffle House," said Don.

"Frankly, I don't give two fucks whether yous twos are fans of me taking a suspension or not. I'm not going to stand up there and apologize to some worthless piece of trailer trash who tried to start a fight and bit off more than he could chew—especially when I never laid a hand on him."

"Phillip, be reasonable."

"What's there to be reasonable about? This is bullshit."

"So what if it's bullshit?" said Lou. "I hate to be the one to tell ya, but the world is full of bullshit. It practically runs on the stuff. Get used to it."

"I am fucking used to it. That's why I'm telling you to give me the goddamned hearing. If you don't like it, you can speak with my union rep."

The hearing was scheduled for two days later. The commissioner arrived by plane from Arizona, where he'd been running the usual media gauntlet of press conferences and broadcast booth appearances that he now had to interrupt to deal with this public relations flare up. Reardon explained to Casey that the commissioner had a bit of a personal vendetta against him, mostly fueled by the public embarrassment Reardon had caused when he'd avoided the penalty they tried to slap him with over the butter incident.

"At least that time I'd allegedly done something meriting a suspension."

Casey had been roped into attending the hearing and was now in his only suit—badly wrinkled—standing in front of the Residence Inn by Marriott in downtown Clearwater. It wasn't much of a downtown. In fact, the surrounding landscape was so flat that they'd seen the hotel's tower rise above the rooftops from miles away. As Casey and Reardon walked into the lobby, one of the team's PR reps, Jenny Schwartz, was there to greet them. She shook their hands and gestured for them to take a seat. Coffee was brought to their table in white ceramic mugs.

She spent a long time explaining a great many things that Casey couldn't fairly say he fully, or even partly, understood, which of course wasn't helped by his mind drifting in and out of focus like a camera lens. Meanwhile, Reardon didn't even attempt to listen as he worked the gaps between his teeth using a one of the complimentary picks that had arrived with the refreshments. Finally, she got annoyed and said, "Well, it looks like my services aren't needed here."

"Don't take this the wrong way, lady, but I've been through this whole song and dance before. It'll take more than a few lies and that lousy commissioner to put ol' Reardon on ice."

The hearing lasted nearly two hours, with league representatives describing to the arbitrators all of Reardon's past misdemeanours in detail. The commissioner had interrupted multiple times to point out the serial nature of these infractions, and pressed the arbitrators to deliver the reasonable three-game suspension that his office had proposed.

But the arbitrators had difficulty in identifying which league policy Reardon could be found in violation of. He could not be said to be in violation of the league's domestic violence and sexual assault policy, and the DA was refusing to press charges based on a social media witch hunt. "How, exactly, are we supposed to justify a three-game suspension to the Players' Association?" asked one of the arbitrators, echoing the Players' Association representative, Mel Schott.

"With collective bargaining coming up in the next year, it would send the wrong message to our members to deliver suspensions unwarranted by any agreed upon policy or writ."

After hearing both sides of the debate, the arbitrators ultimately decided against the three-game suspension, much to the anger of the commissioner, who as soon as he heard the verdict, stood up and exited the room with his entourage in tow.

"See?" said Reardon, as they got back into the Beast to head to the training facility. "Told you we had 'em licked."

Casey and Reardon had been training together all this time, but had yet to form a battery and play a little pitch and catch. This was due to Lou wanting to give Ramirez as long a leash as possible, hoping to prove to the front office that he could handle the closer. Unfortunately, the four appearances Reardon had made so far had proven just the opposite. Ramirez, who was better known for his bat than for his defense, had proven incapable of handling both Reardon's high heat and Amuro's knuckler, and now the pressure was on to get Casey and Reardon started with bullpens.

Reardon stood on the mound, came set, reached into his glove, and found his grip. Next thing Casey knew, Reardon had thrown the ball. It blipped into nothingness before reappearing as a beachball and striking Casey in the face so hard the mask flew off his head and clattered to the ground. Casey looked down at its bent metal frame in wonder as medical staff mobbed the scene and began interrogating him about numbers of fingers. "Relax, would ya," shouted Reardon from the top of the mound. "He didn't have much going on up there in the first place."

After Casey had sufficiently assured them that he wasn't concussed, the bullpen session was allowed to resume. They both got set and Reardon delivered the ball. The pitch was another scorching heater, this time at the bottom left-hand corner of the zone, and Casey was able to reach across his body to get his mitt on it. The ball struck the heel of Casey's glove and rolled off into the grass as pain shot from his palm to his wrist and forearm.

The next few pitches yielded similar results, with the medical staff stepping on the field a several times after Casey had taken a ball off his mask or the chest protector. The ball came in so fast that Casey hardly even saw it before it hit him. He started to find it around the twenty-first pitch, a throw that exploded right over the heart of the plate. This time, Casey's glove hand came up, darkened his vision, and pocketed the ball with a crack.

Regular Season

Customs was no less of a drag on the return flight than it had been on the way south. Once again, they pulled Casey out of the queue to pass through the security checkpoint and led him down a maze of hallways. He found himself back in the room with the glass boxes, standing at gunpoint with beads of sweat trickling down the back of his neck. They were by no means gentle in removing the contents of his bag, even slitting open a pile of t-shirts with a bayonette knife to expedite their examination. Meanwhile, Reardon, who had for some reason been allowed to tag along, ate a bag of Doritos and laughed.

"You may step forward," said the guard standing behind the examination table as he peeled off his gloves. Casey could hear the clink of the guard behind him lowering his carbine. Reardon signed an autograph for one of the security personnel while Casey zipped what was left of his belongings back into the duffle and slung it over his shoulder.

"Do they always give you so much shit when you're crossing the border?" asked Reardon. He'd waited until they'd touched down, collected their baggage, handed their arrival cards to the agent, and coasted through the doors into arrivals before broaching the subject.

"Pretty much," said Casey.

"You know why that happens, don't ya?

"I don't know. They've probably got me on some list."

"Bitch, the only list you're on is the shitlist of public opinion. They ain't fucking with you because you're on some fuckin' list."

"Well then, the fuck if I know why they're doing it."

"You know what your problem is? Your problem is you make it too enticing for them."

"And how do I do that?"

"By standing there looking like you want to shit yourself. It plays right into their game when they can get you spooked. They get off on that shit. They're hardwired to get off on it. That's why they went and became customs agents. The trick is to play it cool and not let them get under your skin."

"I'm sure you'd be real calm if it was your head in front of the gun."

"Brother, I wouldn't even let it get that far."

"Why'd they let you follow me in?"

"Because they're pigs and dumber than a sack of bricks. If you know how to play them right, you could murder some poor son of a bitch right in front of one and they'd help you dispose of the body."

"Bullshit."

The two men traversed the terminal, crossed the bridge over to the longterm parking facility, took the elevator up to the top floor, and stepped out into the lot. It was easy to spot Reardon's car on account of it being the same black Mk. I Golf GTI Reardon had been driving around in Florida.

"Did somebody drive it back for you?" asked Casey as the two men approached the car.

"Naw," said Reardon. He placed their bags in the trunk. "I told you, I left the real thing up here at Pearson. The one in Florida's just a spare."

Out on the 401, the Beast let out its banshee wail across the desolate early spring landscape. Casey didn't much feel like talking after the flight and Reardon seemed content to let him stare out the window at all the streetlights and houses and shopping malls. The city arose gradually amongst these fields of suburban homes, and soon they found themselves flying past old brick warehouses recently converted into chic, loft-style dwellings. Proceeding further into the city, clusters of mid- and highrise condo and apartment buildings, both old and new, began to appear on both sides of the highway. It was on an overpass overlooking this part of the city that Reardon pulled the car over.

"Is there something wrong?"

"Nope," said Reardon, hitting Casey on the chest with a flask. "We gotta have ourselves a little celebratory drink."

"You mean in here?"

"I mean out there," said Reardon, gesturing with the flask towards the passenger door. "Get out and we'll have ourselves a sip or two."

Reardon would hear no protest, and soon enough the two men were standing on the shoulder of the overpass staring up at two mammoth, twin condo buildings. They passed the flask back and forth and watched as the towers and their green lights flickered on and off. In truth, Casey was only pretending to drink, still mindful of how the doctors at the clinic had warned him that alcohol was probably what set him off. "The alcohol is what gives you permission to go further," his therapist would say, looking at Casey from over his glasses. "Alcohol has the powerful effect of giving us the permission to do things we would not otherwise dream of doing, and that effect is dangerous when our self-control is already suspect."

"This here's the good shit," said Reardon, winking as he took another slug and wiped his beard clean with the sleeve of his coat. "Crown Royal, a favourite of the old man himself, 'til it killed him. Burns all the way down the way proper hooch ought to, don't it?"

"You never struck me as much of a drinker."

"Well, I ain't," said Reardon, running his fingers over the back of his head. "But ain't it great to be back home? A fella ought to celebrate."

"I guess," said Casey. "I don't exactly got a home right now."

"What you talking about, kid?"

"I gave my notice the day I signed the contract."

"Alright. Where the fuck are you staying?"

"I figured I'd probably stay at the hotel until I was able to track a place down."

"You should have said something, brother. I've got a spare room at my place if you want to crash there until you can get your shit together."

"Are you sure? That would be a pretty big favour."

"It's like I told you before, friend: so long as you's got my back you can be sure as shit I've got yours. Besides, it might not be so bad to have an extra pair of hands and eyes around. We can find ways of putting your lazy ass to work. You can be sure of that."

"I could pay you for it."

"What? You think I look like the kind of guy who needs your money?"

"No—"

"Then don't fucking worry about it. Stay as long as you want; it won't cost me nothin' but havin' to look at ya," said Reardon, taking a swig from the flask before passing it back to Casey. "Besides, if I'm gonna keep my word, I oughta keep an eye on the situation, don't you think? Keep your coke-crazy ass on the straight and narrow."

"Is that what you call this?" asked Casey, nodding toward the flask.

"Sure. Why not?" said Reardon, screwing the lid back on the flask and slipping it back into the pocket of his jacket.

They exited the highway at McCowan and drove through a familiar mixture of mid-to-high-rise buildings and seventies subdivisions until they made a left onto Lawrence. Casey knew which building was Reardon's from a distance: it was the tallest around—a sixteen storey monster that arose from the crest of a hill on the corner of Golf Club and Lawrence, a black monolith against the light-polluted sky. As they turned right into the building's sloping driveway, Reardon popped open the glove-box, pulled out a fob, and waved it in front of a receiver, causing the big garage door to creak open so the Beast could roll through.

"Penthouse, seventeenth floor," chimed the elevator's female voice before its doors slid apart to release the ballplayers into the hallway. The carpet was so faded that Casey could only observe that it had once had a pattern, but couldn't have told you what that pattern might have been. The walls were painted the same eggshell white as those of the clinic, except here it had started to flake off and the old beige colour could be seen underneath. The light at the far end of the hallway was out, so that only the faint, red glow of the emergency exit sign could be made out.

"This is me," said Reardon as he stood in front of the door next to the elevator, unit PH17. He unlocked a number of dead-bolts and swung the door open.

Standing here in the "foyer" to Reardon's apartment, Casey took a moment to take in his new environment. The first thing he noticed was that living room was practically wall-to-wall books—a feature that might have given the room a touch of class had they not all been repair manuals for every conceivable make and model of automobile and motorcycle, or had the shelves on which they perched not been the grotesque metal things used for storage at fast-food restaurants. For furniture there was nothing but a pair of armchairs with holes in the fabric with an endtable positioned between them. The kitchen was your standard fare: an electric range and oven with no ventilation to speak of, along with an undersized sink with a wire dry-ing rack. The only peculiarity was the big chest freezer standing next to the refrigerator. One thing the place had going for it was plenty of cupboard space, but even that was limited due to Reardon repurposing what might have been a large pantry into a small-scale grow-op.

"Nothin' special," said Reardon, opening the door to show off the four-foot plants he'd been cultivating. Casey stepped inside and examined one of them, finding the buds thick, dense, and purple. Casey salivated just looking at them.

"Damn! This shit looks good."

"These puppies ain't quite ready to be smoked yet. I like to push 'em a little further along in their life cycle—then, of course, I've gots to cure 'em—but never fear, I've always got plenty of bud stowed away in the freezer."

"What're you planning on doing with all this?" said Casey.

"Smoke it. What else?"

"Bullshit, you're never going to smoke that much. There's gotta be twelve pounds of weed here."

"If you think that's a lot, you oughta see the icebox."

Cold air foamed from the mouth of the chest freezer as the two men stood looking inside. Reardon hadn't been lying. The freezer was full of litre-sized Ziploc bags of weed labeled in permanent marker with their strains and dates. "Jesus," said Casey, gazing down at the hoard.

"Beautiful, ain't it?"

"You must have everything here."

"If you can name it, I've probably got it."

"Are you sure it's a good idea to have all this?"

"Why not? Where else would I keep it?"

"It's just that if someone were to ever rat you out, you could go to prison for a long fucking time, man. This here's intent to distribute."

Reardon reached into the freezer, grabbed two of the baggies, and held them up for Casey's inspection.

"Nigerian Prince or Purple Tangie?"

The kitchen had another entryway that fed back into the living room. Through it Casey could see sodium-coloured streets and the moon hanging over the lake, which reflected it back as an imperfect twin. Casey walked into the living room and braced himself with his hands on the sill of the window, looking out at the night landscape, and wondered what he was doing here. Something wasn't right about this. Something wasn't right at all.

A tap on the shoulder jogged Casey from his contemplation and caused him to nearly knock over a bookshelf.

"Hey, hey, relax. What's got you all bugged out? We ain't even smoked nothing yet."

"I don't know, I was just thinking about something," said Casey, pointing to the joint that Reardon had somehow already been able to produce. "What you got there?"

"Let's see if you can guess," said Reardon, sparking it with a lighter.

Reardon pointed to a pair of sandals he expected Casey to put on, and the two men stepped through the door onto the balcony which stretched almost the length of the apartment. They walked to the end, where they could make out the glow of the Toronto skyline.

"Hell of a view, right?" he said, passing Casey the joint. The wind came in stiff off the lake so that Casey could feel the goosebumps rising on the exposed skin of his arms. The CN Tower could just be made out in the distance, its needle rising above the bright cluster of lights that was downtown Toronto.

"One of the best views in the city by a long shot," Reardon continued. "You buy a condo in the core and what do you get for it? A view of your neighbour's bedroom. Me? I want a view of the lake, and out here I get it almost for free."

"You're telling me you live all the way out here for the view?"

"That and the fact that there's only one entrance in or out that's accessible by foot, and that everyone living in this shithole knows better than to go putting their noses where they don't belong. They do you the goodness of nodding to you in the hallway and then they leave you the fuck alone. The only ones who give me a lick of trouble are those goddamned middle schoolers from across the street back over thataway."

"Middle schoolers?"

"They've made a game of trying to get photos with me. So far I've been trying to ignore it."

"How's that been working out for you?"

"They ain't bored of it yet," said Reardon, spitting over the rail of the balcony. "Having you around will probably only renew their enthusiasm."

"Great."

"It's not so bad. If the worst paparazzi you've gotta deal with is these little fuckers, you should count yourself lucky. Tell me something, kid, has it sunk in yet for you yet?"

"Has what sunk in yet?"

"*Has what sunk in yet?* Man, you just can't make this shit up. You're in the fuckin' Show, brother! Two days until opening day. I thought you'd be flipping your lid."

"To be honest I don't know how to feel about it. It doesn't quite seem real."

"It's fuckin' real alright, and you've got yours truly to thank for it. Two days from now you'll be standing on that chalk line while they're playing the anthem and I'll tell you how you oughta feel: like you're the luckiest goddamn son of a bitch on this here planet Earth. And do you know why? Because that's exactly what fuck you are. No pressure or anything, but I can't have you fucking this up for me. You know what I'm saying? I've stuck my neck out for you here, so when someone asks you how you're feeling about it, you better act like a humble little fucker and tell 'em you feel like a special fucking snowflake and won't never forget all the kindnesses everybody's done for you, especially ol' Reardon. Got it?"

"You're crystal clear."

Back inside, they crossed the living room and entered a long hallway with four rooms branching off. They stopped at the first room where Reardon swung open the door and flicked on the light. It was large and mostly empty, with the exception a desk, a wooden chair, and a dorm bed. It didn't look all that different from the room he'd had at the clinic. "This is where you sleep," said Reardon.

"Cozy."

"Yeah, it ain't much, but it's something. Who are you to bitch? I wasn't expectin' visitors."

"Relax."

Casey walked up to the big window on the far wall and looked out at where they'd been standing on the balcony.

"Come see the rest of the place."

The next room shared a wall with Casey's and was set up in almost the exact same manner, complete with the single dorm bed and desk.

"This here's where I sleep, so you can mostly come and go at your leisure, though I don't see why you'd go in since I'm hardly ever in here. That over there is the bathroom, where ya can do all your shittin', showerin', and what-not. And this room," he said, knocking on the door perpendicular to his bedroom, "is the third bedroom."

"What's in there?"

"Nothing special. I've got a workbench in there since I usually got two or three projects on the go and that's where I choose to do 'em. Truth be told I was thinking of expanding my operations to your room, but now that it looks like you'll be sticking around a while I'll have to change my plans."

"I never said I was staying for long."

"Now, at this point in this here tour," said Reardon, clearing his throat, "I should probably mention that I don't got many rules except that you clean the fuck up after yerself and stay the fuck out of this room. No offense, but I don't trust you not to fuck something up in there."

"If you want to jerk off in there, it's nobody's business," said Casey.

"And here I thought you didn't have a sense of humour," said Reardon, wrapping an arm around Casey's shoulder. "This is going to be great. Can you feel it?"

The two ballplayers stood on a muddy patch of ground near the old railroad roundhouse. Historic trains dotted the lawn, each with a little plaque stating its historical value for anyone who took interest. It was terrifically cold and both Casey and Reardon were underdressed for the weather, but it only seemed to be bothering Casey, whose fingers were so numb he could barely hold onto the joint he and Reardon were passing back and forth.

Reardon was going off in his usual manner, lecturing on one of the many subjects on which he had an opinion. Casey was hardly listening. He was too captivated by the steady aural rush of early morning traffic as it echoed off the glass of the surrounding condo towers and the cawing of the gulls as they hung in the stiff wind, so Casey just muttered affirmations whenever it seemed appropriate. He was only broken from this trance when Reardon dropped the roach into the mud and stomped it out.

They walked over to Bremner, waited for a gap in traffic before crossing to the north side, and were about to enter the stadium through the gate when Reardon barred Casey's progress with his arm and pointed up to the CN Tower. "You ever been up top?" he asked.

Casey's gaze followed the outline of the tower until it disappeared behind the shifting cloud cover. Its surface was splotchy from where the rain had soaked into the cement.

"Not that I can remember."

"You mean you're from here and you've never even experienced our greatest monument? You've gotta be fucking kidding me."

"I guess I just never found the time."

Reardon changed direction and started walking towards the tower's entrance, beckoning for Casey to follow.

"But we'll be late," said Casey, casting an anxious glance back at the gate.

"Relax, would ya? It's eight—we're plenty early. In fact, we've got all the time in the world. How am I supposed to stand idly by after you've just finished telling me you ain't ever even been to the top. Surely we can spare two fuckin' minutes to take in some of the local flavour."

"I mean, is it even open?"

They entered through the front door. Reardon lead the way, marching resolutely past the ticket desk, through security, and onto the elevator without the slightest interference from the attraction's staff, who merely nodded complicitly as the two men rushed past.

They stepped off the elevator into the circular corridor of the observation deck. The only two others there were dressed in tower staff uniforms. They seemed to be having a heated conversation, so Casey and Reardon walked in the opposite direction. They walked until they came to one of the sections of glass floor, which stood before the polymer observation windows that bowed out in front of them to provide a panoramic view of the city. Skyscrapers gleamed in the sunlight, the clouds having moved on to reveal blue skies. Plumes of exhuast spilled from rooftop ventilation systems, drifting into the atmosphere in long white tracers.

Looking through the glass floor, the streets appeared nothing more than mottled grey ribbons woven together into a grid, carving the city up into cluttered tiles that stretched out all directions before disappearing in the throng of towers and trees that made up the horizon.

Casey stood at the edge of the floor, wondering what it might be like to fall from this height. His thoughts were interrupted by a faint gurgling sound and an all-too-familiar aroma. Looking in the direction of the sound, he found Reardon standing in the middle of the glass floor, holding what looked like an e-cigarette to his lips. He gave a mighty pull before letting out a thick jet of green-white vapour.

"What the fuck are you doing?" whispered Casey, casting a paranoid glance in both directions.

"Relax, kid. It's odourless."

"I can fucking smell it, man."

"Yeah? Well, the smoke detectors can't, so quit being a baby and take a hit. You know, you'd do better to be a little more appreciative. Here I take you up top—free of charge—then I offer you some high-grade wax of yours truly's own personal manufacture, and all you do is bitch."

Casey snatched the vaporizer from Reardon's hand, held down the button, and brewed himself a hit. He stared down the mouthpiece into the chamber where the foamy, greenish vapour built up until he could no longer see the red glow of the coil through the haze. Then he sucked it in.

The vapour had hardly entered his lungs before he was doubled over coughing it out.

"What's the matter?" asked Reardon, laughing and slapping Casey on the back. "Bite off more than you can chew?"

Casey hacked up a wad of phlegm and spat it onto the carpet.

"Jesus. Not cool, man. Now them two squabblin' employees is looking this way. Come on, let's walk over here. The best view's over here anyway."

They walked along the corridor until they reached another section of glass floor. Reardon stopped at its edge and stood staring down at the city below.

"You sure seem to know your way around here," said Casey, still coughing. "Why'd they let us in without a ticket?"

"That's just one of the many perks of being the hometown hero," said Reardon, spitting into his cup. "I mean, just look at this city, do you really think any of its doors are locked to a bonafide superstar like old Phil Reardon? Not fucking likely, brother."

"Whatever. Being famous isn't all its cracked up to be."

"Yeah? What makes you so sure?"

"It didn't help me when I wrapped my car around that telephone pole."

"Kept you out of prison, didn't it? And here you are getting paid five hundred thousand bucks to ride my coattails. Pretty soft landing after getting booked for a DUI, if you ask me. Besides, you weren't even famous. You were just some top prospect that only them baseball worshippin' stat wonks had ever heard of. In terms of athletic celebrity, you were on like the D-list. You get what I'm saying? But even as a D-lister, you're better off than most of the dumb fucks slinkin' around down there," said Reardon, gesturing towards the glass floor. "You can trust if they pulled what you pulled, they'd be up shit creek, but good."

"Maybe," said Casey.

"Well then don't go telling me being famous ain't worth shit. We both know better than that. In this world you're either somebody, or you're nobody—just another cockroach scurrying around, fightin' other cockroaches for a few scraps and crumbs."

"Do you think you'd look any different to them, if they were the ones up here and you were down there?"

"Yeah, brother, but that's just it—they *ain't* up here, now are they? I bet most of thems are just like you, they've scuttled around this hole for the better part of their lives and they ain't never even sniffed the top. How do you suppose that can be?"

"Probably because it's fucking expensive when you don't just barge into the place."

"Exactly," said Reardon. "It's priced that way on purpose. All those people down there? This ain't for them. This tower's for people like you and me—the powerful and the exceptional—those who can do things others can't. We get to stand up here and take in the view, while everyone else gets to scuttle around. Like I said, a bunch of cockroaches."

"And you think you're not a cockroach?"

"That's just it, isn't it? Being a celebrity, not being a celebrity, neither of those things changes what's coded into the old DNA. I may be a cockroach, but comparing me with any one of them ain't much of a fuckin' contest. You see, the difference is any of these poor bastards could be stomped out of existence this very moment and seconds later there would be another rushing to fill the pathetic little niche their predecessor was able to carve out during their miserable little lifespan. On the world would go a-chuggin' and none would be the wiser. But suppose someone were to try to stomp out ol' Reardon, the alpha roach? You can bet his absence would be felt by just about everybody, especially the little runts who make a name for themselves feeding off the alpha roach's scraps."

"Yeah," said Casey. "They'd probably be relieved."

"You know what? Go fuck yourself," said Reardon, taking another hit. The closer took some time to take in the view before continuing his monologue.

"Last season I would come up here two or three times a week during home stands just to take in the view. I made it a point to get real cozy with the management, by signing autographs and handing out free merch. In exchange, they'd let me come up after the place was closed, so I could have it to myself. Pretty good trade, eh? After night games, I'd get stoned as a motherfucker, come up here, stand on this glass floor just like I'm doing right now, and the whole city would be all lit up like the fourth of fucking July, with all the buildings and the headlights and taillights of the traffic stopping and going—shit's bananas. You can't see it the same way in the daytime.

"Anyway, one night I was feeling a little adventurous and macked on a fistful of 'shrooms before heading up top. So here I was, high as a kite, and all of a sudden it all started comin' to life on me. It took the form of some sorta, I don't know, some sorta organism. It was like one of those videos they show you in grade school, where the different parts of your body are illustrated by something you're more familiar with, like say a backhoe for your arm, or a dump-truck to represent your shithole. I remember there was this one where they showed how yer circulatory system worked, where yer veins and arteries were compared to a highway system and all them blood cells were nothin' but cars zoomin' this way and that carrying oxygen and shit to all yer appendages. You remember that one? Well from up here the cars and trucks and bikes, with all their taillights and headlights pulsing through them streets, glowing red and white, reminded me of that. I got to thinking that all these suckers—the people in the cars, I mean—will probably spend their whole lives doing just what they were now. They'd just keep circulating. Day and night, rain or shine, they'd just ferry themselves around and take their kids to school, and cook lousy dinners, and work themselves to the bone—and for what?"

Reardon waited for a response, but Casey didn't know what to say so he remained silent as Reardon took another big rip from the vape. "Go on, tell me for what."

"I don't know, to keep themselves and their families alive, I guess. Fuck if I know."

"Wrong," said Reardon, spitting into his cup. "They may think that they're acting in their own self-interest—after all, it must look that way to them on the ground—but from up here we can see that they're no more independent than an ant or a goddamn honeybee. Everybody's just scurrying around for the sake of the hive. Come on over here and see for yerself."

Casey peered over the edge of the glass floor. "I think I'm good."

"Don't be such a chicken shit."

"I don't like heights."

"All the more reason to step aboard," said Reardon. "How do you expect to overcome your fears if you don't never face 'em?"

"I guess I don't expect to."

The two men argued in this way for some time until Casey finally relented.

"See," said Reardon, passing Casey the vape as he stepped into the middle of the glass floor. This was when Casey made the mistake of looking down. His knees buckled and he lowered himself down, feeling with his hand for the floor, where he sat looking at the ground between his feet.

"That happens to most people their first time," said Reardon.

Just then the doors to the nearby elevator chimed and a group of uniformed schoolchildren ran out onto the observation deck. They ran and skipped across the glass floor without even noticing the vast distance between their feet and the ground. Their teacher was eventually able to corral them back into a line against the railing so they could be counted. A few must have recognized Reardon because they whispered to one another and pointed in the direction of the two ballplayers. Then, their teacher called them to attention and led them in a single file line towards the apex of the circular corridor and out of sight.

"Don't sweat it," said Reardon. "Children are fearless. They haven't been around long enough to have the spirit crushed out of 'em yet."

Neither man said anything for a few moments as they looked out over the vista of tower blocks. A flock of pigeons erupted from the roof of one of the towers beneath their feet and flew as one dark shimmering mass before being vacuumed up by that same tower's rooftop. Suddenly both men broke into laughter.

"Dude," said Casey, wiping a tear from his eyes. "We really shouldn't've got so baked before Opening Day."

From where Casey stood on the third baseline, the people in the stands were nothing but a field of blue and white dots that rippled in the windless atmosphere.

The Dome wasn't at all like Casey remembered it, the old patchwork turf having been replaced with a permanent artificial playing surface that the local fans and media had been raving about ever since its installation. It really was quite remarkable. For one thing, the engineers had designed it to have cushioning equivalent to actual grass, and during day games with the roof open, it was visually indistinguishable. At night it was a different story. Then, under the glow of the newly installed arrays of LED lighting rimming the upper deck, it glowed a neon green. The players and anything else that happened to be on the surface radiated light as if they themselves were the source. The old metal roof was gone. In its stead they'd erected a transparent plastic one. Standing below, with the roof closed, Casey could see the mass of condo towers looming large over the lip of the stadium's bowl. The seats were new, as was the black batter's eye the team had installed in straightaway centre. The old cement walls were the only thing that remained unchanged.

Opening Day in Toronto always draws a sellout crowd, and this year was no exception. The stadium announcer introduced the players as the cameramen strode across the baselines, projecting the Blue Birds' smiling faces on the jumbotron as they were introduced to their hometown crowd. The catchers went first, so Casey was the second man to step forward and raise his cap to the crowd. His introduction was met with a chorus of boos and shouted insults, with one voice from behind the home dugout calling for someone to get this piece of human filth off the field. Casey turned around and briefly met the eyes of his slanderer: a tattooed woman with a toddler on her hip flipping Casey the bird.

The rest of the players were met mostly with polite applause, until the introductions made their way down to Steele, who lifted his hat high in the air and turned to bask in the swell of the stadium's roar. Camera flashes rippled through the seats as he stepped forward. The fans loved him and the stats up on the screen said why. He was a bonafide superstar.

From the position players they moved on to the starting pitchers, through the early and middle relief corps, and into the late innings specialists. The stadium began to buzz as the acknowledgments made their way down to Reardon who, when he raised his hand to greet the fans, Casey could have sworn their adulation was causing the ground to tremble beneath his feet.

The only thing that brought the crowd to heel was the announcement that Francine Cole would now sing the national anthems. Attendees stood at attention as two rows of flag-bearing mounties in full dress regalia marched toward the mound. The cameramen kneeled, holding out their equipment at arm's length in front of the young woman who stood on the rubber. Her face was projected on the jumbotron above, and she smiled and waved to the camera. Steele, Tubs, and several of the other athletes and team staff took a knee. Then, when the anthems were over, the field was cleared and it was time for the regular season to officially begin.

Up in the broadcast booth, Zach Sadler and Jack Rodriguez were ready for their first broadcast. There was no cameraman in the room because the corporate broadcaster had purchased an array of Canon LCX, the latest in automated camera technology. There was now a large digital timer where the cameraman once stood, relaying to the broadcast team how long it was until they were on. The stylist was frantically making final adjustments to Rodriguez's hair as the timer showed ten. A last speck of Sadler's dandruff was brushed off his shoulder by the wardrobe coordinator just as the red light came on, letting the crew know it was time to clear the set. There was a moment of total silence and then:

"Hello, and welcome to another beautiful Opening Day here in Toronto. It's a balmy ten degrees at the start of play today, so once again the Dome is closed, but the bunting is out and as you can see the fans are on their feet and ready to see things get started, hoping the team can put last year's disappointing finish behind them."

"They weren't supposed to be good last year, and they weren't," said Sadler. "Granted, there was some bad luck involved, like when the infamous buttered floor incident caused them to lose Davis—who they had pencilled in at third base— right out of the gate."

As the players re-entered the dugout, Lou, who had positioned himself at the top of the stairs, held out his hand to block Casey's entrance.

"Not you," he said.

"What? You want me in the field?"

"Kid, let me tell you that's just about the last place I'll ever want ya. You might be the worst ballplayer I've had the misfortune of being saddled with."

Casey looked to Tubs and then back to Lou. "Then where do you want me?"

"You can head out to the bullpen. We've got a spot all warmed up for ya out there on the bench," said Lou, leaning over and spitting seed husks onto Casey's shoe. "Well? Don't just stand there with your pretty mug hanging open! Go on!"

Lou watched as Casey jogged along the sideline and disappeared behind the bullpen's gate. The skipper backhanded Tubs shoulder, leaned in, and said, "I'm telling ya, that kid's gonna be the death of us."

"He might a little slow, but he's alright."

Lou spat ·on the turf and looked out towards the bullpen. "Whaddya mean he's *alright*? You've seen him: the kid can't play. And, more importantly, I think he was born under a bad sign. He's bad luck, I tell ya. I can feel it in my knees."

"I don't think that's what's doing it to your knees," said Tubs, glancing down at Lou's protruding belly, "and it don't matter if he can play or not. If the boss says he's on the roster, then he's on the roster. Nothing you or I can do about it."

"That's just what I hate most about this horse's ass of a situation," said Lou, taking his hat off and running his fingers over his balding crown. "How am I supposed to run this nuthouse when the boss won't give me the stick I need to beat them with? I've never been on any team where somebody other than the skipper was calling the shots. I'm of a mind to quit, you know that? If these bean counters think they know everything, let them come down and do the job themselves."

"They'd replace your ass in a minute," said Tubs.

"You're damn right they would. That's what's wrong in this world—nobody's got no goddamned loyalty these days."

The skipper's conversation with his bench coach was interrupted by the crack of a bat hitting the baseball, which bounced right by the home dugout along the baseline. The third baseman ran to his right, his glove down, anticipating the short hop. Just then the ball took an awkward bounce and trickled over the heel of Schopenhauer's mitt and into the outfield. Lou checked the umpire, who was signaling that the play was fair. Tony Anchovy, the Tabbies' shortstop and leadoff hitter, had reached first and was rounding the bag for second when Hernandez came up with the ball and fired it back toward the infield. He might have got Anchovy at second if his throw hadn't been slightly off-line and pulled Steele off the bag.

Lou sighed and shoved a fistful of seeds into his mouth. "At least we know everything's right with the world," he said, retreating down the dugout steps.

"How do you figure?"

"The season's just started and it's already got its dick in my ass."

Some of the buzz had already been taken out of the stadium as the Tabbies' first baseman, Hugh Pickle, stepped into the box. Bonfiglio, the longman, was already starting to get himself stretched out down in the bullpen, while the rest of the relief arms kicked back on the bench. The Aucoin twins were busily cracking and downing peanuts from a bag tossed to them by one of the yellow-shirted vendors, and Reardon kept depositing thick gobs of brown saliva into his Gatorade cup.

Hardy went 0-1 on Pickle, then 0-2 on a slider that swept across the plate for a strike. The next pitch was supposed to be a curveball in the dirt to induce the strikeout, but Hardy hung the pitch up in the zone and Pickle tee'd off on it. The ball came screaming the other way, towards left field on a line until it was nearly at the outfield wall. Everybody in the bullpen ducked as the ball shot past and ricocheted around before finally rolling to a stop. By the time they'd all sat up again, Pickle was nearly done his home run trot.

"Gimme that there ball," Reardon shouted to one of the bullpen catchers, who tossed it to him. Reardon held it up to his eye as if he were inspecting it. "Ain't nothing special about it."

"Why should there be?" asked Casey. "It's just a baseball."

Reardon laughed and tossed the ball behind him into the crowd where a sea of eager hands rose to meet it. The ball was lost until the crowd began to disperse and two men were left holding on. A tug-of-war over the ball ensued until one finally shoved the other lose and turned back to the crowd, holding up his prize.

"Would you look at that," said Reardon, backhanding Casey's shoulder with his cup hand. "Those chumps seemed to think it was worth something. I mean, it's not like it takes much to hit one off this loser—he's terrible."

"He's Chet Hardy."

"He's an old ox past his prime."

Detroit's right fielder smacked another line drive that arced right past the outstretched glove of Thompson towards the first base line. The crowd roared with disapproval as the ball landed just fair and bounced over to the wall where eager hands scooped it off the turf in front of the right fielder for a ground rule double. Nuñez shook his head disapprovingly as he jogged back to position. Now there was a man on second with no outs and two runs already on the board.

Chet dug deep, found his command, and was able to get out of the first without giving up any further damage, and now it was the Birds' turn to bat. Hernandez led off the inning and swung at the first pitch, sending a ground ball back up the middle, but Detroit's shortstop had been shading to his left and was able to intercept it. Hernandez legged it out of the box, but it wasn't enough as the umpire pumped his fist and called him out at first.

The offense did nothing to follow up Hernandez's effort. Over the next three innings their only baserunner was Steele, who hit a ball the other way into right field for a single to lead off the second inning. From there he set to work, taking healthy leads as the pitcher got ahead of Cruz 0-2. On the third pitch, a ball in the dirt, Cruz swung at and missed. Steele had taken off as the pitcher started his wind-up and Detroit's catcher came up throwing, but he put too much on the ball and it went over the head of the second baseman into centre field. Steele popped up from his slide and kept going, hustling to third base as the centre fielder made a throw that sailed over Steele's shoulder. The umpire stood over the bag as the tag was applied to Steele's arm and hesitated a moment before declaring that the runner safe on third with one out.

The crowd began to crackle to life again. For the last inning they'd been sitting on their hands waiting for something to happen. But the celebration was shortlived as the next three Blue Birds struck out. They weren't even able to put a ball in play.

Meanwhile, Hardy continued to struggle keeping his pitches on the outer portions of the strikezone, and when he wasn't throwing meatballs he was missing badly. By the middle of the third he'd already thrown seventy-eight pitches and allowed the Tabbies to cash in five runs on eight hits. Bonfiglio was now up and throwing in earnest. The pop of the ball hitting the catcher's mitt echoed off the walls of the bullpen. By the time Bonfiglio took the mound in the top half of the fourth, some fans were already making for the exits. The Tabbies had led off the inning with a bloop single to left that those in the know understood to be the final nail.

Living with Reardon exposed Casey to more of his roommate's eccentricities, one of the strangest being that Reardon didn't have a cell phone, just a landline that fed into a cordless that was rarely, if ever, used. When Casey asked about it, Reardon explained that he didn't feel like it was his job to be on call all the time and that if somebody really wanted to get a hold of him, they could leave a message.

"But what if you want to call somebody?" asked Casey.

"Anybody I'd dream of calling, I keep in this here black book," said Reardon, tapping a worn looking notebook that sat next to the phone.

"What if you're not home?"

"Then I guess I can't make a phone call, can I?"

"Is my number in there?" asked Casey.

"Not fucking likely."

The man was like clockwork. He would read in the living room with Casey—who had turned to reading pulp novels in the absence of a television—until the latter got tired and decided to call it a night. Then the two men would take the walk down the narrow hallway together and bid each other adieu as Casey entered his room and Reardon entered his "workshop."

For the hour or so it would take Casey to fall asleep, he would hear all sorts of strange sounds emanating through the walls. Sometimes there was the hammering of metal, at others the squeal of a drill as it perforated some unknown material. Occasionally, there would occur the wheezing of a handsaw.

Meals at Casa Reardon were surprisingly healthy in addition to being homemade. Casey was expected to contribute to both their preparation and clean-up and was adjusting well to these expectations, but didn't understand why everything had to be so laborious. When Casey pointed out that Reardon didn't have to bother making his own meals on account of how inordinately wealthy he was, Reardon replied that you didn't get rich by spending money. "And besides," he said, "nobody is going to make it better than yours truly," a point with which Casey strongly disagreed.

There was no need to set an alarm, because every morning at exactly 8:15 AM Reardon would wake Casey up by banging a metal pot with a wooden spoon right next to his ear. "Get up, shithead," the closer would say. "We've got work to do."

Breakfast consisted of cereal, fruit, and instant coffee Reardon made so stiff it bordered on undrinkable. There wasn't much time for Casey to enjoy his meal, because almost as soon as he started eating Reardon would already be badgering him about getting ready to leave. If they left any later than 9:30, the closer would flip his lid and begin insisting he would have to start charging for his wasted time.

The drive to the stadium was a long one. To avoid the constant traffic of the DVP, Reardon stuck to the municipal roadways, zipping from one lane to the next to avoid the slower vehicles while Casey held his tongue and silently prayed for a safe deliverance. He found it strange how they were never pulled over, even though he often saw the white hood of a police cruiser streak by the window. When queried about this phenomenon, Reardon would just shrug his shoulders and smile.

The Blue Birds opened the season with a thirteen game homestand, a situation many pundits had described as favourable. It turned out to be a disaster. The Birds were swept in their opening series against Detroit and in the following series against Tampa Bay. They were able to take the first of a four-game series against the Sams, trouncing New York by a score of 12-6, where a poor outing from Amuro was erased by Steele accruing twelve total bases by hitting a pair of home runs and two doubles. Every player in the lineup that night reached base, which somewhat revived the optimism of the clubhouse, but what little celebration there was proved shortlived as the team went on to not score a single run for the remainder of the series.

With all this underperformance, there weren't many at-bats to be had for Casey. Lou was playing his vision of the starting lineup every night, and every night during the media scrum the only answer he had in response to the press' demands for explanations was that the offence was better than this. "You saw them last year, they were one of the better offences in the league. They didn't just forget how to hit."

You could have fooled the fans, who watched in dismay as their team went 1-11 to start the season. Searching for signs of life proved a fruitless activity. Every night the team took the field looking flat and defeated, leading several bloggers to openly question the coaching. But the team's lack of success could not be blamed on a lack of preparation on the part of the players and coaches, who showed up early every day, putting in their allotted time and then some in an effort to get the monkey off the team's back.

In these tough times, many of the players had fallen back on superstition. A few of the more eccentric ones began murmuring that maybe there was some sort of curse.

Casey was more than happy to be out in the bullpen where nobody noticed him, where he couldn't be blamed for any curses. The only time Lou ever called on him was to catch Reardon, and so long as Casey did his job, nobody complained. He liked the guys out there in the bullpen, too. He appreciated that they didn't give a fuck if he belonged there or not. Most of them, truth be told, seemed rather ambivalent about the team's fortunes. Nobody knew better than a reliever that this game was, first and foremost, a business. They weren't going to lose any sleep over the ship sinking since they figured to be the first ones in the lifeboats come the trade deadline.

Casey was starting to feel comfortable in his new role as the team entered the last game of their series against the Fishermen. He looked forward to sitting out there in the bullpen and taking in the game from a vantage he could have only dreamed of when he used to go to games as a kid. Part of him wondered if he should pinch himself. How could this be real? Another part of him hoped that maybe it could go on like this forever, with him sitting out there in the bullpen and nobody expecting anything from him except to trot out there with Reardon whenever he was given the call.

This fantasy was shattered in the ninth inning of the team's thirteenth game. Martinez came to bat in what had to this point been a rare bases loaded situation and swung at the first pitch: a high fastball he crushed to left field. It hit the wall just below the yellow line and dropped onto the warning track, where Seattle's left fielder picked it up and fired to second. Cruz had already crossed the plate and Schaupenhauer was right behind him. Martinez slid feet first into second, but the second baseman's glove was already there to apply the tag. The catcher was slow in getting up after getting called out, and the umpire signaled to the dugout for someone to come out and assist him. Martinez sat there holding his ankle while AC and the team's trainers jogged out to examine him.

"It's broken," Lou told the team in the locker room after the game. "His goddamned ankle is broken."

And just like that Casey became the starting catcher for the Toronto Blue Birds.

April hadn't gone as well as Don had hoped. The offence was anemic and the starting pitching terrible. Amuro had been shelled so hard in his first six starts that his ERA now stood at an even 9.00. Don and his colleagues were discussing the possibility of sending him down. That decision would have been made easier had anybody in Buffalo been performing to expectation, but to this point both the team's top pitching prospects were struggling with the increased level of competition in the International League. There was also the obvious difficulty of justifying to corporate why they were paying someone fourteen million to play in Buffalo, a stand Don was loath to take, given his increasingly tenuous relationship with the parent company.

The usually reliable Chet Hardy had been consistently mediocre, not exceeding six innings in any of his starts, but not allowing too many runs either, so that his ERA sat at a modest 5.43. This early season "success" gave Don little in the way of reassurance, as his peripherals and many of the team's in-house metrics suggested Hardy had been extremely lucky and was probably headed toward some negative regression.

To make matters worse, the unthinkable had happened when Martinez broke his ankle, leaving the Birds with Casey as their starting catcher. The transition had been ugly. On the defensive side of the ball, Casey had been spotless. He'd already thrown out five baserunners and called decent games, even with the lack of execution from the pitching staff. The trouble was the bat. He had yet to reach base in twenty-nine plate appearances and already struck out twenty times. He was quite simply overmatched by the high-nineties heat that had become endemic throughout the Big Leagues. Lou had been campaigning to move Olivier—who the Birds had selected from Buffalo to fill Martinez's empty spot on the twenty-six man roster—into the starter's role. When Don pointed out Olivier's track record of defensive miscues in the minor leagues, Lou responded by claiming that he would do anything to get Casey's black hole off the lineup card.

The one bright spot on the ball club was the bullpen. The Aucoin twins had both pitched to an exact 3.33 ERA and had a combined twenty-one shutout innings. After his rocky outing on Opening Day against Detroit, Bonfiglio was called on to mop up after the starting staff on multiple occasions and earned two of the eight wins amassed by the pitching staff. Reardon had been perfect. He only had eight saves, but that number equaled the number of Bird wins in April. He hadn't allowed an opposing baserunner in any of his twelve appearances, seven of which had spanned multiple innings.

Don took to crushing his daily aspirin between his teeth and washing it down with coffee. He was doing this now, as he read a blog post that amounted to little more than a half-baked call to arms. It was written by some nearly illiterate fellow who had joined the throng of self-styled experts saturating the blogosphere. The author demanded the team call up Singh to at least make it appear like were trying to salvage the season, and used Singh's early results in Buffalo as a justification for placement on the twenty-six-man roster. Don could do little but shake his head as he waded through this imbecile's nonsense.

If it were as simple as that, Singh would have already received the call and be slotted into the lineup. He was tearing up the International League, getting on-base at a .440 clip, but Don didn't have anywhere for the boy to play. Shortstop and second base were manned by the only two players in the lineup who were producing, so it made no sense for Manny to play there. He could slot Manny into one of the outfield positions, but Don had faith in the Dominicans turning things around, as they'd been very unlucky so far this season. That left third and first, neither of which seemed to Don like an ideal option. The best course was probably to call Singh up and use him as a super-sub, allowing players some much needed rest while also getting Singh's potent bat and blistering speed into the lineup. But even this seemingly simple solution was compromised. It was curious that little was ever said about the looming Super Two deadline—about the massive financial consequences of bringing up Singh before the beginning of June. These amateur pundits never thought about the ballooning arbitration costs or the significant blow to the team's leverage in extension negotiations.

Don was sitting in the waiting room of Huntsman, Brazeau, and Turner thinking about what he was going to do. The place was just as Don had remembered it: low-sitting leather sofas, white walls with limited edition prints of Group of Seven paintings, a portrait of Queen Elizabeth II in her hayday. On the coffee table before him magazines such as *Esquire* and *The Walrus* were meticulously fanned, to be perused at the leisure of the firm's clients. Don normally didn't go in for print media, but today one of the magazine covers caught his eye. It was an issue of *Sports Illustrated* with Reardon's grinning face on the cover. Beneath his ugly mug was printed in the piped font of the Blue Birds, "Mr. Perfect." Don chuckled as he picked it up and flipped through the pages until he found the interview. He hadn't read more than a line when he was interrupted by Stuart, Francine Goldman's personal assistant.

"Good morning, Mr. Billingsley. Mrs. Goldman is ready to see you now," said the young man with a smile.

They exchanged the usual pleasantries and then Stuart took the lead, ferrying Don through the firm's corridors. The office doors were all shut, but the muffled sounds of many conversations could be heard through the paper-thin walls. Looking around, Don recognized what he considered to be the tell-tale signs of corporate decay: dark splotches on the carpets from years of spillage, chipped picture frames, streaky office windows, the clutter of documents that had accumulated and ossified over the decades and now sat stacked in manila folders, not even stowed away in bankers' boxes. It all felt a little too lived in. It lacked any sense of urgency. Indeed, even as the phones rung off the hook, they seemed to do so lazily. The women who answered them could scarcely be heard over the choppy whirr of desktop fans. Don was worried he might sweat through and ruin the new solid navy suit he'd just purchased. Stuart, anticipating Don's discomfort, hastened to explain that the building's air conditioner was broken. It had actually broke the previous fall, but nobody was expecting a heatwave this early in May.

"Pretty crazy weather, huh?"

They reached a familiar door. It was the corner office of Francine Goldman, the estate lawyer he held on retainer. As Don and Stuart stepped inside, she was yelling into the handset of her office phone, "Okay! Good-bye, Mrs. Lieberman. Talk again soon!" She hung up the phone and stood to shake Don's hand. "Mrs. Lieberman. Sweet old bird, but I'm afraid she's gone a little batty. Keeps calling me Carlyle. How are you, Don?"

"Things could be better."

"Things could always be better."

"I noticed things around here are in a bit of disarray," said Don, wiping his forehead with his lapel handkerchief.

"You're telling me. We're going paperless right now and it's just about killing me."

"But most places have been paperless for years!"

Francine shrugged. "We write contracts here, Don. Paper's our currency."

"Your staff don't seem too excited about the transition."

"Yeah? What do you expect? I mean, half the reason we have so goddamned many of them is that we've been running so much paper around. Once we've gone completely paperless, we'll be axing three quarters of them. That's when we'll start making a real tidy profit."

"And the carpet?"

"We're blazing a new trail here, Don. We're doing away with the whole office concept. Soon I'll be operating from home."

"But how will you meet with your clients?"

"Meetings with clients can be held remotely," said Francine, sticking a piece of gum in her mouth. "We're not living in the nineteenth century, you know. Now what can I do for ya, Donnie?"

"Well, you know how it is. Just want to make sure everything's up to date."

Francine's lips flattened. "Don, this is your will we're talking about here. What could have changed in the last six months? If anything needed changing, we'd call you. You really don't have to worry about it."

"All the same," said Don. "I would rest easier knowing I've got this thing taken care of."

"You've already taken care of it! I've already taken care of it! We've all already taken care of it! Nobody needs to take care of it any further. It's on cruise control, auto-pilot, set it and forget it. All you've gotta do is keep breathing, so I don't have to go and execute the damned thing. You wanna know something? I've got a word for people like you. Donnie, I hate to say it, but you're a clinger."

"Excuse me?"

"I see this all the time. For some people this whole business of the will is a bit of a head trip. And I get it: what we're ulti-mately talking about here is what's going to happen to your stuff when you get knocked off. People have a hard time letting go, so it helps them to come in here. It helps them—I don't know—get used to the idea that they're going to die or something. Most of them come in three, maybe four times. It's pretty annoying, if I'm being honest. It's not like I'm getting paid to be their thera-pist, but over the years I've learned just to put up with it and sooner or later they move on and let me get on with doing my actual job, which is writing wills in case you were wondering. But every once in a while, Donnie, every once in a while you get a client and they *don't* stop coming. They keep coming, year after year after year. I'll put up with it. I mean, you pay me, so what the hell, right? But you, sir, you have been coming here twice a year for the past decade and I can't in good conscience take any more of your money without letting you know this is unhealthy behaviour."

"You're saying that this is unusual?"

"I've only had one other clinger cling this long."

"I see," said Don, staring down at his hands.

"It turned out he had plotting to fake his own death and had been obsessing over the details. You wouldn't be thinking of pulling something like that on me, now would ya?"

"Heavens no," said Don. "I just—I just need to be sure."

"What the hell's there to be sure about? Once you're knocked off, all your property will be transferred to your ex-wife, one—" Francine glanced at the folder she had open on her desk. "'Mindy Schaeffer.'"

"But she hates me!"

"What do you want me to do about it? If you'd rather leave it to somebody else, we can set that up. Do you have any children? Sisters? Brothers? You can leave it to charity for all I care."

"We didn't get around to having children," said Don. "And both my brothers are dead."

"So you mean…"

"I've got nobody. Mindy hates me. I can't stomach the thought of her getting everything. I mean, think about what she'll do to all my suits."

Francine cleared her throat. "I don't mean to be rude or anything—so don't take this the wrong way—but once you're in the dirt, will you really give a shit what happens to your suits?"

All the same, Francine agreed to run through the details this one last time, with the caveat that this was *it*, at least for the next twenty-four months. They were in the middle of ironing out what would happen to his rather impressive collection of baseball memorabilia when a new idea or premonition surfaced in Don's mind, sending him into a state of complete distraction. Right now, as he was re-finalizing the fate of his possessions, it occurred to him that he was done. Finished. He felt certain that there was some act of fate afoot against him and he was so taken up with the thought, he didn't even realize that Francine had finished speaking. He found himself staring at the screen of her computer monitor.

"Are you alright, Mr. Billingsley?" asked Francine.

"Never better," said Don, snapping back to attention and forcing a smile.

"It's just that you don't look so hot. You're pale. You're shvitzing—and I mean, who isn't?—but you're shvitzing so much that it looks like you got rained on. Maybe you ought to just go home and take it easy."

"If only," said Don as he glanced at his phone. "Are we finished here?"

It was apparently six days past garbage day in the financial district, because the whole place stank of whatever was rotting in the overflowing bins. Don had to pinch his nose the few steps between the entrance of Scotia Plaza and the waiting Rolls Royce. It was a relief to enter the scented cabin of the vehicle and be sealed in by the door that Tom slammed shut.

Brenda, the receptionist, filled Don in on what had happened in his absence. It was mostly small business: extra funds here, so-and-so wants you to call him back, etc.

"Oh and Nickelbrook wants to schedule a lunch meeting for sometime next week."

"What about?" asked Don, hoping he didn't sound too defensive.

"Oh I don't know," said Brenda. "Nobody tells me anything."

"I hear you're going on vacation."

"They've got someone temping for me. I was told by the powers that this is the best time of year to go. Four days and then I'm going to let loose."

He found it quaint that this woman could feel so enamoured with a budget vacation to Mexico, where the biggest perks were that she and her husband could get as wasted as they wanted with no judgment and that she wouldn't have to cook for seven glorious days.

"I'm sure you'll have a wonderful time."

Don was the only solid object in the buzzing atmosphere of his front office. Phones rang, people were scrambling, walking with purpose, whizzing this way and that. Don, on the other hand, walked steadily, his thumbs typing methodically as he stared into his phone. People parted—even dove out of his way—as he approached.

He only looked up once he'd reached his office door and had to fish around in the breast pocket of his blazer for the keycard. Susan, the assistant general manager, was leaning against the wall.

"Good morning," she said.

"Good morning," Don replied, finding the keycard and pressing it against the reader. It blipped green and Don swung open the door. His office lights turned on instantly as he and

Susan entered and took their seats on their respective sides of Don's desk.

"You're awful late," Susan said, replying to an email on her phone.

"On the contrary. I'm never late because I'm always working."

"Touchy. You know there's no need to be so sensitive, Donnie. I'm just poking you in the ribs a little bit. Where ya been?"

"The dentist," Don said.

"Your teeth look awful funky for a guy who's just been to the dentist."

"They said it's all the coffee."

"Right," said Susan, leaning back in her seat. "That's why it's usually so noticeable when you go to the dentist."

"Don't you have some work to do?" said Don, turning on his desktop computer.

"There's always something. It's just that this morning I got a phone call from Pete in Los Angeles. He heard from a guy in their office that the Corporation has been making calls about Baum, and that Letner is worried they're going to lose him."

"Phone calls, you say?"

"Only of the *exploratory* variety, according to Pete."

"I didn't think it would be this soon."

"We look like we're out of the playoff picture in mid-May. What did you expect?"

"To make it to the trade deadline."

"The trade deadline? Are you kidding me? If the team keeps playing like this we could be out the door by next week."

"Does anybody else know?"

"Nobody but you, me, and Pete."

"Let's keep it that way. Everyone's already anticipating the fall of the axe, we don't need to heighten tension by telling them we've spotted the headsman."

"You know what this means, don't you?"

"Unfortunately, yes."

"We've already got all the promotional stuff ready to go. All it would take is a word."

Don rubbed the bridge of his nose. "Just give me a few days so we get the extra year of control."

The bar was called "The Blue Moose" according to the back-lit plastic sign. The establishment made its home in the basement of an old-Toronto tenement that faced south onto King East. Casey was surprised there were even any of these places left, what with all the construction that had been going on lately. The entrance was recessed from the sidewalk so that it might have been mistaken for a storefront if it weren't for the neon beer signs hanging from chains in the windows. The light's glow was shrouded by black curtains that prevented any sort of surveillance. A row of Harleys stood out front.

It was well after eleven when Reardon and Casey stepped into The Blue Moose, and even though their entrance was declared by the tinkling bell tied to a nail on the big wooden door, they seemed to produce none of their usual reaction. The two Italian men seated at the ancient bar just kept on gesticulating with the smoking tips of their cigars. Each of them wore a rather serious looking set of rings and dark-hued linen shirts beneath their pinstripe suits. They were absorbed by the soccer match playing on a tiny CRT set rigged to the ceiling like it was an emergency room. The bartender leaned against the cash register, drying a glass with a rag.

Reardon rapped his knuckles on the bar, but the bartender kept watching the game. "Ahem," he said, clearing his throat.

"Yeah?" said the bartender, turning around. "What do you want?"

"Can I order a fuckin' drink or what?"

"I don't know—can you?"

Reardon sucked his teeth.

Crowd noise crackled from the television. One of the Italians poked the other in the chest with a pair of fingers and said something in his mother tongue which caused the bartender to laugh.

"I don't know who you think you're talkin' to, pal," said Reardon.

"What? You think just because you two play for a shitty baseball team that makes you somebody?"

"No brother, seven million a year says I'm somebody."

"I'll tell you something," said the bartender, leaning in conspiratorially, "you don't make seven million. And even if you did, if you aren't winning, nobody gives a shit. Now what'll it be?"

The room was poorly lit and thick with smoke, so that Casey could hardly see ten feet in front of him. Figures appeared and disappeared in the haze like apparitions as the two men advanced toward the back of the establishment. The glasses they carried frothed over their lips with the rancid smelling house brew's foam. Not far from the bar, a man wearing a teal polymer jogging suit appeared. He was writing something on a folded-up newspaper. On the table in front of him he had a cup of coffee and an actual pager that buzzed irritably as Casey and Reardon walked by. The man in the track suit picked it up, gazed at the display, and returned to writing on the newspaper without so much as looking at the two ballplayers.

Further back, just before a landing that now crept into Casey's field of vision, a row of tables had been assembled for a group of bikers who sat smoking and swilling beer from bottles. The two ballplayers moved past them and slid into the booth furthest from the door.

"Like I told you before, kid, there ain't nothin' to worry about. Plenty of perfectly respectable fellas in this here establishment."

"Regardless, I'm not really supposed to drink."

"Why the fuck not?"

"The doctors at the clinic told me it would lead to relapse."

"Bullshit! You can't tell me you really believe that."

"Of course I believe it."

"You can't never trust no doctor. All they're out to do is line their own pockets and all they end up doing is spreading misinformation. This is a classic case of misdiagnosis."

"Oh yeah? What's wrong with me then?"

"See, what you had was a clingy relationship with the old funny stuff. By the sounds of it, you were probably stage eleven and you're better off steering clear when you see 'er around the neighbourhood. But you and liquor? It's like yous twos just met and you're takin' 'er real slow. You know what I'm saying?"

"No," said Casey.

"Point being," said Reardon, spitting out a wad of tobacco and chugging half his beer. "That coke ain't got nothin' to do with hooch—and don't never let anyone tell you otherwise."

"I don't know about that. If you saw some of the people I met at the clinic, you might think differently."

"What? You mean those losers? They just can't handle it because they don't have what it takes to say no. If you ask me, a man oughta do drugs, if for no other reason than to test his mettle, just to see if he's fit."

"Fit for what?"

"Fit for livin'! What else? How can you know you've got discipline unless you go and test it every once and a while? I tell ya, instead of all these commercials telling parents to keep their kids away from drugs they should have ads where good, loving people ram a fistful of pills into their toddler's little yap. Ya gotta see if the little fucker is worth the time and effort of raisin'."

"Sounds like euthanasia."

"Naw," said Reardon, finishing his beer. "They haven't caught on to the Reardon method of parentin' over there yet."

The conversation halted for a moment.

"But Reardon, *I* was in rehab."

"Key word there bein' *was*."

"And you aren't exactly a walking, talking example of sobriety, either."

"What's that s'posed to mean?"

Casey gestured towards the tobacco cup.

"I could quit chewin' and smokin' tomorrow if I damn well wanted to."

"Then why don't you?"

"'Cause I don't fucking want to, dumb-dumb. What's up your ass anyway?"

The Blue Birds had been swept in three straight series by the Monuments, Stars, and Swordfish, and were currently in the thick of a ten-game losing streak that had sent them to the very bottom of the division. Casey was still hitless on the season. Lou, unable to stand the sight of him, considering him a cancerous spot on the face of his roster, kept him out in the bullpen while the other position players hung around the dugout. In other words, he couldn't escape Reardon, who was always in the middle of subjecting Casey to his opinions on subjects as wide-ranging as what it *really* took to climb Mount Everest (he had, with no damned Sherpa, neither) to why the Big Leagues should switch to Mizuno as the manufacturer of their baseballs ("Why in the hell are we still using Mississippi mud when it could come out of the box sticky as your mother's tits?").

It wasn't just the longwinded soliloquies that had gotten to Casey. It was becoming increasingly clear to him that most, if not all, of his teammates hated him and were going out of their way to let him know it. He was constantly being shoved and bumped into as the other players went about their business: during drills, as they exited the locker room onto the field, in the various corridors of the different stadiums in which they played. One time, he returned to his locker to find a shoebox filled with human feces with his name written on the lid in permanent marker. Another time somebody had Scotch-taped a printed article detailing Casey's DUI the previous fall with a Post-it suggesting he kill himself. The only players—other than Reardon—who didn't seem to hate him were the twins, who took pity on him if for no other reason than to have someone listen to them talk to one another.

"Why are we here, Reardon?" Casey asked. "If anyone in the media gets word of us going out in the middle of a losing streak, they'll think we don't give a shit. Optics, remember?"

"You heard the man, nobody really gives a shit," said Reardon. "It's not like we're in it anyways. Besides, all these kooks got one thing right with all their rabbits' feet and their stitch switching. That being: when shit ain't workin', you gotta shake it the fuck up. Go on and live a little."

The bell hanging from the door rang.

"After all, it's just a drink or two and that never hurt nobody. And as to your concern over us getting 'found out'—how paranoid is that? Look around. There's nobody here. Who's gonna rat us out?"

"Maybe them," said Casey, nodding towards the bar. Reardon turned around and squinted through the haze to see Amuro and Saito speaking quietly to the bartender.

"Well, would you look at that," said Reardon.

Now all three of the men—the pitcher, his translator, and the bartender—were climbing the three steps to the landing. A moment later they were standing beside the booth. Amuro rapped his knuckles on the tabletop, looking first to Casey, then to Reardon, and then back to Casey before letting out a grunt and gesturing for Saito to intervene.

"Amuro-San has reserved this table."

"This table?" asked Reardon, pointing at it.

"Specifically," said Saito. "I'm afraid you must move."

"I don't see his name on it," said Reardon, pretending to look.

Amuro reached down, grabbed Reardon's glass, peeled a cocktail napkin off its base, and held it under the light so everyone could see. There was something written in green ink. It was little more than a Rorschach test now that the moisture had bled it.

"It said *reserved*," said the bartender.

"Well it sure as hell doesn't say it now," said Reardon.

Amuro must have understood something of what was said, because he started yelling in Japanese words Saito opted not to translate and violently jabbing his index finger against the surface of the table.

Reardon just kept repeating, "Well it ain't there no more, is it? It ain't there no more, is it?" as spittle flew from his mouth in great gobs.

"If you all don't sit down and shut the fuck up, I'll have you thrown out!" yelled the bartender. Everybody was staring in their direction: the two men smoking cigars, the mustached man with his newspaper, and the bikers, who stood ready and willing to do the bartender's bidding.

Reardon smiled. "Relax, would ya? We're just having a bit of a disagreement is all—nothing to get your panties in a bunch over. Tell you what, Saito, how's about you explain to your compadre that this has all just been one big misunderstanding. Why don't yous twos just sit yer keisters down and have a coupla brewskies on us. You understand? Gratis. My Treat. Then we'll up and move along and leave yas to your business."

Saito spoke quietly while Amuro looked around the room. The only other available table was the booth directly across from Casey and Reardon where someone's half-eaten dinner sat waiting to be discarded. Amuro made a face as he watched some flies scuttle around the plate and finally said, "Baka!" in resignation. He sat down, took out a pack of long-cut cigarettes, and tapped one out into a waiting pair of fingers before lighting it with a match. Then, with a single motion of his wrist, he put the match out and deposited it into the glass ashtray sitting in the middle of the table. He let the smoke pool and trickle out of his mouth before inhaling it through his nostrils.

"See, that's what I'm talking about," said Reardon. "What's the big deal? We're just a coupla teammates going out for a few beers on our night off. I mean, we're supposed to be chums, right?"

Amuro nudged Saito and said something in Japanese. "Amuro-san says he's seen how you treat your friends and would rather keep his distance."

"I treat my friends just fine. I mean just look at Casey here. Let this fine young man be a testimonial to my good fucking nature. I've picked him up out of squalor and brought him under my wing when nobody else wanted to even look at the poor son of a bitch. Here he is now, with a bona fide big league contract and a second chance at life. And who does he have to thank for it? Yours truly, of course. No, brother, I'm afraid you've got it all wrong. My friends are golden because I take care of them. It's my enemies that have to worry."

"And why is that?"

Reardon took out a joint and lit it. "Because I take care of them, too."

"Amuro-san says he would like to know how it is you came about this place."

"You know—it's the strangest thing—we were just walking by and decided to come inside out of the heat and have ourselves a brewskie, it being the off day and all. Had no idea I'd be bumping into yous twos here. But, ya know, now that we're all here in the same place, drinking a few beers, smoking a few ciggies, I've gotta say it's a real pleasant surprise. What do you think, Casey? Is this a real pleasant surprise or what?"

"Sure, I guess."

Amuro said nothing even after Saito had finished translating. A long ribbon of smoke trickled from the corner of his mouth as he stared across the table at Reardon.

"Seems like you two come here often," said Casey, to break the silence.

"Yes," said Saito, turning to Casey. "This country has very prohibitive smoking laws. This is the only bar in the city where patrons can enjoy a cigarette along with their drink."

"There're others if you know where to look," said Reardon. "Ask him if he'd like me to show ya."

"We're okay," said Saito.

"I bet you are," said Reardon. "So the old stone buddha comes here to smoke, eh? Nasty little habit for a ballplayer, if you ask me."

"Yes," said Saito, gesturing towards Reardon's lit joint, "I'm afraid we've all got our crutches."

"Speak for yourself. I don't got no stinking crutches."

"You're entitled to your opinion."

"It ain't my opinion. That, sir, is the gold fucking standard of facts." Reardon spat into his cup and stood up. "I'm gonna take a piss and check on the drinks, fellas."

Casey watched Amuro's gaze follow Reardon down the stairwell that led to the bathrooms, identifiable by a hand-painted wooden sign that simply read: SHITTER. He said something to Saito, who then asked, "What are you two doing here?"

"It was Reardon's idea; he's been talking about it ever since we drove past the place on our way to the park on Monday. Kept going on and on about how this looked like his sort of joint."

"It seems like a strange coincidence, does it not?"

"Sure does," said Casey, polishing off the rest of his drink.

Nothing else was said between Casey and his interrogators, who conversed rapidly in their mother tongue. Based on their body language, Casey figured they were debating whether to stick around or split. Before they could reach any decision, Reardon returned with four pints in hand. He plopped them down on the table, and the head sloshed over the lips of the glasses onto the tabletop. Amuro and Saito looked at each other and stood up as if they were about to leave.

"Well shit, fellas," said Reardon, hanging his face. "If I knew you were gonna be so sore about it, I wouldn't have gone and insisted we have a few beers together. I paid for these, you know. The least you could do is stay and have a drink with a coupla your teammates. Whaddya say."

Saito looked to Amuro for a decision. The pitcher sat back down and thought a while, letting the stub of ash on his cigarette grow long. "Baka," he said as he shook his head and ashed the smoke.

"That's the spirit," said Reardon, slapping the table. "And here my boy Casey said you didn't have much of a fun side."

"Leave me out of it," said Casey.

"Temper, temper. See, that's what I like about our friend Amuro over here. This motherfucker's what my moms used to call level fucking headed. It's too bad he can't pitch, because he's sure as fuck got the mental equipment to keep it all together."

Amuro's ominous, baritone laugh rent the conversation like a crack of thunder as he put out what was left of his cigarette and pulled out another. He let the cigarette hang from his smile as he watched Reardon from across the table. "Baka," he said.

"You know, he keeps saying that. What the fuck's it mean?"

"It means 'idiot,'" said Amuro, ashing his cigarette on the lip of the ashtray.

"It speaks!"

"Of course he can speak!" shrieked Saito.

"Then why's he got a nerd like you on the keep?"

"Part of my function is to provide Amuro-San with language instruction. The other to translate for him. I doubt even most native English speakers can understand what you are saying half the time."

"That's on account of my first language being Scarborese. I mean, who's got time for learning the Queen's proper English? She's just another stuck-up old broad, anyway."

"Point being," said Saito, his voice resuming its usual, controlled cadence. "Most English speakers use idioms or slang that doesn't make sense to people only just learning the language."

"What's he mean by calling me an idiot?"

"I mean," said Amuro, leaning forward, "that you talk too much. Always flexing your muscles. Always making trouble. You are a typical American."

"That's where you're wrong, pal. I'm a local."

"Ah, yes, Canadian! Excuse me. Sometimes I have hard time seeing difference."

"I'll show you the difference in a minute," said Reardon.

"You seem agitated," said Saito. "Perhaps it would be better if we left."

Reardon shook his head as if he had just remembered something and stood up.

"Under absolutely no circumstances will I allow you to leave on my account. I just thought—since we all happened to be here at the same time—it might be nice for all of us to sit down here and have ourselves a brewskie, but it's clear that yous twos would rather be left the fuck alone. I get it—it's your night off. You're out on the town, maybe going to see the dancing girls. You don't want ol' Reardon cramping your style. Fair enough, boys, fair enough. Me 'n' the kid will just mosey on over to that table there where that pervert was sittin' before, and leave yous twos to enjoy the rest of yer night. And here," said Reardon, slapping a several hundred-dollar bills onto the table. "This oughta cover your drinks for the evening."

All this beer was not achieving its expected effect. Casey was already on his fifth drink and he didn't feel any more intoxicated than when he'd finished the first. In fact, he almost felt *more* sober, and certainly more awake than when they'd arrived at the bar. The words he spoke came out eloquent and enthusiastic in a way that somehow didn't surprise him. He drank beer like water, slurping it back in huge mouthfuls and wiping his lips dry with his sweaty palm.

Reardon had started a conversation with the bikers at the next table, which seemed like a natural enough progression to Casey. Everyone was just shooting the shit, trading war stories from times when they'd been fucked up or else when they fucked someone else up. They talked about old-school Harleys, a subject on which Reardon turned out to be something of an expert. After Reardon had bought them a third round, the bikers made it clear they were thinking of heading out. One asked Reardon to come outside and sign his bike.

Amuro and Saito stepped out onto the sidewalk. They were much more amiable now, having shed all their former rigidity. They were laughing as they approached Casey, Reardon, and the bikers.

"Where are you guys headed?" asked Saito.

"Don't know yet, why?"

"They're clearing out, so we need to find somewhere else to go."

Reardon's face lit up. "Why, sure! You've come to the right guy. We'll get a cab."

"Shit, don't bother with that," said one of the bikers in a husky southwestern accent. "We'll take you where you need to go, so long as we're headin' in the same direction."

Next they were firing through the chrome chute of King Street. This late on a weeknight, the core was a ghost-town and the only sounds that could be heard were the hawgs' many-cc'd engines echoing off the checkerboard-lit glass faces of the Financial District's skyscrapers. They zoomed past Yonge Street, and Bay, and University Avenue. Casey loved the texture of the biker's leather vest. He was rubbing his face against it, unsure of if he was supposed to have his arms wrapped around the biker like he did, but worries were unable to enter his head and make a home for long. Somehow, everything just felt right.

Up ahead, Casey could see Saito on the back of a red Honda with his arms stretched out like they were the wings of an airplane. The old biker he was with kept shouting at him over his shoulder to knock it off. Reardon was actually piloting the bike at the head of the motorcade while the man with the mullet took photos using a selfie-stick. Amuro was yelling "Sugoi! Sugoi!" with his fist in the air.

The time of night was unknown, but assuredly late, certainly past most places' last call. It was alright, though. They would figure it out. *Tonight*, he felt, *anything is possible.*

"Wake up, shithead! We've got work to do."

Reardon was standing by the door spooning heaps of shredded wheat into his mouth and chewing as he talked. "Some night last night, huh?"

"What night?" croaked Casey as he sat up in his bed and rubbed his eye with his palm. For some reason his throat was the texture of sandpaper and his tongue so swollen that these two words were all he could manage.

"I said 'last night,' didn't I?"

"Why? What happened last night?"

"You mean you don't remember?"

But Casey couldn't respond because he was on his feet, a man possessed by need. Reardon stepped out of the way as he charged down the hallway to the bathroom where a flick of the faucet sent cold water gushing from the tap into his open mouth. He drank with abandon, his thirst unquenchable, and when he finally stood up to look in the mirror his gaze was met by a pair of yellow, bloodshot eyes.

It couldn't be that...

But the thought ended there, as the throbbing pressure at the back of his skull disabled all such consideration. A churning in his stomach brought him to the rim of the toilet bowl, which he held with both hands as he heaved up bile. When he looked up from the porcelain, he found Reardon leaning against the bathroom's doorframe still chowing down on his breakfast.

"Hell of a night, huh?"

"How much did we fucking drink?" asked Casey, wiping his mouth with some toilet paper.

"Oh we had enough. But don't worry, it's not like we went too crazy."

"Then why the fuck do I feel this way?"

Reardon's mouth moved, but Casey couldn't discern what it was saying.

"You what?"

"I said you probably feel like shit because I put a little emm in our drinks."

Casey sat up and pressed his palms into his eyes to keep out the light.

"You did what?"

"I said I put emm in our drinks. You know: emm, Molly, MDMA—fucking ecstasy, brother."

"Listen, man. This is important. Did we do anything fucked up?" asked Casey once he'd stood up from the bathroom floor.

"Us? Naw. I wouldn't worry about that. I kept you on a tight leash. Saito and Amuro, though?"

Reardon started laughing.

"You aren't saying…"

"Kid, I ain't saying nothing," said Reardon, punctuating his sentence with his spoon. "All I'm sayin' is we couldn't possibly have stolen the show with them two as gone as they were."

It took Casey a while to think this over. "You crossed a line this time, Reardon."

"Oh yeah? What line's that?"

"The fucking legal one. What were you fucking thinking?"

"Calm down," said Reardon, sweeping the spoon in front of him. "I told you we needed to shake things up. Let's not overreact."

"*Overreact?*"

"They were consenting adults."

"Bullshit, man. There's no way they would have agreed to that. You fucking drugged them!"

"Now that's a very dangerous and illicit assertion right there. I hope you won't be going and saying that to anyone who asks you about it."

"Asks me about it?"

"That's right, you can't be going around making allegations about things you don't know one way or the fucking other about. The way I see it, or—I should say—the way *we* see it, we were all just having a good time, had a few too many drinks. That's what you say to Don or any of his cronies if they come asking about it. It won't even be in our system in a few hours, so if we just play it cool and don't talk to the media it will all blow over."

"You must be out of your fucking mind."

"I ain't out of my fuckin' anythin'. Quit being such a wimp. If anything, I did you a favour."

"I don't know if you noticed, but I am a fucking recovering coke addict."

"How was I supposed to know a thing like that? I mean, it's not like you tell me about it every ten seconds or anything. Relax. All we did was help that old stick in the mud and his little oompa loompa loosen up for once. Besides, you've got nothing to worry about. If anyone's going to get in shit for this, it'll be yours truly. And old Reardon doesn't intend on taking no shit from nobody."

"Jesus, you didn't even tell me you were spiking the drinks."

"Sure I did."

"Yeah? When the fuck was that?"

"You just don't remember. You were drinking an awful fuckin' lot. We wound up at a rave and then we went a few other places."

"Did anybody see us?"

"Well it's not like we was goin' over to have a drink in Mikey's parents' basement now was we. Of course people saw us, dipshit. That's why I'm here telling you to keep quiet about it. Now get off the floor and get yourself cleaned up. We've got a long day ahead of us."

"I need to know exactly what happened last night," said Casey as they got into the car.

"Are you sure you don't remember?" asked Reardon.

"For the tenth fucking time: I don't remember a thing."

"Well, after we left the bar, we caught a ride with those bikers you seemed to like so damn much. Somehow, we wound up at a rave at this warehouse. Like I said, it was a great night. Or at least it was a great night until tweedle dee and tweedle dumb wound up getting a little too fuck-faced for public display. You know, I'd have never thought that little guy had it in him, but he got up on a stage without his pants. You thought it was hilarious at the time. Of course, when you go around doing things like that it sometimes garners attention."

"What sort of attention?"

"Oh, you know—pics, cell phone videos, the usual."

"Jesus."

"Will you relax? It's not like it was the biggest rave I've ever been to. After that we took a cab to the strip club."

"What strip club?"

"Alright, so we rented a hotel room near the airport and ordered strippers. What of it."

"Jesus."

"It wasn't my idea. Anyway, somebody called in a noise complaint and we got the boot, so we bounced."

"Do you even know if they got home okay?"

"Yeah, sure. I mean, we dropped them off and everything. I even had to fish out our friend Amuro's wallet to figure out where the son of a bitch is holed up. You and me had to carry them up to his condo. You're sure you don't remember?"

"You know, you've really gone and fucked things up this time."

"You gotta quit making mountains out of molehills, brother. How are you ever going to play with the big boys if you can't overstep decorum on occasion? If you just keep your mouth shut and let me handle things, everything will blow over. You'll see."

Reardon turned into the parking lot of the old Guild Inn, a once dilapidated building that stood at the head of a circular drive. The white stucco exterior had been redone and repainted and a huge outdoor patio had been installed. The Guild Inn was presently being arranged for a wedding, with flowers, décor, and food being ferried this way and that by men and women in black vests and white longsleeves.

The two men went unnoticed as they took a gravel path from the parking lot leading down a slope. The chalky gravel was wet and squelched beneath their feet, staining the sides of their shoes white as they marched towards God knew where.

It was at this moment—looking up at the sunlight drifting between the laden branches of the trees overhead, feeling the earth give messily beneath each step—that Casey started to wonder what he was still doing here. After all, hadn't this son of a bitch walking in front of him just spiked his drink with an illicit substance and not told him about it? Shouldn't that have by all rights been the end of their little partnership?

They arrived at a series of switchbacks wrapping around rows of pines, leading to an old service road. As they approached the foot of the cliffs, Casey could hear the cawing of gulls and the wush-wush from the waves as they crashed into the breakwater below.

Reardon had brought along a duffle bag and metal pail. As they walked along the breakwater, he told Casey to start filling the bucket with rocks.

"Just make sure they ain't too big. You don't want 'em to be much bigger than a jawbreaker."

It wasn't long before the bucket was full to the brim with stones that clinked against the metal as Reardon lifted the pail and set it down on top of the breakwater. They had no baseball, just a couple of Casey's bats in the duffle bag.

"Take one out and get on up there," said Reardon.

"What? You gonna push me off?"

"No, shithead. I've got a new drill for you. I think it'll help you out," said Reardon. "You really oughta forget about what happened last night."

"What do you mean forget about it? I couldn't remember if I wanted to. You fucking drugged me, man. At this point I'm seriously considering moving out."

"Yeah? And where would you go?"

"I could find another place."

"Go ahead and do that then."

"What? Really?"

"Yeah, sure. But remember, that'll be it. I won't be able to help you out no more. You'll have to figure shit out all by your lonesome. How do you suppose that'll go? Then, of course, there's the media to think about. If they get wind of us falling out, well, rumours might spread. The chemistry those two limp dicks up in the broadcast booth keep insisting we've got? Well maybe that's worn off. On the other hand, it probably wouldn't even take that much. I could probably just tell Donny Boy and the Louster that it's no sweat off my back if they decide to send you back to where you belong. Do you see where I'm going with this?"

"Are you threatening me?"

"Not at all, Casey. Not at all. Alls I'm saying is that it would-n't take much."

Casey stared into space for a moment. "I'm not sure I can forget it."

"You just said you couldn't remember."

"I can't remember what happened, but I also can't forget what you did now that you've told me."

"You've got to," said Reardon. "What you ought not to for-get is all I've gone and done for you. Remember our deal? I'm the one who's got your back. You wouldn't even be in the show if it weren't for me. If it were up to anybody else, you'd still be stalking around the hallways of that old condo tower you was working at, playing with your night stick. Or else you'd just be layin' on the couch, eating potato chips and watching guys like me get shit done. Hell, I'm the one teachin' ya all the stuff your little league coach never did. The way I see it, you oughta be grateful."

"Grateful?"

"Why not?"

"You could've killed him, jackass."

"Are you kidding? I carefully measured the dosage. It was fine."

"What's Don going to say when he hears about this?"

"Let me worry about Don," said Reardon, spitting into his cup. "You've got bigger problems, namely that you've been striking out way too fucking much."

"What's that got to do with anything?"

"It's got everything to do with you sticking in the Big Leagues, so I suggest you start giving a damn. Do you realize that your K-rate is up close to fifty percent? Soon enough Lou won't be able to *take no more* of your garbage play and he'll stop letting you handle the bat all-to-fucking-gether. After that you won't get another shot. Lou ain't the type to give folks second chances."

"Quit trying to deflect."

"I'm just telling it like it is. I mean I've watched all your at-bats—all of 'em. I've watched 'em again and again down in the media lab—you see how much I've invested in you?—and you know what struck me? There you are, standing up at the plate, and they're sending the ball right down broadway and you just keep swinging through these beautiful, plump, juicy pitches. It's like the ball teleports right through your bat. You're late."

"Let me guess: you know just what to do about it."

"The way I figure it, your hand-eye coordination must be all shot from being such a lazy, drug-addled son of a bitch. Well we've gone and rebuilt your swing, so who says we can't get you making contact?"

"I feel like shit."

"What's that matter? Your tummy hurt? In case you hadn't noticed, we're running out of time here, dickbrain."

"Fuck off, Reardon. If they send me down it'll be because of all the shit you stirred up last night."

"No, *you* fuck off. You keep harping: *Last night! Last night!* You know what? Fuck last night. I don't give two fucks about last night and neither should you. Did I cross a line? Sure I fucking did, but who cares? Name me somebody worth mentioning who never overstepped the boundaries every now and again. That's part of the cost."

"The cost of what?"

"The cost of greatness. How am I supposed to cook up an omelet if I don't break a few eggs, huh?"

"I fail to see how fucking over your teammates adds to anybody's greatness. That's some twisted fucking logic, man."

"I didn't fuck over nobody. The truth is you and the old Stone Buddha both got the same problem. It's like you're both stuck in quicksand and struggling. But we all know what happens when you struggle in quicksand—you end up in deeper shit than when you started. So, to bust yous twos nuts out of your ruts, I thought I'd teach you how to cut loose a little—to have fun, you know? *Relax.*"

"You're one sick motherfucker, you know that?"

"You're just looking for someone to blame, but I won't be your scapegoat. Not when I've been going out there every damned day getting my job done. Ain't you the one who's been whiffing on pitches any high schooler could crush? You want to play at this level? Well start acting like you got a pair and fucking *play* because right now you're making us both look bad. I know you may not believe this, but you've got a fucking shelf-life. We all do, even old Reardon here. And yours, my friend, is rapidly expiring, with or without my help. Do you catch my drift? Nobody likes a loser, Casey, and the way you've been handling the bat has already got people wondering what you're doing hanging around. The fans blame you for taking up a roster spot that oughta be held by somebody who can help the team win, and it ain't just the fans. Now, if you know what's good for you, you'll shut the fuck up so I can get to teaching you how to hit a goddamned breaking ball."

"I feel like an idiot up here," said Casey once he was standing atop the wavebreak. He pulled on his batting gloves, velcroed them up tight, and Reardon handed him his bat. For a moment Casey fantasized about using it to club Reardon to death right then and there.

"I'm going to throw these here rocks up in the air for you. What you're going to do is track the rock with your eye. It falls in a parabola, you see?"

"Sure," said Casey. "Then I hit it?"

"That's right."

"You brought me down here to hit rocks?"

"Why not? This here's the type of drill that can help bust a fella out of a slump. It teaches timing, contact, you fucking name it. It's a simple drill, I saw it done down in the DR, back when I still played winter ball. I noticed the local kids weren't playin' with your usual equipment. Instead, they were usin' a stick they found by the side of the road for a bat and a big ol' rock for a ball. For practice, they toss up rocks and knock them over the fence or through store windows or whatever. I've since seen similar drill done with bottle caps, but in my opinion the rocks are better for building up contact skills. Are you good and ready up there, or what?"

"I guess," said Casey.

"Here we go."

Don was torn away from his ruminations by the sound of his phone rattling against his desk. At this point he could only function with the aid of a frightening amount of caffeine coursing through his bloodstream. He'd been up all night fielding calls from the media, ownership, the league office, all because of these... *pictures* that had recently surfaced on the internet.

The pictures of tonight's starter and his translator onstage, stripped from the waist down, presumably belting some song into a microphone, had become the stock avatar of this fresh scandal and the subject of many cruel memes, but Don was more concerned with another photo that had been making the rounds, one in which Casey stood vomiting into a trashcan while a flash-lit Reardon gave the finger to the anonymous cameraperson. There was also a video, taken by the translator himself and posted online for only God knew what reason, where he kept panning from his excited face to a fleet of motorcycles piloted by dirty, middle-aged men who, in Don's estimation, appeared to be dyed-in-the-wool professional criminals.

He had been trying to contact the players in question since the photos had surfaced, but so far had only been able to get through to Saito. Even then, the only thing he heard was the whooshing of air and *baka!* before the phone was hastily hung up.

Don rubbed his eyes and thought about the many hours that lay between himself and much-needed rest when his phone went off again. It was a text message from the team's media relations director, Howard Samarasekera, whom Don had charged with handling this recent flare up. Don opened the message hoping that Howard had finally got a hold of Reardon, but the news turned out to be far worse. Just three words:

This is fucked.

He texted Howard back:

meet me in my office.

Howard arrived two minutes later, carrying a tablet on which he put the finishing touches of a draft email he was intending to send to the media relations team. He shared the document with Don, who read the draft on his phone while Howard sat across from him, typing away. It read:

Connectors,

Being the in-touch people you are, you have no doubt heard about certain photographs that have been circulating on the internet for the past eight hours. Many of you may be concerned for the safety and wellbeing of our players and colleagues, but rest assured that they are right as rain.

You may also be concerned with how you are going to respond to the phone calls that will surely be flowing in imminently. It is with this concern in mind—as well as our obsession with transparency and honesty—that we endeavor to share with you the facts as we know them:

- *The players are safe and at home.*
- *The photos and videos were taken over the course of several hours, beginning at 10:07 PM, with the last photo being taken at 3:45 AM.*
- *To our knowledge, absolutely no illicit drug use took place.*
- *The police are presently not involved.*
- *There have been, up until now, no reported assaults.*

We believe that it goes without saying that if we keep to the facts, this situation is more likely to come to a favorable conclusion. We will be dedicating the next few days to the dissemination of the facts as we know them and as we come to know them, in the hopes of securing the best resolution to this situation for our team, for our players, and for ourselves.

It need not be said that while we are being open in our approach to the investigation and the facts as they are, you are expected to exercise a certain level of discression with regards to their dissemination. The bullet list above is <u>not</u> meant to serve as a script to be rattled off to every inquiry. We trust in you, our connectors, to exercise your professional judgment in which facts you choose to disclose and to whom.

In solidarity in these difficult times,
Howard Samarasekera,
Media Relations Director

"You have a divine gift for bullshit, Howard," said Don, looking up from his phone.

"There's nothing divine about it," said Howard, typing away on his tablet. "It's just a practical solution to a predictable problem. Picture yourself in their shoes, fielding calls, not knowing what to say. That's the kind of situation that induces panic. You give them a script—talking points they can keep circling back to—and they're right as rain. It allows our connectors to stick to the truth, to the facts. As the facts change, the strategy changes. But the facts, as they stand, aren't enough to draw conclusions, so why give them more than you need to?"

"The problem is the facts, as they continue to surface, probably won't shine a very positive light on our friend Mr. Reardon."

"It's all in how the information is presented."

"Has anyone actually been able to get in touch with Reardon, or are we just blowing smoke here?"

"Oh it's pure smoke," said Howard. "But if Reardon had somehow wound up in a morgue, we'd have heard about it by now."

"We need to find him, Howard, and we need to find him fast."

"He's not answering his phone."

"The bastard probably isn't home. What about Casey?"

"Nothing but dead air so far. We think his phone might be off."

"Brilliant," said Don.

"They'll show up sooner or later."

"I want them in my office as soon as they arrive. Do you understand?"

"Consider it done."

Casey and Reardon didn't arrive at the ballpark until almost one, and were escorted straight to Don's office as requested. Don scrutinized the players from behind his desk, looking first at one, then the other, waiting for either to offer some sort of explanation for the events that had dominated headlines over the past twelve hours.

"Well?" asked Reardon.

"I was hoping you could tell me," said Don, sipping his coffee. "I was hoping you could tell me what the fuck is going on."

"There's not much to tell."

"Really? Then why hasn't my phone stopped ringing since one in the morning?"

"Well it's not ringing now."

Just then Don's phone began vibrating against the desk. He gestured toward it. "You were saying?"

"Look, the media has a way of blowing things out of proportion."

"You're right about that," said Don, dismissing the call with a swipe of the screen. "That doesn't change the fact that Amuro's fuming. He's thinking of pressing charges."

"Ain't nobody going to press no charges," said Reardon, spitting into his cup. "You've gotta quit talking nonsense if you want me to take this here investigation seriously."

"And you," said Don, turning toward Casey. "Did you have anything to do with this?"

"No."

"Then why do I see your face in all these photos?" said Don, holding out his phone and scrolling through the photos so Casey could see.

"I don't remember any of it."

"That's just wonderful, isn't it? Can you give me one reason I shouldn't—"

"Why are you picking on the kid? You know damned well I'm the one who did it."

"What's that you say?"

"I said that I'm the one who did it. I drugged Casey, Amuro, Amuro's lackey, the whole lot of them. Hit 'em each with 10 milligrams of pure, unadulterated MDMA—the good shit, the highest quality, of my own personal manufacture. What you going to do about it?"

"I'll repeat every word you just said to me," said Don, his eye twitching.

"You don't have the balls to rat me out."

"Then I'll send you down."

"I'd never pass through waivers."

"Damn it, they can have you!"

"You'll thank me later," said Reardon, "once all the dominoes fall into place."

"Fuck the dominoes and fuck you. You're trying to ruin me. Don't you understand? I can't just let this go. You've created a media circus here, Phillip. They're out for blood. They want answers and I need something to tell them. There must be some sort of consequence. The scales of justice must be balanced."

"Let me ask you something, Donny Boy. Has anyone actually made the assertion that your fine ballplayers were, in fact, drugged? Isn't it more likely that we four ballplayers was just having ourselves a night on the town and simply... overimbibed?"

"Are you suggesting—"

"I ain't suggesting nothing," said Reardon, spitting into his cup. "Alls I'm saying is there's more than one way of reading this situation."

Don swiveled in his chair and looked out the window. The grounds crew was busy doing a sweep of the field. As he watched them, he tapped his fingers on his desk and considered what Reardon had just said.

"I just don't think he'd go for it, unless…"

"Unless?"

"Unless you issued an apology."

"I ain't issuing no fuckin' apologies, I can tell you that."

"A closed-door apology."

"Fuck no."

"Listen, Phillip," said Don, turning back around. "You don't have a choice in the matter. The only way your version of the story holds water is if Amuro corroborates it."

"He'll probably just keep his mouth shut and this whole thing will blow over."

"That's not good enough. We need full corroboration if we're going to bury this thing. I won't have any loose ends. It's deliver an apology or I throw you to the wolves. Do you hear?"

"Well then I guess it's been nice knowing ya."

"Damn it, Phillip. You *owe* me. You made this mess and now I'm supposed to clean it up? Well I'm not the maid, Phillip. I'm not here to take out your trash. You've fucked me."

"Don't be weak," said Reardon, spitting into his cup. "What? You want to blame me for your own failure now? Take some responsibility. You knew what you were getting into when you signed me and you did it anyway—at a real bargain price, might I add."

"I'm done for," said Don, running his fingers over his scalp.

"Don't get your titties in a knot, Donny Boy. I mean, relax a little would ya? I told you when I signed, I said I'd take you where you wanna go, and that's exactly what I intend to do. You want me to apologize, but what good is an apology when our friend will know as well as you and me that I ain't sorry for what I've done, that the only reason I'd be apologizin' is on account of orders. Do you really think that's going to get him to play nice?"

"If you have an alternative proposal, I'm all ears."

"There ain't much to propose. I'm just gonna do what I always do and carry this team on my back."

"And how on earth do you propose to do that?"

Reardon just smiled and winked.

"You will answer my question, Phillip."

But Reardon was already walking towards the exit, calling over his shoulder, "I wouldn't want to ruin the surprise."

The sound of the locker room door closing echoed ominously in the otherwise dead silence following the entrance of the team's closer and starting catcher. The players stood in a range of postures: Steele was standing looking into his mirror and working something into his hair; Thompson sat on a stool shaving down the handle of a bat; Lou stood in the doorway of his office, leaning against the frame with his arms folded, working a handful of seeds in his cheek; a few others sat tapping away on their cell phones, their faces bathed in the pale white LED glow. Reardon walked into the middle of the room and cleared his throat to signal he was about to say something, but didn't say anything for quite some time, so that all one could hear was the rasp of the bat shaver, the patter of seed husks and tobacco into paper cups, and the occasional pop of bubblegum.

"Now," began Reardon, "I've been sent here with marching orders to apologize to yous guys on account of my *allegedly* spiking a teammate's drink with emm and him goin' off afterwards and making a complete ass of himself—but I ain't here to do that."

"You must be out of your goddamned mind," shouted Lou.

"Sure am, Lou. Sure am. I've been driven plum fuckin' crazy by all this losing. It was was starting to leave a bad fuckin' taste in my mouth and I couldn't take it no more, so I thought it was time to shake things up. God knows all that voodoo shit you fuckers been practicin' ain't done shit."

"You crossed a line this time, Reardon," said Chandler from his locker at the far end of the room.

"You wanna talk about lines, brother? How about the Mendoza line? You ain't been north of it all fuckin' season." Reardon swept the room with his bloodshot gaze; spit was spraying from his mouth. "Fuck, I'm standing here looking around and you know what I see? A bunch of miserable fuckin' losers who can't get the job done and need someone to blame."

"You aren't the only one stuck on this shit club, brother," said Steele, still looking into the mirror.

"Yeah, but I'm the only one who's got the right to complain about it."

"Why's that?"

"Two days ago," said Reardon, pointing at Steele. "Two days ago I was sitting up in the bullpen when Hally was pitchin' and I fucking saw you. I was sitting up there and I saw you."

"You saw me what?" said Steele, popping a stick of Double Bubble into his mouth. "I've been hittin' just fine."

"Yeah, except your job ain't just hittin', dipshit. You gotta field the ball while you're at it. Hally over there was pitchin' and I fuckin' saw you give up on a ground ball with men on-base. And it wasn't like you went all out and you just couldn't get to it: it was a goddamn playable ball. You just gave up on it. You just fuckin' let it roll on by and plate a run. Where's the damned apology for that?"

"We were losin' already. I could've hurt myself going after that ball."

"That's weak and you know it."

"Yeah, partner, and what are you going and doing about it?" said Thompson, looking up from his bat. "About all the losing, I mean. You're just here closin' out games. Sure, you've found yourself a nice little sweet spot, but I've seen your type before. It won't last. It never does. Next season could come around and someone might figure you out, or maybe that ol' elbow gives out again and then what? I reckon that would be the end of Phil Reardon."

"This is a contract year, brother. Next year, I get paid."

"You might get a big paycheque out of it, but in the end you're still an asshole."

"At least I won't be stuck being mediocre."

"So that's what you think, is it?"

"You've yet to show me otherwise. The whole lot of you have yet to show me otherwise, and yet you motherfuckers walk around like you've got something special going on. Well, let's look at something objective, namely, our record. Does sitting at the bottom of the division sound too fuckin' special? Will the twelve thousand people slated to show up today make you feel special? Because I'll tell you something: it makes me feel right fucking low and I'm the one out there shattering records. What the fuck is the point of it all, if we're just gonna roll over and take it from pretty much every team in the league? We'd be better off with a lineup of little leaguers."

"Everything you say is so goddamned ignorant, Reardon," said Steele. "I'd like to see you even make contact. You probably haven't swung a bat since little league."

"Well, let's find out just how hard it is. Lou, I want you to put me in at DH tonight so I can show these chumps how it's done."

All eyes in the room turned towards Lou.

"What are you all looking at?" said Lou. And then to Reardon: "You don't get to make decisions."

"I can't be any worse than any of these losers," said Reardon. "How's a man supposed to put his money where his mouth is if you won't even give him an opportunity."

"You just drugged one of my starting pitchers, you goddamned lunatic. You're lucky he ain't charging you. You're lucky I'm not making you eat your teeth."

"Go on. Put him in, Lou," said Thompson.

"Yeah, put him in," said Steele, turning back to the mirror. "He ain't got nothing to show. It's all just talk."

"What makes you so sure?" asked Reardon.

"Because you know what your problem is, Reardon? You've got a big fuckin' mouth, and I mean *real* big. Ain't seen nothing like it. You talk and talk and talk and talk like you know it all, seen it all, and can do it all, but you don't, you haven't, and you can't. You're up there, actin' like a hotshot, but nobody's buying it. We know it's all just a big act you're putting on to distract us from the fact that you're one fucked up dude. What? You think it's somehow our fault that you went out and drugged somebody?" said Steele, turning from the mirror, walking towards the pitcher, and poking him in the chest. "You committed a goddamned felony. Do you understand that, motherfucker? And now you're up here criticizing everybody and saying that everybody else's job's no trouble at all. Well, if it's so easy, then I say Lou lets you pick up the bat and show everyone how full of shit you really are."

"What you'll quickly find out," said Reardon, spitting a thick gob of tobacco into his cup, "is how much better I am than you."

"Why don't you do as you say and put your money where your mouth is?"

"You mean like a bet?"

"Sure. Since you like to talk so big, how about putting a little skin in the game?"

"I won't have no gambling in my clubhouse," shouted Lou, but everybody ignored him.

"So what? I've gotta get a hit?"

"You gotta get on-base twice. That doesn't seem like too much to ask for from an expert batsman such as yourself, now does it?"

"No problem. What's in it for me?"

"Well, for one thing Amuro won't charge you."

"Please," said Reardon. "Nobody can touch me."

"Yeah? Well, if that ain't enough, tell me what you want."

"Alright," said Reardon. "If I win, you've gotta give me your Huracán."

"No way."

"Why not? I thought you were so certain I'm bullshitting. Besides, that's too much car for you: she needs somebody who's going to treat her right. You know what I mean?"

"Ain't happenin'."

"Ah! He is—how you say?—chicken. Bawk-bawk-backaw," said Felix, flapping his elbows like a pair of wings and pretending to scuff the ground with his foot.

"Stay out of it, you francophone motherfucker."

"Come on, Eddie," said Thompson. "You ain't got nothing to worry about. Like you said, Reardon here hasn't handled a bat since little league."

"I bet he winds up wearing the golden sombrero," said Chandler.

"Eddie will not do it," said the other Aucoin twin.

"You really are a sick fuck, Reardon. Alright, you can have the car, but if we're setting the stakes so high, let's make it a little more interesting."

"Bring it on."

"Two hits. Walks don't count."

"Done."

"And if you lose," said Steele, "what you got to offer me?"

"Name it."

"There's only one thing I want from you, motherfucker, and that's for you to disappear. I don't care how good you are, homie—you ain't right. You're sick. The game's gone and got you twisted. You need help. You can't be allowed to stick around. You're the type of motherfucker that's bound to get somebody killed one of these days. So, if you lose—and you will—you're gonna quit the game at the end of the season and never come back—not as a manager, not as a scout, not nothin'. I never wanna see you again. Feel me?"

"That's a big ask there, brother."

"And my Lambo ain't?"

"Now listen up," said Lou, breaking his silence. "You must all be out of your goddamned minds. This team's fallin' apart, I tell ya, and up until now I've been loiterin' around holding my dick, waiting to see how it'd all boil over. And you know how it did? With hot, liquid shit. I can smell it from here," he said, pointing at the ground he was standing on. "I won't be having none of it! Nobody mutinies on my watch! No, I ain't givin' you the bat, Reardon. Not on my goddamned life."

"Why not?"

"I don't know what you're up to, but I know one thing for certain and that it can't be nothing good. That much I know. Now, I can't speak for Tubs here, but this all smells to hell of insurgency."

"It sure does," said Tubs, crossing his arms over his chest.

"We wouldn't even be talking about this if y'all had've done the right thing in the first place and suspended his whack ass until the end of the season," said Steele.

"You know what, Eddie? I agree with you. This crazy son of a bitch ought to be suspended, but the powers that be—such as they are—have decided that we *need* him. And do you wanna know somethin'? They're probably right. It's not like the rest of yas are setting the world on fire. He's the only one on this club who's been getting the job done while everyone else has been rotating the deck chairs on this sinking ship. As of today, we've lost eleven in a row. I look around at you boys and in my heart I want to call it quits right here and now. Not one of you is showin' any sense of urgency. I'll tell you something, if we make it to twelve, our gooses are cooked. I feel it in my bones."

"Then put him in," said Casey, not knowing exactly why he said it. A silence ensued in which all eyes in the room turned in Casey's direction before gradually returning to Lou.

Lou spat seed husks right onto the floor and stared Casey down while he considered what he was going to say.

"You know, back in the day... back in the day I would've made a dipshit like you eat your teeth just for breathing the wrong way in front of me. You know that? But it ain't the nineties no more, and now if I sock a two-bit loser like you I've got all these red-tape lovin' HR types running around the place, cryin' abuse and workplace harassment, muddying up the water, and confusing the hell out of everything. It's gotten to the point where all a man can do is stand here and stare at you and wish for you to spontaneously combust. Well? Is it working? I didn't think so." Lou took off his hat and ran his fingers over his balding scalp. "I mean what's next? Is Ernie over there gonna start bossing me around like he's my dear dead mother? You know, I've seen 'em come and I've seen 'em go, but you my friend might be the most thankless piece of shit that ever crawled on God's green earth. If I didn't need someone to catch this piece of human garbage over here, I'd've cut your ass loose long ago."

"But you can't cut nobody loose," said Reardon, spitting into his cup. "You can't cut nobody loose and you know it."

"I'm going to make you eat your teeth in a minute, Reardon, I swear."

"Go on and do it then, I won't do nothin'. I won't even report you. I'll just stand here and take my licks, so long as you give me the bat."

Lou threw his hands up in the air. "Maybe Eddie's got a point. You must be out of your fuckin' mind."

"Just give him the damn bat," said Thompson.

"Absolutely not."

"Give him bat."

"Come on!"

"Let him tie his own noose."

"Get rid of this crazy son of a bitch."

"I tell you it isn't happening! Now get out there on the field and get on with it."

Despite Lou's stated position on the subject, the players pestered him about putting Reardon in the starting lineup all afternoon. He couldn't talk to anyone without the topic bubbling to the surface. Everywhere he turned there was Reardon, or at least someone asking about the sonofabitch.

All this chatter smelled to hell of high mutiny. For Lou, who had spent the better part of forty-four seasons in and around professional baseball, and who—as far as he himself was concerned—had seen everything there was to see, there was no doubt this rat bastard was trying to tear the team apart. But for what purpose? What motive? Lou didn't know. There may not have even been a reason, but one thing was certain—Reardon was letting loose something dark in the clubhouse and whatever that dark thing was, it was infecting the team like a cancer. If they didn't cut out the cancer at its root, namely by getting rid of Reardon, there would be no season left to save.

"Nothing good will come from this mutiny, mark my words," he said to Tubs after a particularly heated exchange with the Aucoin twins.

"Maybe you should just let the man hit."

"What, and let the son of a bitch win? I'm not risking my neck for some clubhouse bet."

"Why not?"

"Do you have any idea what happens during a mutiny?"

"No," said Tubs.

"The captain—not to mention his first mate—end up walking the plank."

With all this badgering, Lou became progressively more irritated as first pitch approached. It got to the point where he thought he might just force feed some teeth to the next sono-fabitch that asked him whether he was going to put Reardon in.

The last straw came when the *Star*'s beat reporter intercepted him on his way into clubhouse. All the journalist did was ask if the rumours of Reardon starting at DH tonight were true. Lou stared at him in silence before spitting seed husks onto the reporter's shoe and looking up to the sky to whisper something to the heavens. Next thing the reporter knew, Lou was ripping off his own hat, throwing it to the dirt, bursting into a stream of profanities, and stomping on the thing over and over in a red-faced rage. So much spittle flew in all directions that the reporter was forced to beat a hasty retreat, holding his cellphone out in front of him in case Lou resorted to the use of violence, as he was promising to. Lou was still cussing under his breath as he walked down the dugout tunnel to his office.

He slammed his office door so hard the windows were still rattling around in their frames when he sat down at his desk. The water cooler glugged as Lou filled a paper cup, which he downed all in one go to wash down the fistful of ibuprofen he'd just swallowed. The lights in his office were off and Lou was happy to keep them that way. His head felt as if it might split open. He imagined his skull spilling its contents all over the blank lineup card lying there on his desk. It was clear things were no longer under control. The team had gone all mutinous over this little incident between Reardon and the goddamned useless tofu-eater. Now what was he going to do about it?

Lou woke frightened and scrambled for the digital clock he kept on his desktop. The face lit up with the touch of a button, but it took a moment for his eyes to focus in on the digits, which told him it was 4:30. He breathed a sigh of relief and was calm a moment before being overcome by his former rage and hurling the clock across the room. It exploded as it hit the concrete, all its circuitry popping loose on impact and scattering across the floor. Lou rubbed his eyelids with his fat fingers to dispel some of the heaviness. Around this time the team would be preparing for batting practice, and since he'd been missing for what must be hours now, he reasoned that he really ought to make an appearance.

Although this need was apparent, his knees hardly felt like they were ready for the hike past the dugout onto the field. As he tried to stand, the old machinery failed and he was forced back down into his chair. He opened the bottle of ibuprofen and knocked a couple more back, washing them down with another paper cup of water.

The truth was that some days his body felt as if it were on the verge of falling apart. His stiff, surgery-addled knees, his chronically arthritic hands, his damned back, his right elbow, his bum ticker—nothing worked right anymore. What had happened to the young man who used to block home plate with his body? Who slid head-first into second on an unlikely steal attempt? Who blocked ninety-plus heat in the dirt to prevent a run from scoring? Sometime in the intervening years it had all slipped away without his even noticing. He'd tried to reverse it: attempting the new training techniques every new crop of prospects carried up with them from the minors, followed the dietary advice of the team's trainers and doctors, applied all the creams and ointments, taken the multivitimins and supplements, and even quit with the tobacco, but all these remedies did nothing to reverse the process. Every year he'd come back just a little bit slower, a little bit weaker, and his injuries nagged him. One day he woke up to find he was nothing more than a bench player. Not long after, his playing days were done.

Lou's vigor had been irrevocably sucked out of him, worn away through years of toil behind the dish and in the dugout, and now all that remained was this short old man with a beer belly and waddling gait. This was the cost, the inevitable result of all the work that had gone into the game so gladly because he had remained largely ignorant of its toll of minutes, turned to days, turned to years, turned to decades. As far back as Lou could remember, baseball had been his life. Even now, his memories of things like school and family felt faint in comparison to those of summer days spent on the parched grass of the little league ballparks of Brooklyn. One thing he did know was that he didn't have as many days ahead of him as he did behind, and if the team's fortunes kept on their current trajectory, heads were going to roll.

The players were assembled around the cage and talking excitedly as Lou emerged from the dugout and began the long trek out to where they were standing. These days he walked with his head down, to prevent people from catching sight of any difficulty, any sign of weakness. He had waddled halfway out to the plate when the deep cork-pop of solid contact froze him in his tracks. He looked up and watched as a ball rifled straight past the infield into left. It continued to climb and climb, right up over the fence and finally ricocheted off a seat in section 241 and into the bullpen. He stood there a moment considering what it might mean, but was interrupted once again by another resounding pop, this time fired into the gap in right-centre and coming down at such a flat trajectory near the base of the wall that it got jammed between the warning track and the scoreboard. A few more balls were sent into the deep part of the outfield, each booming with the satisfying pop of hard contact.

Lou stood there salivating, thinking that maybe he'd lucked out and one of the Dominicans had finally found their touch again, but when he finally looked to see who was taking the hacks, he discovered it was Reardon. The giant sonofabitch was standing up there in the batter's box with a bat that looked like a toothpick in his massive hands. God knew how the bastards had found a batting helmet in his size.

Lou hustled over to the cage, his knees stinging worse and worse with each step. "What the hell is going on here?" he bellowed, pointing towards the man at the plate.

"Reardon's taking his hacks," said Tubs, popping a fistful of seeds into his mouth.

"What the hell are you talking about?"

"Just what I said: he's up there taking his hacks. What does it look like?"

"And you allowed this to happen?"

"Couldn't stop it," said Tubs, shrugging and gesturing towards the players. "They insisted on it."

"I don't give a damn who insisted on what. I said he wasn't going to play and—by God!—I'll be damned if he plays. You know, in any decent institution—the army, for goddamned instance—they'd have a mutinous son of a bitch like you court-martialed."

"Damned good thing this here's no army then, ain't it?"

There was another pop, so loud this time that for Lou the very air seemed to tremble with the weight of the sound: a deep, sweet, hollowed out note that sent a ball to straight-away centre, carrying and carrying, its hang-time so enormous that at first Lou thought it was really nothing more than a noisy fly ball. But it kept going and soon its arc carried it down past the lights, until it was just a white speck against the blue field that was currently on the jumbotron, and disappeared into the black of the batter's eye.

"You sure about that?" said Tubs, placing a hand on Lou's shoulder and leading him back a couple of steps towards the dugout. "I mean, this guy can mash."

"Do you think I give a damn? Does he even have a Big League at-bat? Sure, he might be crushing it in batting practice, but it's another thing to do it in a game."

"Just look over there at Eddie. Boy's gone and turned white."

"Tubs, I need you to get your head in the game. We've got problems."

"Yeah, namely that Reardon hasn't been our DH since day one. Joe's been watching him, says the stroke's clean and I think the same, so what's the problem? It's not like we've got any skin in the game on this little wager of theirs. And what if he can hit? Stranger things have happened. We've been begging Don for a lefty bat all season."

"Jesus! Would you listen to yourself? You think Reardon's the lefty bat we've been begging for? Have you blown your god-damned lid? You're telling me to put this lunatic in the game because the players have gone and forced our hand and bullied us into even considering it? What's next? Are they going decide the lineup as well? Why don't we let them determine the order of the rotation? While we're at it, they can make the call to the bullpen. Are we going to run this team like a goddamned democracy and vote on every little decision? You'll have to make me drink hemlock, because the only way any of that'll be happening is over my dead body."

"Li—"

"No, you listen: a circle ain't got but the one centre and there ain't a ship that's got but one captain. People need to know who's in charge. Otherwise, it all goes to hell."

"Well then I guess you shouldn't've been off takin' your nap then, cap'n," said Tubs, spitting some seed husks to the turf.

"Now, you know I've got your back, Lou. I ain't never given you no reason to think I'm anything but loyal, but if things keep going the way they's going we'll all be working on our resumés in October. Hell, maybe as soon as next week. I mean, look around. What we've got goin' on right now? It ain't working. Maybe we can catch ourselves a little lightnin' in a bottle here and bust out of this slump. He can't be any worse than that fool Chandler."

Lou reached into Tubs' bag of seeds and flung a few of them into his mouth. He cracked them open with his teeth and watched as Reardon finished off with another blast to left-centre. He tracked the ball's long parabola as it flew off the bat, this one carrying all the way to the fifth deck and out of sight to the cheers of the players and the few fans that had made it to the park early enough to catch batting practice. When Lou looked back towards the cage, the entire congregation was turned to face him, including Reardon, who stood at the plate with Casey's bat in hand.

"Alright! Fine! Have it your way!" said Lou, waving his hand dismissively before wheeling around and lurching his way back to the dugout.

Shortly before game time, Lou posted a new lineup card on the clipboard secured to the dugout wall and Reardon's name was right at the top of it. News spread quickly and not just among the players: bloggers and newspapermen hustled to put together posts and articles regarding the lineup change.

Don learned about Reardon leading off via a text message from Howard, who had seen the lineup card posted in a tweet, along with a GIF of Lou stomping his hat into the dirt. Don phoned Lou's cell and got no response, so he went down to the locker room and found Lou bespectacled and alone, poring over a pile of heat maps the advance scouts had provided him.

"Didn't we give you a tablet?" asked Don, closing the door behind him.

"Yeah, well, I guess it's tough teaching an old dog new tricks. I just like the feel of the paper in my hands, you know?"

Don cleared his throat. "Would you mind telling me what the hell is going on?"

"You mean you don't know?" said Lou without looking up from the papers.

"How could I know when the one person who is supposed to keep me in the loop has neglected their duties?"

"It's nice of you to pay us a visit," said Lou.

"You've got a minute to explain to me why Reardon is hitting leadoff tonight before I hand you your pink slip."

Lou stroked his chin as if he weren't sure himself. "I suppose it's because he wanted to start at DH tonight. He's got the whole team on his side for this one. It's all on account of this bet he's got going with Eddie."

"A bet?"

"Where if he hits twice, he gets Eddie's Lambo, and if he doesn't, he calls it quits," said Lou. "This losing streak's gotten into people's heads, and what happened between the Japanese fella and Reardon's got everybody on edge. This ain't nothing new, Don. I told you in the offseason to send that nut packing and now he's got the whole damned club fightin' and bickerin'."

"Let me make something clear: the reason I pay you is to stop things like this from happening, so put a fucking stop to it."

"Yeah? Well, easier said than done. The thing about situations like this is that the best way to deal with 'em is to prevent 'em from happening in the first place. Didn't I tell you Reardon was a bad fuckin' apple? Didn't I tell you he was nothin' but trouble? I'll be damned if the proof ain't in the goddamned puddin'. He's got the whole team actin' all mutinous. In fact, they're out of control. If you want my advice, you oughta ship that sonofabitch out of here before he goes and makes matters worse."

"Who?"

"Reardon! Who else? I want him gone after tonight's game. All he does is keep stirring things up and upsetting everybody. I don't give a damn how hard he can throw; we ain't gonna win many ball games as long as he's on the team. What I need is players who will execute my game plan and help our team win. What I don't need is a giant prick who thinks it's okay to drug his teammates. If you had any sense you'd've suspended the son of a bitch indefinitely, but instead you sent the message that so long as he's throwing gas he can go and do whatever the hell he wants. How am I supposed to manage a team like that?"

"That's for you to figure out."

"Not for much longer, it ain't."

"What's that supposed to mean?"

"Exactly what it sounds like. That sonofabitch better not be on the roster tomorrow or you'll need to go and find yourself a new manager. While you're at it, you can ditch that useless kid he's got tagging along with him. Then maybe you can go about getting me somebody who can go out there and play. I've had enough of this goddamned, two-man sideshow."

Don typed something into his phone. "That won't be happening."

Lou tossed the heat maps aside. "If he's still here tomorrow morning, you can expect my resignation."

Don slid his phone into his breast pocket. "Rest assured, I'll be expecting it either way."

Outside of the 100 level seats behind home plate—which were packed with people who, for the most part, hadn't paid for their tickets—the stands were mostly empty. There were scattered groups: local beer league teams; boy scout troops from places like Sault St. Marie and Cambridge, who'd come to take in a game in the big city; there were the octogenarian season ticket holders with their grandchildren and other hangers-on; and the university students who were there to get drunk and be rowdy. In all, there were just thirteen thousand, four hundred and sixty-three in attendance.

Jack Rodriguez and Zack Sadler were sitting at a desk that looked out onto the field through the open windows of the press-box. Sadler was reading over some of the interesting observations he thought he might share on air, while Jack sat still for the make-up artist to work her magic.

Auxiliary personnel had cleared the box, leaving Jack, Sadler and their semi-regular stat-guru Keith Anderson sitting at the desk. The digital clock that hung over the camera counted down to zero and they were on.

"Hello and welcome to another great evening of Blue Birds baseball here in Toronto. It's a fine May night here in the city, as of now a balmy twenty-six degrees. This evening's match-up is between the visiting Baltimore Robins and the hometown Toronto Blue Birds, who enter tonight's game lurking in the depths of an eleven-game losing streak. Baltimore, winners of eight of their last eleven, will try to capitalize on Toronto's latest skid and take game one in the hopes of eventually sweeping the series."

"The way this season has gone—for both teams—really sets this one up as a David-versus-Goliath-type matchup," said Sadler. "One comes into the series on a tear and the other in the midst of their worst losing streak in almost a decade. A series sweep wouldn't really come as a surprise to anybody, since the Blue Birds have been playing some sloppy baseball lately. The errors on the defensive side of the ball and the baserunning mistakes have really cost them in May."

"It's been the problem since the start the start of the season," said Jack. "And I think you can look even further back in Spring Training, when the team was struggling to make plays and everybody was saying it was just rust. Well now the season's been going for almost two months and they're *still* booting the ball."

"They haven't looked good, that's for sure. They've had those defensive gaffes, the offence has dried up, and the pitchers have been leaving pitches way out over the heart of the plate. It's almost as if everything could go wrong has gone wrong. One thing's for certain: they need to get *something* going and they need to get it going *quick*."

"I'm with you there, Zack. If there was a time for action, it would certainly be now—before they dig themselves too deep a hole to climb out of. But the Birds are going to have their hands full tonight with what might be the hottest offence in all of baseball."

"That's right, Jack. Their three- and four-hitters might be the best offensive combination in the Bigs. They lead the league in runs, extra-base hits and on-base percentage. Max Stamford has already amassed *fifteen* home runs and May's not even over yet. I know if I was the opposing pitcher, I'd think about calling in sick."

"No such luck for Amuro Takazawa, the Birds' starter tonight. Here are his stats over his last five starts. Underwhelming to say the least, but based on what I've heard around the cage and from the players this morning, it sounds like Amuro's all fired up. Hopefully that intensity is reflected in his play this evening."

"Speaking of unorthodox pitchers," said Jack, "the Blue Birds' oft-maligned closer enters tonight's game from the very beginning, and no, he's not the starter. That's right, folks, *Phil Reardon* will be leading off for the Blue Birds in the bottom half."

But Reardon's debut at the plate would have to wait as the defense took the field. From where Casey was standing, tonight's starter didn't look good at all. His skin was the colour of cocaine and his whole body trembled. Casey cast a look over to the dugout and tried to indicate the situation to the bench by nodding towards the mound. If Lou had understood the sign, he made no indication one way or the other, and so Casey returned his attention to the pitcher as he prepared to throw the first pitch.

"First up to bat for the visiting nine is their second baseman, Xavier Brown. He's had a hot start, hitting .358 with an on-base percentage of .421."

Brown stepped into the box and Casey threw down the sign, but it was just a formality. Everybody in the stadium knew what was coming. The batter looked down at the plate and dug his cleats in. Amuro nodded and brought his glove to his chest. He kept his throwing hand hidden, adjusting his grip on the ball until he felt his fingernails bite into the leather. Casey watched him follow through and release the ball: the stitches didn't move, but merely expanded as the ball floated along its sixty-foot trajectory towards home, wobbling from side to side, up and down, before taking its last break and sinking under Brown's swinging bat for a strike. The hitter stood there looking at his bat as Casey fed the ball back to the mound.

They tossed Brown another knuckleball on the second pitch, but this time he didn't bite, letting the pitch tail off outside for a ball. On the third pitch, Casey threw down the sign for fastball and they busted him inside—another strike. One-and-two, they went back to the knuckleball, a four-breaker that floated in high and outside before breaking down and back over the corner of the plate where Casey held it until he heard *stee-rike three*, then sent the ball around the horn.

The next two batters didn't fare much better. The two-hitter popped up on the first pitch, a towering hit that went straight up and hung there for what seemed like minutes while Steele stepped beneath it, adjusted his position to the right, and settled in to make the catch. Jimmy Kesla, the Robins' three-hitter, was next up. He tried to play wait-and-see, looking at the first two pitches for strikes before fighting off a couple of borderline pitches, and finally falling prey to Amuro's inside fastball.

"Swing and a miss and he struck him out!" shouted Jack into the microphone. "Takazawa puts them down in order. And when we come back, the Lumberjack will try to get things started for the home nine. Stay tuned."

When Amuro re-entered the dugout, he was greeted by a truly haggard looking Saito and the bulk of the team's medical staff, who poked and prodded at him until he shooed them away with a sweep of his hand. After he'd rid himself of the pests, he took his usual spot on the bench, wrapped his arm in a towel, and said nothing to anyone. It was business as usual.

"We're back here at the Dome and here is tonight's home nine, and you'll notice a few interesting changes to the lineup. As we mentioned earlier, Chandler's out and he's been replaced by Toronto closer Phil Reardon, who steps to the plate to lead-off the first. A very unusual decision, wouldn't you say, Zack?"

"Unusual is right. Not only is this Reardon's first at-bat of the season, it's his first Big League at-bat since his days with the Mammoths. Looking back at his numbers, I have to say they're pretty good, but we're talking a very small sample size. It does seem like a risky call given where the team is in the standings. I could understand it if maybe there was an injury or some sort of personal emergency, but now, in the middle of an eleven-game losing streak? Something doesn't add up."

A murmur of confusion rippled through the crowd as Reardon stepped out of the on-deck circle and into the batter's box. Visiting players exchanged skeptical glances as Reardon spat into the dirt and lifted his bat.

He watched the first pitch miss the strikezone way outside for ball one. The second pitch came in, a curveball—low, for a ball—leaving the count at 2-0. After that second pitch, Baltimore's starter, Felipe Francisco, was all done with nibbling and shook off a sign for another breaking pitch. This time they challenged Reardon with a fastball right down broadway and he swung at it. There was a crack of hard contact and Reardon was off towards first, having rocketed the ball into the gap in left-centre. The outfielders gave chase, but they had no hope of getting to it before the ball caromed off the wall and back onto the turf, where Xavier Brown picked it up. Looking to first base, he found Reardon already making the turn towards second, so he fired to the keystone. Everyone in the home dugout was on their feet now, whooping as Reardon slid head-first into second base, grabbed hold of the bag, and held on just long enough to get a foot on it. When the dust cleared the umpire signaled Reardon was safe.

Reardon asked for time out and it was granted. He got up and handed his wrist-guard to Herb Zakowski, the Birds' first base coach, who gave Reardon a slap on the ass, leaned in, and whispered something that made Reardon laugh. Back in the dugout, Lou was busy sending out signs for the third base coach to relay to Steele as he stepped into the batter's box. Steele was able to get ahead 3-1 before grounding out on a changeup, low and outside.

Hernandez was up next and he hit the first pitch on the nose, a flyball to the warning track in deep-centre, but Brown got a good break on the ball and was able to flag it down before crashing into the screens. Having tagged up right when the ball left the bat, Reardon was able to advance to third on the throw, but it made no difference since Cruz came up next and struck out on three pitches to end the inning.

After that promising start to the bottom half of the first, the offense couldn't put anything together in the second and third. Francisco struck out both sides, but the game was still tied thanks to Amuro's striking out six and not allowing any baserunners.

Casey's strikeout in the bottom of the third made for Francisco's eighth K on the night and brought Reardon to the plate with two out.

"The lineup turns over as Toronto's closer-turned-DH comes to bat for a second time," said Jack. "He had a double to lead off the first, which to this point has counted for the game's only offense."

"It shouldn't be so surprising. I mean, you look at how big and strong Reardon is and think that maybe he *ought* to be a hitter. He absolutely clobbered that ball in the first because Francisco threw one right down the middle of the plate. I'd be really surprised if they gave him a decent pitch to hit here."

They didn't. They got ahead 0-1 with a heater high and inside that just nipped the plate for a strike, and then got him to foul off a ball on the outer half for strike two. Reardon was able to claw back to two-and-two by holding off on back-to-back sliders, but they finally struck him out on a curveball in the dirt. Reardon bolted towards first, but was beat to the bag by the throw.

The game remained scoreless until the eighth. The Birds scattered their hits, racking up five with no runs to show it. Casey was scheduled to lead off the second half of the inning. As he ran off the field into the dugout, Lou showed no signs of calling on a pinch hitter, so he took off his catcher's gear, grabbed his equipment, and began to get ready. Police officers patrolled the turf just in front of the dugout, gazing up into the stands for any sign of trouble. Casey stepped onto the on-deck circle and started taking practice swings while the fans booed.

Francisco was out of the game now, and Baltimore brought in Powell Brock, who Casey had logged forty at-bats against in VR. He looked different now that he was up there on the mound, since he had a face and tattoos. Casey had seen all his pitches in simulation, and had started to pick them up out of the pitcher's hand and send them deep. He should have felt great stepping into the box, but his seven innings behind the plate had done nothing to alleviate his hangover. His head pounded and his lower back screamed as Brock wound up and threw the first pitch. Casey watched it all the way, his head following the trajectory of the ball as it exploded into sight just in front of the dish. Before he knew what was happening, Casey committed to his swing and *crack*.

The ball wasn't hit hard, just a looper to right field that the outfielder gave chase to as Casey hobbled doggedly towards first. His legs burned, but all he could think was *run with your head down*.

Casey lumbered past first, and had almost reached the outfield wall by the time he slowed down. He turned around to find the first-base coach extending one hand towards him while calling for the ball with the other. "Now I ain't seen you here before," he said, shaking his hand. "You'll be wanting that one."

"Why?" asked Casey.

Herb gave Casey a hard look. "It's just most guys, they want to hold on to their first hit in the Bigs." Polite applause emanated from the crowd as he leaned in and whispered in Casey's ear, "Well, go on, they ain't paying to see you stand here."

Casey turned and waved limply to the crowd as Reardon stepped to the plate to considerably more fanfare than his first trip. Cellphone flashes flickered as the thirteen thousand in attendance rose to their feet. Casey took a small lead. He was under strict instructions to not get thrown out, and even at four feet from the bag he felt untethered, exposed. He watched the pitcher closely; any movement towards first and Casey was going to dive back. Except what if he slipped and was unable to get there?

Thankfully, the pitcher didn't seem too worried about Casey, forgetting about the baserunner after casting a solitary glance over his left shoulder. He got set and made his pitch.

"A slider. A good pitch inside, but Reardon doesn't bite. The count is 1-0."

"Brock's slider is just filthy. He's got that classic pitcher's build, with a big old backside that allows him to generate a lot of power. That slider clocked in at ninety-one."

Casey felt a sense of relief when he stepped back onto the bag between pitches, but it was shortlived. Herb leaned in and whispered into Casey's ear to take a few extra feet, but even that wasn't enough to distract Brock, who merely cast another glance over his shoulder before sending in the second pitch.

"A slider, for ball two."

"They seem afraid of throwing him the fastball. I think if you're the Robins, you should challenge him. This is this guy's forty-fifth Big League at bat. I wouldn't be surprised to see them throw the fastball here."

Sure enough, Reardon got the fastball, a 95 MPH heater right on the lower inside corner of the strikezone. But on a 2-0 count, Reardon was waiting for that pitch and barreled it up. The pop of the ball off his bat silenced the fans, who watched with great anxiety as the ball rocketed out to right field.

"Get up, ball! Get up, ball!"

It was slicing right and for a moment looked like it might go foul, but it stayed fair, hooking around the foul pole and into the utility tunnel.

"And it's gone! Home run! Home run, Blue Birds!"

Reardon wasn't too far behind Casey in stepping onto home plate, but did ham it up a bit, holding his hands out before him like he was gripping a steering wheel and every so often pretending to honk an imaginary horn. Steele stood in the on-deck circle, dumbstruck.

It wasn't long before Steele returned. There were conciliatory ass slaps and sympathetic glances for the second baseman as he peeled off his batting gloves and buried his face in his hands. Brock was able to close out the inning without giving up any further damage. Toronto headed into the top of the ninth with a two-run lead.

Lou had made the call down to the bullpen after Reardon hit the home run. Now, as the defense was preparing to take the field, Lou made a second call to find out if Felix was ready to pitch.

"He says he's good to go," said Drew McMillan, the bullpen coach.

"Send him to the gate. I'm gonna put him in," said Lou, slamming the phone down. His foot was already on the dugout step when someone grabbed his arm. He turned his head to find it was that good-for-nothing punk.

"I'll give you about a second to get your goddamned filthy paw offa me."

Casey removed his hand. "You've gotta keep him in the game."

"Keep who in the game?" said Lou.

"Amuro."

"Let's get one thing straight here. I don't hafta do nothin'."

"You gotta keep him in the game."

"You know something, kid? I really hope you enjoyed having teeth."

"The kid's right," said Reardon, placing a fresh plug of chew in his lip. "You can't take the old Stone Buddha out the way he's been pitchin'."

"I don't give a damn how well he's pitching. You see the score? We lose this game and the season's over."

"I see the score fine. Do you?" asked Reardon, pointing to the scoreboard. Beneath Takazawa's name were three zeroes: zero hits, zero walks, zero runs. Lou blinked and checked again. How hadn't he noticed that?

Lou glanced over at Amuro, who was wiping the corners of his mouth with a towel, having just vomited into the bucket Saito was holding up for him. Lou turned and looked at Casey.

"You want the rock, kid? Alright, show me what you got. But if you fuck this up, tomorrow I'll be shipping your ass to Buffalo."

"You sure about this?" asked Tubs as Amuro walked back out to the mound.

"Nope," said Lou, spitting seed husks onto the step.

Casey stepped behind the plate wondering why he'd gone and opened his big mouth. Amuro looked like a wreck out there, having turned increasingly green as the game progressed. Casey was now catching from one knee, unable to maintain the crouch. His splitting headache made him wonder if hangovers had always felt this bad. How was Amuro still able to stand out there, let alone pitch?

But pitch he did. He was still throwing his nastly knuckle-ball, and it was still lingering, for the most-part, on the edges of the strikezone. He'd struck out fourteen of the twenty-four hitters he'd faced, tallying his fifteenth K against the first batter of the ninth. After they'd popped out the number eight hitter, Casey looked up at the scoreboard to find the guy had already thrown one hundred and twenty-eight pitches.

That brought the last hitter in the Robins' lineup, CD Davis to the plate. He was hitting a clean .255 with a .308 on-base percentage and had so far succumbed twice to Amuro's knuckleball. This time, Casey threw down two fingers instead of one, and Amuro nodded and made his pitch. Casey had his glove held up off the plate outside, but Amuro missed the target. The fastball leaked in over the heart of the plate and Davis took a swing at it, but hit it late, pulling the ball to the right side of the infield—a bad spot for the defense. Thompson, who was playing in, could do little more than look as the ball rolled past. The perfect game and no-hitter were about to be broken up.

Out of nowhere streaked Steele, diving, his glove stretched out as the ball skipped along the turf. He was just able to snag it, but now found himself lying flat on the ground with the speedy Davis racing toward first. There was no time to get to a knee— a play had to be made—so Steele transferred the ball from his glove to his hand and awkwardly flipped it to Thompson, now standing at first. Thompson stretched and gloved the ball from the air *just* before Davis put his foot on the bag. The umpire pumped his fist and the stadium erupted.

"And that will do it. Amuro Takazawa records Big League Baseball's twenty-fourth perfect game under very unlikely circumstances. The crowd is loving it."

Dog Days of Summer

"You've gotta be fucking kidding me," said Reardon, throwing his scratch ticket to the ground and fumbling around in his plastic bag full of Keno tickets.

"I don't know why you bother with that shit," said Casey, shielding his eyes from the glare of the sun as they exited the Jug City. "You never win anything. Besides, what's a guy like you need *Instant Millions* for? You're the 'twenty-million-dollar man,' remember?"

"Hit a few dingers and you get real cocky, huh?" said Reardon, tearing the paper strips to reveal the result of his keno ticket. "Fuck. So close."

"I'm just saying. It's not like you need the money."

"It ain't about the money. I do this because it's fu—God fucking damn it!"

"Hey, Phil! Is that you?"

Casey turned to see who it might be. Whoever it was, he struck Casey as being incredibly short. He wore a Hawaiian shirt and khaki shorts, flip-flops, and he carried a plastic bag that would've been identitical to Reardon's, had it not been bulging with two-litre pop bottles instead of keno tickets.

"Hey there, brother," said Reardon, dropping a ticket to the ground and extending his hand for a fistbump. "It's been ages."

"No doubt. How the fuck you doin'?"

"The sweet taste of victory's still on my lips."

"You mean you guys won again? What's that, like forty in a row or somethin'?"

"We're working on it." said Reardon.

"I'll bet you are," said the man, nodding in Casey's direction. "Who's the kid?"

"You don't recognize him from the broadcast?"

"You know I don't watch that shit, man. I cut the cord years ago."

"Casey," said Casey, shaking the man's hand.

"They call me Joka. Say, now that I think about it, maybe I have heard of you. Ain't you the kid that everybody wants run out of town?"

"That was only when we were losing," said Reardon. "Winning changes everything. And quit bustin' his balls, would ya? The kid's sensitive."

Joka sucked his teeth. "Man, since when did you start giving a fuck about people's feelings. You gettin' soft or somethin'?"

"Speaking of soft, Joka here fancies himself a bit of an artist. How's playing those shitty vapour lounges downtown pay these days, by the way?"

"Naw. I don't fuck around with that shit no more. I'm getting too old. You know what I'm saying? All these kids want is a good beat. Nobody cares what some old, grey-haired bastard's preachin' 'bout."

"Nor should they," said Reardon. "Nobody takes well to preachin'."

"Who the fuck you trying to fool?" said Joka, turning back to Casey. "I swear the way this motherfucker goes on pontificatin' you'd think he was the pope, or some shit. The thing is, everything that comes out of this motherfucker's mouth is one hundred percent, grade-A bullshit—you know what I'm saying? Yet people lap it up like they're drinking the sacred waters of Shangri-la."

"That's one of the perks of fame. You can say or do pretty much anything and people will fucking love you for it."

"Shit. You mean like slipping some molly in your homeboy's drink without him knowin' about it and then lettin' him go and make a public spectacle of himself?"

"Just like that," said Reardon. "That's the way the world works. Nobody gives a damn how something gets done, they just want it over with and the quicker the better."

Joka sucked his teeth. "So the ends justify the means then? Same old Phil."

"Brother, I ain't the one who makes the rules. I'm just the one who benefits. Ends are all anyone really cares about. They're what counts."

"Some people feel differently."

"Some people ain't enough, and anyways they's hypocrites. Just by livin' they're complicit in the accomplishment of ends. In this world you don't have to do much more than get up and brew a pot of coffee and you're already part of some atrocity against your fellow man. I figure if there ain't no help being a villain, I might as well go live up to the fuckin' moniker."

"Mm. So that's how it is, brother?"

"You don't like it? Go on and get famous and see for yourself how easy it is to change it." Reardon pulled a joint out of a tin in his pocket. "Care to smoke?"

They sparked it up and passed it around.

"How do you two know each other?" asked Casey as he exhaled.

"Shit. I've known this motherfucker right here since grade school."

"What was he like then?"

"Quiet," said Joka. "I remember there was one year where he just wouldn't say nothin'. Everybody thought he was a damn mute or something, and nobody ever called on him for shit. We all assumed he was just a big stupid oaf of a whiteboy. Then one day we were in the middle of taking up the math homework—this was fifth grade—and up shoots this motherfucker's hand. None of us knew what to make of it. Even Mrs. Singer looked confused. Was she supposed to call on this idiot, who hadn't even introduced himself on the first day of class? Then we all find out why he's been so quiet all this time: it's because his voice sounds like it should belong to someone's dad, you know what I'm sayin'? He's got a fuckin' *man's* voice. We haven't been able to shut his ass up since."

"That ain't how I remember it," said Reardon.

"Motherfucker, when it suits you what's black becomes white and what's blue becomes red. Nobody aksed you how you remembered it. They don't have to because you're always

broadcasting your perspective all over the goddamned neighbourhood."

"At least I've got the balls to tell it like it is, even if people
don't wanna hear it."

"One day you'll learn," said Joka, smiling. "It's just pearls
before swine, brother. You may think your fame is a platform,
but people see what they wanna see when you're up there on
that stage. You can channel it, but you can't control it."

Joka took a pull from the joint.

"So what do you do now?" asked Casey.

"What's that?"

"I said what do you do now that you don't"—Casey had to
search for the word—"perform."

"Work. What else? I pay the bills, feed the kid, clean the
kitchen."

"Viva la cucaracha," said Reardon, spitting into his cup.

"Anyway, I better scuttle," said Joka, winking at Reardon
and hefting his bag of bottles. "But I oughta let you know, I've
heard tell *she's* been asking around about you. Something about
you not returning her phone calls or some shit."

"Who'd you hear that from?" asked Reardon, stomping out
the roach.

"Through the grapevine. You oughta give her a call."

"Sure, man. I'll call her."

"Good."

"Good."

There really had been a lot of phone calls lately. They'd be
sitting in the living room reading and the phone would start
ringing, but Reardon never answered. It always went to voice-
mail. Some days the counter would climb as far as seven or
eight messages before Reardon unceremoniously deleted them
with the press of a button. As far as Casey knew, Reardon
never listened to the messages. It was odd, but now that
Casey's bat was heating up, he felt disinclined to dig into the
closer's personal life.

Not that he was necessarily knocking the cover off the ball. His .247/.301/.458 slash line since Amuro's perfect game was only slightly above the States League average, but still quite respectable for a catcher. As the cherry on top, he'd tapped into some power and swatted four homers during that stretch.

Seeing Casey's improvement at the plate, the rest of the players began to buy into the VR technology. Surprisingly, the first player to begin using it was Hernandez, who had to make significant adjustments to his long-established routine to accommodate an hour of VR training a day. The VR lab was usually open between one and three in the afternoon, so Casey and Hernandez often found themselves training at the same time. It was strange for Casey to be in such close proximity to someone he hadn't been introduced to and who, so far, had shown little interest in getting to know Casey further. The two men just went about their business, each quietly pretending the other wasn't there.

By early June, Cruz and Nuñez had joined their countryman in the growing list of VR lab regulars after watching Hernandez use it to turn his season around. After a slow start in April, he was now hitting a respectable .255/.348/.511 and .400/.455/.771 since he began training with the VR, making him the hottest hitter on the team. After the Dominicans bought in, it was only a matter of time until the remaining dominoes fell. Steele came in next, and with Steele came Thompson. Soon enough all the position players were taking advantage of the technology.

Whether it was this wholesale buy-in by the players or something else, the team's offense had led the league in runs since the beginning of June. Of course, the pitching hadn't been bad either, with the starters contributing quality start after quality start and the bullpen remaining dominant. The team seemed to be firing on all cylinders, and it showed in the standings. The Birds had passed the Rebels and were now only a game back from Baltimore who, after a terrible month, now sat third in the division.

Casey wasn't sure if it was the victories stacking up, his prolonged exposure to his teammates, or his improved performance, but the attitudes of his teammates began to thaw, so that now when he met one in some corridor or hotel lobby, they might nod in recognition instead of pretending not to notice him. Steele was the only one who still gave Casey the cold shoulder, but Casey didn't take it personally, writing it off as Steele still being sore about having to sign his car over to Reardon—a rage made worse when, arriving to the ballpark the morning after Takazawa's perfect game, Steele had discovered Reardon was still driving the old VW to work, having already sold the Huracán.

Susan recommended Casey get more involved in the community—"you know, to improve your image"—and he had. He enjoyed community service, mostly because it was easy. All he had to do was show up, and the Foundation took the care of the rest. They even provided him with inspiring things to recite from a cue card handed to him on his way in the door. When he was inevitably asked to deliver a few words, he'd pull it out and read it as best he could, and when he stepped away from the microphone, whatever audience he was speaking to would inevitably applaud, regardless of how well he delivered his lines. After the BBQ, or luncheon, or whatever, he'd shake hands, exchange pleasantries, sign autographs, and smile for photos. From there, his handlers were happy to drive him wherever he needed to go.

Returning home from calling a Saturday night bingo game at the Lofty Precipice Retirement Community, Casey was surprised to find neither the handle to the door nor the deadlock secured. Stepping inside, he found the place a mess, with books strewn all over the floor and the rubble of Reardon's smashed flatware littering the kitchen.

He called out his roommate's name, but there was no answer. He began walking towards the bedrooms, but was stopped short by Reardon's massive handprint inked in sickly reddish brown on the wall. When Casey reached out to touch the stain it felt sticky, like half-dried latex paint. A trail of droplets led down the hall towards the third bedroom, which stood ajar. Light poured from the room, illuminating another grisly handprint on the jamb. Casey nudged the door open with his foot and stepped inside. There, at a long workbench spanning the breadth of the room, sat Reardon on a wooden stool, applying a gauze bandage to the right side of his face. He was using a small circular mirror to check his work. "How'd it go, kid?"

"Fine. What the fuck happened to you?"

"What does it look like? My face got all fucked up."

"Jesus, I'll fucking say. You scared the hell out of me. It looks like a goddamned murder scene out there. How'd that happen?"

"I had an accident," said Reardon, pressing on the last piece of adhesive tape.

"What?"

"I said, I had myself a bit of a knife accident."

The gauze was already beginning to saturate with blood.

"But I thought you weren't the kind of guy who had accidents."

"We all have accidents, dipshit. Just look at my fucking face."

"You think it needs stitches or what?"

"I've already taken care of it," said Reardon, indicating the bloody instruments used to suture the wound. "Hell of a job, if you ask me."

"You fucking stitched it up yourself?"

Casey continued to badger his roommate while the two of them cleaned the apartment, but Reardon would not back down from his insistence on this highly implausible knife accident. He had explanations at the ready for each of Casey's questions, so that when Casey asked how the books had flown all over the place and had their pages torn out, Reardon, without missing a beat, informed Casey that he'd thrown them about in a fit of rage after wounding himself so badly with the carving knife. When Casey pointed out that the trail of blood led straight from the kitchen to the third bedroom and so it was impossible for Reardon to have torn out the pages of the books *before* treating his injury, Reardon explained he'd only started to *really* bleed after he'd done a number on the old library. When Casey asked what had happened to the knife in question,

Reardon looked around and said, "I must've thrown it out the goddamned window."

Don and Lou were not impressed when Reardon showed up the next day with the bandage on his face. They couldn't let him step into the batter's box when one of his eyes was covered by a gauze compress, and his assurances that the ol' eyeball was just fine they found in no way reassuring. They compelled him to submit to inspection by the team doctor, who after looking under the bandage was able to confirm that the eye was indeed functioning, but the injury itself was quite substantial, at risk of infection, and would take several days—if not weeks—to fully heal.

The timing of losing Reardon's bat wasn't ideal. Hardy had got the flu earlier that week and was still feeling some of its effects. Many on the training staff thought he looked pale and that he probably shouldn't play, but he swore to Tubs and Lou that he was well enough to make his next start. Out of respect for his veteran, Lou gave the green light for Hardy to take the mound.

This proved a mistake. Hardy managed to hold the Seraphs off the board for the first four innings, but it hadn't been easy. He let the leadoff man reach in every inning and was only averaging around 79 MPH on his fastball. He needed the heater to establish his breaking stuff, so he threw it anyway. Dancing with danger finally caught up with him in the fifth. He wasn't locating well enough to get away with throwing those softballs, so he got smacked around, giving up three runs and loading the bases before Lou finally pulled the plug. Paolo came in to put out the fire and promptly gave up a grand slam to Seraphs slugger Abel Goldhirsch.

They didn't fare much better in game two. Ordoñez pitched seven innings of two-run ball, but without Reardon's bat in the middle of the lineup, the offense came out flat and was shut out.

Reardon made himself available for game three of the series by bullying the team physicians into clearing him for play. There was some debate amongst the players about Reardon possibly playing up his injury. Some even said he was making the whole thing up to get a few extra days' rest. But when he showed up that morning with the bandage off, everybody in the clubhouse conceded that the wound was as serious as it was disgusting. It stretched from just above his right eyebrow down the side of his face, almost to the corner of his mouth. The skin around the stitches was swollen and purple. In the gap between the two flaps of sutured flesh a thick black crust had formed. The closer could barely open his right eye.

Casey was zipping up his fly in front of his locker when someone tapped him on the shoulder.

"Let us outside, mon amis."

Patrice and Felix led him to the end of the dugout tunnel and climbed the steps onto the field.

"What in the hell has happened to Phillipe?" asked Felix.

"You'll have to be more specific," said Casey, tucking in his shirt.

"He is talking about his fucking face," said Patrice. "He looks like—how you say?—Freddy Krug-air."

"According to him, he had a kitchen accident."

"And you believe this?"

"No," said Casey. "I think someone busted into the apartment and fucked him up."

"Sacré-bleu!"

"You didn't see this?" asked Patrice. "Were you not there, mon ami?"

"No," said Casey. "I was at a retirement home."

"Ah, then who is to say? Perhaps he is telling the truth," said Felix.

"He cannot be allowed to play like this," said Patrice, as if Casey had any say in the decision.

Everyone understood that Reardon shouldn't be allowed to play, but at the same time, nobody could see any way around it. The Birds needed Reardon's left-handed bat in the middle of their lineup, they needed his arm in the bullpen, and what they needed most was to put a stop to this skid, even if it was only two games.

Their last match-up in the series was against the fearsome Seraphs righty, Terry Hughs—a long-time Bird-killer. His career ERA against Toronto was 2.06 and this season he was pitching better than ever. So far, he had held opponents to a .210 batting average, and had yet to give the Seraphs fewer than five innings per start. The position players had been preparing for him all week by spending as much time as they could in the VR lab and with the advance scouts, but no matter how much they prepared, they knew he was going to be a formidable opponent. To make matters worse, New York and Boston had each won their last two contests, so New York now led the division by a game and a half over Tampa Bay, with Toronto three and a half games back in third, and Boston, having passed the Robins, breathing down the Birds' necks. These considerations were probably the reason nobody was surprised that morning when the lineup card went up and Reardon's name was slotted into cleanup.

They got to Hughs in the first when Steele ripped a one-strike curveball into the alley in right. Cruz had already gone first to third by the time a Seraph outfielder reached the ball, and was given the sign to head home. Looking over his shoulder, he was surprised to see Steele already rounding second, so he took a wide turn around third and turned on the jets, diving as Reardon signaled for the slide from the on-deck circle. He slid right over the plate, scoring the game's first run. Toronto would finish the bottom half of the first up five runs, while the kid they'd called up from Buffalo for a spot start went on to pitch a gem. Reardon would finish the game with a pair of doubles in four at-bats and earned player of the game honours from Sadler and Ramirez up in the broadcast booth.

Everyone was happy to forget the so-called accident ever happened. It was easy now that the "slump" was over. They went on a tear, winning ten of their next twelve, with big offensive performances by Steele, Reardon, and the Dominicans buoying the team while the starting pitchers got abused by opposing lineups.

Unfortunately for Casey, he couldn't forget so easily. After all, he'd spent hours helping his roommate scrub half-dried blood from the walls and parquet floors using cold water and a brush. The question of how something like this could have happened, and why his roommate kept insisting on it being an accident, nagged at him. It kept him awake at night staring up at the glow-in-the-dark stars the former tenant had left on his bedroom ceiling.

Whatever had happened, it didn't seem to phase Reardon as he continued to rack up innings, appearances, and strikeouts. He still hadn't allowed a hit, let alone a run, and people in the know were beginning to wonder when the shoe was going to fall on this spectacular run. After all, he couldn't sustain this type of dominance over the course of the entire season, could he? Sooner or later, someone would lay into one of his heaters and send it for a ride.

Reardon already had 48.2 innings under his belt by the end of May. The high heat the prognosticators thought would tail off towards the end of the season had, if anything, intensified. Now he was throwing 107-109 and giving batters fits. It didn't seem to matter where he threw the ball because they stood little chance of catching up to it. His fastball had become such a devastating pitch that his zone whiff % shot to a staggering 45.6 percent.

He was also killing it with the bat. He had a .400 OBP since taking a full-time role in the lineup, hitting six bombs. His OPS had climbed to a frightening 1.114, which provided the Bird offense with a considerable boost. The Blue Birds were regularly putting up double-digits in the hit column, a feat which was greatly aided by Steele's average having climbed over the .375 mark. Reardon's stellar offensive play had kept him in the conversation for SL MVP in what was becoming an increasingly narrow field.

The Birds' resurgence had bought Don and his front office some much needed time. Not only were they able to successfully manipulate Singh's service time, but as the Birds' phenomenal play continued, they were now able to eye a new target of June 4—the Super Two deadline. The date came and went. Don waited a few extra days for good measure, and then he made the call to Buffalo. Chandler was DFA'd and Singh called-up.

Singh's call-up gave ticket sales an even bigger boost. The media had done a fantastic job of painting him as the team's saviour all offseason, so now the anticipation was high for the number four prospect in all of baseball. Don intended to exploit that anticipation by milking it for every dollar it was worth.

Weeks ahead of June 4, the team increased the cost of tickets for the series, the first after a nine-game roadtrip, in which Don planned for Singh to make his debut. Howard had been busy with his team preparing montage videos highlighting the young star's rise to the Bigs, which included International League and Eastern League MVP honours and a Northwest League championship run. Howard also arranged interviews for the days leading to the call-up so that Don could drop hints suggesting Singh's promotion was imminent. Replica uniforms had already been stitched and pressed in preparation.

It went off beautifully. Tickets sold out for the first time since opening day. Merchandise flew off the shelves. Most important, however: Singh did not disappoint. Not only did he make several acrobatic defensive plays in his debut, but reached base every time he stepped to the plate and stole three bags.

"You know they're still going to say you should have called him up sooner, don't you? They'll say we wouldn't be in such a deep hole if he'd been on the team all season," mentioned Susan, after the game.

"They can say what they like."

"Yeah? Well, maybe they're right. We've barely lost these past three weeks and we're still sitting third in the division."

Susan wasn't alone in being cheesed with Don for delaying Singh's call-up. Most of the front office staff resented the decision, having spent the last two months worrying over their job security while also preparing for the draft and J2 period. Could he have spared them some suffering if he had called Singh up earlier? Perhaps. But if he had called Singh up back in April, the talking heads would have pivoted from their hollering for Singh to be on the team to claiming Don was only doing it to save his own neck. That's how it was with fools like McTown and Chair: if there wasn't something ready at hand to criticize, they would go and make that something up.

"Irrelevant," said Susan, after Don had explained it for the tenth time. "Manny would still be on the team and the team would be better for it. We aren't trying to win any popularity contests here, Don. We're trying to win ballgames, or maybe you're more worried about the optics."

The barb hurt because there was some truth to it.

"It's not about optics. It's about doing right by my employer."

"Well maybe you ought to be thinking about doing right by your employees," said Susan. "Because you've made this a hell of a lot more stressful than it needed to be. I mean, who gives a shit if you've gained a year of control when you might get the boot next week? In that scenario it comes off as delusional to be worrying about what might happen six years from now."

"Seven," Don reminded her.

Ring, Ring, Ring went Casey's cellphone.

He glanced up from his book and put it down. Reardon was back in his workshop, grinding away at something. *Ring. Ring. Ring.*

"Hello, Casey," said a woman's voice.

"Who is this?"

"A friend, that's all. I'm a friend of Phillip's."

"Do you want me to put him on?"

"No," said the voice. "I called you, didn't I."

"Who is this?"

But the voice had no opportunity to respond. Reardon had materialized from his workshop and snatched the phone from Casey's hand. A second later, it was flying through the open balcony door and over the rail to the parking lot fifteen storeys below.

"What in the fuck—"

"Who was calling?"

"She said she was your friend."

"I don't have any friends. Don't answer the phone unless you know who's calling."

"I just thought—"

"You just thought nothin'. It ain't your job to think, moron. It's your job to do as you're told and not fuck my shit up."

"But my phone…"

"We'll pick you up a new one. Now come on, we've got shit to do."

O'Reilly's wasn't much to look at. Casey guessed it hadn't been renovated in at least fifty years. Photos of the various soccer and hockey teams the restaurant had sponsored over the years hung on imitation wood-paneled walls. There was no air conditioning, just a fan pushing back helplessly against the might of the pizza ovens and charcoal grill. Past the counter there was a naked view of the kitchen—a greasy, grey-tile affair. The men back there hurried about, opening and shutting the ovens to check on the pies, rolling out the dough, flipping burgers with tongs. Everyone's skin was slick with perspiration that gleamed beneath the weak fluorescent lighting. A nona scolded her grandson in Italian while he kept repeating, "I know, I know."

"Look, everybody, Phil is here," said the man behind the counter.

O'Reilly's whole staff stopped what they were doing and came to say hello. Greasy hands were extended, and Casey was forced by good manners to shake each and every one of them.

"I see you two know each other," said Casey to the man behind the counter, whose nametag read *Joe*.

"Well," said Joe, lifting the hinged countertop and stepping out into the restaurant, "there's knowing a fella and then there's *knowing* a fella. A lot of people will tell ya they know so-and-so when they really mean they met them once or twice. They're acquaintances, see? But when I tell you I know somebody? Then I *know* them. So it burns me up when people badmouth this guy in the papers—saying he's this or that—because I know this guy.

He's like my own family. You understand? You can't go believing all them terrible things they say about him. Take it from the source! Take it from the man who's known him since he was just a runt. Phillip over here? He's a good man."

Casey nodded. "You've known Reardon since he was little?"

"Sure have. You need proof? Look no further." Joe pointed to one of the team photos hanging on the wall. "There I am at the end, the coach—a damn good-looking son of a bitch if I may say so—and four in from the right at the back, there's Phil."

Casey would have followed the trail of Joe's finger, but his eyes froze on a pair gazing out of the photograph. They belonged to a little boy whose thick black hair shot out from under his cap in all directions. He was smiling, which would have been reassuring if it weren't for the fact that the boy's eyes, perhaps by virtue of the low-quality print, were nothing but a pair of black dots.

"Who is this," said Casey, indicating the boy.

"E-Excuse me?" asked Joe, sounding agitated.

"Sorry," said Casey. "It's just that I thought I might know him. For some reason he caught my attention."

"That there's Joey Jr. Did you know Joey?"

Casey looked at Reardon, who shook his head. "I guess not. Who is he?"

"He was my son."

"He's dead now," said Reardon, spitting into his cup.

"I'm sorry," said Casey. "I didn't know."

"Don't be," said the man, shaking his head. "It's probably for the best that he's no longer with us. Joey? He wasn't never no good. Gave us—and everybody else he came into contact with—nothing but problems. And animals? Forget about it. I know it's messed up to hear a father talk that way about his own son, but if you'd've knowed Joey, you would understand."

"You wouldn't be the first father to say something like that," said Casey.

"Don't get me wrong. Some people, they'll just say that sort of thing just to say it, because they're bitter, or mad. But like I told you before, there's no bullshit with me and when I say a thing, I mean it. From early on we knew something wasn't right with him. He did things, you know? And it wasn't just your usual 'kids getting into trouble' stuff, neither."

He leaned in close.

"I'm talking about some seriously fucked up shit. Do you understand what I'm saying?"

"He wasn't so bad," said Reardon.

"Wasn't so bad? One time when he was six I walked in on him out in our garage and he had the goddamned dog strapped down to a piece of plywood and a boxcutter in his hand. What do you suppose he had in mind, a tea party?"

The three men stood there looking at the picture for a long time before Joe broke the silence. "The strangest thing though," said Joe, walking back to the counter, "is I never would've said any of that back when he was alive. There was just something about him. He was the kind of guy who could punch a man in the face and ten minutes later be their best friend."

The muggy night air felt cool in contrast to the sweltering heat of O'Reilly's. The parking lot in front of the strip mall was surprisingly crowded for a Wednesday night and Casey couldn't help noticing that most of the cars in the lot were cabs. The cab operators leaned against their machines smoking cigarettes and swilling coffee purchased from the 7-Eleven a few storefronts down. They all raised their hands to greet Reardon as he and Casey crossed the lot. The closer gave them a nod of recognition as he climbed into the Beast.

The hull of the car rattled as it blasted over the pitted surface of Ellesmere Avenue. The sound of a siren could be heard off in the distance. Casey was vaguely aware of Reardon's voice pontificating on this or that bone of contention, but he was too preoccupied with the rush of his own thoughts to pay attention to what was being said.

They took McCowan back down to Lawrence and Lawrence back towards Golf Club, but as Reardon rounded the last corner, Casey observed in the passenger side mirror a pair of blue headlights and realized they'd been there since they'd left the strip mall's parking lot. He looked over his shoulder to find the outline of a black Mercedes S-Class looming just a few metres behind the Beast, its steel grill gleaming in the glow of its head-lamps, its occupants rendered invisible by a tinted windshield. "I think somebody's following us," he said when Reardon finally quit rambling.

"I know," said Reardon, checking the rearview mirror. "They've been following us since O'Reilly's."

"What do you think they want?"

"No clue. They're probably just after an autograph, but I ain't in the mood," said Reardon. "Buckle up."

There was a sudden jolt as the car accelerated into the right-hand lane, tire squeal and smoke as it turned onto Golf Club, and then nothing but a wash of engine noise as Reardon let loose the Beast, the speedometer climbing up past 100 KMPH. The car got a few feet of air as it went over a crest, throwing its occupants forward against their seatbelts as it crashed back down on the road. Casey checked the side mirror again only to find the propeller emblem of the Mercedes still leering at him. There was another jolt as it nudged the Beast's back bumper.

"Jesus. They're trying to fuckin' kill us."

"They'll have to do better than that," yelled Reardon over the roar of the engine. The car shuddered as it drove over the train tracks that ran diagonally across Golf Club, fishtailing for a moment before Reardon was able to regain control. They were coming up fast on Kingston Road. The Beast had gained ground on the straight. The light turned yellow and Reardon braked just before entering the intersection, glancing into his mirror to check the separation between themselves and their pursuers. He drifted into a lefthand turn, letting the tail slide out before righting the car's trajectory and slamming his foot on the gas. Casey looked over his shoulder and found that the Mercedes was no longer in pursuit, its headlights standing still at the intersection. Reardon took a right on Guildwood Parkway, drove down the escarp-ment, turned into a strip mall parking lot, found a secluded spot, and cut the engine.

The two sat there in the darkness for some time without saying a word. Casey was still panting with fear as Reardon pulled a tin of Wintergreen from the dash well and packed another cut of chew into his lip.

"What the fuck was that?" asked Casey, breaking the silence.

"What was what?"

"Don't play dumb with me. That was a fucking car chase! Why was I in a fucking car chase?"

Reardon glanced at Casey and smiled, "Rabid fans, I guess."

"Quit fucking around, man. This is serious."

"Relax, kid. Just relax. We're fine."

"Do I look fine to you?" asked Casey, holding up his shaking hand. "Because I'm not fucking fine, man. I've never had so much adrenaline in my fucking life. I mean—what the fuck?"

"We lost them, didn't we?"

"That's not the point. Who the fuck was chasing us? Why would someone be chasing us?"

Reardon didn't respond; he just spat into his cup.

It was a long time getting back. As a precaution, Reardon drove out to the city's west end via the 401, turned around at Allen Road, and drove all the way back. While Reardon made a few attempts to rekindle the conversation, it remained, for the most part, a silent ride.

Casey's legs were stiff when he got out of the car, and he hobbled around a moment like he was relearning to walk. When he finally got his legs back under him, he leaned down and pulled the paper bag of food from the footwell. By now it was cold, blotted with grease, and incredibly mushy.

They walked towards the door on the far side of the garage, the soles of their shoes rasping each time they peeled off the sticky cement. Casey was thinking about how tired he would be tomorrow when he felt something hard jab against the small of his back. He looked around, but then was told not to.

"You'll act like nothing's happening if you know know what's good for you," said what he thought was a Russian voice. "That's it. Just stop right there. Put your hands behind your back. Do it."

The ballplayers were cuffed and led up a staircase to a grassy parkette that sidled the elbow in the road behind Reardon's apartment building. The S-Class was parked beneath a streetlamp a few metres away. Using the muzzles of their guns, the kidnappers let their captives know they were to get into the back seat. Once everyone was in the car, the man sitting in the passenger seat turned around to face the prisoners. He had a pistol in his hand, and he waved it back and forth.

"I'm glad you decided to be reasonable this time."

Casey hadn't even heard the car start, but soon they were off. He looked up from the window to find the barrel of a handgun staring back at him. The man holding the firearm had a big grin on his face.

"Guess you forgot that we know where you live."

"How could I forget?" said Reardon. "I was just letting the tension settle. If you really wanted to get in touch so bad you could've made a fuckin' phone call or something."

"We tried, but we got no response," said the man with the gun. "Ms. Lyuba wasn't very pleased to have her calls ignored."

"I'm sure she wasn't," said Reardon.

The man with the gun reached back and slammed the butt into the side of Reardon's head, right in his as yet unhealed knife wound.

"Fuck!" shouted Reardon as blood began trickling from the scabs. A few of the stitches had burst open.

"Next time I think you'll find it in your best interest to return our phone calls. Yes?"

"Where the hell are you taking us?" asked Casey.

"If it were up to me," said the man, turning the gun back towards Casey and pressing its muzzle up against his forehead, "I'd put a bullet in your head and dump you in the lake. Unfortunately, Lyuba Ivanovna has asked for us to bring you along."

"Me? Why me?"

"Who is to say why? Why does Lyuba do anything?" said the man as he pulled the gun from Casey's forehead and shrugged.

"Maybe she's got a thing for him," suggested the driver, who wore a Mexican wrestler's mask. A silence ensued. Then the two men burst out laughing.

"What's so funny about that? And who the fuck is Lyuba?" asked Casey.

"Oh, nothing," said the man with the gun. "You'll see."

They hadn't gone very far before the car parked in front of an unkempt two-storey house situated on a deep lot. The house faced onto what could have been any of the tributaries branching off Eglinton Avenue. The tolling bell of a train in the distance told Casey they must be near the tracks. The driver stepped out of the car, removed a gun from a holster he concealed under his blazer, pulled Reardon out of the car, and led him by the arm to the front door with Casey and the Russian falling in behind.

Inside, the house was just as old and worn out as it appeared on the outside. Bits of plaster were missing from the walls, exposing the wooden studs. The original purple paint was so mottled with grey it resembled diseased flesh. The corridor was lit with dusty, cobwebbed wall sconces whose period charm seemed to predate the building's construction by a sizable margin. In the middle of the corridor stood a large stone-and-mortar fireplace over which hung a reproduction print. At the far end stood another door with a man blocking the way. The ballplayers were led to the fireplace.

"Relax with the gun, would ya? It's not like we're going anywhere," said Reardon. "I mean, you know where I live, right? And you can take these damned cuffs off, too. We'll play nice."

The masked driver put the gun in his shoulder holster but showed no signs of removing the handcuffs.

"And just for the record, if you ever go and pistol whip me again, I'll skin you for it," said Reardon, spitting on the Russian's patent leather shoe.

The Russian smiled. "Shall I get my friend here to practice his knife skills on your face again?"

Casey looked around the room. His gaze caught on the print hanging above the fireplace. It featured a giant holding a much smaller person in his hands, or what used to be a person. The head and arm were now gone, with what remained amounting to a couple of bloody stumps. The giant's lips were glossed a guilty, blood red. Its eyes wild, frenzied as it feasted on this gift of flesh in the dark. Casey shuddered at the sight of it, and glanced over at Reardon, at whom the Russian was now threatening to take a swing. Just then the door at the end of the hall opened and the doorman beckoned them to proceed.

This new room was decorated in much the same way. It was lit by a trio of chandeliers hung precariously from the crumbling ceiling. The numerous guests fell silent and made way as the two ballplayers were led to a leather wingback chair, the occupant of which was possibly the most beautiful woman Casey had ever seen.

"How nice for have you to finally have come!" she said merrily. "Vlad said you gave him quite the chase."

"Noticed I was being followed, decided to split rather than to find out by who," said Reardon. "Mind getting us out of these cuffs?"

She nodded to the masked driver, who cut the plastic cuffs with his boot knife.

"Tut, tut, tut. Who else would it have been? And you haven't been answering your phone, either. What's wrong? Aren't you happy to see me?"

"I cut the cord," said Reardon, rubbing at his wrist. "Why'd they bring the kid."

"Why—he's the one I asked them to bring! I've been watching you on TV, you know: two local boys trotting out of the bullpen, striking out your opponents, being oh-so-heroic." She sighed. "I see this little one tagging along behind you like a lost puppy and I think to myself, *Who's this new friend Phillip's got? Why hasn't he introduced us?*"

"I guess it just plain slipped my mind."

"But *nothing* slips your mind, sugarplum. Remember?"

"Well, I guess now you's been introduced, so now we can clear out and let you have your party. Me and Casey here've gotta be up awful early. Ain't that right, Casey?"

The woman turned to Casey. "It's a pleasure to finally make your acquaintance. Lots of people come and visit, but only rarely do I get an honest to goodness celebrity."

"I'm not a celebrity," said Casey.

"Nonsense. I see you on television all the time. I watch all the games. I've even read about you on the internet. It's funny. You wouldn't think you were like that just by looking at you. You wouldn't think you'd been such a naughty, naughty boy." She paused. "Has our friend Phillip here ever mentioned me?"

"Maybe?"

She gasped. "That means he hasn't! Phillip! How could you forget to mention me, your oldest and dearest friend?" She turned back to Casey. "I wonder why that would be. Do you think he might be trying to hide me or something?"

"I don't know," said Casey.

"We used to be high school sweethearts," she prattled. "Weren't we, Phillip?"

"We never dated."

"Oh, but you would have liked it if we had, wouldn't you? And to think, right now I could be Mrs. Phillip Reardon," she said, opening her mouth and pointing towards the back of her throat, making a gagging noise. "That, Casey dear, is what I would call a bullet dodged."

"Listen, I don't know anything about it."

"That much is clear."

"Leave the kid alone, would ya?"

She turned to Reardon. "Oh, but I'm afraid I'm too curious for that. You make me so curious when you don't introduce me to your friends. Why didn't you take any of my calls, Phillip?"

"I wasn't home."

Lyuba stood up from the chair and stepped toward Casey. Taking his face in her hands and inspecting it, she said, "Oh, it doesn't matter anyway. I have what I want now. You always did have great taste, Phillip."

"What are you talking about?"

"Don't play coy with me! Don't think I don't see how he looks at you," said Lyuba. "I've seen it."

"How do I look at him?" asked Casey.

"Like you respect him. Like you like him—him! As if he's worthy of anyone's respect, this dog, this mongrel! Tell me, pretty Casey. How you can respect this filth after he's lied to you? After he's drugged you? You must have the patience of Job himself to have put up with all this monster's nonsense. I didn't think anybody would ever be able to tolerate this lousy mutt and yet here you are. You've been living together how long now?"

"I don't know, a few months," said Casey.

Lyuba patted Casey's cheek. "You know, I've been watching you a long time. Is that odd? That I've been watching? I mean, it's hard not to! You two are everywhere—on TV, in the papers, on the internet, just everywhere!"

"I guess it isn't so odd then," said Casey.

"Of course it doesn't hurt that Phillip here drags this hunk of eye-candy along with him every time he trots out there. You know what I wonder to myself as I watch you step onto the field? I wonder if the reason you respect him is that you hardly know him. I mean, hasn't it ever occurred to you that maybe our friend Phillip here isn't so *nice* and helpful as he *seems*? If maybe your affection for him isn't just a symptom of Stockholm Syndrome?"

"What's Stockholm Syndrome?" asked Casey.

"As I thought," said Lyuba. "Naïve as a newborn child."

"He ain't trapped," said Reardon. "Nobody's holding a gun to his head. I'm just doing the kid a favour."

"Is that what you call it? Is that why you slipped him that MDMA?" asked Lyuba as if she were genuinely curious. "Or why you've hidden this scrumptious young specimen away from *me,* your oldest and dearest friend."

Lyuba offered Casey her hand.

"My name is Lyuba, by the way. Lyuba Ivanovna."

Casey looked over at Reardon.

"What? Do you take orders from this mutt? What's the matter? Can't you think for yourself? Go on and take it."

He did as he was told. Her hand felt cold.

"Now kiss it."

"What?"

"I said kiss my hand. Aren't you a gentleman?" asked Lyuba, looking around at her other guests. "It's not polite to keep a lady waiting."

Casey obliged and lifted her hand to his lips and kissed it.

"That's it. Good boy," said Lyuba, patting him on the cheek. "He's just wonderful, Phillip, a regular prince charming."

"Well, I'm glad you like him so much, but we really oughta get going."

"I'm afraid you won't be going anywhere, Phillip. Now sit."

"Let's get one thing straight, Lyuba. Old Reardon? He marches to the beat of nobody else's drum but his own. He don't go obeying orders like some dog."

"Nonsense! When I tell you to sit, you sit; when I tell you to wait, you wait; and when I tell you to come, well, here you are. Now stop contradicting me, Phillip, or things will become particularly nasty for you."

Reardon looked around the room and spat in his cup. "Have it your way, Lyuba," he said, dropping himself into one of the chairs she was gesturing towards.

Lyuba turned to Casey. "You see? He does as he's told, even if he pouts about it. What other tricks would you like to see him do?"

"Lady, I don't know what's going on between you two, but I'd just as soon stay out of it."

"Tut-tut, you're no fun," said Lyuba, her face becoming exaggeratedly sad. "Don't you even want to see him beg?"

"I think it's time for us to leave," said Reardon.

"You're starting to bore me anyway. We'll save that last trick for later. But don't click your heels just yet, Dorothy! I'll be making sure we see each other again real soon. Just next time leave your pretty friend at home."

"You just had him brought here at gunpoint, ya nut."

"Well then, I guess in the future you'd be better off taking my calls, that way I won't be forced to come and get you. Save us both the trouble."

She handed him an old flip phone.

"Hold on to this. I'll call you when I need you. No sixteenth storey falls this time, capiche?"

They were halfway to the door when she called, "Oh, and Phillip…"

Reardon stopped in his tracks and turned around. "Yes, Lyuba?"

"Aren't you going to say thank you?"

"For what?"

She mimed thinking with a finger on her lip. "For my hospitality."

Reardon spat into his cup.

"Well?"

"Thank you, Lyuba."

Kicked unceremoniously to the curb at the front entrance of the apartment building, they were still getting to their feet as the Mercedes sped away into the night. The ride up to the seventeenth floor was a silent one, and once they were back inside the apartment Reardon walked into the kitchen, took two shot glasses from the cupboard, and filled them with whiskey.

"I'll pass," said Casey.

"Who said either of 'em is for you?" said Reardon, knocking back both shots in quick succession and wiping at the corners of his mouth.

"What the fuck just happened?" asked Casey.

"Whaddya mean?"

"I mean we were just fucking kidnapped."

"I'd hardly call that a kidnapping."

"We were led in there at fucking *gunpoint,* man."

"No harm, no foul," said Reardon, pouring another pair of shots. "Here."

Casey took the shot.

"Did you see that painting on the fucking wall?"

"She's got strange taste in art is all. Don't blow the whole thing out of proportion. Alls we did is pay an old friend of yours truly a visit."

"Are you for real? We got into a fucking car chase."

"No, see, that's where you're going and getting the story all mixed the fuck up, friend," said Reardon, poking Casey in the chest. "The absolute most we did—you hear me?—the absolute most we did was pay an old and dear friend of yours truly a visit, and it wasn't no Lyuba either. We ain't never heard that name, you and me."

"Then who the fuck did we visit?"

"If you're cornered into answering a question, just tell 'em we went to that house 'cause there was a party going on that we just couldn't pass up on account of my old friend being there. But to be honest, it'd be better for us both if, as far as everybody else was concerned, it was just another night at the office."

"Why would someone ask me about that?"

"People asks all sorts of stupid questions. We're just covering our asses, that's all."

"You want me to lie about it?"

"Don't think of it as a lie, just think of it as veiling the truth. Besides, nobody's likely to ask."

"Who the fuck did you just get me involved with, Reardon?"

"Trust me when I say you don't want to know. She's just a nut. You've gotta humour the infirm, you know what I mean?"

"No. I fucking don't. You better start telling me what the fuck is going on."

Reardon stood up from the table and patted Casey on the shoulder, making toward the third bedroom. Casey followed his roommate down the hall demanding answers, but the door was slammed in his face and latched shut. No amount of shouting and pounding on the door could compel the man to reopen it and face interrogation. Soon the grinding sounds resumed, drowning out Casey's voice, forcing him to retreat to his bedroom and wonder what the hell he was still doing here.

Ever since their little visit to Lyuba's, Casey couldn't concentrate. He would try to read, but could only process a handful of words before his mind wandered off the page and into wild dreams of cocaine. He might even have purchased some if he knew where to get it without attracting too much attention, but nobody Casey knew could be relied upon not to rat him out, and the last thing he needed was a scandal. Still, an eight-ball would have been nice right about now. Maybe a bump was just what the doctor ordered to kill the anxiety eating away at the inside of his head.

Casey wasn't sure if it was the fatigue or worry that was caus-ing it, but he was back in the thick of another slump, going 0 for his last 23. When he stepped to the plate, it seemed the plans he developed in the VR training were beginning to backfire. Pitchers around the league had clued into the Birds having deci-phered some of their tendencies, and so they began pitching backwards, offering Casey a heavy dose of breaking balls that he kept whiffing on. The worse the rut got, the worse his approach became, until the brief glimmer of success that had given him so much confidence just a few weeks before seemed an unrepeatable anomaly. The truth was, he might never get hot again, and as he continued to throw up goose eggs in the box score, he could feel the noose tightening around his neck. He couldn't keep playing like this. He had to do *something* to make it stop. If only he could have just one little bump.

Not that his performance was hurting the team much. In fact, his slump had gone largely unnoticed by all but the most livid armchair general managers. This was because practically everybody else was on fire. They had won thirteen of their last eighteen and the Blue Birds now sat just four games shy of the division lead. Everybody in the dugout was watching the score-board, hoping to see crooked numbers put up against Boston, New York, and Tampa Bay. Nowadays everybody was showing up to the park early and ready for business. At all times of day, one might hear the clank of metal from the weight room, or else the crack of bats down in the cage, or some conversation about the finer points of the game. Walking by the VR lab one was liable to find a group of players scouting an upcoming opponent, or micro-analyzing their swings for flaws.

Casey and Reardon were now for the most part avoiding each other. On the road, Reardon was hardly ever in the room, preferring to drive around in a rented car, or in one of the beaters he kept stored in SL East cities. What Reardon did out there was a matter of great speculation for Casey. He imagined his room-mate making illicit exchanges with Hells Angels in some parking lot, or else maybe helping some local hood dispose of a body, a matter on which Reardon probably had plenty of advice to dispense.

When they played at home, Reardon's habits flipped the switch. The man had become a real homebody, hardly ever leaving the apartment outside of driving to and from the stadium. He'd even hired an industrious ten-year-old Senegalese kid who lived down the hall to fetch groceries. Casey no longer spent his evenings sitting in the living room engrossed in some book he'd borrowed from the library. Instead he retreated to his room where he spent most of his time lying in bed, surfing the internet on his phone, listening to the strange grinding and hammering coming from behind that locked door, and dreaming of ways in which he could score without attracting too much attention to himself.

Winning had proven to be a real shot in the arm for the once sick ball club. They were all so hooked on the rush of victory that it felt as if they would do anything just to get another win. The players watched the standings as the number in the W column inched closer and closer to that in the L column and then sur-passed it—by ten games, eleven games, twelve games. Each night seemed to build off the last. People started showing up with those lame signs boasting about how the team may never lose again. The Birds were hot.

Reardon, who one might have expected to crack under the duress of his unravelling life, was playing the best baseball of his career. It was no longer a question in anybody's mind that he was going to achieve what he had bragged about in May's issue of *Sports Illustrated* as he continued racking up innings, strikeouts, and saves. He hadn't been bad with the stick, either. Since the beginning of their current thirteen-game win streak, he had hit seven home runs with an on-base percentage of .532.

While Casey's underperformance was mostly ignored by the media and his teammates, there was one person who took notice. One evening, after Casey had worn the golden sombrero for the third night in a row, Tubs pulled Casey aside and asked if there was something going on.

Casey confessed that he was feeling a little distracted when he was at the plate.

"You should've said something. Come in early tomorrow, say nine-thirty, and we'll have you fixed up right as rain."

The next morning Casey woke at 6:15, hoping to leave the apartment by 7:30. It wasn't until he stepped out of the shower that he realized that Reardon must still be awake. Strange sounds seeped through the door as Casey stood at the sink, brushing his teeth. When he finished in the bathroom, he rapped on the door of Reardon's workshop but received no response, so he knocked again.

"What do you want?" yelled Reardon from behind the door.

"I'm headed out."

"Yeah? And who gives a fuck?"

He ate a bowl of cereal, washed his dishes, and left. On the seventh floor, two men in identical blue jumpsuits got on the elevator. They were in the middle of a conversation in Hindi, which they didn't stop on Casey's account. The doors opened with a ding and Casey followed them off the elevator at a saunter. For some reason, as they reached the entrance, they began speaking more quickly, flung open the door, and ran across the rise of the driveway.

At first, Casey wondered if he had scared them or looked at them the wrong way or something, but as he approached the door he saw the reason for their hustle. The blinking red hand of the crosswalk signal turned solid just as they reached the other side of the street. Stopped at the light was the bus. Casey checked his phone. It wasn't supposed to arrive for another five minutes, yet there it was, pulling away.

The app said the next bus would be in ten, but Casey waited closer to twenty. When he finally did get on, it was crowded on account of the backlog of people who'd missed the last like he had.

He was fifteen minutes late meeting Tubs, who was already waiting on the bench when Casey exited the tunnel into the dugout.

"Took you long enough," said Tubs. "I don't care for my time being wasted."

"Sorry, Tubs. Got held up in transit."

"Mhmm. Well, whatever. You're here now. You got your gear?"

Casey held up his hands to show that he was wearing his gloves.

"We better get at it."

Tubs had had the grounds crew arrange the infield for batting practice and bring out the throwing machine the night before, so there was little for Casey to do other than get stretched out while Tubs adjusted the settings on the machine and loaded the ball hopper.

The session got off to a rocky start. Casey felt just as lost swinging the bat as he had the day before. He seemed to be late on everything.

"That might be the ugliest I've seen that swing in some time. Something wrong with you, boy?"

"No. Why would something be wrong?"

"Well, see, it's just we spent so much time teaching you to hit. It's a little hard to believe you've just plum forgot, ain't it?"

"I guess so."

"Ain't it more likely somethin's got under yo skin."

"I'm fine."

"Really? Because you said you was distracted."

"I guess there's just a lot of stuff I've been thinking about."

"Look, I don't know what's goin' on with you and I don't need to know, but I'll tell you one thing: one way or another you're gonna have to figure how to block it all out. You gotta compartmentalize it. Them boys like your roommate, they think this thing's all mind games, but really, it's the opposite. You gotta wipe that slate clean and keep it clean, you know what I'm sayin'? When you step into that box, you shouldn't be thinking 'bout nothin'. You see the ball. You hit the ball. There ain't much more to it than that."

"First it's I gotta think three pitches ahead, now you're saying I've gotta think about nothing. Just how am I supposed to clear my mind, anyway?"

"I don't know," said Tubs, "count or something."

Casey shook his head as Tubs ambled back up to the mound. Tubs started feeding balls into the machine again.

Casey got set. *Fuck it*, he thought to himself, and started counting *one… two… three… four… whoomph, crack!* This time he made contact off the end of the bat. Pain shot through his forearms as the bat vibrated between his clenched fists and the ball looped just fair over third base.

He fouled off the next pitch, the one after that, and the one after that, but he gradually started making better contact. All he was doing was counting up before each pitch, but it settled him down. Soon enough, balls were flying to all fields and over the fence. Tubs only stopped feeding the machine after he'd emptied the bucket.

"Your swing sure don't look busted no more," he yelled as he stepped out from behind the pitching screen and approached the plate.

"Yeah, but that's just because the machine's feeding me the balls."

"Maybe," said Tubs, spitting seed husks onto the turf. "I wouldn't know either way. Alls I'm sayin' is you've gotta keep your mind good and clear if you expect to do any hittin', so count away."

"Yeah? And what if that doesn't work?"

"Then I guess you're shit out of luck."

Casey must not have looked assured, because Tubs quickly followed up by saying, "Look, sometimes we've got problems that even a little countin' won't fix. Somethin's a-naggin' at you, houndin' you every minute and just won't leave you alone no matter what you do and I'm afraid there's only one way that sort of thing ever gets resolved."

"What's that?"

"You gotta figure out what's getting to ya and root it out."

"Let's hope counting works," said Casey.

"Why don't we test it out?"

"But there isn't anyone here to pitch me."

"I could."

"But you don't throw batting practice."

"I guess there's a first time for everything. What's the matter? Don't think I'm up to it?"

"Well," said Casey, shouldering his bat. "If you say so."

Tubs wheeled the machine off the field and set up behind the pitching screen with a fresh bucket of balls. Even now, at fifty years of age, Tubs still cut an imposing figure at six-foot-five and nearly three hundred pounds. He picked up the ball, rubbed it with his palms, and called out, "What you want?"

Casey asked for the fastball by holding up his index finger and began counting *one… two… three…* Tubs' began his wind-up and let fly. It was a lifeless pitch, with hardly any zip and next to no movement; Casey was able to square it up, the barrel of the bat cutting through the zone before he'd even thought about swinging. The pop of contact echoed off the empty stadium and Casey watched the white blip sail higher, higher, reaching the peak of its parabola before dropping onto the fifth deck just left of the right field foul line.

"That was a terrible pitch," yelled Casey.

"I never did have a good heater," Tubs hollered back as he picked up a new ball. "Let's see if you can hit my curve."

This time the pitch came in high, slow and tempting. Casey tracked it in with his eyes and it grew like a melon. Time slowed down, his breathing was steady, and he couldn't help but take a big healthy cut at the juicy pitch. He'd have knocked it a good four hundred feet if, in the pitch's last moments, it hadn't gone straight from twelve to six, catching the strike zone right at Casey's knees well after Casey had swung at it.

Casey spat in the dirt. "That's some curveball."

"I told you I still had it."

"You think so? I dare you to give me another one."

Tubs obliged, another twelve-sixer just where he'd located it before, but this time Casey resisted the urge to swing until that last millisecond. Once he saw the pitch break, he pulled the trigger.

Crack! It was a laser beam off the bat, flying straight and low, deep to the left field alley where it hit the wall and bounced back across the warning track to rest in the turf. When Casey looked back to the mound, Tubs was still staring at the left field wall.

"I see how it is," said Tubs as he turned around. "Guess I'm gon' have to mix things up."

And he did. He started using a changeup and a slider and because there was no count going, Casey never knew what to expect. All he could do was keep counting *one… two… three…* as he waited for the next pitch. He started reading the ball out of Tubs hand, watching for spin, trying to figure out how to time his swing and at times he looked downright foolish, swinging out of his shoes; at others, he was rewarded with that satisfying *pop* and would watch the ball sail past the outfield fence. By the time Tubs had emptied the bucket both men were gleaming with sweat.

"Where'd you go and learn to hit the curve like that?" asked Tubs as they toweled off in the dugout.

"Hitting rocks, I guess," said Casey.

"That what Reardon has you doin'?"

"Sometimes," said Casey.

"Listen, I don't mean to pry, but this trouble you been havin'—it has somethin' to do with the big man, don't it?"

"What makes you say that?"

Tubs shook his head. "Jus' seems like whenever there's trouble, Phil can't be too far away."

At some point in the next twelve games Casey found his stroke again. Over the first two weeks of July, he hit .348 with eight extra-base hits, but even though Casey was performing on the field, he felt like a wreck off it. He would lie awake rolling questions over in his mind. Reardon occasionally clomped up and down the hall from the kitchen to the third bedroom and back, slamming the door behind him. The closer now spent almost all his time sealed off in his little workshop. All sorts of strange noises emanated through the walls. At one point there would be the schnick of metal scraping other metal; at another it sounded as if Reardon might be smashing two rocks together. Sometimes the fire alarm would start to go off and some dog would howl until long after it abated; and there was always the squeal of the elevator pulleys.

He listened for so long that he began to recognize patterns. He observed that different intervals of pulley activity signified to the careful listener the distance the cars had travelled, or if they were carrying passengers or just ferrying up and down uselessly. Another pattern was that his roommate left his room only after solid three-hour intervals in his workshop, so that if he had recently returned from one of his forays into the kitchen, he could be trusted not to be seen again for quite some time.

Casey couldn't have said why this information was of interest to him until the moment he made use of it. He was lying in bed one night when he heard the sound of Reardon's heavy footsteps and the clack of the latch bolt. Quietly, Casey got up, walked over to the closed bedroom door, pressed his ear against it, and listened. He could hear Reardon's drilling and hammering clear as noonday, so he opened the door and advanced to the kitchen where he picked up Reardon's black book from the side-table. Shutting the batwing doors behind him, he flicked on the light and flipped through the pages until he reached the section for J. The sound of something heavy falling, followed by Reardon yelling *Fuck!* interrupted Casey's thoughts. He was about to put the book down and beat it back to his room, but shook his head and resolved to continue. His eyes returned to the page—there it was:

Joka—647-555-2825

There was no address. Casey copied the number into his phone before putting the book back where he found it and turning off the kitchen light.

He took the elevator downstairs, exited the building through the main entrance, and crossed the street to a bench that overlooked the school's playground. He sat in the dark a long time before he initiated the call.

"Hello. Who is this? I don't got this number."

"It's Casey. I met you at the Jug City, remember? I was with Reardon. We smoked a joint."

"Yeah? I guess so. Mind splainin' to me how the fuck you got this number?"

"Reardon gave it to me."

"Is that so? Funny. We don't ever give out each other's numbers."

Casey bit his lip.

"Hello?"

"Alright, I stole it."

"Now why would you go and do a thing like that? That shit ain't real smart."

"I had to talk to you."

"Well start squawkin'. I've gotta be up in the morning. Unlike you motherfuckers, some of us have to be up by five."

"It's about Reardon. I think he might be in trouble."

"Yeah? What else is new? Boy was born in trouble."

"You ever heard of Lyuba?"

Nothing but dead air on the other end of the line.

"Hello?"

"Where you at? You in the apartment?"

Casey looked around. "I'm sitting out back of the school across the street."

"Tecumseh? I ain't far from there. You think you can make it down to Orton Park in fifteen?"

"Sure."

"Alright, I'm texting you the address. I'll see you."

Joka's apartment was not a bad size, but poorly maintained, like the occupants had lived there for many years. There were toys everywhere—on the floors, on end-tables, in boxes. Out on the counter was a plate with last night's dinner with a few flies hovering overhead, anticipating an easy meal.

"Sit," said Joka, gesturing toward the couch. As Casey stepped through the threshold, he noticed that there was a woman standing in the living room in a bathrobe, her arms folded over her chest.

"Don't got nothing better to do than to go waking folks at all hours of the night?" she asked.

"I'm sorry to bother you," said Casey.

"You know something? Whatever."

"Just go back to bed," said Joka. "You gonna wake the kids."

"She sure doesn't seem to like me much," said Casey after the woman had shut the bedroom door.

"You done woke her up, homie. What'd you expect her to do? Thank you for it? Couldn't you have called during the day? The fuck's the matter with you, anyway?"

"I don't know," said Casey.

"Well," said Joka, tapping a pack of cigarettes against the table. "We might as well get down to what you came here for."

"You asked me here."

"That's because you never know who might be listening. You stupid?"

"Who'd be listening?"

"I don't know—the cops maybe, Lyuba's people maybe, maybe nobody. Who the fuck knows? You don't go phoning people up and asking about what's going on between Phil and Lyuba, especially not me. That's too much smoke."

"Alright," said Casey.

"Do you mind explaining how the fuck you know about Lyuba?"

Joka listened while Casey described for him how he and Reardon had been abducted by Lyuba's men on their way home from O'Reilly's.

"And I remember what you said about some lady wanting to see him. I figured you might know something."

"Now you haven't gone running your mouth about what happened that night, have you?"

"Other than Reardon, you're the only person I've spoken to about it."

"You better keep it that way," said Joka, cradling his forehead with his palm. "I mean, Lyuba's one crazy bitch. She don't take to people nosing around in her business."

"I just have to know."

"Motherfucker, you don't need to know nothin'."

"I have to know why he does what she tells him."

Joka sucked his teeth.

"Come on, man. If you weren't gonna tell me, why'd you call me over?"

"To let you know that I think you're done barking up the wrong tree, homie. Fuck," said Joka, locking his gaze on the window-mounted air conditioner as he considered something. "If I tell you what you wanna know, I need a guarantee that you won't go around asking any more questions. Ya hear? After this, you're done."

"Fine. Whatever you want, man."

Joka took a long look around the room, as if making sure that nobody else was listening in.

"Now I don't know much more than what I've heard, so you can't take everything I say as gospel. You know how Phil likes to gamble, right?"

"Sure. He's always buying those scratch tickets."

"See, I used to think that was where it ended. I always saw him playing those damned scratch cards, but never thought a thing of it because so many people do, right? Except with Phil, he apparently don't just play the lotto. He does it all—cock fights, boxing matches, you name it—and he don't know when to stop. You know what I'm saying?"

"No," said Casey.

"I'm saying the dude's an addict."

"And what does that have to do with Lyuba?"

"About a year ago I start hearing these rumours, and you know how it is: most of the time people is just talkin'. Folks down at the corner store were talkin', buyin' lotto tickets. I was just getting myself some drank from the fridge in the back when

I hear Phil's name come up. Fat Jeffrey's reporting that he's heard from his bookie that Phil'd taken the windfall from his contract and laid it all down and he'd heard Phil lost it all—every dime and then some."

"Jesus," said Casey.

"That ain't the worst of it. Word is, he managed to con the local bookies into loaning him money on the back of his future earnings, and that's when he got himself really deep into the hole."

"How much does he owe?"

"I've heard some folks say he's on the hook for over fifty million, but you know how it is; these things get exaggerated. One way or another it must be a hell of a lot of money for it to be making so much noise."

"But how does Lyuba factor into this?"

"Phil made it clear to the books that he had no intention of ever paying them back, banking on none of them having the balls to go after him, what with the stir it would cause and the potential for exposure and everything. The crazy thing is that it worked. The bookies figured it was easier to blacklist him than it was to make an example of him.

"What Phil hadn't counted on was Lyuba. When she heard about all these debts he was reneging on, she started buying them up at the fraction of the cost. As far as the bookies was concerned, they'd been handed a golden ticket. They pretty much jumped at the opportunity to dump the bad debt."

"Why'd she do it?"

"She wants to kill him," said Joka, flatly.

"It seems like she wouldn't need his debts to do that."

"Even criminals gotta play according to a rulebook. You can't just have someone out there killing people whenever they feel like it, especially not nobody like Phil, who people will notice has gone missing. You've gotta have some pretty good reasons for doing something like that."

"And I guess that much money squares it."

"As good a reason as any in this world. Besides, she's willing to do what the rest of them won't. She may be a fine-looking woman, but she's as hard a case as you'll likely ever see."

"But why would she want him dead?"

"There's bad blood between those two, let's leave it at that."

"Jesus," said Casey.

"You want my advice?" asked Joka as he lit a cigarette he had extracted from the package. "Stay the fuck out of it. There ain't nothin' good can come from fucking with Lyuba. People say she's struck·a deal with the devil hisself."

"People say a lot of shit."

"Well, I guess we gon' find out, now ain't we?"

Casey sat there and stared into his lap for some time before finally lifting his head and saying, "But if she wants him dead, why hasn't she gone and offed him yet?"

"Yo, you wanna know somethin'?" said Joka, standing up from the table.

"What?"

"You're as good as dog meat."

Casey returned home to find the lights on and Reardon sitting at the table with a forty of vodka in front of him, smoking a fat blunt. Neither man said anything while Casey stood there, his feet frozen to the door mat. Reardon made a show of leafing through his black book, which was laid open before him. "Been making a few house calls, have ya?"

"How'd you guess?"

"I can always tell when somebody's been tamperin' with my shit," said Reardon. "That, and about half an hour ago I get a phone call from my old pal, Joka. He tells me you went and paid him a little visit, been asking him about Lyuba. Now what the fuck am I supposed to make of that? You're poking your nose in where it don't belong."

"Well you haven't exactly been honest with me about what's going on, so I went to find out for myself."

"Yeah? And what'd you hear?"

"He told me everything."

"How can he tell you everything when he don't even fucking know all there is to tell?" asked Reardon. "When it ain't his damn story to tell. Go on and explain, Casey. What is it that you think you know?"

"I know you're in pretty fucking deep with this Lyuba chick."

Reardon laughed. "That's putting it mildly, brother."

"He said it was personal," said Casey. "That she wants to see you dead and you owe her a lot of money."

"That's a bit of an exaggeration. I don't know if she wants to see me dead, but she sure as fuck hates my guts."

"What's the matter? You get her knocked up?"

"No."

"Bad breakup?"

"If only," said Reardon. "No, it wasn't no breakup. I told you before, we never got that far."

"What happened then?"

Reardon inhaled deeply, exhaled, and then poured himself a shot. He downed it and wiped his lips with his hand, grimacing at the taste. "I don't know if I can do this, kid. It's a hard story to tell. Doesn't exactly shed the most positive light on yours truly."

"Come on, man. You've involved me in your bullshit, the least you owe me is an explanation."

"I guess you won't quit diggin' unless I tell ya. See, back in high school I was on the baseball team," said Reardon. "As you know, back in grades eleven and twelve I was something of a hometown hero, but it didn't start out that way. Grade ten was just my second year on the team and, sure, I was bigger than the rest of the guys by a long shot, but there was still the element of exclusion that you've always got in them jailhouses they call places of education. The older kids hold the keys to power, while the younger ones are expected to wait their turn. It's the same old bullshit. Well, in grade ten nobody liked me, with some even calling me a freak on account of how big I was.

"I was the kid who always sat alone in the school cafeteria and never said a word to nobody. By way of listening, I knew that people thought that one day I'd shoot up the school and make all of them little Catholic rats holier than a block of Swiss cheese. I was real quiet, stuck to myself, kept my nose in the books whenever I wasn't at some practice. One day, I'm just sitting there staring down at my empty tray, waiting for the lunch period to be over, when this girl walks up to my table out of nowhere and drops her bagged lunch onto it. It was in one of them brown paper bags, like you'd see in the movies. I wondered if I was having a fuckin' dream or some shit, because—well, you've seen her.

"So there I'm sitting, dumb as a goddamned board and sweating so bad it was starting to bleed through the armpits of my uniform. She asks if anyone's sitting there and all I could think to say to her was no, and that's how it all started. From that moment we started eating lunch together every day. To be honest, she was the only person in the whole world who ever gave a shit about me. I spent almost all my free afternoons with her just talking.

"Well, you know how it goes at that age: you fall in 'love' fast and you fall hard. I was sad when I had to spend most of that summer riding coach buses and playing ball. I'd call her on payphones using calling cards that would muck everything up so I could barely hear her over all the static. As the summer went on our conversations grew shorter and shorter, until sometimes she wouldn't even take my calls. Meanwhile, I'm hearing from my new buddies—my teammates, that is—that they had it on good authority from people back home she'd been partyin' like a goddamned animal, making out with people. In other words, doing the same mostly innocent shit any other sixteen-year-old would do when their parents aren't looking, but I lost it. To me it was a personal betrayal, even though neither of us promised the other anything. Anyway, my new buddies and me spent a good bit of our time on the bus shit-talking her as just another slut.

"When I came back home that fall, it was clear Lyuba and I'd drifted apart. I'd put up some crooked numbers that summer, earning an invite to national juniors. I returned to school a god. You see, they knew all about me on account of all the profiles the papers ran, claiming I was the next Canadian baseball superstar. Suddenly everybody wanted a piece of the action; all the best lookin' girls would say hi to me in the halls. They'd get all giggly and reserved when I walked past, as if it were some sort of secret they'd been sharing about yours truly. All our teachers were ex-jocks themselves and they'd shake hands with me if we met in the halls, just like they was shakin' hands with a grown-ass man. That's when Joey, the self-elected captain of our school's baseball team, decided to take me under his wing. My school-mates and I were all suddenly real tight, like a pack, or a gang. I won't lie: it felt good. It was almost like we'd always been good friends. It was almost like we were brothers.

"Lyuba, on the other hand, wanted nothing to do with old Reardon. I mean, sure we'd nod our heads whenever we passed each other in the hallway, but neither of us would say nothin'. She was the only one who didn't seem at all impressed with my baseball exploits.

"But me and the boys? Man, we went everywhere together—the same parties, the same practices. In the winter we'd go down and hold sessions on the beach, struggling to keep our poorly rolled joints lit against the wind. These guys were just as eager to shit-talk Lyuba as my buddies from Triple-A. One guy, Mikey, even claimed he had gone all the way with her, but Joey shot that down, calling it bullshit, then he turns to me and says, in all his eighteen years of wisdom, 'The problem is she's too damn stuck-up, thinks she's too good for a fine lookin' fella like you, Phil, when she oughta consider herself lucky that you'd give her the time of day. She's the sort of bitch that needs to learn her place. Don't make the mistake of being soft on women, Phil. In the end, what they all want is the alpha dog.'"

"And what did you say to that?"

"The hell if I can remember."

"Somehow I doubt that."

"The way I managed it," said Reardon, as if he hadn't heard Casey's last comment, "was by avoiding her, which was easy enough given that it was like two separate worlds we was livin' in: she with her alternative friends and me with the athletes and cheerleaders and whatnot. It was just like one of them teen movie stereotypes. Anyhow, one night we both end up attendin' the same house party. My teammates and I spent most of the night trying to avoid her by standing out in the backyard around the keg. Around eleven, our right fielder Benny Anderson, comes crashing through the screen door into the backyard and tells us that we've gotta get our asses upstairs, that there's something all of us just *had* to see. He leaps up them stairs two steps at a time and we all tramp up after him, wondering what the fuck could be so important. He leads us down the hall, over to a closed door, and opens it.

"Well this room must've belonged to the sister of our host or something, because from what I remember there were horses everywhere. Statues of horses, a ceiling border of horses, god-damned horse wall-paper—I mean horses everywhere. And there's Lyuba: layin' face down on the bed, muttering something I can't understand. We all pile into the room and Benny shuts the door behind us. At this point, yours truly will admit that he was freaking the fuck out. A few of the guys were chuckling and winking at each other, and Benny turns to Joey and asks what he thinks they oughta do.

"People used to say that it never would've happened if Joey'd not been drinking, but I was there and I can tell ya that he wasn't so drunk that he didn't know what he was doing. I stood there watching Lyuba's limp body and that's when I clue into what's going on and I says, 'Joey, maybe we shouldn't be doing this,' like the pussy I was. And you know what that motherfucker turns to me and says? He says, 'What? You some sort of faggot or something? What's this stuck-up bitch to you anyway? Here's your chance to show her what she's missin'.' And that's when I left."

"Jesus, Reardon. You mean…?"

"Don't get things confused. I didn't have nothing to do with it."

"You were fucking *there*, man."

"Sure, I left her there. But what was I supposed to do? It was all eight of them against me. I knew that if I narc'd on them they'd find a way to make me pay for it."

"How could they do that?"

"You know how jocks are: we're tribal. There was a peckin' order and I was on the bottom rung. You couldn't expect to fuck with Joey and not have him dish out a little payback. Sometimes they'd make you sit on a broom handle, other times they'd strap a guy down while two or three of the guys teabagged the poor sonofabitch. That was how Joey kept everybody under his thumb."

"You could have called the cops."

"Yeah? What the fuck were they gonna do about it? By the time they got there the deed would probably already been done. Besides, the cops don't give a shit."

"Fuck, man," said Casey. "That's low."

"Don't I fucking know it. Had I known what would happen next, I swear to you I'd have intervened."

"What do you mean?"

"Within' a month everyone had seen the pictures. People stared at her as she walked through the hall—a few would even laugh as she quickened her step. She started cutting classes and eventually dropped out. After that it was like she was dead. Every now and then you'd hear rumours—that she was whoring, that she'd killed herself. Eventually, everyone just got bored of the story and forgot about her.

"Anyway, a few years passed. To be honest with you, I was almost able to forget the whole thing ever happened. Then one day, about five years ago, I get an email from Joey's dad—you met him at O'Reilly's—telling me he's gone missing. Around this time last season, I see in the newspaper that old Benny'd been bludgeoned to death from behind while taking a piss in the goddamned Stone Cottage latrine. Well, that there was enough to get my attention. A month later a chunk of Keith O'Malley's jawbone's discovered by an unfortunate rave attendee on Cherry Beach. I've looked into it. Every player that was there that night has either suffered some sort of accident or gone and disappeared. You know what I'm saying? I'm the only one left. The rest were all hunted down, one by one."

"So why were you spared?"

"I guess she's saving the best for last."

"There's no way to link her to the other murders?"

"Oh there's plenty of evidence, but it's all of the fuckin' circumstantial variety. No doubt the cops have figured out we're all dropping like flies, but the only thing that holds us together is that we all played on the same baseball team seventeen years ago. And I mean, they must keep tabs on Lyuba, given the kind of business she's been runnin' out of that house, but I doubt they'd make the connection between her and those disappearances. As far as they're concerned, I'd be as likely a suspect."

"Well, why don't you go to the cops now and try to save your own neck?"

"Are you out of your mind? Nobody's gonna talk about it who knows what's good for 'em. Hell, we probably shouldn't even be fucking talking about it right now. The woman's got rats everywhere. She may have this whole place bugged, for all we know."

"You're fucking paranoid, man."

"What, you don't believe me?" asked Reardon, fishing in the pocket of his shorts and pulling out a piece of narrow, white PVC tubing with a piece of wire mesh surgically grafted to the end of it.

"What's that?"

"That's a fuckin' bug, friend," said Reardon spitting into his cup.

"Where'd you get it?"

"Found it in the trunk of the Beast."

"Is it recording us right now?"

"No. I've disabled it. Bet you can guess how it got there. I know she's got plants on the team's staff too."

"And how do you know that?"

"Call it intuition."

"You wanna know something? You're one fucked up dude."

"Don't I know it," said Reardon, uncorking the bottle and pouring himself another shot. He lifted the the glass in the air, as if proposing a toast. "Don't go thinking I'm the only one she's keeping tabs on. The only way to be safe is to keep your nose out of this business with Lyuba. Got it?"

Casey could only nod.

TRADE DEADLINE

Waiver claims were always messy business and unfortunately for Stephenson, Toronto's claim of Brown required his spot on the 26-man roster. Stephenson was the only reliever with options, so the decision was a no-brainer. Don phoned down to Lou and broke the news as soon as the paperwork had been filed. He knew it was a lot to ask of Lou to understand the overarching strategy and be appropriately elated at the prospect of suddenly having starting pitching depth, but the old laggard's response failed to even *attempt* to meet Don halfway. Instead of saying thank you for the arm, he spent several minutes chewing Don out for what he considered a boneheaded move.

"Anyhow," said Don, after Lou had finished spitting vitriol at him through the phone. "I want to be the one to tell him."

"*You* want to tell him? Are you nuts?"

"It will be better if he hears it from me."

A quarter of an hour later Don was sitting with Lou and Stephenson in the manager's office.

"I can't believe what I'm hearing. I've been pitching great lately," said Stephenson.

"This has nothing to do with your performance," said Don in a tone he hoped expressed both patience and sympathy. "We've been nothing but impressed with you. You've played some great baseball this season."

"Then why the fuck are you demoting me?"

"It's a numbers game, Nick. I know you're new to this, but this sort of thing happens all the time. People get sent down; people get called up. Unfortunately for you, you've got options and nobody else in the bullpen does."

"Who are you replacing me with?"

Don hoped he wouldn't have to respond.

"I said who the fuck are you replacing me with?"

"Brown," said Don.

"Are you kidding me? He's terrible."

"I need you to listen to me," said Don. "This has nothing to do with your performance. This isn't your fault. It's just, sometimes, life happens. Is it fair? No. It doesn't have to be. But when unfair things happen to us, we must find a way to persist. I'm being straight with you, Nick. The reason I'm sending you down is that I need your roster spot to claim Brown. I need him in case any of the rotation goes down. We need bulk innings, do you understand? You're not stretched out. We'll call you back up as soon as there's an injury. September at the latest. Do you follow me?"

Stephenson seemed to think this over a moment before standing up, sweeping everything from the top of Lou's desk onto the floor, storming out, and trashing whatever he could lay his hands on in the locker room.

Lou kneeled on the ground, gingerly picking up the broken remains of a bobblehead in his likeness. "You see what you've done?" he yelled at Don, holding up the dislodged head. "You see what you've done!"

Stephenson was still raging and throwing various pieces of equipment around as Don left the clubhouse. Members of the media were laying in wait with their phones thrust out, shouting their questions. The press gang followed him all the way to the front office lobby, where security prevented them from entry. Don texted Howard, and a moment later he appeared.

"Take a seat," said Don.

"I have to tell you that they are not happy. I think you're going to have to hold a press conference."

"Too formal. It makes it look like we have something to apologize for," said Don, typing something into his phone. "I need you to arrange some talk show appearances. We also need to come up with a boilerplate explanation as to why these moves have been made."

"Forget what you've done. It's what you didn't do that you're going to have to answer for," said Howard. "What people are pissed about is the trade deadline, but as you know it's all in how we present it."

"That's right."

Howard looked down at his phone. "I've secured an interview with Talon and Zuccharini this afternoon at four. Radio interview with McTown at noon."

"Not McTown. He's had it in for me ever since I called him a bonehead on his program."

"You shouldn't have said that."

"I couldn't help it. The man is a cretin and he doesn't let go of his grudges, so you better forget about it."

"I don't see how we can wiggle out of this one. He'll slag you even worse if you don't show up. He'll call you a coward."

"A coward? A coward hides behind sunglasses and a microphone," said Don. "Alright. If there's no getting out of it, I'll go. After all, I know how to deal with him." He took a sip of coffee. "I would just prefer not to."

"Messaging," said Howard, finishing an email on his phone.

"The whole point of this little tête-à-tête," said Don, sending a text message.

"I think," said Howard, leaning back in his seat, "we should just be honest."

"Honest? What does that even mean?"

"It means that you accept full accountability for the team."

"Still not following. I am obviously accountable for the state of the team."

"I mean," said Howard, leaning forward, "you have to make it seem like everything is going according to plan."

Don put down his phone. "That's what you've come up with?"

Howard shrugged.

"Howard, I'm going to sound delusional if I say that—like I am totally out of touch with the gravity of the situation. Is that really the best we can do?"

"Well, do you believe in this team you've built, or not?"

After Howard left, Don busied himself sending a few inessential emails while he waited for a text saying Stephenson was finally cleared out of the locker room. When it arrived, he marched back down the corridor, reporters once again in pursuit. Don simply ignored their questioning. As he walked, he composed in his head the speech he would deliver to the players, laying each word down carefully in place so that it might achieve its desired effect. He entered the locker room and what little chatter there was immediately died out. He waited to hear the clack of the door closing before launching into his planned explanation.

"Pardon me," he began. "I won't take up too much of your time, but I wanted to apologize for the scene here this morning. I tried to reasonably explain the situation to Nick, but I think we can all agree he didn't handle the news as we would have hoped."

"You did send him down for somebody who's worse than he is," said Reardon.

"Yes. It is unfortunate, but—and this must be said—essential."

"Exactly what was so essential about it?" asked Steele. "The whole point of the trade deadline is to get better."

"By sending Nick to Buffalo and bringing Brown into the fold, we were able to achieve depth."

The players collectively groaned.

"Nobody gives a damn about depth, Mr. Billingsley, not when the Sams and Sharks just loaded up."

"Come now, Nick will be back in September."

"We might be out of it by then if Brown has to pitch much," said Thompson.

Don could feel the sweat soaking through his clothing.

"He won't if you all do your jobs."

"So, you're saying we've got to carry dead weight around on our backs for the next month," said Lou, tossing a fistful of seeds into his mouth.

"No," said Don. "I'd hardly call him dead weight. He is a Big League caliber pitcher. He has good stuff. He's just played somewhat poorly this year. You should be thrilled, Lou. You'll have an extra Big League pitcher on the roster come September."

"And less one in August," said Reardon, spitting into his cup.

"Do you understand what I'm trying to do here? This was all that could be done. We had to hedge our bets."

"Well thank you for joining us, Mr. Billingsley," said Lou, rolling his eyes. "But if you'll excuse us, we've got some work to do before game time."

"Certainly," said Don. "Carry on."

"That guy is so full of shit," said Steele once Don had left the room. "Dude fucked up and now he's acting like it's all part of some master plan."

"We're worse now than when we started."

"Why don't you go and cry about it," said Reardon, spitting into his cup. "Donny Boy may be incompetent, but he's right. This shit is in our hands now. We'll go as far as our play takes us."

Don was presently in the backseat of the Rolls Royce, responding to emails as the car crept along the sun-softened blacktop. He arrived at the corporate radio station with just ten minutes to spare. Thankfully, they'd sent an intern to meet him in the foyer and lead him to the studio, where he found McTown already on the air. Through the window into the studio, Don watched McTown pontificate while wearing his usual smug expression and those hideous sunglasses. This bozo didn't even know they made separate frames for polarized lenses. Don mused that this foul lump of human excrement was probably under the influence of the unfortunate misconception that he in some way looked cool or hip.

The ON AIR light went dark and Don was ushered into the room. He sat down behind a microphone across from McTown.

Like most of the daytime sports radio on the corporate network, this show was also being lo-fi broadcast on television by two automated cameras. One of the cameras was fixed on McTown and his producer, Lindsay Starr. Don liked her if for no other reason than she despised McTown as much as Don did. The other camera was pointed toward where Don now sat.

He shook Lindsay's hand amicably and asked about her daughter, who she said was fine and pulled out a picture to show off while McTown scowled into his microphone.

"Good luck," said McTown as the digital clock on the wall counted down the final seconds till airtime. "And we're back. As promised, we're joined by the President of the Toronto Blue Birds, Mr. Don Billingsley. Thank you for coming on the air today, Mr. Billingsley."

"My pleasure," said Don cheerfully.

"I trust your ride here was pleasant. It certainly took you a long time, considering you were just down at the Dome."

"Ah yes, my apologies. The traffic was terrible."

"Oh yes, traffic. I forgot you had yourself carted around in that Rolls Royce instead of riding the rocket like the rest of us schmucks. How's the MPG on the Rolls, by the way? You know what? Nevermind. We're here to talk baseball, not cars."

"Although if you'd like to talk cars, I'd be happy to do so."

"This being August first, there's only one thing people want to hear about, and that's the trade deadline."

"Yes, let's talk about it."

"A lot of people," said McTown, pausing to collect himself. "A lot of people are saying that you didn't do enough to improve the team. How would you respond to that?"

"If the season ended today, we would be playing in the post-season."

"Yeah, in the one-game wildcard series. But you can't be totally ignorant of the things people have been saying about you online."

"Why? What have people been saying about me?"

"Understand that this is people saying this—not me—but people are looking at some of the names out there, some of the players who were moved, and they're asking themselves if it was really impossible for Toronto to trade for say a Montes, or a Geerman? Really, all it would have taken was a small upgrade."

"Yes, we—"

"You're going to say you made a waiver claim and signed a couple minor leaguers to contracts. That's fine and dandy, but many are saying that by making the claim for Brown, you've made the team worse. How do you respond to that?"

"Yes, well," said Don, clearing his throat, "there have to be deals on the table in the first place. There was activity and interest, but most of that interest was in our Big League players. There may have been opportunities to improve if we moved the right players, but it would have meant shipping a household name out of town. Who knows if it would even come out in our favour, in the end."

"You're saying the offers you had on the table were Big Leaguers for Big Leaguers."

"I wouldn't characterize our interactions as offers, per say. They were more... discussions."

Don tried to read what McTown was thinking through those horrible glasses, but the man's expression remained entirely neutral.

"Care to give us some details?"

"You know I can't do that," said Don, feigning a smile.

"Yes, of course, negotiation confidentiality and all that. Forgive me, I just thought I might throw you a bone here, because any example or evidence might improve the overall plausibility of your claim."

"I can't give you that, because like I said, we never got to the point of real negotiation. It was all just idle chatter."

"But you just said there was plenty of interest."

"Because there was. Plenty of teams were interested in our players. We were not so interested in theirs."

"So what I'm hearing is the lines were effectively dead."

Don hated looking at this fat, sweatsuit-clad nitwit. To the audience listening on the radio or to those watching the televised version at home, McTown must have seemed the very font of rationality and impartiality, the way he sat there, expressionless, toneless. Don stared at this this lump of hypocrisy with malice. For the first time in many years he fantasized about doing physical violence to another person. After all, how good would it feel to reach across the table and wring this fool's neck?

"Well?" asked McTown, not letting the point slip.

"Like I said, there wasn't much available."

"I suppose that's why New York went out and got Montes and Tampa Bay landed Geerman. I suppose there were limitations. Many said that the team wouldn't be able to make upgrades because you didn't have any dry powder left. There weren't any prospects to trade."

"Yes," said Don, seeking an opportunity to get back on message. "We have been fortunate to have several of our top prospects graduate recently."

"By several, do you mean one?"

"Yes," admitted Don.

"The truth is," said McTown, leaning back in his seat, "you didn't have any prospect capital because you went and spent it all at last year's trade deadline."

"The truth is," said Don, brushing this criticism away with a swish of his hand, "that this is already a very good team. I will admit that we got off to a slow start, but since the middle of June, the team has been light's out. That is why we are currently in the playoff picture after spending a month in fifth place."

"What makes you think it will last?"

"Nothing lasts," said Don. "Sooner or later someone is going to get hurt, someone else will go into a slump, the team might flag in the standings. Of course it's equally possible that should that happen, someone else might suddenly get hot and fill the gap. Perhaps someone on the roster takes a step forward and makes the team that much more dangerous down the stretch. There are a few players I can think of who I believe have made big strides over the past several months."

"What, you mean Casey?"

"Sure. Why not?"

"I don't think he can be counted on," said McTown, covering one nostril and inhaling.

Don threw up his hands.

"I must say, this isn't a polite way to treat a guest. I feel as if I'm being interrogated. When you extended an invitation onto your show, I didn't expect to be poked by some local sports radio toady. I might take greater offence to your malevolence if I took the opinion of a man who dresses like he still lives in his mother's basement at the age of fifty-five seriously, or if I thought his opinion might make one difference with regards to the outcome of events. You'll eat your words when the team is leading the SL East in September."

After concluding his statement, Don tore off his headphones, threw them on the table and exited the studio, leaving nothing but dead air in his wake.

"I guess you pissed him off," observed Lindsay, taking a sip of water. "Well? Say something."

"That man is insane! I think it's time for a commercial break."

The TV interview took place in the back seat of the Rolls Royce as Tom drove Don up to Yorkville for his afternoon appointment with his tailor. Thankfully, the two young people who hosted the show were more interested in playing looped footage of Don's interview on McTown's show than asking any hard-hitting questions. They were particularly enamored with the segment where Don threw the headphones on the table, which they played in slow motion overlayed with metal music.

"So what do you think, boss? Are you going to challenge Joe Cool to a cage match?"

Tom pulled up along the curb outside the Park Hyatt and got out to open the door for Don, who stepped onto the sunlit sidewalk feeling like a new man. The television interview had confirmed that the smoke was already disapating. He would survive this PR crisis just like he'd survived the others.

Walking into Tony's Fine Menswear was like walking into a dream. One was always greeted with a smile by Tony himself, who had the properly powerful handshake of a man who performed manual labour. It was no pleasure to receive, thanks to Tony's many rings, but Don was willing to grit his teeth and bear it for the sake of what this man had to offer. Not only did he have the finest cuts and materials in the city, but he ran a tight ship. Fresh measurements were taken and fabrics brought out while Tony schmoozed the customer and walked him through the plethora of options. Each swatch was held up like a museum artifact for Don's personal inspection. There were fabrics of many colours and textures and materials. A few samples caused Don to raise an eyebrow. Did anyone ever come in here searching for a mustard-yellow, paisley suit? Perhaps this would do for one of those fools on television—those dandyish chasers of the fame monster—but no person who wished to be respected could ever be seen in such a thing. Power could only be attained by a refinement of self. A person had to carry oneself with dignity and restraint. In Don's estimation, it was far better to be in the background pulling the strings than the person in front of the lens, and one certainly couldn't hide in the shadows wearing a mustard yellow suit.

He narrowed it down to three swatches: a navy linen, a charcoal wool with grey pinstripes, and a respectable green tweed number that was sure to knock more than a few socks off this fall. He took the invoice cheerfully and stepped out the door.

Outside, Tom was leaning against the car smoking a cigarette. As Don approached, he cleared his throat and made eyes at the car as if to say *what the hell are you doing?* So Tom broke from his ruminating and slowly lifted himself from the hood.

"Where to next?"

"Back to the Dome."

Tom tossed the still-smoking butt into the street and opened the door for Don. They drove for some time while Don dealt with the emails he'd received during the fitting. He realized Tom was asking him something.

"Pardon?"

"It's nothing."

"That just makes it look like you wish to retract. Out with it!"

"I was just asking what you were planning to do."

"About what?" asked Don.

"If you get fired."

"I'm not going to be fired."

"Whatever you say. It's just, if I were you, I'd be worried about how I'd be able to afford it all."

"What all?"

Tom gestured around the car. "Everything."

August was the month in which seasons were won and lost and Don knew it. If the team was to make a go of it, they had to pull up their bootstraps and own the month of August. Fortunately for him, they were doing just that, having not lost a game since the trade deadline, winning fourteen in a row. Home games were now easy sell-outs, merchandise was flying off the racks, and money was flowing in. Everything was finally working out.

But Don still felt uneasy. Cracks were beginning to form. The pitching had faltered slightly of late, with Hardy and Haliburton going ice cold and only completing six innings combined over their past four starts. Thankfully, the offense had kept going strong. Over their past sixteen games the lineup had averaged 6.3 runs, and on the rare occasion the offense hadn't shown up, Amuro or Ordoñez threw up a gem and the bullpen had taken the team the rest of the way. They hadn't lost a series since the middle of July.

But something was wrong—Don could feel it. Beneath this veneer of success was a disease he couldn't diagnose. Of course, he had no evidence. It was nothing more than a feeling, he would remind himself. It had no basis in reality. After all, hadn't they just surpassed the Sharks for the first wildcard slot? Weren't they just four games behind the Sams? If the season ended today, they would be in the playoffs. A one-game playoff, but postseason nonetheless. The team was healthy, pounding the ball, and playing great defense, so what was Don so worried about?

He couldn't have explained it, and that's why he kept it to himself. Was it a problem that, after years of things going wrong, of best-laid plans constantly blowing up in his face, things were suddenly going better than expected? Weren't the scales just finally returning to balance? So what if for years the players his front office brought in consistently underperformed the analytics, or went down with significant injuries? His luck had simply turned. The winds had lifted the sails after all these years of hanging slack. What difficulty was there in that?

The difficulty was that it was too good to be true. The whole thing had taken on this mythic, magical quality for the sportswriters, bloggers, and broadcasters, who spoke about the team as if it were on a date with destiny. These tales were all well and good for the masses, mired as they were in a permanent state of intellectual adolescence, but they did not work on him—a man of the world—as they did the rabble. There was no such thing as fate or destiny, only probability and result, and Don had to admit that the team's turnaround was at the very least improbable.

He was in this state of mind when he received a call from Tubs, who said he had thrown an extra BP for Casey a couple weeks ago. The player had apparently confided that he had been feeling "distracted" as some sort of explanation for his underperformance the week and a half prior to the incident.

"I think it's got something to do with Reardon," Tubs said.

"Is that what the boy said?"

"Not in so many words."

Why was this only coming out now? And why was this tactless, guileless lout suddenly turning so sketchy? If he was hiding something—which Don felt now, for certain, he was—then it could only be for Reardon's benefit. And if he was hiding something for Reardon's benefit, it could only mean trouble for Don somewhere down the road.

Speculation! It was all speculation and paranoia, and Don knew better. This was almost as bad as the magical thinking being peddled by the pundits. He tried to reason with himself: the team he had put together was finally tuned and humming along—this was merely the long-expected result of the processes he had put in place.

On the other hand, something had rattled the boy. What that something could be, Don feared to guess. Nothing good, he could be sure of that. And yet whatever was going on had no perceptible ill-effect on the closer's performance. If anything, Reardon's play had shown slight statistical improvement, if such can be said about an unblemished statline. Reardon was throwing harder, with better control, and striking out more batters than he had at the beginning of the season, while his bat had proven to be a viable middle-of-the-order weapon. There was no reason to believe that anything was amiss, but what harm could come from investigating?

A few hours before first pitch, he picked up his phone and texted Casey:

Come to my office immediately.

wut now?

Yes. Now!

What did they think you meant when you said immediately? Don was able to send a few emails before Casey, half-dressed, finally appeared.

"I suppose you could have taken a moment to finish clothing yourself."

"What's this about?" asked Casey, shutting the door behind him.

"Take a seat."

The two men sat silently a few moments before Don decided to break the ice. "You see, I think you know why I've called you up here."

"Did Tubs say something?"

This was too easy.

"Nothing, other than you seemed a little rattled."

"I'll get over it."

"He said you were… distracted."

"Sure. There's a lot going on."

"To be sure, my boy. To be sure. I just wanted to be certain we are doing everything we can to support you in your development. If you're feeling distracted, or anxious, we have in-house psychiatric services of which you could avail yourself. These are resources that we have secured for your benefit, but it's up to the individual player to take advantage of them."

"I see."

"What do you think? Should we schedule an appointment with Dr. Shaw? Say, tomorrow at noon?"

"I've been feeling better lately, really."

"You're sure?"

"Absolutely."

Don nodded, as if accepting Casey's proclamation. The boy was a terrible liar: he was clearly a disheveled wreck.

"Very well. I just wanted to make sure your feeling of distraction had nothing to do with our friend Phillip. Speaking of which, how *have* things been on the home front?"

"Same as they've ever been," said Casey.

"Are you certain?"

"Absolutely."

"There has been no change?"

"None that I can see."

"Well, that's good. Because let's say there were something going on and you kept it to yourself, it wouldn't be a very good look—would it?"

"I guess not."

"I mean, it would essentially necessitate that I personally ensure your career in baseball come to an abrupt and—needless to say—permanent end."

"Right."

"So just for my own peace of mind," said Don, leaning across his desk and fixing his gaze on Casey. "Look me in the eye and tell me there's nothing going on with Reardon."

Casey looked Don in the eye and said, "There's nothing going on with Reardon."

This was not the response Don had anticipated. He had expected the boy to crumble and confess to it all—whatever there was to confess—right then and there. Or perhaps give the response he gave, but deliver it poorly, so that his actions might betray the truth. Instead, the boy had looked Don right in the eye, and without so much as a twitch, or a clearing of the throat, said straight out what Don hoped to be true. Why was he disappointed this was evidently the case?

"You can go," said Don.

"Thanks," said Casey, and he got up and left.

Down in the locker room, Reardon wandered over to Casey's locker and asked what Don had called him up for.

"A pep talk," said Casey. "Don't worry about it."

Second Half

The heat was getting to Casey. For the past few weeks daytime temps had sat in the low thirties, with the humidex some days making it feel over forty. No sooner would Casey step onto the field than his skin would take on a sheen of glistening sweat. During day games he felt like he was being boiled alive in his plastic shell, like a lobster, and prayed for the shadows to move in. When shade finally crept past home plate there was some relief, but not much. There was no escaping feeling wet and slimy and hot. Worse, he developed a bad case of jock itch for which the High Performance Department had yet to find a remedy.

Still, it was better to be out there on the field than stuck with Reardon at the apartment, where there wasn't any air conditioning because Reardon maintained that it was bad for a person's respiratory system. All day the heat built up, rising from the ground floor up to the penthouse, where it was trapped by the roof. Reardon's idea of a remedy was to place a standing fan in each room and keep the windows open. Casey had expressed doubts of this method's sufficiency back during the May heat wave, when the place was already a sauna. Reardon had dismissed Casey's concern outright, saying that Casey would get used to it. It wasn't so bad.

Well now it was August, and there was no getting used to it. The whole place reeked of BO and the disinfectant they used to try to mask the BO. Casey could no sooner put on a fresh t-shirt than find it soaked through at the armpits. The best place was out on the balcony, where one could escape into the cool night air. The problem was, no sooner would Casey step out there for a toke, than Reardon would come out, fresh joint in hand, angling for a session. There was no escaping him, not in the apartment at least, so Casey had taken to late night walks, east on Lawrence Ave to a drive-thru Timmies booth situated behind a gas station. The women on the night shift would let him in through the locked lobby door. He would order what he wanted, pay for it, and moments later be out on the street again, ice capp in hand, ready to wander the night.

This wasn't the downtown. The streets were for the most part empty outside of the Afghani and Syrian families enjoying the night air on the lawns of their apartment buildings and the modded BMWs, Hondas, and Mercedes spitting flames from their tailpipes as they raced each other down the street.

Casey'd been fiending for coke lately. On these night walks he couldn't help but think that maybe he could just have himself a little stash from which to take a bump every now and again, until he was able to get himself out of this bullshit situation. He just needed a little bit of an edge, a little confidence. After all, a little bump now and again never hurt anyone. It'd been so long since he'd had any that it would take forever to get as bad as it was before.

No. He couldn't go down that road. There were no short trips on the wagon, he reminded himself, and what if the coke he purchased wound up being laced with fentanyl? He would end up like Corey Crowley over on the Bootleggers, dead in a bathroom stall with a line of white powder on the toilet paper dispenser, leaving no doubt as to the cause of his untimely demise.

Casey realized he was shaking hands with someone underneath the awning of an apartment building entranceway. A typical hood—white, possibly a skinhead, with facial tattoos and plaque so thick Casey wondered how this guy's gums were able to contain it. He was showing off a knife he said he used to stab snitches. Finally he said, "You want anything?"

"What do you got?"

"You ain't a cop, right?"

"No."

"Say, haven't I seen you somewhere?"

"I live nearby—do my grocery shopping across the street."

"Naw, I mean I've seen you somewhere else, like on MeScreen or some shit."

"I've never been on MeScreen. Your mind's probably just playing tricks on you."

"Why don't we just skip the crap then," said the hood as he lit a cigarette, "and tell me what you're looking for."

"Coke," mumbled Casey.

"What?"

"I said I want some coke."

"Jesus, motherfucker. Keep it down. You want heat?"

"Do you have any or what?"

"Sure, I got it. I mean, I can get it."

"Is it pure?"

"Pure as it's gonna get around here. Won't kill ya. How much you need?"

"Just an eight-ball."

"That'll cost you a hundred, brother."

Highway robbery.

"I was thinking sixty."

"The absolute best I can do for you is eighty. You got the money on you or what?"

"I'd have to go get it."

"Well the closest open ATM is all the way down at Bellamy. Thirty-minute walk there and back. You get the money. By the time you get back, I'll have the shit."

What am I even doing? thought Casey as he walked down Eglinton Avenue. The ATM was just where the guy said it would be. The machine took a while to take Casey's information and count out the money, but finally delivered the goods. He couldn't remember the last time he'd held money in his hand. He'd almost forgotten that bills existed. He was surprised to find the balance in his bank account sitting in the hundreds of thousands of dollars. "Where'd all that come from?" he asked aloud before remembering how much he was supposedly being paid. He waited for the machine to unlock his debit card before shoving it back into his wallet along with the cash. The plastic bills felt strange, too light somehow. He ran his thumb over the braille bumps and thought about how drug deals were probably one of the few transactions remaining for which such things were still essential.

Back he went, the entire time debating whether to chicken out or not. Soon he found himself standing once again under the awning, placing four of the rolled-up bills into the young man's hand as the two pretended to shake. Casey felt the money slip away. In it's place was pressed a small plastic baggie.

"Thanks."

"Don't mention it," said the young man, showing his disgusting teeth. "Any time."

Casey hurried home with the dime bag held fast in the hand he kept crammed in his pocket. Had he gone too far? Had he made a mistake? It didn't matter. Now that he had the stuff, he knew what he was going to do with it.

Into the apartment he slipped, quietly bolting the door and inserting the chain. Casey could tell Reardon was in his workshop by the sliver of light that shot out from beneath the door. The catcher hastened to remove his shoes and crept to his bedroom. Approaching his desk, he peeked out the window to make sure Reardon wasn't out there having a smoke. Satisfied, he closed the blinds and turned on the lamp so that it cast a ring of light onto the desktop, in the centre of which he poured some white powder from the baggie.

It didn't give off much of an aroma. Unusual. Casey figured it must have been cut with something, which gave him pause. But the craving proved substantial. What were the odds that they'd put something like *that* in there? It was probably just ground up glass or something—nothing Casey couldn't handle. He rubbed at his nostrils as he gazed at the cocaine and pondered. He had promised himself only a bump, but what good would that do? He wanted a solid buzz. He wanted to really feel it. Using his debit card, he separated a chunk from the mound, broke up the clumps, and worked the powder into a thick line. From his wallet he fished out the last of his twenties and rolled it into a straw. Casey took a second look at the mound. Would there still be enough for a few bumps later? At least now he knew where to go for more. He leaned down, held the bill up to his nostril, and hoovered up the line in one quick snort.

"Fuck," he said, throwing the bill down and tilting his head back. It burned bad. For a moment, Casey was worried he'd gotten a hot shot and would die here right then and there, choking on his vomit with Reardon just two doors down, fucking around in his stupid goddamned workshop.

He waited for the coke to kick in or for his body to drop dead, but nothing happened. His nasal cavity burned like hell. He coughed and wheezed as mucus trickled down the back of his throat.

When his coughing fit finally abated, Casey picked up the bag, smelled it from a distance, and realized that whatever was in there didn't have that sweet, floral cocaine scent, even in trace amount. He stuck his finger in the bag and licked it. It didn't taste right, either. Casey took the bag with him to the kitchen and dumped what was left into a bowl. Rummaging under the sink, he pulled out the bottle of vinegar and poured it over the white powder.

When Reardon finally came out from his workshop, he found Casey sitting on the kitchen floor laughing.

"What the fuck's gotten into you?" said the closer, pouring himself a bowl of cereal. Seeing what was left of Casey's cocaine he said, "I think we're a little old to be making volcanos."

"I think we need to hire a private investigator," said Don.

Susan was sitting across from him. She didn't look up from her phone.

"I think that is a very bad idea."

"Is it?'

"Yes," she said, finally looking up. "The PA would be all over you. Imagine if word got out that you were *spying* on one of your players."

"Of course. What good's a union if it can't protect all the crooks and lowlifes."

"Have you considered maybe it's all in your head? I hate to say it, but it sounds to me like you're cracking under the pressure just a little bit." She smiled as she said it. "I mean, if you think about it, it's a perfectly rational psychological response from Casey. He's in a slump, he hasn't been getting along with his roommate lately, so he—perhaps inadvertently—blames said roommate."

"That's just the thing, he didn't lump it on his roommate. He took full accountability for his performance."

"Then I don't get it. What's the problem?"

"The problem is he said he was *distracted*."

"Fuck, Don. He's twenty-four. He might be a recovering addict, but he's still just a kid. He could be distracted by any-thing—performance anxiety, his family, girls. What makes you so sure this has something to do with Reardon?"

"He may have performance anxiety, but the kid's family doesn't even talk to him, outside of one uncle. As for girls, Phillip keeps the boy on a pretty tight leash, so I don't think he's been seeing anyone."

"You sound like you've already hired a private eye," she said, laughing.

"That information has been easy enough to come by. If I want any more than that, I'll have to pay for it."

She sat there thinking this over for some time, her face pinched in concentration. Don began to wonder if he had made a mistake in sharing this with his subordinate—if it had, in fact, been inappropriate.

"Suppose," she said, typing something into her phone, "there is something wrong. Suppose Reardon is up to something. Would it do us any good to know?"

"Whatever do you mean? If we knew something was up, we could put a stop to it."

"I don't see how you could put a stop to it without either benching or suspending our star player, which seems to run counter to the goal of everyone keeping their jobs."

"The goal," said Don, "is to win a championship."

"Of course, if we suspended said player, we would have to provide some sort of explanation and accompanying evidence in order to substantiate to the PA, the league, and the public the merit of any suspension, and would have to disclose just how it was we were able to come by said evidence."

"The damned union again!"

"It's for the best. They're the only thing standing between you and full-blown crazy."

"I was only half serious about the PI."

"Whatever you say."

It was 8:37 AM when the team arrived at Pearson. They were fresh off a road swing through the SL East and eager to return home after twelve days of living out of hotel rooms. Their plane was delayed three hours at JFK due to a severe tropical storm coming off the Atlantic and nobody was permitted to disembark. The players were thus understandably cranky when they finally got off the plane in Toronto. Reading the room as they waited in line for customs, Lou went ahead and cancelled the next day's fielding and batting practice to give his players some rest. That didn't stop Reardon from rousing Casey at the usual hour and carting him down to the ballpark for one o'clock.

Casey spent the afternoon in the VR simulator, taking sliders from that night's starter until he was able to recognize whether the pitch was going to be a strike, a ball, or a hanger he could hit four hundred feet. Then he turned the simulation to game mode, where he took at-bat after at-bat until he was launching baseballs into the outfield. He could have spent all day in this endless repetition, thinking of nothing but the bat and the ball and the faceless man on the mound, had Tubs not tapped him on the shoulder and told him the players were getting dressed and taking the field.

Casey was rehydrating after the warmup when Felix slapped him on the back, causing him to spit out his beverage. Felix pointed past the third base dugout to where a woman in a black dress was waving and calling Casey's name.

"Who is ze babe?" asked Felix.

Ignoring the question, Casey started walking toward the dugout. As he approached the woman in the stands, the world around him slowed down, his stomach lurched, and he had to fight the compulsion to turn around and walk the other way. It was, after all, Lyuba standing there in the black dress, a matching clutch resting with her hand on the guardrail. She wore big sunglasses that covered her face and a floppy, broad-brimmed hat. She looked like an attendee of the Kentucky Derby rather than a Blue Birds game.

"Aloha," she said as he approached the guard rail.

"What do you want?"

"Tut! Is that any way to speak to a lady come to see her knight errant on the field of battle to bestow upon him a prize?"

"Knight what? And what prize?"

Casey realized that her clasped hand was already extended. She was waiting for him to take whatever she held in it. He lifted his palm and some scant piece of lacy black fabric was pressed into it. Lyuba closed his fingers around it.

"What is it?" he asked skeptically.

"If you're so curious, why don't you take a look?"

He opened his hand and took out the piece of crumpled silk and started pulling it apart. He nearly dropped it on the turf when he realized what it was.

"Jesus."

"You like them?"

Casey said nothing as he stuffed the panties into his pocket.

"That's a good boy. That's what makes you different, Casey—your humble spirit. Now do as your lady commands and be waiting in the lobby of that roach hotel you're staying in at one o'clock. Don't be late!"

"For what?"

But she had already turned and begun ascending the stairs.

"Woah-ho! Who was that?" asked Patrice when Casey returned.

"Trust me, man. You don't wanna know."

"That is where you are wrong, mon ami," said Felix. "She was—how you say?—perfect ten."

"A sexy maman."

"A sex kitten."

"A p—"

"I get the idea," said Casey.

"And what is it she gave to you, eh?" said Patrice, fishing around in Casey's back pocket and extracting the black panties before Casey could slap his hand away. "Oh-ho-ho! Very nice!"

"Please tell me you got her nombre."

"I'm afraid she's got mine."

"All the better," said Felix. "Let them come to you."

"Ooo, look everyone!" shouted Lyuba, lifting her dress as she ran on tiptoes down the red carpet that led to her throne. Casey was ushered through the double doors by his elbows. "Look everyone! My boys brought me a present. But couldn't you have tied it with a bow?"

"We'll remember next time, Ms. Lyuba," said the driver.

"I'll forgive you, but only because you brought me something so… delectable. What do you all think? Isn't he just delectable?" she asked her guests, who were already nodding their approval. "Well now that I've got my present, I guess the polite thing to do would be to open it up. Strip him down, boys."

The masked driver poked him in the back with his gun, saying, "You heard the lady."

Casey took off his clothes so that he was left standing in his underwear in the centre of the room.

"And of course, we'll have to check him for a wire."

"But we're the ones who picked *him* up, Miss Lyuba."

"One can never be certain, now can one? Maybe he told Phillip about our little rendezvous. He might want to see what I'm about, abducting his poor wittle sidekick. Why, I'm half expecting him to come crashing through the door. Now, let's see…" she said, reaching around and giving Casey's ass a squeeze. "He's clean! How wonderful! Wonderful!" And now stroking his chest, "Darling, how are you? I've missed you. Tell me: what's happening? What's good?"

"Listen, lady, when you asked me to meet you downstairs you didn't say anything about getting pistol whipped and tossed in the trunk."

"Sh-sh-sh," she said, pressing her finger to his lips. "It's better when you don't talk. We don't want to ruin something so beautiful with something ugly, now do we?"

"But you asked me—"

"So I did," she cried, clapping her hands together. "That certainly was rude of me."

"It's fine," said Casey, rubbing his head.

"That's so sweet. Isn't he just so sweet?"

There was a lot of mhmming and yessing from Lyuba's guests.

"Can I go now?"

"What? Leave? But, my dear, you just got here. If you leave now, you'll miss all the fun!"

"That whole coming here thing was pretty much against my will."

"Nonsense! By being where I wanted you to be, when I wanted you to be, weren't you basically signaling that you in fact wanted to visit the woman with the black panties?"

A few of the guests whooped.

"I lost interest after the whole getting pistol-whipping thing."

Lyuba pinched his nose and swung his head from side to side as she said, "And why do you suppose I brought clean, chiseled, handsome Casey all the way over here for a visit?"

"Your guess is as good as mine."

"I brought you here," her voice now a fortune teller's, "as a warning."

"Whatever you're trying to warn me of, it's working."

"Oh you! You can't be scared of wittle ol' me, now can ya?"

Casey gulped.

"You don't need to worry. I've got *your* best interest at heart. Say, I bet that's the sort of thing *he* tells you, isn't it? I mean, how else could he have duped you into being his little minion? *Stick with me, kid. I've got all this bullshit figured out.* Oh, he is so… *hopeful,* that Phillip. He's also a liar."

"Look, lady, I don't know what's going on between you two, but it's been made pretty clear that it isn't any business of mine."

"See: you say you know, but I'm not sure that you really, really, truly know. Because you're just so… *snoopy*, you know? Like a little puppy. *Where's the bone? Where's the bone?*"

"You can trust me, lady. My snooping days are over."

"But here's the thing," she said, caressing his nipple. "How can I know *for sure* that I can really, *truly* trust you. Because I've been hearing from little birdies that you've been making phone calls and paying little visits and been up to all sorts of mischief. Yes. *Yes, you have.*"

"I found out what I needed to know and now I'm done with it. I'll never tell a soul."

"Take an addict at his word? Unlikely. But I'm curious, what is it you discovered?"

"I found out you bought up all Reardon's debts and that's how you've got him under your thumb."

"Casey, Casey, Casey. If that's all you wanted to know, all you had to do was ask! Instead, you run around behind my back and do all this snooping. I want our relationship to be built on a foundation of trust. And of course, you know why I bought up all those debts of his, don't you?"

"I know," said Casey, looking away as he said it.

"You don't know shit."

"Lady, I don't pretend to know what actually happened. All I know is he says he didn't do it."

"And you believe him. Why? Just because he told you so?"

"Yeah," said Casey.

"I think we've all seen what weight his word carries by now," she said, putting her fists together as if she were holding a stick. "He's the sort who likes to bend the truth. It's like he can't help but bend it and bend it, until sooner or later… *snap!* The truth comes out in splinters. You'll see! You want to know what the funny thing is? Phillip probably believes the garbage that's always coming out of his mouth. He might even believe he's not a rapist because he didn't stick his tiny dick in me."

"But then he really *wouldn't* have… done it."

Lyuba reached back as if she were going to slap him. Casey winced in anticipation, but the blow never arrived. Instead, he felt her fingers gently caressing his jawline. He opened his eyes to find hers staring back.

"Poor, naïve, stupid Casey. Is that really what you think? After he told you about the whole… episode? Didn't it ever occur to you that maybe—after I categorically turned him down—maybe he *wanted* something bad to happen to me? Especially since he has such a knack for arranging things, doesn't he? Like when he put MDMA in your and your teammate's drinks without telling you about it. Do you remember that? Or when he was able to secure you a roster spot on a team on which you didn't belong. All he had to do was stomp his foot and they let him keep you around like a stray dog. That's the one thing that always impressed me about Phillip. He's just so good at making things happen, except getting with me of course. At least, not until that night."

"You don't mean—"

"Ah, so you're finally clueing in," she said, her lips pursed in simulated sympathy. "But let's give him the benefit of the doubt for a moment and assume that—in spite of all the humiliation and anger he was experiencing due to my simply not wanting to fuck him—that he didn't plan it all. Let's suppose he didn't put his buddies up to it like a pack of filthy animals. We can allow for that possibility, can't we? There's still the issue that he was still there, wasn't he? In the room, I mean."

"He told me as much."

"Well then he could have tried to stop them, couldn't he?"

"I guess so," said Casey, feeling less certain.

"I didn't hear anything from him afterwards either—no apology, no phone call, no nothing! And to think, before he was all but tearing his heart out over me! *But Lyuba, I love you*, he used to say. *I'd sooner die than let anything happen to you.* Bullshit!"

"I'm sorry," said Casey, not knowing what else to say.

"I don't need your apology and I don't need his either. If there's one thing that bastard has taught me, it's that apologies are nothing but consolation for the weak. The strong exact retribution, since it sends a clearer message. Phillip will get what's coming to him, just like his old pal Joey. Want to know what happened to his old pal Joey?"

"I don't think so."

"Don't be such a poor sport," said Lyuba, stomping her foot and twisting Casey's nipple.

"Fuck!"

"Well," said Lyuba, touching a finger to her lip, "not exactly. Although I suppose he thought he had a chance for another go when I called him up a few years later. Though, looking back, it was all quite transparent, really. I'm surprised he fell for it. I guess he thought I was one of those girls who falls in love with her attacker."

"I think you oughta let me go," said Casey.

"One moment," she said, stepping back to her throne to retrieve her phone. "What do you think?" she asked, lifting the screen to Casey's face.

"Nice?"

"Psh! Not me, sugar plum. I mean all that blood!"

"It looks almost real," said Casey.

"I would hope so. It is real. You can see where I got it from right… here." She pointed to the bottom right corner of the screen. "You see, that's Joey."

Casey lifted his hand to his mouth.

"Did you know there's about five-and-a-half litres of blood in the human body? I didn't either, until I bled this one like a pig and measured for myself."

"Jesus."

"Now watch your tongue, young man. That's no way to talk to a lady," said Lyuba, putting her phone away.

"I don't get it," said Casey. "If you're so convinced Reardon was in on it, why haven't you just knocked him off already? I mean you've already got all his loans lined up. Wouldn't it be easier just to get it over with?"

"Because don't you think," she said, standing on tiptoes so she could whisper into his ear, "that it'll be so much better after I've made him wait?"

Then she slapped Casey in the crotch and laughed before walking back down the red carpet to her throne. From the armrest she picked up a pair of metal scissors and turned around, holding them open so Casey could see them in the light. She began snipping at the air. Casey attempted to turn and run, but was met by the hands of his abductors, who pushed him to the ground and held him down.

"Please, Lyuba, please."

"I told you I could make a grown man beg," said Lyuba, straddling his chest and holding the scissors before his eyes.

"Wh-what are you going to do?" asked Casey.

"It's called neutering your dog, Charlie Brown."

"God! No!"

"Hold still, or I'll have to sedate you."

"Fuck. I'll do anything."

"That's right," she said, squeezing his cheeks together to make his lips move. "*I'll do anything, just no snip-snip.*"

"No snip-snip," Casey agreed.

This didn't satisfy her. She slapped his face and moved further down his body.

"No snip-snip!" he cried, struggling to break himself free. He stopped when he felt the cold metal of scissors press against his neck. Lyuba lifted his chin so their eyes met.

"If I ever hear about you snooping around about my business again, I'll cut your fucking balls off. Got it?"

"Y-yes."

"Good boy," said Lyuba. "You may yet live to sire if you do as you're told. Alright, I think he's had enough. See him out."

"Where ya bin?" asked Reardon as Casey stepped through the door.

"Where the fuck you think I've *bin*?" said Casey. "That crazy stalker of yours abducted me again, motherfucker."

"What do you mean she abducted you?"

"I mean like last time. Remember? When we are held at fucking gunpoint? That fucking happened again."

"Shit."

"Yeah, shit."

"What the fuck could she want with you?"

"She told me to keep my nose out of her business and that's exactly what I aim to do. You're involved with some fucked up people, man."

"Jesus, kid. What the fuck did she say?"

"A lot of things. Fuck."

"Kid, you've gotta calm the fuck down. You're shiverin'. You've gotta get your shit together."

"Who the fuck are you to tell me to get my shit together? Lyuba owns you. Do you fucking understand that? Do you fucking understand the shit you've gotten yourself into? That you've gotten *me* into? Of course you don't!"

"Lis—"

"No, I'm done fucking listening. I've done nothing but listen to all your crazy bullshit for months on end. There's no end to it. You just talk and talk and talk and talk. You act as if you've got it all figured out, but you wanna know something? The truth is your life is going to shit right in front of you and there's nothing you can do about it, so don't you go telling me to listen. I mean, I guess I owe thanks and all that for the opportunity, but I think it would be best if, after this thing is over, we just go our separate ways."

"So that's how it is, is it?" said Reardon.

"That's right."

"You're a big boy now, huh?" said Reardon, spitting into his cup. "How far do you think you'll get without me, anyway?"

"You know what, man? It doesn't fucking matter. Because you know where I won't be? Fucking dead."

"Yeah? Well, go ahead. You're only delaying the inevitable."

WEST COAST SWING

Nobody was happier than Casey when the Blue Birds' twelve game home stand ended on the Monday of the August long weekend. In their infinite wisdom, the league office had scheduled the away game for 1:07 PM EST, making for the third damned day game in a row, and in the middle of a record-setting heatwave no less. He was looking forward to the road trip if only to escape the the blazing heat of Reardon's apartment. Hotel air conditioning, here we come.

The team was scheduled to embark on their last west coast swing, a thirteen-game road trip that began in Oakland before backtracking east to Denver, on to LA, and up to Seattle for a series that, according to the Aucoin twins, would be just like being the home team, except on the far side of the continent. As far as Casey was concerned, the plane couldn't leave the tarmac soon enough. Aside from the weather, he also couldn't wait to be away from all this drama. Of course it meant being in even closer quarters with his battery mate, but at least he would only have to deal with Reardon, and not the criminally insane woman hunting him.

Besides, Casey had developed strategies for avoiding his roommate even in close proximity. Take now, for example, flying tens of thousands of feet above the surface of the earth in this passenger aircraft. The two were seated next to each other, with Casey looking down through the window, his headphones on, music blaring to ward off any possible conversation, and Reardon reading the repair manual for a Harley Davidson XR-1000.

It was a long flight, made longer by the pilot having to circle around SFO a few times while waiting for permission to land. Casey turned off the music and chewed a piece of gum as the plane descended toward the runway. Reardon leaned past Casey and peered through the window at the tawny ground below. "Good ol' Frisco," he said, spitting into his cup. "We meet again."

The team shuttle dropped them off at the Westin St. Francis. There was a flurry of activity as bellhops unloaded the shuttle van and ferried the ballplayers' belongings up to their rooms. Each man was given a key to their shared suite for the series. Casey was about to head up to the room when he felt a hand on his shoulder.

"Where ya goin', kid?"

"It's been a long day," he said. "I thought I'd get some sleep."

"There will be time for napping later."

"I'm really tired, man."

"You ever even been to 'Frisco?"

"No."

"Well then how can you in good conscience go up there and sleep?"

"Easy."

"Well, there won't be time for sightseeing tomorrow."

"Who says I wanna do any sightseeing at all?"

Reardon spat into his cup. "You know something, I know we ain't been on the best of terms lately and all, but that ain't no reason for you to be such a dickhead when I've got somethin' in mind."

What he had in mind was a storage locker out in East Palo Alto. Casey wasn't even particularly surprised when Reardon lifted the rolling garage door to find another mint Mk. I Golf, but he did wonder just how many of these caches this son of a bitch had lying around, waiting for the rainy day when Reardon might show up and make his claim.

"Good old locker 192," said the closer, running his fingers across the glossy black hood of the vehicle.

"Where are we going?" asked Casey, his hands in his pockets.

"What makes you think we're going somewheres?"

"Cut the shit. There's a car."

"The beach," said Reardon, spitting into his cup. "Where else?"

Off they blasted, back up the 101 towards San Francisco. They took exit 414B for the California 92 towards Half Moon Bay. At some point on the drive through the canyon, the uniformly blue sky turned grey and ominous, the temperature dropped, and they rolled up the windows. They drove past greenhouses before finally reaching the town of Half Moon Bay, where they took a left onto Highway 1 and passed signs for state parks and beaches, groves of cypress and oak, fruit stands, and fields of strawberries—fields that teetered over cliffs, threatening to slide into the ocean.

They drove until they reached a parking lot with a placard reading *Bean Hollow State Beach*. Stepping out of the car, Casey instantly felt cold. Goosebumps began to form. He rubbed his arms to warm himself.

"Here," said Reardon, offering Casey a rain jacket.

The two men took a narrow, winding path that skirted through patches of what Reardon assured Casey was poison oak. A pod of seals lazed on the jagged black rocks below, arfing half-hearted warnings to each other as the two men walked towards them without speaking. The sound of waves crashing against the rocks was constant, along with the cawing of gulls far larger than those back home. A squadron of brown pelicans flew low over the incoming waves, their flight indifferent to the stiff wind coming in off the water.

They found a staircase leading down to a beach that not only boasted its own bathroom, but also its own parking lot, making their little hike superfluous. They took off their shoes and left them next to a log by the staircase before stepping down to the water's edge. With every lapping wave, the water crept further and further up the beach towards their feet. The two men stood there gazing out at the ocean for some time before Reardon finally cleared his throat and said, "Don't it just make you wanna hit some rocks?"

"Yeah? Well we don't have a bat and there aren't any rocks."

"There's a few."

Casey said nothing.

"I guess not."

"You know something, Reardon? Cut the shit."

"What shit?" said Reardon, spitting into his cup.

"Quit pretending you're my friend."

"Is that what you think? That I'm pretending? Maybe I am. What of it? Even by just pretending, I'm probably the best friend you've ever had. I mean, yeah, I may have been pretending at first, but now it feels real, you know?"

"You don't quit, do you?"

"Never learned it."

"You should've."

"I'd be a little less judgmental if I were you, seeing as the only reason your ass is even on the team is because you were too big a dummy to even check whether or not the cocaine ya bought off some hood was real. Here I thought you were holdin' your shit together pretty good and then you go and pull something like that."

"I would've thought you'd approve."

"I wouldn't recommend your coke-addicted ass go and buy blow off some guy you met in the goddamned projects, ya nut."

"Well, if you've got a better connection, feel free to hook me up."

Reardon spat into his cup.

"Listen, kid, we've come a long way here. We're close to the finish line. I know things have been fucked up lately, but I need you to hold it together, for your sake as much as mine. You've been playing better. We're winning."

"It isn't just that."

"Then what? Lyuba? I told you to keep your nose out of it. You're the one who had to go and dig."

"Whatever you say."

"I mean, take some responsibility."

"That's rich," said Casey, picking up a rock. He chucked it out across the water, trying to skip it, but it just disappeared into a crashing wave.

"How ya figure?"

"Since you're all about taking responsibility, how about telling me what you're going to do about Lyuba?"

"What's there to do?"

"She's going to fucking kill you and she'll probably off me while she's at it."

"Instead of concentrating what little brain matter you have on ponderin' what the hell Reardon's gonna do, you oughta be worrying what *you* are going to do. If you want my advice, the best course of action is to pretend like nothing's happening and keep out of it. Let me worry about ol' Reardon. I mean, that should be easy enough, right? Seein' as we ain't friends anyway."

They didn't spend much more time together during their stay in San Francisco. In fact, Casey hardly ever saw the closer off the field outside of the few moments they happened to be in the hotel room at the same time. Casey was pissed that Reardon had squandered his afternoon by taking him to that stupid beach for no apparent reason while Manny and the Aucoin Twins had gone and gorged themselves on dungeness crab on Fisherman's Wharf.

"Ah. C'est bon, mon ami. C'est bon."

Casey didn't play well in the Oakland series. In eighteen plate appearances, he only managed a a single hit and got clunked by a pitch, while the rest of the team cranked out a staggering thirty-two runs. To make matters worse, he lost a few pop ups in the lights, turning free outs into mere foul balls. The strikeouts? Forget about it. It seemed he no sooner stepped to the plate than he came back shaking his head in consternation. His frustration came to a head in game three when he struck out with the bases loaded to end the third. Instead of picking up his equipment from the bench, he walked straight down the dugout tunnel and smashed his bat to pieces before collapsing against the cement wall with his head in his hands.

"Man, what in the hell are you doing?" asked Steele, having come to check on him.

"I just need a minute."

"Commercial break's gonna be over before you even get your damned pads on."

"I said I just need a minute."

Steele sucked his teeth. "Man, whatever."

They went on to win the game 7-2.

It was a short flight from San Francisco to Denver, so they were able to get to the Westin by two in the morning. Dropping his bag in his room, Casey went out in search of the ice machine, as his elbow was still sore from the last game. Finding the correct alcove, he was surprised to see Eddie there, smacking the side of a vending machine.

"Damned thing just ate my Lincoln," he said, turning to Casey.

"Sorry," said Casey, fishing around in his pocket. "I don't have one."

"Don't worry about it. You here for ice?" asked Steele, gesturing toward Casey's bucket.

"Yeah."

"Somethin' hurt?"

"Nothing serious."

"Cool, man. Cool."

The two men stood there saying nothing for some time.

"So, I don't mean to pry or nothin', but what was that shit down in the tunnel today all about."

"What shit?"

"Oh, I don't know, the shit where you shattered your damned bat into a million pieces."

"Just letting off a little steam, I guess."

"Yeah?

"It was nothing, really."

"Sure didn't look like nothing to me."

"Look, I had a bad series."

"True enough."

"There's a lot going on."

"What, exactly, is going on?"

Casey said nothing.

"Your boy's probably got something to do with it, knowing him. That fool's always up to no good."

"I'd better get some sleep," said Casey, turning toward the hallway.

"Hold on. Don't go nowhere. I didn't mean nothing by it."

"See you tomorrow."

"Ain't you going to get some ice?"

To say that Casey liked hitting at Corona Field would be an understatement. He knew as soon as he sent a pitch the other way out of the park in batting practice that the ball was going to fly here. He finished the series with a pair of home runs and six doubles, going 12 for 16. He had to remind himself it was just one series. It didn't mean anything. He had to keep his focus and ignore Reardon as much as possible if he wanted to get out of this slump.

That last bit was easy enough. The only time Casey saw the closer during the series was at the ballpark. Where he went at night, what he was doing—Casey didn't know and didn't care. It was sweet relief to come back to the hotel room and find it empty, to be able to fall asleep without being blathered at for hours first.

In the mornings, he would get up and meet the Aucoin twins for the complimentary breakfast. The twins would load up on fried eggs, bacon, and toast, and spend the whole time bragging about the previous night's conquests. Much of this Casey couldn't understand, as the two often lapsed into French, forgetting—perhaps—that Casey couldn't speak it.

They gained an hour flying west to Los Angeles and Casey was able to get some much-needed sleep thanks to Reardon's absence. He didn't see the closer again until breakfast the next morning.

"How's it going, boys?" asked Reardon, approaching the table where Casey and Manny were in the middle of a game of cards.

"'Sup, Reardon?" said Manny, pounding Reardon's extended fist.

"Got yourselves a game of chance going, do ya?"

"What do you want?" asked Casey, laying his cards face down on the table.

"Say, Manny, you wouldn't mind me cutting short your game with old Casey here a few minutes, would ya? I'm giving him a ride to the park."

"Can I get a ride? The shuttle's taking forever."

"No—I mean, I would, but it's just that I've gotta talk with ol' Casey here about some bits of strategy and whatnot. You know how it is. You can't play your cards too close."

"I'd rather take the shuttle," said Casey, picking up his cards.

"Yo, is something going on?" Manny asked as they rode to Seraph Stadium in the shuttle.

"What do you mean?"

"I mean the way you talked to Reardon back there. I thought, *Damn. Casey is pissed.*"

"I'm just sick of his bullshit," said Casey.

"Still," said Manny, "he's your boy, you know?"

"Why? Because we're both from Scarborough? That's just a convenient narrative."

"No, because that motherfucker's had your back. He's an asshole, no doubt, but he's had your back since day one."

"Don't take this the wrong way, Manny," said Casey, looking out the window at the suburban desert landscape. "But you don't know what the fuck you're talking about."

Reardon finally secured his interview by already being there when Casey arrived at the hotel room after the game.

"What do you want, Reardon?" Casey asked, dropping his duffle bag to the floor.

"I think I've got it figured out."

"Figured what out?"

"Why Lyuba hasn't offed me yet. It's bad, Casey. Real bad."

"I don't want to know. You said it yourself: the less I know the better. Why do you suddenly want to keep me informed, huh?"

"So that's how it is now? Everything I say or do, you're going to put under the microscope?"

"Seems like I have to. Just looking after number one, right?"

The Birds swept the Seraphs and flew to Seattle where they stayed at the Fairmont Olympic, a grand old place with wood paneling in the lobby. Casey spent the time between breakfast and when the shuttle arrived lounging in the hotel's hot tub, staring up through the glass enclosure at the cloud-laden sky, thinking nothing. Time passed without notice until he was interrupted by his phone's alarm, letting him know it was time to head to the stadium.

Steele found Casey at his locker and asked if he might want to take a walk in the outfield with him—ostensibly to give him some pointers, places to aim for, and the like. This was unusual, and Casey wondered why Eddie was suddenly taking so much interest in him. But he agreed to the walk anyway, hoping there was some sincerity in the offer.

"You know something?" said Eddie, blowing a bubble as they walked the warning track. "I don't know why the ball don't fly here the same way it does other places, but it don't. Here them towering fly balls that would normally land in the bullpen, they just drop right in front of the fence, and that's if you're lucky. Most of the time the damned thing just ends up in the left fielder's mitt and the difference? Just three feet. I don't know if it's that we're at sea level down here or what, but the ball just won't fly."

"Shit," said Casey.

"Yeah. Shit," said Steele. "And the way teams've been defending you the past few series, you've basically been hitting over them and finding holes. That shit won't fly here at B-Cellular. I think you've gotta be thinking up the middle and the other way."

"Jesus. Most of the time I'm just trying to hit it."

"Outer half," said Steele. "You've gotta be thinking outer half. You gotta be thinking the other way."

"But I'm a pull hitter."

"Bitch, at the beginning of this season you wasn't even any sort of hitter. I mean, shit, you picked up hitting taters to left field quick enough. What makes you think you can't learn to hit no other way?"

"Nothing, I guess."

"It's all in your mentality. Are you the sort of motherfucker who knows who they are and is just gonna keep doing that? Or are you lookin' in all them little nooks and crannies to find where you can get better?"

"You're starting to sound like Reardon."

"Say that shit to me again and I'mma slap your ass all the way back Tuesday," said Steele, blowing another bubble.

Casey was able to cash a couple base-hits in game one, both going the other way, which forced Seattle to give up on the shift and go back to playing him straight up. In game two, he collected another hit—a home run—and a walk. Steele caught him by the arm in the Fairmont lobby to say, "See! Ain't it better going the opposite way." They made plans to meet at the hotel gym the next morning to work out.

The Fairmont's streamlined, modern equipment barely made a sound as the players pumped iron and rode stationary bikes. Steele taught Casey a few new stretches to lengthen his range of motion, and they capped their workout off with protein shakes and a soak in the tub.

"You know something?" said Steele, closing the cap on his plastic cup. "When you first arrived in camp? I thought you was some coked-out, cracker-ass punk, but it turns out you're aight."

"You weren't wrong. If you want to know the truth, if you put some coke in my hand right now, I probably wouldn't hesitate to do it."

"That's just nerves talkin'."

"What do you mean?"

"I mean that when a person really wants something like blow, there ain't much that's gonna stop 'em from gettin' it. Way I see it, is if you really wanted it, you probably would've already got it."

Casey gulped down some shake. "Yeah, maybe you're right."

"And there's been some extenuating circumstances, you feel me?"

"What extenuating circumstances?"

"Like your damned crazy fool of a roommate."

"He hasn't done anything lately."

"Exactly. He's too quiet. Motherfucker's got something cooking."

"Nah. He's harmless—too busy chasing records."

"But say he were up to something—"

"He's not up to anything," said Casey, wanting to tell Steele about Lyuba, the abductions, and the accusations—everything— just to get it off his chest. "Not that I'd know if he was. Son of a bitch doesn't keep me in the loop on anything, not even the damned play call."

The Aucoin twins hadn't been lying when they said B-Cellular was like home away from home. Every night the bleachers were a sea of blue jerseys with rowdy fans from Vancouver chanting, *Go-Birds-Go, Go-Birds-Go* and *Let's Go Blue Birds*. It caught Casey by surprise when *OK, Blue Birds* didn't come on during the seventh inning stretch. Autograph lines before the games were enormous and Casey signed so many balls, bats, and hats that his hand felt sore. The fans were so riled up they gave Hardy a standing ovation after he delivered five innings of three-run ball in game three.

Everybody was in a celebratory mood as the team's jet took off that afternoon. They played loud music over the stereo system and many of the players cracked beers to toast the successful road trip. They now found themselves first in the SL East standings for the first time since the start of the season. Reardon was the only player who wasn't on the flight.

Casey found the closer vacuum-sealing his crop at the kitchen table when he stepped into the apartment around midnight.

"You got back quick."

"Caught the first flight."

"And who's that for?" asked Casey, gesturing toward the weed. "Last I checked, the freezer was full."

"Friend's taking care of it."

"Friend?"

"Acquaintance then," said Reardon, spitting into his cup. "Who gives a shit? You asked for an explanation and now you're standing there busting my balls over the particulars."

"I'm sorry. It's just that I know how you like to exaggerate."

"You see what she's done to us? She's got us bickering like an old married couple. She's trying to isolate us. You know that, right? It makes us vulnerable."

"You mean it makes *you* vulnerable."

"What if it does? You keep forgetting that I stuck my neck out when nobody wanted nothin' to do with yas. I'm the reason you're even fuckin' here. Now you have the fuckin' gall to stand there, look me in the eye, and act like you're better than me or some shit? That's fuckin' rich, buddy."

"I don't think I'm better than anybody."

"Yeah? Well you're sure acting like you fuckin' do. You act like your past is so squeaky clean. I'll admit I've made some mistakes, but you're treating me like a goddamned leper just 'cause you got caught up in some shit. I mean, does it disqualify all I've done for you? Now you're saying we ain't friends and shit after I've treated you like family."

"Fuck, man," said Casey, sitting down at the table and brushing back his hair. "It's just there's been a lot of heat lately."

"Yeah," said Reardon, spitting into his cup.

"Well, what are you gonna do about it?"

"About what?"

"About Lyuba."

"To be honest, kid, fuck if I know."

HOME STRETCH

Fall had descended hard on the city by the third week of September. The heat was driven off by stiff, northwesterly winds that tore the leaves from the maples, oaks, sycamores and ash dotting boulevards and populating city parks. Beach-themed window displays were suddenly displaced by the mustards, browns, reds, and oranges that festooned the sleek plastic mannequins. Here they stood, miming, in a carefree sort of way, the determined gestures of the people trudging to-and-fro on the other side of the glass.

The cold air brought an end to the languid movement of summer and replaced it with the rigor of fall. The students were back in full force, decked out in their black pea coats, Jansport backpacks, and athletic shoes. Some could be seen wobbling home from parties and bars; others were up early, already heading to class, coffee in hand, ready for the lectures, tutorials, and shift-work that constituted their daily schedules.

Businesspeople, too, had found their way back from their summer trips and vacation properties. Anyone who saw them a few weeks ago, when they sported flannel shirts and cargo shorts as they canoed across the surfaces of perfectly still lakes, or swam the electric blue waters of some Caribbean island, or rode down the rapids of the Columbia River, would hardly recognize them now. They flooded out of Union Station, a swarm of men in black and navy suits and women in autumn-hued attire, the tails of their beige, black, and pink rain jackets fluttering behind them as they marched in columns, fanning out through the gridded streets toward their various places of employment.

TTC drivers now donned their maroon jackets. They could be seen walking in pairs along the station platforms, laughing at each other's jokes, and exchanging professional gossip as they stood holding still-steaming cups of coffee, waiting for the next train.

Young people on bikes rung their bells as they swerved out of the way of opening car doors, shouting *Watch it!* or worse over their shoulders, holding on to their backwards blue ballcaps for dear life. Walking past the bars, day or night, one could see men and women in Blue Birds apparel on the patios, laughing drunkenly, and taking in a game as they enjoyed these final days of tolerable weather before the dread cold of winter.

The Birds' phenomenal second half had made them the toast of the town. Outside of that minor three-game slump at the end of August, they'd been playing lights-out baseball in front of sold-out crowds every night. As they came into their final home stand of the season, they had increased their lead on the SL East by two games and now turned their attention to the slumping Regents and their league-leading 92 wins.

Reardon was everywhere you looked—on billboards, on evening newscasts, on bus stop advertisements. Wherever one went, one found young men of all backgrounds with long, sometimes patchy beards grown in imitation of Reardon's trademark neo-Spartan look. It was as if they thought that by growing a beard they could somehow tap into the source of the closer's magic.

And magic was the only word most could think of to describe Reardon's performance. Now that the season was drawing to a close, Reardon's earlier prediction of a perfect season was a foregone conclusion. The team's beat bloggers and television pundits were debating whether he was now one of the favourites to win the SL Cy Young. After all, there was a case to be made: he had already pitched 128.2 innings in relief and the season wasn't over yet; his ERA was still rock bottom, a true 0.00; and he had held opponents to twelve hits and no walks. Some even wondered if he might be considered for MVP due to his superb work with the stick and the incredible run the team had gone on when Reardon had taken over full-time as the DH.

Fans coming out to the games these days were rowdier and more opinionated than they had been all season. They hollered jibes at the opposing players. They stomped on the bleachers in appreciation of a big hit. When an umpire blew an obvious strike call and Lou walked out of the dugout to make his case, the fans made his case for him by screaming profanities and demanding the lousy bum of an ump be hauled off the field.

Even with everything going in the Blue Birds' favour, there was little room for error. At some point in August, the old-timers in the Sams clubhouse found a second wind and went on a big run, winning thirteen of seventeen and on pace with the Birds. Toronto had only just managed to maintain a two-game lead.

The Rebels were the Birds' last scheduled opponent, and they rolled into town for the first of a three-game set on September 28. The Rebels' new hands from Pawtucket hadn't let the team's elimination spoil the party. They'd just capped off a championship run before being called up at the end of the month, and continued where they'd left off. It was largely on the back of their offence that the Rebels had gone seven for their last ten.

But the Birds were not intimidated by the new look Rebels. In fact, everyone in the clubhouse expected to trounce these upstarts and lock down the division for keeps. The facility staff had wheeled in four massive steel troughs and filled them with ice and beer prior to the first game of the series. Champagne had been set out on a long rectangular table in a twenty-by-three array. White ski goggles had been laid out to shield the players' eyes from the corks that would inevitably be flying. When the team filed out of the locker room into the dugout, some players had even been cheeky enough to bring their goggles with them and sport the eyewear through the warmup. Who could blame them? Hardy was slated to start. He'd improved his numbers in the second half. The old, plucked goose was now doing slightly better than his typical 3.82 ERA. The full starting lineup—or as Tubs referred to them, the walking wounded—were playing. Several of the veterans were looking forward to a couple days of rest once the team clinched.

The game got off to a bad start when, with two outs in the top of the first, one of the Rebels' new hands, right-fielder Octavio Sanchez, came to the plate. Sanchez was getting his first cup of coffee in the Bigs after spending the past three years as Boston's top prospect. On the second pitch of the at-bat, Hardy missed his spot and the ball found the upper-inside portion of the strike zone, well out over the plate. Sanchez didn't miss the mistake, keeping his elbows in as he swung and drove the ball hard to left. It carried deep, forcing Hernandez to give chase all the way to the wall, only to watch the ball sail into the visitors' bullpen.

Long-time Rebels' slugger, Manny Olivio, then stepped up to the plate. He had been one of the few holdouts from July 31's mass exodus. Indeed, even though this was probably his final season, it would have been almost unthinkable to trade him. The three-time MVP had done it all: he'd been a playoff hero, won the Globe Series, and been its most valuable player. So when Olivio asked the team before the trade deadline to allow him the opportunity to retire as a member of the Rebels, the front office didn't even bother to ask him if he would reconsider.

Stepping into the batter's box, Olivio balanced the knob of his bat against his crotch, spat into his gloved hands, and rubbed them together as he stared Hardy down with his glinty yellow eyes. The two had faced off more than sixty times over the years, and the result usually came down to not who played the better game of chess, but simply who executed their game plan better, meaning it all hinged upon whether or not Chet was able to spot his pitches.

It wasn't Chet's night. At first, it appeared he was getting the better of Olivio. He'd started off the slugger 0-2 with a pair of fastballs. Then Casey called for the slider down and away, hoping to get the punchout. The problem was, that slider just hung over the plate like a piñata, and Olivio smashed it the other way along the third base line where it fell just fair before scampering into foul territory.

Hernandez had to hustle from the shift in left-centre in order to get to the ball. Olivio, meanwhile, had already stepped on first and was well on his way to second. The DH had to stop there as Hernandez came up with the ball and threatened to make a throw. That ended the play, leaving the one-day Hall of Famer standing in scoring position.

Casey looked at the dugout, shook his head, and called for a changeup on the next pitch, figuring that was the only one they hadn't tried. That too managed to hang and get clobbered for the second home run of the inning. The next batter, sixth in the order, they managed to pop out to centre.

Those three first-inning runs would prove fatal, as not only would they be piled upon over the next four frames, but the Birds were so deflated by the trouncing that the casual observer might be forgiven for thinking they'd forgotten how to hit. The only two Bird hits came off Casey's bat in the third and seventh innings, by which point nobody was wearing their goggles anymore.

When the players returned to the clubhouse, all the ice and liquor were gone, quietly stowed away somewhere while the team was busy getting curb-stomped. Nobody seemed to mind or notice. After all, they would probably clinch tomorrow.

But the next day the Blue Birds didn't fare much better. The team got off to another rocky start when Ordoñez gave up four runs in the first—a deficit from which the Birds wouldn't recover. They ended up losing 8-2.

The atmosphere in the locker room for game three was decidedly more somber. Everyone arrived early at the park that morning, and Steele—who was so far 0/10 in the series with four strikeouts—was the first. He and his personal hitting instructor spent all morning down in the cage making an adjustment to his swing to help him get a better handle on the fastballs up and inside that Boston had been smothering him with the whole series. They set up a pitching screen in one of the batting cages so that its edge sat just about in the middle of home plate, where it obstructed Steele's swing path if he didn't keep the barrel of the bat over the inside part of the plate.

The only people who dared to wear a pair of goggles for game three of the series were a few September call-ups, but they quickly put them away when Reardon instructed them to knock it the fuck off. All the good humour that had saturated the locker room in the preceding days and weeks was gone now that New York was threatening to take the division.

Don could do nothing but watch as the team let their slim lead in the standings disappear. And now the threat of being bounced down to the first wildcard position? This was simply too much. The mob was already sharpening its farm implements, and those in the media could already be heard murmuring the word *choke*. The Birds' general manager couldn't help but wonder if this could really be the end. After all the sacrifices, all the hours, all the effort put into transforming this team into a winner, would he really wind up emptyhanded? It left a bad taste in his mouth to think about this contingency and what it would mean for him personally, spiritually, and professionally. One thing was certain: if the team didn't pull out of this tailspin, Don would never get the opportunity to run another ball club. Just the thought of working in a diminished role, say as assistant to the head of scouting—or worse, as a regular rank-and-file scout—for some other team appalled him. That sort of humiliation could not be tolerated.

The radio shows were abuzz. Angry fans who had called for Don's head at the beginning of the season were dialing in once again. They claimed Don should have sold what was left of the farm at the deadline to bring in some pieces to bolster the roster. He should have brought in a starting pitcher to replace the rapidly decaying Chet Hardy. Of course, had such a deal been available, Don would have jumped on it in a heartbeat.

This was the way these things went. You bust your ass for years, give your life to the team, and in the end they run you out of town based on a bunch of what-ifs and nonsense. This was the lifecycle of your run-of-the-mill Big League general manager, and he'd been fool enough to believe he was above it.

Susan came in carrying a bottle of Prosecco.

"Good news," she said.

Don looked at the bottle like it was a hand grenade.

"Get that out of here."

"You're almost as superstitious as they are," said Susan, nodding her head towards the field. "Don't worry, I'm not going to open it until after we've locked up the division."

"What makes you so sure we'll lock it up?"

"The Rebels decided to rest Bargain. They've got Spencer pencilled in for tonight."

"Why would they do that?"

Susan winked. "I guess they hate the Sams more than they hate us."

"Evidently," said Don. "But it doesn't mean anything. The way our boys have been playing, we could still lose this in a blowout."

The game certainly didn't get off to an ideal start. Boston's centre-fielder hit a leadoff double off Clessinger and made it to third on a fielder's choice. Sanchez followed that up with a home run to dead centre. Clessinger managed to get out of the inning on a pair of ground balls, but the damage had been done. All Don could do was bite his fingernails and watch.

Thankfully, the Rebels' starter was, as predicted, ineffective. The Birds were able to tie it with two runs in the bottom half of the second inning. Casey hit a lead-off single along the right field baseline to beat the shift, bringing up Cruz, who walked after working the count full, so that there were baserunners on first and second. Next, Thompson took a first-pitch curveball into the right field alley for a bases-clearing double. Don groaned as he watched Thompson get thrown out by falling flat on his face while trying to get back to the bag on a check throw. The next two batters struck out swinging to end the inning.

More fireworks followed in the fifth, when Boston knocked Clessinger out of the game with four consecutive doubles. Lou called on Patrice to face the three upcoming righties and Patrice delivered with three strikeouts to strand the runner on second.

Don had shut the window some time ago and was now watching the game on TV with the sound muted. His hand shook as he mechanically raised his coffee cup to his lips and watched his team crumble.

"I just knew something like this would happen," he said.

"The game's not over," said Susan.

Sure enough, the Blue Birds came back in the bottom half, plating three runs to bring them even. That's how it remained until the bottom half of the eighth, when Reardon crushed a full-count fastball into the seats in right. After the closer finished running the bases, he trotted out to the bullpen and started warming up. When he came out to pitch in the top of the ninth, he was met with much fan appreciation, and made short work of the Boston rookies, striking out the side.

Don could hear the crowd explode seconds before he saw the final strike land in Casey's glove. He couldn't help but stand and pump his fist along with the umpire. Tears welled in his eyes as he watched the team exchange high-fives and make a slow exit toward the dugout. Sharon Mao had pulled Reardon aside for a post-game interview, but Don couldn't hear the question or answer; all he could hear was the muted howl of the crowd as it seeped through the concrete, the pop of the cork as Susan opened the Prosecco, and the tinkling of bubbly as it was poured into the glass.

Down in the locker room, it was mayhem. The goggles were back on and the champagne was being uncorked and sprayed over the throng of players decked out in matching Division Championship t-shirts. Lou sat with his feet on a stool, a fat cigar in one hand and a tumbler full of scotch in the other. The twins busied themselves with seeing who could shotgun the most beers consecutively, while the rest of the players butchered a round "Alouette". Tubs was downing daiquiri after daiquiri from the comfort of the locker room hot tub. Manny Singh was the first— and last—to volunteer to do a keg stand. The Dominican players were all gorging on Hernandez's mother's rice and beans, which they washed down with bottles of Presidente. Everybody was having a great time—that is, except for Casey and Reardon, who had snuck out of the Dome and were now cruising along the DVP in the direction of the 401. They had to wake up early. They had shit to do.

POSTSEASON

The Blue Birds' SLDS opponents were the Texas Gunslingers, who had clinched the SL West weeks ago, finishing 4 games ahead of Oakland, who had held on, just barely, to the second wildcard spot. By putting their boots to the Sportsmen in the Wildcard Game, New York advanced to the SLDS against Kansas City.

Toronto had dominated the season series against the Gunslingers 6-1, so nobody was too worried about them. They were more troubled by who they would have to face next. It wasn't that they were looking past the Gunslingers. Far from it: they were adhering to the old cliché of *one game at a time,* but the hard numbers showed the teams matched up in a way that could only be described as favourable for the Birds. The same could not be said for the Regents or the Sams. The Birds records against those teams was a wash, with the Birds holding a slight advantage over the Sams at 10-9 and having tied their season series against the Regents 3-3.

Even with the favourable first round matchup, the team came to the ballpark with a purpose. They were by now all VR rats, with most of the hitters forgoing on-field batting practice during home games in favour of an extra hour wearing the headset. They had spent the days leading up to game one of the SLDS hammering every pitcher on the Gunslingers' staff and were thus confident they could beat their opponent, so long as the pitching held up. It helped that the first two games were scheduled to be played in Toronto, with the next two in Arlington and, if it came to it, a Game 5 back in Hogtown.

Fans in Canada were not happy with the scheduling. Social media was abuzz with angry Birds fans complaining about Toronto drawing the short straw. Games One and Two were set to begin at 1:07 PM EST on the Monday and Tuesday, while games Three and Four in Arlington were set for 4:05 PM EST. While Texas fans assumed this was no more than the legendary eastern bias in sports media, Blue Birds fans took it as a slight. Of course the league would schedule games in the least desirable timeslot for the Birds' first playoff run in nearly a quarter century. It was typical that those who wished to watch the games would have to play hookie from work. That was only sensible, wasn't it? It was only fair.

Coinciding with the Gunslingers' arrival in Toronto on the eve of Game One, there was a marked increase in media presence in and around the clubhouse. So far, the reporters had mostly left Casey alone. They were too busy hounding his teammates for interviews and one-liners. Still, they did press him for comments, they did holler questions at him as he walked into the clubhouse, and they did expect him to respond. Casey kept it light, sticking to the scripted responses he practiced in the mirror each morning.

Unfortunately, a lot of the questions were about Reardon—what he liked about Reardon, what he thought about Reardon's pitches, what he thought of Reardon as a teammate—Reardon, Reardon, Reardon. It was the name on the tip of everybody's tongue. There were no scripted responses for these questions, so Casey would say what he thought everybody wanted to hear: that Reardon's stuff was the best he'd ever seen and that Reardon led by example, modelling for other players in the clubhouse how to be a top-level big leaguer.

"And what about you?" asked one reporter.

"Me?

"Yes. After all, you two are roommates at home and on the road. What is the closer like in private? You know, when there aren't any cameras around."

"Just the same as when they are around."

But Reardon wasn't the same at home as he was on the field, at least not anymore. He spent all his time in his workshop hammering away. He didn't leave the house and had hired more of the hallway's kids to run errands for him. Casey could tell Reardon was afraid by the way he checked behind doors for intruders and under his car for unwanted devices.

But as soon as they were back in front of the cameras, back would come the old braggadocio:

"Horseshit," Reardon said to a question about the scheduling of the SLDS. "Pure horseshit, not to mention typical."

"What do you mean by typical?" the reporter asked, extending her cell phone towards him.

"I mean," said Reardon, spitting into his cup, "that it's typical American horseshit, is what it is. Of course, we Canucks are used to it. We're always playing second fiddle to these Sam assholes. I mean, being born Canadian is about the same as being born a second-class citizen in the eyes of an American. Don't believe me? Just ask one. Nobody oughta be surprised they bumped us down to daytime television to compete with fuckin' *Maury* and *Ellen*. Just another jab in the rib from our so-called allies."

"You're making it sound like this is some sort of foreign relations crisis."

"Ain't it?"

This created a stir almost immediately. ESPN and SI simultaneously published articles claiming that the Blue Birds star closer was an anti-American bigot. Others wrote that this recent blow-up was evidence that he was some sort of extremist. While the American media blew its collective lid, the Canadian media and fans ate it up. Viewing parties numbering in the tens of thousands were organized to take place in public parks, squares, arenas, and football stadiums across the country, and many of the eventual attendees would arrive draped in Canadian flags as often as Blue Birds gear.

Steele, meanwhile, had to field questions relating to his future with the club. Around the end of August, the beat reporters had begun publishing articles discussing this very topic and these pieces were growing more regular, bloated and speculative by the day. Now it seemed like every time he agreed to an interview, or to answer a few questions shouted by the pack of reporters constantly tailing him, he was inevitably asked whether he would re-sign with the team. That was just fine with Steele and his agent. It meant the reporters desperately wanted him to stay and would take up his cause against the corporation in this battle for public opinion.

Lou found himself even busier than usual. Along with all the gameplanning, scheduling, and preparation, he was now expected to make the rounds of the various local and American sports talk shows. He was forced to spend at least an hour each morning answering questions about the upcoming series via teleconference. Most of it was bullshit, just him smiling and nodding and a few *gee, fellas* as people asked how great it must feel to be managing the Blue Birds. A few brave reporters had the temerity to ask about comments he had made in Spring Training about the team being a bunch of losers, etc., to which Lou responded with threats and profanity.

The team's PR took hit after hit after hit. In the days leading up to Game One a new fear began to dawn on the General Manager: that perhaps his team could not withstand the magnification of the postseason. Surely, any crack in the armour was bound to be exposed under such intense scrutiny. Who knew what would come of any of it?

When he expressed these fears to Susan, she laughed and told him he was being an idiot.

"Do you see what's happening out there? We're getting murdered."

"Not in our market. Eddie's the one who's going to end up with egg on his face."

"What makes you so sure?"

"Because the fans won't blame ownership. It's easier to blame the greedy player who left for money."

"And what about Reardon?"

"If anything, his comments have actually improved our chances of signing him. Americans can't stand him."

"I'm afraid we Americans aren't as thin-skinned as you Canadians. They'll all forget once he's put on their uniform," said Don, leaning back and sipping his coffee. "All the same, he isn't very good at this contract negotiation thing, is he?"

"He isn't helping his brand, let's put it that way."

"On the contrary, he just knows where his bread is buttered. Part of me hopes all these scandals really are nothing but some sort of national theatre to appeal to pub-goers and farm yokels. You know, all it would take is one serious scandal right now and we could kiss this season goodbye."

"God," she said, palming her face. "You're being such a baby."

The Dome was an absolute gongshow at the start of Game One. Fans who'd lined up at the gates hours before opening were still waiting to enter the stadium as the first pitch was being thrown. Reporters were everywhere, lurking in corridors with microphones, cameras, and phones at the ready to capture any potential behind-the-scenes action.

Casey stood with his hands behind his back. If he had been asked to speak, he wouldn't have been able to. There was a lump in his throat that couldn't be cleared. It was true the team had been playing in front of sell-out crowds for the past two months, but none of those games had felt anything like this. The lights were brighter, the field greener, the fans louder. Standing out here on the baseline, he'd never felt more exposed.

He was torn from his thoughts by the sudden calling of his name over the PA system. He stepped forward, raising his hand and smiling what must have appeared an incredibly false smile. He felt relieved as he stepped back to the baseline.

The fans began to lose it long before Reardon's name was read, but when he finally stepped out of the line the whole stadium went crazy. The noise, amplified by the closed dome, made the very air vibrate. Looking across the diamond, Casey saw several opposing players cast nervous glances at the crowd.

This being the playoffs, the ceremonies at the start of the game took a considerable amount of time, so that first pitch was almost twenty-minutes behind schedule, but still—as said before—well ahead of the last fan entering the stadium. Amuro was to be the first pitcher to take the mound for the Blue Birds, and this decision was made mostly due to rest and Amuro being the hottest hand on the staff. It was a decision that Lou was not altogether comfortable with, but what was he supposed to do when the starting rotation had been the team's achilles heel all season long?

Everyone knew going into the series that there were going to be fireworks. Both teams had finished top five in the SL in runs scored and in the bottom-half in runs allowed by starting pitching. The one area where Toronto had a definite edge was in the relief corps, which ranked the best in the States League by FIP-, ERA, WHIP and a host of other metrics.

Watching the players take the field from his office, Don only felt dread. Inside, hidden from any potential onlookers by his cold, emotionless exterior, he was tied up in knots of worry and anxiety. He mentally rehearsed all the different nightmare scenarios that might occur out there on the field as he sipped whiskey from a tumbler.

There was a knock on the door.

"Come in."

"Is now a good time?"

It was Howard.

"Good a time as any. Come in, take a seat."

"Are you... drinking, sir?"

"Why not? It's all in the hands of fate now."

"What's all in the hands of fate?"

"Everything. Come on in and pour yourself a drink."

"I don't think I should."

"First rule of business, my boy," said Don, unstopping the decanter and filling a second tumbler. "Never say no when the boss asks you to sit down and take a drink."

Howard took a few polite sips before putting the tumbler down.

"I wanted to talk about the Steele contract."

"Well then it ought to be a short conversation," said Don, taking a long sip of his whiskey.

"We need to get out in front of this thing. These comments he's making are killing us."

"It's all just posturing," said Don, glancing down into his suddenly empty tumbler before pouring himself a refill. "Besides, what way is there to spin it? The picture they're painting is cheap ownership doesn't want to pay the money necessary to put a quality product on the field, and what can we say? He's right."

"We could mention that he's turned down multiple offers."

"An old trick and a bad one. Especially so if the details were to somehow get leaked. They would be exposed as the truly unserious, low-ball offers they were."

"We could use his own tactic against him and demonize him in the media."

"Doesn't make for a very good look. It's never productive when laundry gets aired in front of the media. No, Howard. It won't do. After all, what we want to do is re-sign the man."

"But—"

"Howard, believe me when I say there is nothing left to do but take a drink. You're right, we could slander him, but what good would that do? The last thing we need is our best player distracted by public contract negotiations. That sort of thing could lead to Eddie second-guessing his loyalties and becoming demotivated."

"But—"

"Damn it, Howard, don't you understand? I know what you're going to say: we need to do something. We need to get ahead, otherwise we'll look like fools come free agency. But I'll let you in on a little secret"—here Don hiccupped—"there won't be any free agency for us if we don't go and win it all."

"You're drunk."

"Doesn't make me wrong," said Don, sipping from his drink.

"Give me that," said Howard, snatching the glass. "How often do you do this, Mr. Billingsley?"

"This is the first time in… ten! Ten years," said Don with a big grin on his face.

"I don't think you should leave this office, Mr. Billingsley. At least not until the game is over."

"Who said I wanted to leave. Eh, my boy? I do say, I practically live here anyway."

Howard broke into a sweat.

"Listen," the head of communications hissed. "I need you to stay put. Do you understand? There are too many reporters around for you to be wandering around drunk. You just sit down here and watch the ballgame. Can you do that for me?"

"For you, Howard? Anything."

It was some time before Don realized Howard had left the room. The game had already started. By his best reckoning of the scoreboard he thought it must be the seventh inning, although it may have been the fifth. It was hard to say. He was drinking whiskey straight from the decanter now. He heard the door open.

"Whaddya want?"

"It's me," came Howard's voice.

Don turned from the field to greet his visitors.

"Holy shit," said Tom after taking one look at his boss. "Dude's slammered."

"I'll have you know," said Don, raising his index finger. "That I am the president of the Toronto Blue Birds!"

"Not for long, buddy," said Tom.

"I need you to take him home. Nobody can see him like this," Howard said.

"How the hell am I supposed to get him out of here without anybody noticing? It's like goddamned D-Day down there."

"Take him down the utility stairwell and circle back to the garage. I'll radio security to clear the way. Just move. The sooner Mr. Billingsley is out of here, the better."

Don lay face-down across the backseat of the Rolls. The cold leather felt good against his skin. A rivulet of drool trickled from the corner of his mouth as he sometimes mumbled, sometimes shouted, sometimes sang while Tom sat in the front seat staring stoically through the windshield.

Whenever Don opened his eyes, the cabin of the car spun, so he kept them shut. Inside, it felt like his guts were boiling. Hot molten lava rose up his esophagus and filled his cheeks before finally building enough pressure to erupt onto the seat and carpet of the car.

Tom slammed on the brakes, causing Don to spill over the seat into the well, where he lay face down in his own vomit. The chauffeur turned around and shook his head when he saw where Don had wound up. He discovered his boss wasn't moving by poking his side.

"Shit," Tom said, signaling right and pulling over. He got out of the car and cautiously opened the rear door. "Mr. Billingsley?"

Don moaned in response.

Tom rolled his boss back onto the seat and overcame Don's feeble resistance to check his mouth for foreign objects. Finding nothing, the chauffeur stepped back from the car and ran his fingers through his hair, allowing himself to exhale. "You son of a bitch," he said. "You son of a bitch."

They reached Don's building without further incident. Mercifully, there wasn't a soul to be seen in the garage. Tom got out of the car and opened the rear door again to find Don just where he'd left him. The chauffeur was now able to get a better look at the damage: the leather was no big deal, that could be wiped off, but the large orange-brown spot that by now had probably worked its way deep into the carpet's fibres? "Fuck," he said, taking a step back from the smell. A moment out here in the garage's fresh air had been enough to re-sensitize him to it.

"My boy," said Don, trying to raise himself up on his elbows before failing and falling back down.

"Up you get," said Tom, pulling Don into a seated position. "Up you get, big guy. There you go."

As they walked away from the car through what appeared to be a violently undulating garage, Don asked, "To what godforsaken hell have you—hic—taken me?"

"We're at your condo building, Mr. Billingsley."

"Ah, Tom," said Don, slumping down against his driver. "You're a good lad. Have I... have I told you that?" He hiccuped.

"You won't stop telling me."

"Do you understand? A good egg!"

"Thank you, Mr. Billingsley."

"I live on the one millionth floor," said Don, breaking into a giggle as they stepped onto the elevator. Tom pressed the button for the Penthouse and swept his fob against the sensor to make the thing work. Don stared at his pale reflection in the mirror.

"I've grown old, Tom."

Tom was relieved when the elevator door opened and he was able to lead his boss back to his unit. It was a pain in the ass getting this fat son of a bitch to bed, but Tom did it and rewarded himself with a hit from his vaporizer as he went and got Don a glass of water. When he returned, Don was still lying as he had left him.

"Sit up, Mr. Billingsley."

"A good lad," mumbled Don, letting Tom pour some water into his quivering maw.

"Drink up, it will help."

The chauffeur was about to get up and leave when Don said, "Wait!"

"What is it, Mr. Billingsley?"

"The score?"

Tom took his phone out of his pocket and checked. "Looks like you won."

"We won!"

"We won, Mr. Billingsley."

"Let's have ourselves a drink!" said Don, attempting to sit up.

"I think you've had enough. You're pretty drunk, man."

"Man!" said Don mockingly. He fell back on the bed. "Man!"

"Goodnight, Mr. Billingsley."

According to Don's phone, it was 8:47 AM. How could it be so late in the day? It must be mistaken. After sitting unplugged all night it was down to five percent, so perhaps there had been some error? A quick check of his messages let him know this was not the case. There was a text from Tom, received at 6:28 AM, saying he'd come by and been unable to wake him. He was supposed to text Tom when he got up.

He couldn't remember anything after Howard had entered his office and sat down for a drink. Whatever muscles, tendons, veins, and ligaments were in his head had turned against him and were attempting to crush his skull through sheer constriction. His throat was raw and hot from he knew not what. He drank four glasses of water, but they did no good, so he brewed himself a coffee. The thought of food made him feel ill.

Soon Tom arrived with a six-pack of donuts and a smirk on his face. "How you feelin' this morning, boss?"

"How do you think I'm feeling?"

"I brought you something."

Don looked at the box, skeptically. "You expect me to eat that?"

The donuts and coffee proved good medicine. Don wondered if this explained the immense popularity of this country's coffee chain for the rabble. He still felt terrible, it was true, but at least now he could function, even if in a reduced capacity.

He gasped when Tom opened the rear door of the Rolls. In the seat well, below where Don normally sat, was a pale orange blotch.

"Heavens! What on earth happened here?"

"You puked on it."

Don raised his hand to his mouth as he gazed ruefully at the stain.

"I took it to a cleaner this morning. They said this was the best they could do."

"Tom, I believe I owe you an apology."

"You don't owe me anything," said Tom. "Just get in the car."

"Really though," said Don as they were driving down Davenport Avenue. "There has to be something I can do for you."

Tom thought this over a moment.

"Well there is one thing."

"What's that?"

"It's just something I've always wanted to know."

"What's that?"

"What's with the fake British accent?"

"I'm not sure what you mean."

"I mean," said Tom. "Why the hell do you speak with a fucking British accent when you're from New York?"

"Brewerton."

"What's that supposed to mean?"

"It's the boarding school for boys in Connecticut, where I was educated. We all spoke like that."

"That's it? A fucking *boarding* school?" said Tom. "How about weekends off?"

"You had your chance," said Don, typing something into his phone.

Nobody looked up from their desk when Don walked into the office five hours later than usual. He had expected sniggering, an elephant in the room, but as he stepped over the threshold there was nothing. Evidently they didn't find it particularly disagreeable that he was arriving so late. Everybody just kept on with business as usual, and this felt very strange, considering Don had gotten blackout drunk at work the evening before.

He was no sooner seated behind his desk than Howard and Susan stepped into his office. Howard locked the door behind them and the two approached cautiously, their lips curled into forced smiles as they sat down.

"What's this all about?"

"You tell us," said Susan, crossing her arms.

"Your—let's call it an episode—yesterday, could have got ugly," said Howard.

"I mean," said Susan. "You're so preoccupied with this paranoia. You're scared shitless that Reardon is going to cause a scandal, but last night you nearly walked into one yourself."

"What Susan is trying to say," said Howard, "is that you can't be acting that way during the postseason. What if someone had seen you?"

"Does anybody else know?" asked Don, rubbing his eyes.

"Only us, Tom, and a few security guards," said Susan.

"Very good," said Don. "Let's keep it that way."

In the heat of being interrogated so immediately after his arrival, Don had forgot to take out his phone and place it on his desk, so that now it rumbled against his chest. He pulled it out and read the text:

meet 2nite 7:30. ur condo

"Are you okay?" asked Susan after some time had passed. "You look kind of pale."

Why tonight?

"I must still be recovering," said Don, recomposing himself, "from having over-imbibed."

got the info u wanted

"Maybe you should take the night off," said Howard. "Get some rest."

Alright. Make sure you're not followed.

"You know, I think you're right," said Don, putting down his phone.

"Really?" said Howard, his face betraying a certain surprise. "I mean, you definitely should."

"You don't think it will be a bad look?"

"Not if you give everyone the night off," said Susan.

Don pretended to spend some time thinking about it, before finally instructing his subordinates to make it so.

The early dismissal was an easy request to grant on account of the game being played so bloody early. It was a welcome reprieve for Don's staff, who worked eighty, sometimes one hundred hours a week, which was nothing compared to the number of hours Don himself spent on baseball-related activities.

Not that this was any vacation for Don—far from it. He didn't know what to do with himself when he wasn't working, so he'd no sooner applied the hot compress Tom had prepared to his forehead than he'd begun thinking of different scenarios, emails he could be sending, affairs needing his attention. Laying here with this ridiculous hot handtowl on his forehead like some sort of invalid, all he wanted to do was get back to work.

It wasn't the same for Howard or Susan. They both had families, families they probably felt like they didn't spend enough time with—were neglecting, if everyone was being honest. They both relished this opportunity, surely. A few hours off to spend with the kids—time one could never get back. That was the main difference between Don and his subordinates. It was one of the many reasons they had probably risen as far as they ever would.

But at least they still had a future, limited though it may be. Don had lately begun to suspect that none of this—his efforts, the playoffs, even winning the damned Globe Series—none of it mattered. It was ineffectual. It would change nothing. He was sunk. After all, hadn't they committed to his replacement the second they began sending out feelers on potential candidates? Would a trophy even be enough to shake the board's resolve? Don knew if he were sitting on the opposite side of the boardroom table, it wouldn't be enough for him. His underlings at least had the hope that they might be retained by Don's replacement. For Don, his only way out of this mess was for the team to win it all. Then some ownership group might be desperate enough to give the man who built the Globe Series champions a shot. But wasn't that putting the cart before the horse? The odds of this team even reaching the Globe Series—let alone winning it—were suboptimal. Just because they beat up on Texas in games One and Two didn't mean they would have such an easy time with whoever they faced in the SLCS. Then again, who knew? Perhaps Texas wasn't down and out yet. Maybe they still had a comeback left in them to render all Don's handwringing for nought.

His visitor was punctual, arriving at exactly 7:30. Don buzzed him up and poured himself a club soda while he waited. Eventually he heard a knock on the door and walked over to let his guest inside. There was something greasy, distasteful about the man he had hired to spy on Reardon. His hair—which he kept pulled back in a ponytail—looked like it hadn't been washed in weeks and he wore a long grey trench coat, like a flasher. Thankfully, the man was fully clothed under his trench, albeit shabbily, and wore a utility belt which held a number of what Don presumed to be surveillance devices. He was a fat man, acned, bad teeth. His belly protruded from his too-tight sweater, which was probably purchased years before he had morphed into a slob. There was a mustard stain on his jeans. He was, in a word, pathetic.

How had Don found this disgusting person? Through the internet, where else? There had been a website detailing his services: infidelity, location of missing persons, unsolved crimes, fraud, process serving, the list went on; a small bio page with pictures of this slob in police uniform. He looked younger in these photos, but still disheveled, uncouth.

The man walked right into Don's living room without even taking off his shoes and flopped down on the Italian leather sofa.

"I was starting to think I wouldn't hear from you," said Don, sipping from his club soda.

"Always follow up on work paid."

Don had almost forgotten that he'd paid this man thousands of dollars, against Susan's advice—or rather, before he had solicited her advice—to spy on Reardon and let Don know if anything was afoot. But now that the man was here, the deed presumably done, Don was overcome with a sincere sense of regret.

"Very good," said Don, adding hopefully, "I assume everything's in order."

"Not quite," said the PI, pulling out his cellphone.

"Is Reardon up to something?"

The PI extended his arm to show Don what was on the phone's screen: a picture of Casey standing in front of a door to a derelict looking abode shadowed by two men in black suits, waiting to be let inside.

"What's this?"

"This is a photo I took near the end of August. Had to do a bit of legwork to figure out why two armed thugs were leading

Casey to this place," said the PI, zooming in on the gun held in the larger thug's hand. "Found out the house is owned by one Lyuba Ivanovna Svidrigailova. I did some digging and it turns out her family has Russian mob ties, that this woman is of some notoriety. People I talked to seemed scared of her."

"What sort of business does she run out of there?"

"Hard to be sure. What I can tell you is that people are constantly in and out of the place. Outside of that, all I've got is hearsay. It sounds like she's mostly into gambling and drugs, although I haven't seen anything being moved around."

"Drugs, you say?"

The PI nodded.

"What about Phillip?"

"Mostly a homebody. Doesn't leave his apartment except to run errands and go to the ballpark. Keeps destroying the bugs I've planted, so it's been tough getting any dirt."

"What do you mean, destroying?"

"As in I plant them, he finds them, and then he breaks them."

"Jesus, so you mean he knows we're watching him?"

"He definitely knows that *someone*'s watching him, but I doubt he's put two and two together yet. There's another photo, I took it later that night."

The PI swiped to another image, this one of Casey kneeling on the ground. Next, a video of Casey running down the pavement barefoot.

"Jesus," said Don, covering his mouth. "What the hell is he doing?"

"They threw him out on the sidewalk like that."

"Could just be a love affair," said Don.

"Quite the lady to fall in love with," said the PI, tapping a pack of cigarettes against his knee.

"You don't suppose he's frequenting a crackhouse, do you?"

"Hard to say," said the PI. "But given his history it can't be ruled out entirely. What I can tell you is that he hasn't been back since. You'd think he'd eventually go back if he were using."

"What then?"

"Your guess is as good as mine," said the PI. "It's something, though."

Don thought he would be glad when this filthy buffoon finally removed himself from the condo, but once he'd shut the door he immediately wished for the fool to return. Alone with his thoughts, he was overcome with fear. He was fucked. What had he been thinking, hiring a private investigator to spy on one of his players? It was one thing to hire sports psychologists, trainers and coaches with an eye to their potential as informants. It was another thing entirely to out-and-out snoop. The players didn't take kindly to that.

It was only now that he fully understood the exposure he'd risked in hiring this man. People would think he was some sort of crook if this came out. All this time he had been driven by his compulsion to know, but what good was knowing now? A few crummy photos of Casey standing out front of a house happening to belong to some local criminal, or whatever this Lyuba woman perported to be. It was circumstantial at best and misleading at worst. After all, what proof did he have that the boy was back on the wagon? Had his play suffered any for it? Whatever the truth was, it wasn't worth the pursuit—not with the potential fallout for those around him. As he lay down in bed he promised himself he was done with this paranoid nonsense. It could go no further.

Toronto entered Game Three in a position to eliminate Texas on their home turf. They'd won Games One and Two the best way they knew how: by hitting a ton of dingers. They had already hit eight home runs in the series and Casey felt fortunate to be the owner of two of them. The catcher was off to a hot start, batting 6 for 12.

Don forbade the team's VR equipment from crossing the border, so the players prepared as much as they could while still in Toronto. Casey spent almost four hours taking at-bats against the faceless Game Three starter. Near the end, he started making contact and felt like he was seeing the ball better, but his average was still abysmal no matter what statistical sample you cherrypicked.

"You know," Reardon said on their flight down to Arlington, "the machine can only tell you what the pitcher would normally do—what would happen in your usual, run-of-the-mill situation. One thing the machine won't never tell you is what's actually gonna happen. And even if it could, so what? I say fuck it. Show that fucker the future's yours for the making."

Casey stared at his roommate blankly. Things were just that simple, huh?

The players made their way through the terminal, past the baggage carousel, to the customs desk opened specially to expedite the players' exit. Everything proceeded in an orderly and efficient fashion as passports were rubber-stamped without the agents even really looking at them. A couple of blue-gloved men in bulletproof vests appeared and Casey and Reardon followed them to the door marked *Airport Employees Only*. Casey was about to walk right through when one of the gloved men turned around and held up a hand.

"Not you."

Casey stood there for some time, staring at the door through which the gloved men and Reardon had disappeared. By now they were probably standing in a glass box somewhere deep in the belly of the airport. Finally, Casey realized that Reardon's return was not imminent, and made his way back to the customs desk to have his passport stamped.

The closer didn't show up until 3:30 in the morning, or at least that was when Casey awoke to someone jerking his arm. It took a few moments for Casey to sit up and shake the cobwebs loose. Reardon had turned on the lights and was pacing around the room, holding his bald head in his hand, muttering obscenities. Casey sensed this as an invitation to inquire about what happened, and obliged.

"What happened? I'll tell ya what fuckin' happened. Those motherfuckers tried to prevent me from entering the country."

"Why?"

"On account of this High Times cover I was on last year. On account of my being a pot smoker. What else? Oh yeah, because I intimidated some asshole in Florida who tried to start a fight with me. I made a few disparaging remarks about America. Who the hell cares if I'm only telling the truth?"

"Maybe you should quit making those sorts of comments."

"Over my dead body," said Reardon, spitting into his cup. "Nobody silences old Reardon."

At some point during this conversation, Casey fell back asleep. He woke up to his phone's alarm buzzing, and fumbled with the screen to get it to turn off. Reardon, for once, was sleeping soundly. The big man looked so vulnerable lying there with his jaw slack, snoring away. Casey reached down and gave Reardon's arm a shake, but got no response, so he shook it again.

"Wuh? Huh?" said Reardon.

"Wake up, asshole," said Casey. "We've got shit to do."

By breakfast, Reardon's good mood had returned. He shoveled pancakes and sausage onto his plate from the buffet table and set about devouring the mountain of food. When he was done, all that remained were a few spongy crumbs and little puddles of syrup and grease. Impressed with the sheer volume Reardon had managed to consume, the twins stood up and applauded. They encouraged others to follow suit as the last of the sausage disappeared into Reardon's mouth, at which point the big man leaned back, patted his stomach, and released a loud belch.

"Très impressionant, mon ami," said Felix, his fist held to Reardon's face as if he were grasping a microphone. "Do you have any word to say to your fan?"

"Sure," said Reardon. "Never give up, take what you can, and god bless America."

Reardon had already given his teammates the slip by the time the players began boarding the bus. It was probably for the best, as a mob of angry protesters were waiting for the players at the top of the hotel's looping drive. Mob may be a slight exaggeration—there were maybe forty or fifty of them—but they behaved like a mob, and what they lacked in numerical strength they nearly made up for in fervor. They weren't fans, necessarily. In fact, only around half of the picketers were wearing any Gunslingers' paraphernalia at all, and while they booed and jeered the players as they boarded the bus, their signs and slogans were universally directed at Reardon. One gentleman even held a sign with Reardon's ugly mug in the crosshairs of a sniper rifle. It read, *Dead Man Walking*.

Casey found Reardon at his locker in the visitors' clubhouse. The closer laughed when Casey told him about the picketers and the sign with the threat written on it.

"What's so funny?"

"It's kinda fuckin' true. Ain't it?"

Members of the media were eager to transform this incident into a narrative.

"What do you think of all the protesters?" asked John Smelt of ESPN as he and an enthusiastic Reardon sat in the visitors' dugout just over an hour before the game was scheduled to begin.

Don had only begrudgingly consented to the interview. He didn't like the angle from which ESPN was approaching this story, and was even more perturbed by the possibility of Reardon saying more damaging stuff while unattended in a one-on-one interview. On the other hand, even if Don tried to deny the network access to the team's star closer, he knew perfectly well that he could in no way enforce such an order. Reardon would almost certainly go behind his back and do the interview anyway, just to make Don look weak. So now a cameraman stood not a few feet away, broadcasting the interview live to the pre-game audience.

"I think they're a joke," said Reardon, spitting into his cup.

"Do you care to elaborate?"

"Sure. I'd wager that if you took a little survey of these so-called protesters, you'd find they're mostly octagenarians, white supremecists, militia, true believers in the lizard people, and unemployed men over thirty who still live in their moms' basements. And there's significant overlap in those demographics, if ya know what I mean."

"You have said and done some pretty controversial things. Surely you can understand why people are so upset."

"You know, that's what bugs me about this stuff. People say I'm controversial because I chew 'baccy, smoke pot, and say what's on my mind. What I wanna know is, why's it so controversial to tell it like it is?"

"You do have a rather long rap sheet. I've got it pulled up on here," said Smelt, indicating his phone.

"Do ya now? Let's hear it."

"Assault, assault, assault, threats of violence, possession of narcotics, possession of weapons, driving under the influence, and that's just the old stuff. Of late you've been accused of buttering your team's shower floor to get back at a teammate, accosting a patron of a Waffle House in Florida, and drugging your teammates with an unknown substance."

"You know something, John? I thought we lived in free and fair society, you know, where innocence is presumed unless you've gone and got convicted of somethin', and I've never been convicted for no crime or any damned misdemeanor neither. Yet people like you, who've got a microphone and a platform, go around acting like I'm some sort of criminal on a bit of hearsay and some sour grapes."

"Some have accused you of being anti-American."

"I ain't anti-American. If anything I'm pro-American. At heart I'm just another freedom lover like yous guys claim to be."

"You said, 'claim to be.' What did you mean by that?"

"Just what I said," said Reardon. "It's one thing to be able to parrot a damned word; whole nother thing to live it."

The moment Reardon stepped into the on-deck circle, the fans began to boo. And by the time he finally knocked off the ring and walked over to the plate they were irate, shouting profanities, shaking fists, some yelling for him to go home. Casey watched from the dugout as the fans let Reardon have it. Their faces were so contorted with hate it scared Casey a little.

Their vitriol appeared to have no effect on Reardon whatsoever. He walked up to the plate laughing, greeted the umpire with a wave and a few words, and got into the batter's box to lead off the top of the second inning. Jan Visser, the Gunslingers' third starter, had dominated the top of the order in the first, relying heavily on his curveball as he cruised to a pair of strikeouts and a popout. Here, though, he made the mistake of throwing a first-pitch fastball, which was just the pitch Reardon was sitting on and proceeded to crush into the alley in left centre. The ball bounced all the way to the wall while Texas' outfielders chased it down. Reardon legged it to first, rounded for second, and was just able to make it safely to the bag on a headfirst slide. It was a bang-bang play, so close that Leroy Barnhardt, Texas' skipper, challenged it. They played the video up on the scoreboard and from where Casey was standing it looked like Reardon was—just barely—out. Whatever the true outcome, league officials in New York must have found the evidence inconclusive, as they upheld the call. Texas fans didn't like that at all and voiced their displeasure by roundly booing the umpires.

Visser returned to relying on his curveball after the Reardon at-bat. Through 1.2 innings, 25 of his 30 pitches were curveballs, a far cry from his season CB% of 18.89. It helped that the movement on the pitch was sharp tonight. Casey could see that from the on-deck circle. It had more break than in the VR and it was more accurate.

It was only natural then that Casey went to the plate expecting to get a curveball, which was why he was so late on the fastball that cruised over the plate at ninety-five miles per hour. Casey took his foot out of the box and looked back into the dugout for a sign, but none came. Back in the box now, Casey stared down the pitcher and thought *fastball*. Visser was going to throw a fastball, hoping Casey would still be sitting curveball after getting the heater on the first pitch. Visser got into the stretch, sent one look back at Reardon, and fired the second pitch of the at-bat, a fastball. Casey swung out of his shoes, clipping the ball foul, and finding himself down 0-2.

Now he would get the slider. Casey knew from the simulation that Visser could throw the pitch for a strike and liked to use it when the batter was behind. Here the pitch came: spinning, spinning, spinning in towards Casey's hands, or rather where his hands had been formerly, as they were now up at his ears, initiating his swing. Casey followed the ball with his eyes until it erupted in a plume of dust off the barrel of his bat. A great crack resounded and the fans fell quiet. They watched as the ball made a lazy arc over the centre field wall.

They booed again as first Reardon, then Casey, touched home plate. The two men slapped hands in celebration and were greeted with fist bumps and slaps on the ass from their teammates in the dugout.

Whatever hope still existed in the Gunslingers' dugout evaporated when that ball left the park. This event opened a floodgate, a string of six straight singles that rocketed the Birds to a five-run lead and chased Visser from the game.

This would have been a comfortable margin had Ordoñez been pitching well, but he wasn't. Everything was up, and every so often he'd throw a pitch that sent the batter diving out of the way to avoid getting beaned in the head. The umpire told Casey that if Ordoñez didn't get things under control, he—the umpire—would be forced to intervene.

In the first two innings, Ordoñez was able to tiptoe around walking both leadoff batters, but in the bottom of the third it finally came back to haunt him. He walked the Gunslingers' left fielder to lead off the inning. He wasn't so lucky with the next batter, Oh, who replicated Casey's feat of knocking one out with a man on-base.

Ordoñez was able to get out of the third without giving up any further damage, but they got to him again in the fourth with a single and a pair of back-to-back homers to tie it and knock Ordoñez out of the game.

Lou took the ball from the starting pitcher, saying, "Don't worry about it," and giving him a slap on the ass, but as soon as Ordoñez was out of earshot, Lou changed his tune.

"Jesus. Did he fuck that up or what?"

Patrice came in and shut things down. The next two batters, third and fourth in the order, he punched out using the side-arm slider that made hitters think he was trying to plug them in the knees. They jumped out of the way of pitches that wound up on the outer half of the plate. He'd been so efficient that Lou decided to send him out there again for the bottom of the fifth. Patrice responded by picking up another two strikeouts.

The Birds wouldn't strike again until the top of the seventh, when Singh managed to bunt his way on and proceeded to steal second and third while Steele stood there with the bat on his shoulder, which left the count 1-1 with a man on third. He took the next pitch, low, for a strike, and the next one, high, for a ball. 2-2, he swung at an offspeed pitch and smacked it the other way, past the reaching mitt of the first baseman. The Gunslingers had no chance to stop the run, so the right fielder sent the ball to second to prevent Steele from advancing.

But the damage was done. Felix came out in the bottom of the seventh, shut down the side, came back out for the eighth, and punched out three more. The Gunslingers were left to face Reardon in the ninth in front of a rapidly emptying stadium. They all knew what the result would be before the first pitch of the inning was even thrown: the Birds were going to the SLCS.

While their teammates celebrated making it to the Championship Series, Casey and Reardon slipped out and ordered an Uber to take them back to the Sheraton where they silently packed for their flight the next morning.

Casey was tired—of travelling, of practicing, of playing. Worn out, he needed a break. He fell asleep almost immediately after lying down and was woken up by Reardon's violent shaking of his arm.

"Wake up, shithead. We've got a plane to catch."

Even though they were the first team to clinch, there was little rest for the Blue Birds. They spent their afternoons practicing and using the VR to prepare for the two teams they might have to face in the SLCS. In the UL, the Mammoths won the Divisional Series against the St. Louis Red Birds 3-1, and the Monuments lost 3-2 to the Bootleggers.

The series between New York and Kansas City was the last to be decided. It had, predictably, been a more competitive that the Birds' series against Texas. The two teams went blow for blow, with Kansas City taking the first game, New York taking the next, a pattern which repeated itself through game four when New York forced a Game Five with a big offensive night against Kansas City's ace pitcher, Billy Stuber.

Whatever pixie dust the Sams possessed must have been liberally applied prior to the final game of the series, because they came out swinging. The Birds had gathered in the locker room after practice to watch the game and were not at all comforted by the performance of the geriatric Sam lineup. The Sams laid down so bad a beating that the fans began heading for the exit in the top of the sixth. New York ended up winning the game 12-2.

Steele turned off the TV just as the Sams players and staff stormed the field and mobbed the mound in celebration of their series victory. He turned to his teammates and said, "Well, boys, looks like them Sams'll be paying us a little visit. So let's be good hosts and put the boots to 'em."

Gripes over timeslots disappeared when the schedule for the SLCS was released. The first five games were all scheduled for primetime, meaning that Birds fans were able to watch the games without having to play hookie from work. Games One and Two were to be played in Toronto, with games Three, Four, and Five scheduled to take place in the Big Apple. Tickets sold out almost instantly, and now seats in the nosebleeds were being scalped for thousands of dollars. There was always something for the fans to complain about.

In the days leading up to Game One, Casey spent hours in the VR preparing for the Sams pitchers, and when he was not at the stadium working on his game, he and Reardon were making appearances at various charity and publicity events around the city. Casey found he hardly had a moment to himself.

The morning of Game One they visited Sick Kids, where they were led by the hospital's public relations rep through the various wards. Walking through these corridors, with their medical equipment, wall decals of cartoon characters, large stuffed animals, and balloons emblazoned with get well soon messages, Casey felt like an interloper who would soon be exposed.

The last stop of the tour of the hospital was the cancer ward, where the terminally ill children were housed. The children had been gathered in the common area and they cheered as the ballplayers entered the room. A doctor came forward and welcomed them with a sweep of his hand. Casey didn't hear much of what the man said, but he was surely making some sort of introduction. The children smiled expectantly while their parents sat in the common area chairs, clearly exhausted, clearly nervous. For some reason a clown stood in the corner of the room, honking a horn and wearing a made-up grin. *Jesus*, thought Casey. Didn't these kids have enough to worry about?

As they walked with the doctor and shook hands with the children and their families, Casey was overwhelmed by a sensation of self-disgust. He couldn't quite pull off the act of sincere interaction with the kids the way Reardon seemed able to, laughing and pretending to punch the kids in the arm, slapping them on the back like they were old chums, and smiling for photos that Casey hoped wouldn't later betray how he was feeling. Looking into their eyes, he saw a complete lack of recognition. They were blissfully ignorant of this whole event being a charade. Casey did his best to keep it that way.

They toured the children's rooms. In each one they found stacks of merchandise, most of it unopened, which had been brought by those who came before. The ballplayers made their contribution in the form baseballs, mitts and ballcaps, which the kids wore for a group photo at the end of the visit. After many photos, handshakes, signatures and fond farewells, the ballplayers were led to the elevator that took them down to the lot. To exit, Reardon inserted the ticket in the machine and the arm lifted without Reardon having to pay.

"Shit deal, huh?" asked Reardon, to break the silence.

"Sure."

"Something eating you, kid?"

"It's just that I had this thought in there, like maybe it was better this way. Like maybe they're better off dying now, so they don't have to suffer."

"What's wrong with sufferin'? They're already sufferin'," said Reardon. "What I wanna know is what they end up doing with all that merch. I bet by the time everything's over them parents have themselves quite the swag bag of memorabilia. I mean, they gotta sell it, right?"

"That's fucked up, Reardon."

"Why? I'd do the same fuckin' thing if I were in their shoes."

Even after their victory that night, Casey was left feeling low and couldn't sleep, so he slipped out of the apartment and walked west on Lawrence towards the mall. The night was brisk. It had been raining intermittently, so the pavement was dark and wet with small puddles forming where the cement had buckled and warped.

He knocked on the door of the Tim Hortons and one of the staff walked over to let him in. He was in luck: they had just pulled out a fresh batch of donuts, so he bought half a dozen. The woman locked the door behind him. He took out a donut—maple glaze—and closed the box with the heel of his hand. Three donuts had been consumed by the time he reached the building, and one more by the time the elevator chimed and announced the penthouse. He regretted not having taken any napkins as he reached into his jacket pocket in search of his keys.

Sounds were still emanating from behind the closed door of Reardon's workshop as Casey stepped into his bedroom to devour the last two donuts. Before he could open the box again, he got a call from an unlisted number.

"Hello?"

"Hewwo, handsome."

"Lyuba?"

"Good guess," said Lyuba. "Although, I've been told that I'm fairly unforgettable. Then again, you're pretty unforgettable yourself. I just can't stop thinking about you. I've been following you, you know," she said, and when Casey didn't respond, added, "Oh not like that (but yes, like *that*) on TV, you silly goof! So handsome up there in your blue uniform, cleanshaven, under all those bright lights. It gets me all hot and bothered, seeing you out there in your cute wittle pads. You really make me crazy."

"I don't think I'm the one making you crazy, lady."

"That's where you're wrong," said Lyuba. "You see, the problem is I keep going around in circles. I simply don't know what to do with you. I wonder: should I get rid of you? Should I let you be? It's just so, like, hard to make the right call, you know?"

"I'd lean toward the latter."

"I'm sure you would," said Lyuba. "Of course, you could make my decision easier if you were willing to be a good boy and do as you're told."

Casey swallowed. "What do you want me to do?"

"Oh, not much," said Lyuba, laughing. "Nothing too complicated—I know better! It's best to keep things simple, isn't it? You see, all I need you to do is keep an eye on our little friend for me. If he starts acting a little funny, then you give me a call so I can take care of it. Think you can handle that, schnookums?"

"I guess."

"You guess?"

Casey sighed, "Alright. I'll do it."

"That's a good boy. And Casey?"

"Yeah?"

"I hope you enjoyed those donuts."

There were, blessedly, no prior engagements on the day of Game Two. Reardon even let Casey sleep in, which was a good thing because Casey hadn't slept very well on account of the phone call.

"What did she want?" asked Reardon, inserting a plug of dip upon finishing his bowl of Cheerios. Casey had suspected Reardon of listening in on the call from the hallway.

"She wants me to spy on you."

"You gonna do it?"

"I told her I would, but I won't."

"That's good of ya," said Reardon. "Of course, there won't be any funny business, if you know what I mean."

Casey glanced down at his phone.

"I mean, things are gonna run as straight as a fuckin' arrow. Don't worry about it."

Most of the team had arrived at the ballpark by two o'clock. The position players spent most of their time in the VR lab taking hacks against that night's starter, Raul Rojo. This was followed by the truncated gambit of workouts and practices the team had been using throughout the postseason in order to prevent fatigue.

The Blue Birds came out of the gate swinging and knocked Rojo out of the game two outs into the third, but that was no help seeing as the Sam bullpen was second only to Toronto in run-prevention. New York's relievers stifled the Bird bats, preventing them from scoring the remainder of the game, which made things interesting as the Sam offense clawed its way back to within a run in the top of eighth, but a run was as close as they would get as Reardon closed the book on them.

Lou tabbed Hardy to make the Game Three start, because he looked at his options and thought: Who else? Maybe the old-timer would be able to find something out there and give the team five or six innings and give them a chance to win this thing.

Hardy did a hell of a lot better than that. The potent Sam offense was having a hard time catching up to the 83 MPH heaters he was throwing, partly because of how well Hardy was locating them—right on the corners—and partly due to the effectiveness of his curveball, which he was throwing for strikes. He struck out seven and had only thrown ninety pitches when Lou took him out of the game in favour of Stephenson, which wasn't a terrible decision on paper, given that the team was up by five runs. In practice, however, it was a catastrophic mistake. No sooner had Stephenson stepped on the mound than he began serving up meatballs that were getting sent straight into the seats. Lou tried to keep his cool after the first home run, but after New York went back-to-back-to-back he was ready to blow his top and was practically screaming into the phone receiver for the bullpen to get somebody up—anybody up—who could stop the bleeding.

The fans groaned as Paolo stepped out of the bullpen. He hadn't pitched well in the only opportunity he'd had in the SLDS and had been terrible with men on-base all season long. What he did have, however, were good career numbers against the next three Sam batters. When he mowed all three down, those same fans saw him off the field with a standing ovation. From that little scare, the game became automatic. Lou followed the formula of Patrice, Felix and Reardon, and the team held on to its one run lead to put a 3-0 stranglehold on the Sams.

New York didn't put up much of a fight in what remained of the series. They wound up getting swept at Sam Stadium in front of fifty-four thousand frustrated fans, although nobody should have been surprised considering the Sams were a wildcard team and were lucky to be in the SLCS in the first place.

GLOBE SERIES

The Blue Birds had to wait three days for San Francisco to finally punch their ticket to the Globe Series. The Birds, having finished with the better regular season record, would hold home-field advantage for four of the seven games, with the remaining three games played at Delphi Park using Union League rules. Reardon seemed unusually excited by the prospect of playing against his former club.

"I'm going to make those sons of bitches regret the day they shipped out old Reardon," said the closer as Casey groggily poured coffee into a nondescript ceramic mug. He hadn't been listening and had to ask Reardon to repeat himself.

"Here," said Reardon, tossing a newspaper across the table.

It was the front page of the *Sun* sports section and it read, "San Francisco Advances to the Dance." The article described how the Mammoths had played a back-and-forth series, taking the first two games only to hand Milwaukee the next two. San Francisco won the next game—their last home game—before heading back to Milwaukee for Games Six and Seven. The Bootleggers had won Game Six by walking off the Mammoths in the bottom of the ninth on a single to right field that had allowed the runner standing on second to make it home to break the tie. The Mammoths were finally able to put the Bootleggers away by scoring twelve runs in Game Seven.

Game One of the Globe Series was scheduled two days hence, and Game Two two nights later, followed by a day of travel before the first of potentially three games to take place at Delphi Park.

"It would be San Francisco," said Reardon, ashing his joint.

The Blue Birds didn't have much trouble handling the Mammoths in Games One and Two. In fact, the games were routs, as the Bird offense simply beat the cover off the ball, scoring twenty-five runs over the two games. The pitching also held steady. Amuro, in his Game One start, delivered seven innings of scoreless baseball, and Hardy found a little fire somewhere way down in the tank, pitching another six-inning quality start before handing the game over to the bullpen with an eight-run lead.

Casey continued his hot streak at the plate, hitting .433 with three extra-base hits, but this was nothing next to Steele, who reached base in all but one of his plate appearances so far in the Series. The Dominicans and Thompson also hit well, and Manny was wreaking havoc on the basepaths. The apparatus was working, and all was well in Blue Birds land as the team prepared for their trip to San Francisco for games Three, Four and Five.

Or at least all was well for everyone but Lou, who watched games One and Two from the dugout and had paid attention to how badly Reardon had performed, whiffing in nearly half his at-bats, offering up several lazy flies, a few double plays grounded into, and not one hit or walk. What gave? Had the big oaf suddenly forgotten how to hit? Did the Mammoths simply have his number? Something didn't add up. Of course, it was always possible—as Tubs pointed out—the big man was simply having a cold streak. It happened to everybody. It was only two games for Christ's sake, nothing to go jumping to conclusions over. Yet try as he might, Lou couldn't rationalize away this feeling that something wasn't right.

Don and Tubs weren't much help. They both insisted that everything was fine. Whatever was causing Reardon to underperform, it would go away eventually. He'd played a lot of baseball, with almost four-hundred at-bats and—if you included the postseason—almost two hundred innings pitched. Perhaps he was just tired, they speculated.

Lou didn't buy that for a second. He didn't trust Reardon any further than he could throw him, but he held his tongue. There was no sense rocking the boat when the team was winning, but he would be watching Reardon and the second that sonofabitch stepped out of line, Lou would be there to make the bastard eat his teeth.

Casey intended to reward himself with donuts after the team's Game Two victory and had almost reached the Timmies when a jet-black Maybach with tinted windows pulled up next to him. The rear window rolled down a few inches and a gloved hand reached out and beckoned Casey. He stepped toward the car, bending down to look inside. He swallowed when he realized who it was.

"Get in."

He felt the hard thing poke him in the back again and turned around to find the masked driver leering at him.

"You heard the lady."

He got in the car.

"Make yourself comfortable," said Lyuba, pouring two glasses of champagne.

"What do you want now?"

"Who says I want anything?" said Lyuba, feigning offense. "I only want to celebrate."

She put the bottle back in the ice bucket and handed Casey a glass.

"To your success," she said, raising her glass.

Casey raised his glass, tapped it against hers, and pretended to take a sip.

"Of course, you must know I want *something*. I need a favour."

"I don't do favours," said Casey.

"I think you'll want to do me this one."

"What makes you so sure?"

"Because if you don't," she said, her voice sugary, "maybe our friend Phillip ends up a victim of some horrible act of random violence. Maybe if you don't, then snip-snip."

"I thought that was what you had in mind for us anyway."

Lyuba looked shocked. "Never! Who would I toy with if he suddenly wound up in some ditch somewhere? No, if I have my way our friend Phillip will live a good, long time. I might even let him grow some grey whiskers, but that's only if he decides to play nice."

"What are you talking about?"

"There's this thing I want him to do, you see. It's a thing he *really* doesn't want to do, but believe me when I say it's in his own best interest."

"What is it you want him to do?"

"Tut, tut, tut. Hasn't he taught you anything? Loose lips sink ships, you know. The point is, I'm afraid Phillip might get cold feet and, you know, refuse to do it. I need someone he trusts to coax him into cooperating. You could point out how whatever I'm asking him to do can't be worse than the alternative. Do you understand my meaning?"

"Perfectly."

"Then you'll do it?"

"I don't see what choice I have," said Casey.

"I was hoping you would say that."

It was a balmy seventy-two degrees Fahrenheit when they stepped out of the sliding glass doors of SFO. The Indian summer blazed through late October, and after so many days spent playing in the increasingly frigid SL East, it was nice to step back in time a month and savour summer's end once again. Reardon had Casey order an Uber to take them from the airport to the storage facility in East Palo Alto so they could pick up the car. Then they took the 101 back the way they'd come, past Menlo Park, Atherton, Redwood City, San Carlos, Foster City, San Mateo, Burlingame and Millbrae. Reardon parked the car in the garage of the Marriot, where the team was staying.

Casey woke early the next morning feeling completely refreshed and free of jet lag. They ate breakfast at Denny's on their way to the stadium, which Reardon should have known was a terrible idea considering parking in San Francisco was a nightmare at any time of day. The stench of piss lingered in the streets, and everywhere Casey looked he saw men in hoodies walking in packs of three and four engaged in intense conversations while simultaneously typing on their phones. Men in suit pants and polo shirts distinguished themselves by sporting smart watches and designer sunglasses. Their faces were almost completely hairless and gleamed in the morning sunshine like Roman busts. Mexican women stood at the counters of the few bodegas remaining in this expensive part of town, while the homeless wandered through the heavy traffic, staring through the windshields of morning commuters and holding up their recepticals for change. Reardon cranked down the Beast's window and gave a guy a fifty.

"God bless," said the man, holding the bill up in front of his eyes with both hands. "God bless you, sir."

"Couldn't you've got us any closer?" asked Casey as they pulled into a vacant spot in the Pier 27 lot off of the Embarcadero. His phone said they were still a forty-five-minute walk from Delphi Park.

"I could've, but we ain't headed to the park just yet."

They strolled down the Embarcadero until they reached Pier 33 and signage for tours of Alcatraz. Reardon had of course already purchased tickets, so the two men marched past the ticket booth, through the turnstile and into a holding area, where they waited for the ferry.

A family of Canadians approached the ballplayers about signing their hats. Reardon was only too happy to oblige, scribbling his signature across each hat's bill. Casey was surprised when the father asked if he'd also sign the hats. When the family moved off and were sufficiently distant, Casey turned to Reardon and said, "You know, back in April they probably would've told me to go jump off a cliff, or that I deserve to rot in prison, or some shit."

"Victory has the peculiar effect of turning even the most earnest moralist into a hypocrite."

The ferry's horn went off and a pre-recorded voice notified the passengers that it was time to queue up. They boarded the boat and found a spot along the railing of the second deck. Casey turned to watch the harbour retreat, and saw a pair of seals swimming in the ship's wake. Small waves lapped against the hull of the boat as it cut through the water towards Alcatraz. A narrator explained everything the eager passengers would see when they disembarked on the island, while Casey shielded a joint from the wind with his hands so Reardon could spark up.

"Hell of a place to build a slammer," said Reardon, letting out a long trickle of smoke.

Disembarking, the passengers casually ambled up the slope before entering the prison. Inside, they were each handed a headset to listen to the audio tour. Reardon took one, but opted not to use it, claiming to have already heard the thing a million times. Casey allowed himself to follow in the footsteps of these criminals, from where they took their morning showers to where they slept. He heard statistics and stories narrated in the voices of old guards and inmates. He saw artifacts. A voice told Casey to look up and see the gun gallery where armed guards would have been posted to quell any insurrection. By the time he made it out to the yard, Casey had decided he'd had enough and removed the headphones.

He found Reardon at the far end of the prison yard, spitting tobacco into his cup. "Finished the tour?"

Casey looked down at the device. "No."

"Can't blame ya," said Reardon. "You know, considering these cats were in prison, they sure did have a hell of a view."

"I'm sure that was a real consolation."

"I'm sure it was torture. If I'd've been locked up in this coop, I would've done what Frank Harris and them Anglin brothers did and flown it."

"That so?"

"Sure, better to be on the lam out there than a slave in here."

"I'm not so sure. They'd probably shoot you if you tried."

"They might shoot you anyway, just for breathing the wrong way. No, brother, anybody with any sort self-respect would make a break for it, or at least die trying."

Casey glanced at his roommate. "This from Mr. Freedom himself."

"Pardon?"

"All this talk and yet here you are, under someone else's thumb."

"What?" said Reardon, surprised.

"So what is it she wants you to do?"

"What makes you think she wants me to do anything?"

"You said so yourself."

"I might have."

"And she wants to make you suffer."

"She's doing a good job of it," said Reardon, "but she hasn't got me licked just yet."

By the time they reached the stadium it was nearly 1:00. The position players were to meet with the advance scouts at 1:30 to review the potential matchups. This was followed by another meeting for pitchers and catchers at 1:50. At 2:30 they broke for lunch and Reardon drove Casey down to Pier 39 and the Boudin Bakery where tourists sat devouring sandwiches and soups served up and with their famous bread. The ballplayers took their sandwiches to Fisherman's Wharf and found a spot near the docks where they could watch the harbour seals compete for space on the sun-bleached deck. Glances were cast in the ballplayers' direction, whispers were made but nobody approached, so they were able to enjoy their sandwiches unmolested.

"Man, that hit the spot," said Reardon with a belch as they walked back to the car.

"You never told me what she wants from you," said Casey, licking the last saucy remnants of lunch from his fingers.

"And I ain't gonna tell ya. You were right before when you said you was better off not knowin'. Haven't you seen enough by now, kid? She's crazy. She wants all sorts of things, just like some spoiled brat. It don't mean she's gonna get 'em."

"Well maybe you ought to just give her what she wants."

Reardon cocked an eyebrow. "What, she recruit you or something?"

"I already told you she didn't. It just seems like whatever she wants you to do, resisting it ain't worth dying over."

"Is that so? Well I'm glad to have the advice of a regular expert. I'll be sure to take it into consideration."

"Quit fucking around. I'm just trying to be your friend."

"So we're friends again, are we? You'd be a better friend if you kept your mouth shut."

"Maybe she'll let you off."

"She ain't never letting me off," said Reardon as he stopped and glanced around for eavesdroppers. His volume lowered to a whisper. "Don't you get it? There ain't no forgivin' what she thinks I've done. No, she'll grind me down, make me suffer 'til there's no more sufferin' to be had, and then she'll put me in an unmarked, possibly watery grave. When and if you next hear of ol' Reardon, it'll be on the six o'clock fucking news."

"What are you gonna do?"

"Fuck if I know. Win the Globe Series and take it from there."

The rest of the afternoon was spent in the usual sequence of drills and practices while Don looked on, arms crossed, from a seat in the otherwise empty section 115. With two of the necessary four wins in the books, things were looking good for the team, and yet he found no comfort in it. Two games ahead or no, something didn't feel right. He didn't want to give this feeling credence. There was nothing rational about it, he told himself, there was nothing tangible, just his paranoia playing its usual dirty tricks.

Don shook his head. Why couldn't he compartmentalize this feeling like he did all the rest? While it was true that there were still potentially five games left to play and that anything could happen, did it necessarily follow that he ought to be so distraught when his team was already up two games to nil? He thought about maybe telling someone about it, but who? Howard? Susan? One of the team's sports psychologists? No. That would be patently absurd.

He couldn't stomach watching the game. Not from here and not from the executive suite. Instead, he set himself up in the visiting manager's office with a television and a direct cable feed of the broadcast.

The grounds crew had turned on the floodlights shortly before the red disk disappeared over the watery horizon. The clouds were still distant, but the breeze was picking up fast. The weather report had fog rolling in around 9:30, and Lou figured whoever had the lead by then would probably go on to keep it.

He looked at the lineup card. No DH meant no Reardon, which meant no problem other than having to fill Reardon's usual cleanup spot. He looked over the list of available players. He didn't want to mess with the top of the order, so he looked to the bottom half. He could have chosen Nuñez or Thompson, but finally decided on Casey. He pencilled the kid in based on nothing more than the manager's instinct to ride the hot hand. Casey already had five postseason dingers to his credit, which was five more than Lou ever hit. Besides, Lou was starting to like the kid, outside of his association with Reardon. Lou figured, why not bat the kid cleanup and see if he could make good on his manager's faith?

Don stormed down to the office when he saw the tweeted pic of the lineup card and wasted no time in challenging Lou on the call, pointing to the small sample size, pointing out that past success was not predictive of future success, telling him to bat Nuñez cleanup. Lou had no problem telling Mr. Billingsley where he could stick his sample size. He'd be damned if some beancounter who'd never picked up a bat nor ball in his life was going to tell him how to manage his baseball team in the god-damned Globe Series.

"You're being just as bull-headed as when you didn't want Casey on the team in the first place. Now you want to bat him fourth."

"Maybe I'm being bull-headed and maybe I ain't," said Lou, "but this ain't about numbers, this is about instinct. The kid is hot, and in the short game hot's what matters."

Don hadn't liked that at all, but he didn't have to. After all, what was he going to do? Fire Lou? That wasn't happening and Lou knew it. As far as Lou was concerned, the beancounter's work was done. The power to call the shots was finally back in the right hands, and now gut came before numbers. He'd be damned if he'd be told otherwise.

★

The players lined up along their respective baselines, hats over hearts, while some woman Casey'd never heard of belted out what might have been a decent rendition of "O Canada" had the crowd at Delphi Park not booed it with gusto. They booed right to the end of the song, and the singer had to wait for them to quiet down before she could start "The Star-Spangled Banner." The fans remained respectfully silent until the final two lines, when they began whooping and applauding.

The Blue Birds' opponent was the soft-tossing changeup specialist Jesus Romero, whose off-speed offering had been giving the hitters fits all week in the VR. It was a hard pitch to pick up, especially when you were sitting on his 88 MPH fastball.

Through the first two innings he held the Bird offense to a single hit, but the floodgates opened in the top of the third, when the Birds scored two runs to take the lead. The Mammoths responded in the bottom half with a solo shot to right field.

In the fifth inning, the Mammoths were able to pull even after Baba hit a triple to centre field with one out. McTeague, the Mammoths' first baseman, was able to to bring him home on the sacrifice fly and the game was tied. The Mammoth fans were on their feet, letting Ordoñez have it as he entered the dugout.

Five innings was enough for Lou, who made the call to the bullpen after the run plated, initiating double-barreled action with both Paolo and Stephenson. Paolo came out with two men on base, threw gas, and kept it around the corners. The Mammoths weren't ready for the high heat and got sent down in order. Lou brought in Patrice in the bottom half of the sixth, and Felix in the seventhth, and both men were able to hold the fort. In the top of the eighth, Toronto broke out of their offensive slump when Steele hit another dinger to give the team a one-run lead. Lou wasted no time in calling the bullpen and instructing them to get Reardon warming up.

The fog was just starting to creep in when the closer took the mound, seeping in around the players' feet and slowly rising. Reardon came into the game to face Vazquez, who hadn't yet managed a hit in the series. Casey called for the fastball and got one, but not high and inside like he asked. Instead, the ball shot right over the heart of the plate and Vazquez didn't miss. *Crack* went the bat and the ball rifled along the baseline, falling fair before bouncing into foul territory. Nuñez came up throwing, but had no shot getting the speedy Vazquez out at second base.

Casey glanced up at the scoreboard. That pitch had only clocked in at 95 MPH. Baba was next. The defense had to play Baba straight due to his ability to hit to all fields, and they were caught flat-footed when he promptly laid down a bunt. Casey chased the ball along the baseline and gathered it up quickly. It was already too late to get Vazquez at third, so he made a strong throw to first for the out, which left a man on third, one out in the bottom of the eighth.

Next was McTeague, who wasn't scared at all to be stepping into the box against Reardon. The two had been teammates in the minors and McTeague had always been able to get the better of the matchup, so that he now got set with a smirk on his face. In came the pitch, a slider that instead of breaking just hung there for McTeague to tee off on. The Blue Birds defense froze. There was nothing they could do but watch the ball sail over the right field wall and splash into McCovey Cove. The fans went wild as McTeague rounded the bases and Reardon stood on the mound waiting, the maw of his glove open, his face expressionless.

Lou kept looking from the wall to the baserunner to Reardon and back to the wall. He couldn't believe it, and yet the run column next to San Francisco on the scoreboard confirmed what he'd just seen. He tossed a fistful of seeds in his mouth and began chewing mechanically.

"You see that?" he said to Tubs.

"Mhm."

"Is it still all in my head?"

"Maybe it is and maybe it ain't," said Tubs, leaning over the dugout railing. "Gotta test it out."

"I'll test it out alright," said Lou, looking up at the lineup card. "He's going in."

Lou made no call to the bullpen. After the two-run homer, Reardon settled down as the velocity on his fastball shot back up.

It wasn't his usual level of performance, but it was enough to sit the next three batters in order. As the closer re-entered the dugout, Lou grabbed him by the arm.

"Mind telling me what in the hell just happened?"

"I gave up a two-run homer," said Reardon, spitting on the floor.

"Exactly. How the hell did you give up a two-run dinger in Game Three of the goddamned Globe Series."

"I guess I missed my spot."

Lou gave Reardon a hard look.

"I guess you better get ready to bat, then."

"You're the boss."

Casey followed Reardon to the end of the bench, where the closer was selecting a bat from the rack.

"You alright?"

"Yeah, brother. As good as I can be after that."

"It's just th—"

"We'll talk about it later," said Reardon, spitting on the floor and brushing past Casey.

The fog was thick now, but the umpires were hesitant to delay the game in the top of the ninth. Sanchez, the Mammoths' well-rested closer, trotted out of the bullpen and took the mound. The crowd was into it now, letting the Birds know what they thought of them.

Sanchez made easy work of the first two Blue Bird hitters, getting them out on a pair of groundballs, which brought Reardon to the plate. They started him off with a curveball for ball one. Next, they threw him a fastball over the inner half that he sat on for a strike. On the third pitch they went with the fastball again and this time Reardon bit, but he was early and swung right through it. The crowd clapped as Sanchez got set for the 1-2 pitch and fired it in. Reardon swung right over a breaking ball in the dirt and the catcher picked it up to apply the tag. Up went the umpire's fist and the game was over.

It was a quiet ride back to the Marriot, and a quieter ride still up to the sixth floor. Casey waited until they were safely back in the room before he asked the question he'd been dying to ask since they'd hit the showers.

"What the fuck happened out there?"

Reardon spat into his cup.

"What? You aren't going to talk now?" Casey said.

"It was what it was."

"That pitch you threw McTeague was only ninety-five."

"*Only* niney-five. What can I say? Must've been a faulty reading. Maybe I just made a bad pitch."

"Don't fuck with me, man."

"I ain't fuckin' with nobody."

"Does this have something to do with Lyuba?"

"No, it don't got nothing to do with no Lyuba. Where do you come up with this shit?"

"You're lying," said Casey.

"So what?" said Reardon. "What's it matter when you've already gone and decided what the truth is?"

"I haven't decided anything. I just wanna know what the fuck is going on."

"Well, whatever you think the worst is, it probably ain't far off the mark."

"Are you telling me you didn't see how that punk threw that game?" Lou asked Don over the phone later that night.

"Isn't it possible that he simply had a bad night?"

"Are you kidding me? Reardon doesn't have bad nights. He's been perfect all goddamned season, and now he's giving up taters?"

"He got the next three guys out."

"So what? Too little, too late. Only makes things fishier, if you ask me."

"But why would he throw the game?"

"Don't you play dumb with me, Billingsley. You know *exactly* why somebody would throw a game in the goddamned Globe Series."

Don took a sip from his coffee. "That's quite the accusation to make. You ought to make sure you have enough evidence before you go shouting it from the rooftops."

"I'm just telling you to keep you in the loop. You know, doing my job? I figured you might have some thoughts on how to deal with this situation, since you seem keen on meddling."

"What is it you intend to do?"

"Nothing for now," said Lou, scooping a handful of seeds into his mouth and chewing noisily into the receiver. "After all, you're right: there ain't no evidence. But I'm gathering evidence, Billingsley. I'm filing it away. Any further slipups and I'm pulling the plug."

Don stared at his phone absentmindedly as the screen cut to black. He was disturbed by the phone call. Unlike Lou, Don had evidence. He knew at least one of the two batterymates had recently been in contact with a known criminal who was purportedly involved in gambling. There was nothing that could be clearly pointed to as a violation of Rule 21, but the photos on Don's flash drive would be enough to initiate a league investigation if he handed them over.

He didn't sleep well that night, even by his standards. By the time he woke the next morning, he felt like he'd been lying there for an eternity. The hotel coffee did little to alleviate his fatigue.

Don's inbox was flooded with stuff that would likely be irrelevant to him in a few days. All the same, he went to work on his correspondence in the backseat of an Uber and had cleared the queue by the time he arrived at Delphi Park and made straight for Lou's office in the visitor's clubhouse.

Lou was sitting there with his feet on the desk, taking a nap when Don arrived. Don cleared his throat.

"Huh?" said Lou, nearly falling out of his chair. "What?"

"Good morning," said Don, shutting the door behind him. "Sleep well?"

"Not as well as I'd like to," said Lou, rubbing at the back of his neck. "This Reardon business kept me up."

"I wanted to talk to you about that," said Don.

"I thought we already discussed it."

"Nobody else can know about your… feeling. You haven't been hollering about it, have you?"

"Not a soul, other than Tubs."

"Make sure he doesn't say anything to anyone."

"He never does. You seem a tad spooked yourself, Mr. Billingsley. You doing alright?"

"Right as rain," said Don, rubbing his eyes. "We'll keep watch on the situation. If you see or hear anything—and I do mean *anything*—regarding our friend, I want you to report it directly to me and no one else. Is that clear?"

Game Four wouldn't offer any further opportunities to assess Reardon's loyalty. The offense put five runs on the board in the top of the first. Steele provided another spectacular 4/4 performance, collecting a further two base-on-balls, a double and a home run; Manny stole four bases and scored three runs; Hernandez hit two doubles and a triple; and Cruz earned three walks. Takazawa started the game and delivered another gem, a six-and-a-third-inning clinic where he K'd eight batters and allowed only a single run. Lou only took him out in case he needed him to start Game Seven on short rest. The effort proved to be enough, bringing the Birds within a game of winning it all.

But it wasn't to be a five-game series. Now, within a game of elimination, the Mammoths came out ready to play while, unfortunately for Toronto, Clessinger came out flat. San Francisco wasted no time in teeing up on his 90 MPH heater, and his breaking pitches either missed badly or hung there and got clobbered. While the offense did its best to keep the game close by scoring six runs, the Mammoths tallied eleven before the end of the fifth, which proved too big a deficit to overcome.

Even though they lost two of three games in San Francisco, the Blue Birds' spirits remained high. After all, they were still leading the Mammoths by a game and were one win away from being the champs. Still, the long flight back from California was a quiet one, with most of the players turning off the lights and trying to get some sleep. Casey was dozing under a blanket when someone shook him by the shoulder.

"Mr. Billingsley wants to see ya," said Lou, jerking his thumb over his shoulder towards the rear of the plane.

"What about?" asked Casey, rubbing the sleep from his eyes.

"Hell if I know," said Lou, spitting seeds into his cup. "Alls I know is he wants you back there."

Casey found Don in a seat in coach, typing on his laptop.

"Sit down," he said, pointing to an empty seat across the aisle.

"What's this about, Mr. Billingsley."

"Do you remember that thing I asked you about a few weeks ago?"

"Yeah."

"I know you were lying to me."

"What?" said Casey, casting a glance towards the front of the plane.

Don closed his laptop.

"I know you lied. I asked you if you knew if something was going on, and you lied."

"What are you talking about?"

"Don't play innocent. We both know what I'm talking about."

Casey sat silently.

"Well?"

"All I can say is that whatever is going on—if there even *is* something going on—I'm as in the dark about it as you are."

"Is that why you've been paying visits to certain infamous ladies late at night when you think nobody is watching?"

"How—"

"Forget about how. It doesn't matter how. The point is why. As in: why are you lying? Unless you can give me a good reason why you've been going over there."

"I'm fucking her," said Casey, not knowing what else to say.

"You expect me to believe that?"

"I mean, have you seen her?"

"No, but that seems beside the point."

"Believe me, it's the whole point. I don't see what reason I've given you to doubt me. Haven't I been playing my ass off the whole series?"

"I told you what would happen if I found out you were lying to me," said Don, typing something into his phone.

"Are we done here?" asked Casey.

"You're looking a little shook, kid," said Reardon, glancing up from his repair manual as Casey returned to his seat. "Boss give you shit for something?"

"Shut the fuck up," said Casey, pulling his phone from his pocket and typing something into it before holding it up for Reardon to read:

don knos

"Whaddya mean, Don knows?"

abt lyuba

Reardon swiped the phone from Casey's hand.

wut does he kno

"I'm not sure," whispered Casey.

he dont got nuthin

Game Six would prove to be the most competitive game of the series. Lou opted to skip Hardy, tabbing Ordoñez to start, and he didn't disappoint. He threw seven innings of two-run ball that gave Toronto a 4-2 lead going into the top of the eighth. Patrice was the first man out of the bullpen and sat all three of his opponents down on strikes, which meant Lou had to decide if he was going to call on Reardon to close out the game or let Patrice throw another inning.

In the end, he sent Reardon from the dugout out to the bullpen. The closer came out with his usual swagger and made Lou's decision look pretty good by fanning the first two batters he faced.

But Reardon's first pitch to Baba was a slider that didn't spin or break enough. Baba loaded up and clubbed it into the alley in right field, where Cruz ran it down and hurried to make a throw, but it was too late.

And that two-out double was only the beginning. The next batter singled on a mid-nineties fastball, and the fifth batter teed off on a curveball, sending it to the batter's eye. The Mammoths ran out of the dugout to dump Gatorade on the hitter as he stepped on home plate.

Members of the press were still hollering their questions from the hallway as the heavy metal doors slammed shut. They'd been herded out by the security staff at the request of Lou, who now stood in the middle of the room calling a team meeting to order. The players stood with their backs to their lockers exchanging uncertain glances. Tubs counted heads to make sure nobody had given them the slip, while Lou tossed back a fistful of seeds and began chewing.

"Is everybody here? Good."

"What's the hold-up, Lou?" asked Steele as he undressed. "You gonna start losing your shit again?"

"No. As a matter of fact, Eddie, I was hoping to keep it short and sweet, but the more people keep opening their yaps and asking stupid questions, the longer it's gonna take. Capiche?"

"Yeah? Well some of us got places to be," said Hernandez.

There was a murmur of agreement amongst the players.

"Are you kiddin' me?" said Lou. "Tubs, back me up here."

"It's been a long day, Lou. Maybe what you got to say can wait until mornin'."

"My ass it can wait! You're telling me I'm the only one who was disturbed by what I just saw out there?"

"We got beat fair and square," said Thompson. "What's there to say?"

"It may have been fair, but I'll tell you what, it sure as hell wasn't square."

"Are you sure you wanna be sayin' this?" asked Tubs.

"I'm telling you that game wasn't straight."

"You think they were cheating?" asked Cruz.

"Not them," said Lou.

"You think the umps were crooked?" asked Manny.

"One or two calls may have gone against us, but no, I don't think the umps were trying to pull any fast ones."

"Then who the hell do you think had the fix in?" said Steele.

"Well, if I'm not accusing the other side and I ain't blaming the umpires, then it stands to reason that I must be suggesting that it was one of us."

There was a murmur amongst the players.

"But who would do this thing?" asked Patrice.

"You know, Patrick, that's a great question. I mean, the person in question would have to be smart enough to cover his tracks so that none of us could know with certainty he was in fact throwing the game. He would have to be a very slippery character—one who manages to find himself in enough high-leverage situations that he can be reasonably certain he'll be able to dictate the game's outcome."

Everyone's eyes turned to Reardon.

Reardon looked up and spat into his cup. "Why's everyone looking at me?"

"You did give up that three-run homer in the bottom of the eighth," said Steele.

"And two runs in Game Three," added Cruz.

"He hasn't hit a thing all series," said Hardy, spitting into his cup.

"The one time he was on the base, he get picked off," said Nuñez.

Lou walked over to Reardon and poked him in the chest. "Got anything to say for yourself?"

"Got any proof?"

"I don't need any goddamned proof. I know it. I know it the same as I know that rain is wet and that the sun makes heat: because it's happening right there in front of me. You think I don't know a rat when I see one? Now I may not have all the facts, but we've all just seen you blow two consecutive leads after shutting the door for us all season long."

"I've just gone a little cold, is all."

"You've gone a little cold? Did you all here that? Mr. Perfect's just gone a little cold, all of a sudden."

"That's just a name the media gave me, Lou. You know that."

"Like hell I do. You think I'm going to buy that garbage after what I saw you do this year? You're telling me the guy who shattered Big League records all season long just happened to go ice cold when his team's playing in the goddamned Globe Series? Pretty convenient if you ask me."

"You know what I think's awful convenient?" said Reardon. "That when things go south there's someone conveniently underperforming that you can blame for your ineptitude. Well, let me be the first to tell you that ol' Reardon ain't going to be nobody's scapegoat, especially when the only evidence you've got against me are your feelings. Let me know when you've got something substantial. I get the feeling I'll be waiting a hell of a long time, old man."

"What about you?" asked Lou, turning to Casey.

Casey felt a lump forming in his throat.

"What about him?" asked Reardon.

"The kid can speak for himself."

"What about me?"

"What did you think about your roommate's pitching tonight?"

Casey glanced toward Reardon, then back to Lou.

"Well?"

"I guess it was pretty lousy."

"I pitched like shit," confirmed Reardon.

"One more word out of you and I swear to God the cleaning staff will still be finding your teeth ten years from now."

"Come on, Lou," said Tubs. "That's enough."

"I've just got one question," said Lou, turning back to Casey. "Is there something going on we all ought to know about?"

Casey glanced around at his teammates.

"No."

"He might not even know about it," said Thompson.

"You want to know something?" said Reardon. "I think you all forget everything I've done for you. I mean, where were you before I went and carried this team on my back, huh? Dead in the water—that's where. Why would I have gone through all that trouble if I was just going to throw it all away on purpose?"

"Don't think for a second anybody here buys your bullshit, Reardon," said Lou. "I knew you was bad news from the start. If you think I'm letting you anywhere near the mound from here on out, you're out of your goddamned mind."

"Have it your way," said Reardon, inserting a new plug of chew into his mouth and picking up his towel. "You're the one who's gonna have to explain to Don why you're sitting his best player."

"Oh he knows. We ain't gonna let a rat sink this ship."

"Fuck that," said Reardon. "I'm the only one keeping this boat afloat."

Game Seven

What the hell is going on with Reardon? read the text from Susan. Don responded:

Don't know. Seems fishy, doesn't it?

Metrics are way off. Is he playing hurt or something?

He hasn't reported any injury.

The blinking ellipses let him know she was typing a response. It was a long time in coming.

Call me.

"Are you telling me he's throwing the games?" she said, answering the phone.

"That seems to be the prevailing opinion."

"Opinions are not evidence. For all we know he's developing a blister or something and keeping it to himself."

Don cleared his throat. "There's more."

"What do you mean, there's more?"

"Do you remember that thing we discussed before?"

"You're going to have to be more specific, Don," said Susan, sounding annoyed.

"That thing about finding out what Reardon might be up to?"

Dead air.

"Susan?"

"You didn't…"

"I'm afraid I did."

"Donald Billingsley!" she yelled so loudly that Don had to pull the phone from his ear. "I thought I told you not to fucking do that. Fuck, I need a cigarette."

He listened as she rummaged around somewhere. He heard the click of a lighter. Don imagined her exhaling through an open window, so that her kids wouldn't know she was smoking.

"Fuck."

"I'm sorry. I know it was stupid, but it turns out there *is* something going on."

She listened while Don explained about the PI, the photographs, and the woman. When he finally finished telling the story, Susan was unimpressed.

"Is that it? The kid's boning some cougar?"

"I'd hardly call her a cougar, and anyway she's not just *any* cougar. This woman has... connections. She runs certain illicit businesses, including gambling, bookkeeping, and narcotics. He was brought into the house at gunpoint, for Christ's sake."

"I don't know, Don. Are you sure the pictures are real?"

"Trust me."

"Alright," she said. "Fuck."

Casey didn't leave the park with Reardon after the game. Instead, he went to the VR lab and spent some time in the simulation. Reardon was fucked, but that didn't mean Casey had to be. A strong Game Seven performance would be the cherry on top of what could only be described as an excellent rookie season.

His at-bats in the simulation were mediocre, at best. The Mammoths' pitches had so much late movement that it was hard to get a read on them and Casey felt like most of the time he was guessing. He was reaching for pitches out of the zone and coming up empty, and after his hundred-and-first strikeout he finally ripped off his headset and decided he'd had enough. He had just emerged from the shower when Rahim walked in with a load of fresh uniforms.

"I thought you'd still be hanging around somewhere," said Rahim. "Where's the big man?"

"What do you mean?"

"I mean his car is still in the lot. I thought you two might be getting some extra work in the cage or something."

"I thought he'd already gone home."

Rahim shrugged. "Maybe he took the bus?"

Casey knew where to find the closer. He got changed, exited the stadium through the staff entrance, and headed to the tower where the guard recognized Casey and let him in. He ascended in the elevator; blue LED light washed around him as he rose above the rooftops. Spotlights scattered across the city pierced the purple overcast with their brilliant white beams. The doors gasped open at the observation deck where Casey stepped off and found the closer sitting on the glass floor.

"Followed my trail of breadcrumbs, did ya?" said Reardon, spitting into his cup.

"Rahim said your car was still in the lot, so I thought I'd look around for you."

"You found me."

"What are you doing?"

"Asking the gods."

"What gods?"

Reardon held up a baggy of blue-veined mushrooms.

"*Psilocybe semilanceata.* Fourteen ounces. A very strong dose—maybe too strong."

"You sure you wanna take that much?"

"No," said Reardon, spitting what remained of his dip into his cup. "I was kind of hoping you'd split it with me."

Casey glanced around.

"Is that a good idea?"

"There have been worse ones. Besides, depending on how things go, this might be the last opportunity we've got, so to speak."

Casey gazed doubtfully at the bag of mushrooms.

"Come on, brother. Humour me."

They tasted awful. Casey gagged several times as he attempted to get all seven grams down. He drank from his water bottle to get the taste out of his mouth, but it was useless.

"How long does this shit take to work?"

"Depends," said Reardon, putting in a fresh plug of chew. "An hour maybe?"

Nothing was said for some time.

"I guess you're probably wonderin'," said Reardon, at last.

"What?"

"If I'm gonna throw it tomorrow."

"I don't think Lou's gonna give you the chance."

"He'll give me the chance, alright," said Reardon. "He won't have no choice. In the end, it will make its way down to me—it always does. See, I ain't lucky like you are. Fate don't intend on letting me skip this test."

"What are you gonna do then?"

"We'll let the gods decide."

Nothing happened for a long time, so that Casey began to wonder if the mushrooms were duds. Slowly, the edges of everything—the walls, the lights, the buildings, and streets below—began to undulate.

"I think it's working," said Reardon, lying down on the floor.

Casey looked down at the city through the glass. The lights, the traffic, the wisps of exhaust in the cool October night made him feel like the place was alive. When he lay down, he could feel the city breathing. With each inhalation he felt his body curve against the floor as if he were lying on the surface of a balloon. With each exhalation, he flattened as everything returned to level. He closed his eyes and the roof opened, the stars came out, and he saw them constellate into fantastic shapes, laden with meaning. He laughed to himself, saying, "None of this shit matters."

"Welcome to another beautiful fall evening here in Toronto for Game Seven of what has been a back-and-forth Globe Series. This will be the final matchup between these two teams, with the winner of tonight's game taking home the Interleague Trophy."

"You know something, Jack? Had you asked me at the start of the year if the Blue Birds would be competing in the Globe Series, I'd have called you nuts, but here we are in a packed house with a chance of hanging another banner up there in the rafters."

"But it's going to be an uphill battle for the Blue Birds, who've lost all the momentum after blowing two late leads, including in Game Six, which would have sealed the deal. On paper, the Mammoths hold the advantage in tonight's starting pitching matchup, tapping Byung-Hyuk Jeong to start. Toronto has opted to go with Amuro Takazawa, their best starter in the regular season. Amuro has certainly cemented his position as the staff ace this postseason."

Amuro was coming off short rest, but you wouldn't have known it from the way the ball was leaving his hand in warmup. The movement was good, with the ball breaking three or four times on every pitch, and Amuro's command was about as good as Casey had seen it all season.

As the two teams stood at attention along the baselines for "The Star-Spangled Banner" and "O Canada" a giant Canadian flag was unfurled in the outfield. Casey watched it float its way atop the throng. Instead of the warm glow of patriotism, he felt nothing. Finally the crowd broke into applause and Casey got set behind home plate.

Amuro's first pitch didn't break at all. It just hung there in the middle of the strikezone—in the darkest red part of the hitter's heat map—and Vazquez wasted no time in smashing it hard back up the middle for what Casey was sure was going to be a base hit.

Singh was shading ever-so-slightly toward third and had a long run to get to the ball, but he managed to intercept it by diving and batting it down with his glove. Getting to one knee, he scooped the ball from the turf and flung it to first. But it wasn't enough to beat the speedy Vazquez to the bag and the result was a man on first with none out.

Now the threat of a stolen base was significant. Casey knew he had to keep the double play in order, but with Amuro on the mound tossing floaters, it wouldn't be easy. Casey called for a couple of check throws to first before putting his index finger down for another knuckler, this time with Yuuto Baba—the Mammoths' left fielder—standing in the batter's box. The pitch moved much better this time, breaking this way and that before finally clipping the bottom inside corner of the strikezone.

Vazquez broke for second and Casey came up firing, a nice low throw right at the bag, but by the time Steele put on the tag Vazquez's fingers were already touching second. Casey lifted his mask and spat into the dirt, angry with himself for having let the baserunner get so far. He looked to the dugout. There was no signal waiting for him, so he called for a pickoff play himself. Amuro nodded in recognition and threw in a fastball, well out of the strikezone. Casey stepped out from behind the plate, caught the ball while Baba swung uselessly for strike two, and fired to second. Vazquez had taken a big lead and was thinking about going for third, but the play caught him by surprise. By the time he thought to dive back to the base, Casey had already made the throw. Vazquez scrambled for safety, but there would be no return for him. Casey's throw was on the money, and this time Steele's tag landed on the baserunner's wrist *just* before he was able to touch second base.

"Would you look at that," said Sadler. "The kid makes a big play in Game Seven of the Globe Series and barely bats an eye. Just gets right back down in his crouch and ready for the next pitch."

"You've got that right," said Rodriguez. "We've watched this young man develop all season, and I tell you what, he's never looked as good as he does right now—both with the bat and with the glove. There may have been questions about his ability and commitment at the beginning of the year, but at this point I think we can say Casey's a ballplayer."

"He's got great instincts behind the plate," said Sadler. "It looked like he called that play himself."

"And what a pitch for strike three. The fans are into it."

"Baba walked back to the dugout shaking his head."

"But the Birds aren't out of the woods just yet, not with McTeague stepping into the batter's box."

McTeague went through the motions, staring at his bat and taking a deep breath, kicking his spikes into the dirt, and finally getting set, his bat waving over his shoulder. Casey called for another knuckler and was rewarded with a perfect pitch, a four-breaker that finished right there at the bottom of the zone where

Casey was able to present it for a strike. The next pitch followed a similar path, but this time was called a ball.

"Just outside for ball one. I don't know about you, Zack, but this might be the most controlled I've seen Amuro this entire postseason. Other than that first pitch, there's been nothing out over the heart of the pla—and there it goes! Deep to left. Going, going, and it's gone! Home run, San Francisco. That will give them a one-to-nothing lead."

Amuro stood there, his face expressionless, holding his glove up for a new ball as McTeague rounded the bases. Lou had his head in his hands, cursing. Amuro struck the last batter out on four pitches and disappeared into the tunnel after entering the dugout.

"And we're back," said Jack. "And we'll introduce tonight's starter, Byung-Hyuk Jeong. He really needs no introduction, Zack."

"I'll say! This guy's been one of the best starters over the past six seasons, winning the Ty Johnson twice and finishing top five in ERA six times. That's not even talking about his postseason performance, which has been—to say the least—exceptional."

"And there you have the numbers: over twenty starts, he's had a one-point-eight-nine earned run average, and one hundred twenty-nine strikeouts over one hundred twenty-eight and two thirds innings: a real postseason performer. Outside of Game One he's been absolutely phenomenal."

Manny stepped into the box, spat into the dirt, and promptly laid down a bunt along the third-base line. Along the chalk it trickled, while Zapatista charged in from third. He scooped up the ball and fired it to first. Manny would have been called out if the ball hadn't sailed left, clipped the pocket of McTeague's glove, and gone bouncing into foul territory towards the visitors' dugout. Manny wasted no time rounding for second, almost as if he'd been anticipating the mistake. McTeague was quick in getting to the ball, but by the time he retrieved it Manny was well on his way to third. McTeague made a good throw, but it was too late. The baserunner went headfirst into the bag well ahead of the tag and was called safe.

"That's some heads-up baserunning!" said Sadler, pounding his fist on the broadcast table.

"Speed will do that for you. I'd score that as a base hit followed by an error."

"And that brings Eddie Steele to the plate with none out and a man on third. He's been on fire all postseason, the only batter in the Globe Series hitting above four hundred."

"Twenty doubles, ten home runs, and a triple," said Rodriguez. "Those are some bigtime numbers. While he may not be the biggest guy out there on the field, he might be the strongest."

"Steele takes a fastball, for a strike."

"That was a good take there: too low. He's looking for something above the belt, something he can drive."

"Curveball, low, for a ball," said Jack. "He's got such a good eye. Tracked that ball all the way to the catcher's mitt."

"I think he's sitting fastball here."

"Jeong must have thought the same thing because there's a slider on the outside corner. Eddie doesn't like it, but from up here it looked like the right call."

"A tough pitch. Now he's going to have to defend the dish."

"Jeong gets set, the pitch, and Steele hits it hard! Deep to right. Get up, ball! Get up! And it's—he's out. Singh tags and charges toward home plate and he's safe. Just barely. He was almost home when he realized the ball was going to find the glove and had to go back and tag up. The throw almost got him. Just like that the game is tied, with none on, one out in the bottom of the first."

There wouldn't be any more offence that inning. Hernandez went up and whiffed at three pitches and Nuñez popped out to short to bring the inning to a close.

Amuro came out of the dugout for the top of the second and immediately began dealing. The knuckleball was wobbling so much Casey had a hard time keeping it in front of him. He had to toss the ball to first twice in order to complete the two strikeouts Amuro racked up. Unfortunately, Toronto did nothing to capitalize on the strong inning from their starter in the bottom half, making three consecutive outs on groundballs. Amuro was just as effective in the top half of the third, inducing a strikeout and two flyouts.

Casey came to the plate to lead off the bottom of the inning. Barely aware of what was going on around him—the crowd, the catcher, the other position players—he saw only the long stretch of green carpet, the mound, and the pitcher standing atop it, slowly rotating the ball in his hand. The pitcher got set and, just like in VR, his hand cranked back behind his shoulder and he fired the ball. Casey recognized the spin of the ball as it came out of the pitcher's hand. Outside of this recognition, his mind did nothing. His instincts took charge, waited, waited, and finally pounced on the hanging curveball, smashing it to straightaway centre.

"Swing and a drive!"

Brown raced back, head craned over his shoulder, following the ball as it got lost somewhere in the lights and suddenly reappeared. His long strides were effortless and efficient, and he was able to make it to the wall well ahead of the ball. It was then that the crowd, which had fallen silent with the loud crack of Casey's bat, finally came back to life and began to cheer.

"Get up, ball! Get up!"

Up it went, up over the wall and into the flight deck where the fans went nuts. Casey, who had been on his way to second when he realized the ball would clear, just kept trotting with his head down.

Even though he felt like a phoney returning to the dugout, his teammates seemed not to notice. It was business as usual with the high-fives and the slaps on the ass and the seeds raining down on his head. He was surprised. After all, they must have suspected he was in some way complicit in whatever Reardon was involved in.

There wasn't much time to ruminate. He got up and walked past Amuro, who was staring dead-eyed into the middle distance. The pitcher's hand shot out and grabbed Casey by the wrist. The catcher turned to look at his battery mate.

"Arigato," said Amuro, without looking at Casey.

"For what?"

"The lead."

"Amuro comes out to start the fourth and I have to say, Zack, that he's pitched a pretty decent game so far, outside of that one at-bat in the first."

"He really hung that knuckler and McTeague was able was get to it and take it over the wall. Thankfully," said Sadler, "a sac-fly from Eddie Steele and a dinger from Casey have erased the deficit and given Amuro the lead."

"The man behind the plate has held this thing together, both with his glove and with his bat. He's a big reason the Birds are in the lead right now. And what a story he's been for this team. This time last year, he was working as a security guard in a condo building just up Yonge Street. Now he's playing here at one Blue Birds Way for his hometown team in the Globe Series. McTeague steps in to start the fourth. Amuro gets set. And the pitch: low, ball one."

Casey threw the ball back to Amuro and got set for the next pitch. Down Casey's index finger went for the knuckleball and Amuro nodded in affirmation.

The pitch came in high. Released too early, it sailed, drifting this way and that before finally beaning McTeague on the shoulder.

"Well it didn't hit him very hard, but he'll take the base anyway," said Jack. "And that will bring Zapatista to the plate."

Another glance to the dugout. This time Lou was signaling the defense to play Zapatista straight up. Casey thought of the fastball and put down two fingers.

"Amuro nods. Gets set, deals… and he hits him. That will bring Mayberry out of the dugout, pointing out to the mound. I think he's saying they struck Zap on purpose."

"The umpire has handed out a warning to both sides… and now Lou is leaving the dugout. He doesn't look happy."

While the two managers bickered with the umpire, Tubs made the call to the bullpen. Felix was already up and throwing by the time Lou returned to the dugout.

"That sonofabitch gets one more batter. If he fucks it up, I'm pulling the plug."

The next three pitches were more in control, which allowed Amuro to get to two strikes before missing a close call on a ball that finished at the very edge of the lower inside corner. The next pitch was worse. He hung it, and Brown struck it out front.

Manny's long, spidery legs were a blur as he shot into the trajectory of the ball and intercepted it before it hit the ground. There was a smooth exchange of ball from glove to hand before the ball was back in the air again, fired toward second base as the runner who'd been halfway to third tried to race back to avoid the out, but there was no chance. Steele turned and fired back to first. Zap misjudged the distance in his dive to the bag, landing chin-first in the dirt and scrambling on all fours to reach the base. Thompson stepped on the bag and the umpire pumped his fist to signal the completion of the triple play.

The fans cheered, and many waved towels in appreciation as the players jogged off the field and high-fived in the dugout, but the Birds couldn't do anything to expand their lead in the bottom half. First Singh popped out, then Steele was robbed on a line-drive, and finally Hernandez struck out to end the inning, bringing the home defense right back onto the field.

Felix was still standing in the bullpen, staying loose, but Lou opted to stick with Amuro for one more inning. Once again, the hurler was shakey, but effective. He gave up another single, but got out of the inning on a convenient double play and a line drive Cruz ran down deep in the right field alley.

Meanwhile, Jeong had found his rhythm and was mowing down Bird batters with his hard slider, making them look silly on pitches way off the plate. He'd sat down nine in a row by the time he capped off the fifth.

Lou had seen enough. He didn't hesitate in putting Felix in to begin the sixth, banking on his shutdown bullpen to hold on to the lead.

Felix pitched a flawless inning, but then Lou put in Paolo to start the seventh and the result was less than ideal. Two singles and a double and Paulo's evening was over without recording an out. In came Patrice, who was able to get the three outs, but not without giving up the single that scored the man on second.

"Jesus," said Tubs as the players entered the dugout. "That was *messy*."

A few seconds later, the dugout phone started ringing.

"Who the hell could this be?" asked Lou, picking up the phone.

"Would you quit managing like an idiot and play it straight, already?" came the voice on the other end.

"Who let you get on the phone, Reardon?" said Lou.

"Nobody tells me what to do, Lou. When I wanna phone a friend and have myself a friendly chat, I damn well will."

"You know something? I don't find your tone none too friendly."

"Yeah? Well, I don't find your bullpen management too effective. You just coughed up the lead with all your fancy switches when you could've just played it straight. Felix, Patrice, myself—that's the fuckin' formula."

"Let's get one thing straight, Reardon," said Lou, holding the receiver to his ear with his shoulder while spitting some seeds into his cup. "There is no way in hell that I'll be putting you into this game. Do you understand me? Over my dead body!"

"Whatever you say, pal," said Reardon. "Gimme a call when you're ready for old Reardon to save you yet again."

"You son of a bitch," Lou yelled, but there was nobody on the other end of the line—it was dead. Lou stood there a moment, the anger welling inside him until he couldn't stand it anymore. He began smashing the phone's base with the receiver until it was little more than a few bits of plastic and shattered circuitry scattered amongst the usual refuse lining the dugout floor.

"Welcome back, we're here in the bottom of what has been a tumultuous seventh inning for the Blue Birds, to say the least."

"You've got that right, Jack. They were looking good with a one-run lead to start the inning, but for some reason decided to stray from the recipe that had been working for them all postseason."

"It really brings into question what's going on with Reardon. I don't think he's hurt, because we saw him down there in batting practice and he looked fine. And it seems somewhat premature to bench a pitcher because they've had a couple of rough outings."

"He's not in the lineup and he seems to be unavailable out of the bullpen. He must have gotten himself into Lou's doghouse with his performance the past two games, but the postseason is no time to get petty."

Don switched off the broadcast and leaned back in his chair.

"What did you turn it off for?" asked Susan.

"We're fucked."

Don opened a new document on his computer.

"What are you doing?"

"Penning my resignation letter, what does it look like? I've never been fired before, and I certainly won't allow myself to be fired now."

They could hear the boos through the walls.

"Quit being such a baby. You might as well see it through."

"I have become acclimated to disappointment."

"You're so dramatic."

"You think so?" said Don, not looking up from the screen.

"Yeah," said Susan, folding her arms.

He tapped away on his keyboard, then deleted everything he'd written and started over. No matter how he began the letter he couldn't seem to make it sound any less pathetic. They heard cheering through the walls, so Don turned the game back on. Manny had once again reached base. The broadcast replayed the event: a seeing-eye single through the left side of the infield that left Singh at first with one out and Steele stepping to the plate.

"Steele looks like he means business now with a runner on first. Three runs down, with two and two thirds innings left to play and the shark smells blood in the water," observed Jack Rodriguez. "Do they send Singh here and risk distracting Steele at the plate?"

"I don't think they do. This late in the game, you're not playing for a run here or there, you're playing for *runs* and lots of them. Don't take the bat out of your star player's hand. Not when he's been swinging it this well."

Don was on his feet now, hands on the windowsill as he looked out onto the field. The crowd was going mad and Don could feel the buzz through the concrete.

"And the pitch: in there, for strike one."

Steele blew a bubble, took one foot out of the batter's box, looked into the dugout for a sign, and then stepped back in and waited for the pitch. It was a curveball, and Steele took a hack at it for strike two. Then he got another curveball for ball one.

"A fastball, inside... chew-and-chew," observed Jack, somberly.

Jeong must have thought Steele was sitting slider, because the next pitch was a fastball, well placed at the edge of the strike-zone. But not placed well enough, it turned out. Eddie was somehow able to square up the pitch and send it deep to right.

"Get up, ball! Get up! Up!"

Up it soared, up into the glove of a young fan sitting deep in the second deck, who held it up as if to prove what had just transpired. She began jumping and cheering with the rest of the crowd while Steele rounded the bases, blowing his trademark bubble.

Lou did a double take at the scoreboard. Could this really be happening? A glance at the television broadcast told him that Del Toro had just started warming up in the Mammoth pen. Hernandez was next up, and after getting ahead 2-0, sent the third pitch deep into the left field alley, where it found the grass. The Mammoths' centre fielder tracked down the ball and made a strong throw to second, but not in time. Hernandez was now in scoring position.

He was knocked in a moment later, when Thompson sent a ball screeching over the third-baseman's mitt into left field. Hernandez touched home plate ahead of the tag on a headfirst slide. And just like that, the game was tied.

Casey was up next and hit another single. That was enough for the Mammoths' skipper, who went to Del Torro to put out the fire, which he did by striking out Cruz and Nuñez to end the inning.

Lou had Tubs write Stephenson's number on a whiteboard and hold it up so the bullpen coach could see, and then walked over to Patrice as the latter removed a towel from his throwing arm.

"I need you to give me two outs," said Lou. "Can you do that?"

"I can get you three, mon ami."

"Patrice Aucoin comes back into the game to start the eighth inning, after striking out two to begin the seventh."

"Yeah, but he will be on a short leash with Stephenson already getting loose in the bullpen."

"It certainly appears that way. I wouldn't be surprised if this was the last batter Patrice sees. Lou's not going to take any chances."

"Baba steps into the batter's box and we're on our way. Aucoin winds up... the pitch... strike one."

"That was a *nasty* fastball. StatMan had that one at ninety-nine miles per hour."

"I don't think we've seen him throw the ball that hard all season. Winds up... the pitch... a strike on the bottom inside corner. And now he's up o-and-two."

"Ninety-eight miles per hour. That's something from a sidearmer. He'll be looking for the out with that slider here."

"The pitch... and Baba swings over it, the ump rings him up, and that's one out."

Which brought up McTeague once again. Casey had assumed that Lou was going to pull Patrice with Stephenson now warmed up and ready in the bullpen, so he started walking out toward the mound. Surprised to see Patrice staring at him in disgust, he glanced back over his shoulder to find Lou still on the steps, throwing a fistful of seeds into his mouth.

"Boy did Casey look confused there."

"Well the reason he looked so confused is because he was probably thinking what the rest of us were thinking, but Lou has opted to go with the hot hand here after his reliever has struck out the first four batters he's faced."

"I love the call. Your player has risen to the occasion, is dominating hitters, and getting the job done. You've gotta reward him."

Casey called for the slider at the heel and Patrice put it where he wanted it for a swinging strike, but then the battery fell behind by throwing two more sliders and a changeup leading to a hitter's count. After the changeup, Casey stood up and spat into the dirt. He didn't want to use the fastball, but in this count he felt like there was no other choice, not with two out in the bottom of the eighth. The fastball came in on the hands of McTeague, who swung and hit the ball only to have his bat shatter and the ball float fifteen feet in the air. Casey's mask was off, tossed to the ground as he scrambled to position himself under the ball, but he bumped into someone, got knocked off-course, and was unable to recover in time to make the play. He could only watch as the ball bounced helplessly into foul territory.

"Foul ball!" shouted the home plate umpire.

Lou was out of the dugout now, but not to pull Patrice from the game. He wanted to ask the umpires what the hell just happened. Could they be serious? Maybe they needed to get their eyes checked, because the batter had stood in Casey's way and that was clearly interference. It ought to have been an out.

The umpire nodded and pretended to listen while Lou made his case. How could they have missed it? It was plain as day! He even tried to get Casey to do a bit of role play so that they could re-enact the event, to show how the hitter had in fact impeded Casey's pursuit of the ball. But all this "evidence" made no difference to the umpire, who just kept nodding. Lou finally got so fed up with this wise guy's blank stare that he demanded they phone it into New York to review the play.

Off the umps ambled to the sideline, where the crew chief donned the headphones and listened to whomever was on the other end of the line. Meanwhile, the jumbotron projected replays of the incident in question. After a few minutes, the crew chief took off the headphones and pumped his fist to call the hitter out.

No sooner had the fist gone up than Mayberry was out of the visitor's dugout and arguing, pointing from home plate, gesturing with both arms, but it was too late—New York had made their call and that was all there was to it. Mayberry was eventually subdued and dragged back to the dugout so his team's defense could take the field.

"And we're back with the game headed into the bottom of the eighth, knotted up at six a piece."

"Now would be a great time for the bottom of the Bird order to wake up. They haven't really done too much all game. If even one could get on base and turn the order over with less than two outs, that would be huge."

"It looks like they sat down Del Torro and are sending in O'Malley, their set-up man. He's been solid all postseason long, giving up only three runs. The changeup is his best pitch after the fastball, and he's been using it very effectively against the Blue Birds this series. He gets set... and the pitch... fastball for strike one."

Cruz wasn't even able to make contact, striking out on three pitches. That brought up Nuñez, who swung at the first pitch he saw and pulled it into left field for a single to turn the order over and bring the fans to their feet.

Next, Manny Singh stepped to the plate. He watched a few pitches—a curveball for a ball, a fastball for a strike, and a change-up for a strike—before hitting the ball along the third base line. In came Zapatista, who fired the ball to second, but this was a mistake. Lou had called for the hit-and-run, and Nuñez reached safely. The Mammoths' second baseman tried to save the play by throwing the ball on to first, hoping to get Manny. The ball and player arrived at the bag at the same time and the umpire pumped his fist.

"Aaaand... he's out."

Lou didn't even have to demand they look at it this time. The crew chief called an umpire's review to ensure they got it right. The fans began to boo as they watched replays on the scoreboard that made it appear Manny had indeed been safe, but they were only getting the most convincing angles.

"I hate to say it," said Sadler, shaking his head. "But I think Singh's out."

The crew chief confirmed Zack's assessment when he removed the headphones and pumped his fist. The fans didn't like that, but when all was said and done, Nuñez was standing on second with Steele coming to the plate and two out.

O'Malley got behind Steele 3-1, but was determined not to give in. He challenged Steele with a curveball, hoping to get a whiff, but it came in flat as a rake and Steele hammered it. *Pop* went the bat, and up the ball sailed into left field.

"Get up, ball! Get up! That's a home run! Steele raises his fist as he rounds the bases. The Birds now have a two-run lead off the bat of Eddie Steele—his second home run of the game."

While everybody else in the dugout celebrated, Lou scratched at his neck and thought about who to get started down in the bullpen. There weren't many names left on the list after that whopper of an eighth inning. And getting a starter to close it out? Forgetaboutit. There was, of course, the obvious to consider, but putting Reardon out there was just as unthinkable as calling on Chet or Ordoñez.

Sure, Reardon had denied throwing the games on purpose, but what mook would be stupid enough to incriminate themselves by admitting to such an allegation? There was also the matter of the timing. How was it possible that suddenly, during the Globe Series, the sonofabitch had suddenly lost his touch? That didn't pass the smell test. He knew in his gut Reardon threw those games. And that could only mean one thing, couldn't it? Lou turned to the problem of the optics: what were they going to write about him in the papers if he didn't put Reardon in? How would he justify sidelining the guy who had basically got them here?

Lou bit the cap off the whiteboard marker, scribbled down the number eighteen, and paused. He didn't like this number at all; he hesitated before erasing and re-writing it again, this time smaller so he could fit in a forward slash and the number thirteen. He raised it up high so they could see it out in the bullpen. A minute later he was getting a call on his cellphone. The display said it was Don, so Lou waddled down the tunnel and took the call.

"Hello?" he said.

"Can you explain to me what is going on?"

"Bigwood is warming up."

"I can see that. Why is Reardon also warming up?"

"I don't know what to tell ya, Mr. Billingsley. I didn't request that."

"I just saw you holding the whiteboard up with his number on it. Why are you using that whiteboard, by the way? Why aren't you using the phone?"

"The phone's a little out of order at the moment," said Lou, glancing at the phone's shattered remains on the dugout floor.

"Why is that?"

"Who's to say? It was probably Paolo. Hell, he's back there tearing the locker room to shreds as we speak."

"Never mind about the phone," said Don, sounding impatient. "Phillip cannot be allowed to enter the game. Do I make myself clear?"

"With all due respect, Mr. Billingsley, there ain't exactly many other options."

"You have Ordoñez, you have Chet, and Bigwood."

"You're ready to stake your championship on one of them?"

"Sooner one of them than the man we *know* has been throwing games."

"But do we know it?"

"He didn't just forget to play overnight," said Don. "What if I told you that he and his confederates have been seen in the proximity of properties associated with organized crime?"

"That's all whatchamacallit—circumstantial. And besides, how do you know they've been doing business with mobsters?"

Silence.

"Mr. Billingsley?"

"Never mind *how* I know. You know he's a gambler. Put two and two together."

"You know, Mr. Billingsley," said Lou tossing some seeds into his mouth and chewing while he spoke. "I'm planning on putting Bigwood in, even though I think it's a mistake. I'll do things your way for now, but if push comes to shove and our backs are against the wall—I'm going with Reardon."

"Be sensible."

"I am being sensible. Do you know what the fans are going to do to me if I don't put Reardon in and we lose? It ain't happenin'. You can expect my resignation in the morning."

"Y—"

But Lou had already hung up the phone.

"What'd he want?" asked Tubs when Lou returned to the dugout.

"He wants me to keep Reardon out of the game."

"I suppose that boy *did* throw them games."

"We don't have any proof of that. Who knows? Hopefully Ernie will shut things down and we won't need to call on the son of a bitch."

"I sure do hope you know what you're doin'."

"You and me both, pal."

"He hung up on me," said Don, staring at his phone in disbelief. "I should have fired the lout last winter when I had the chance."

"Who's going in?"

"Looks like it's Bigwood," said Don, gesturing towards the monitor.

"Then what's the problem?"

There was some booing as Bigwood trotted onto the field. Fans looked to each other in confusion and disbelief. *Where was Reardon?* Even the broadcast crew was baffled.

"Interesting decision in the bottom of the ninth in Game Seven of the Globe Series."

"Yeah, I don't know about this one. Bigwood's a big, strong guy, but who do you want out there with the game on the line? I think you want your seven-foot closer who throws one-o-five-plus, not the guy who's maybe the fifth option out of the bullpen."

"We'll see how this plays out."

Casey thought Ernie did well with his first three pitches by getting ahead 1-2, but his fourth pitch wasn't so good: a change-up that came in right over the heart of the plate. They were lucky the batter swung early and popped it up just in front of home. The ball spun in the air for what seemed like an eternity while Casey ripped off his mask and charged towards it, but he wasn't quick enough. The ball landed in the grass, fair, and this time there was no interference call to save him. Once Casey caught up with it, he scooped up the ball barehanded and flung it to first. It was a laser beam right into Thompson's mitt, but the ump had already swung his hands out to call the runner safe.

"And the Mammoths leadoff hitter reaches base in the bottom of the ninth, with his team down two runs in Game Seven of the Globe Series," said Jack. "The single turns the lineup over and brings Vazquez to the plate. He's three-for-four tonight with a double."

"The top of the lineup has done most of the damage tonight against the Blue Birds. With Brown on base, you have to think the Mammoths are going to try to run here."

"Here's the pickoff! And he's safe. The Blue Birds must be thinking the same thing you are, Zack. Thompson sends the ball back to Bigwood, who looks over his shoulder and gets set, the pitch out of the stretch. Brown is off, and he's safe with the head-first slide."

"Casey made it close on the throw. With that big strong arm of his he can put a lot of mustard on that ball. StatMan says ninety-seven miles per hour on a rope. What an effort."

"And now there's a man at second with none out in the bottom of the ninth of the Globe Series. The count is 0-and-one. Casey changes up the signs, worried the runner on second might tip off the batter. The pitch, a change up for a ball. 0-and-two."

Next, Casey called for the curveball, hoping for the punchout, but it bounced in the dirt for ball one. He went right back to the breaking pitch on 1-2, but again Vazquez didn't offer at it and now the count was even.

Meanwhile, the fans were stomping, catcalling and scream-ing, making as much noise as they could. The dome amplified the sound to a deafening roar. Casey could hardly put two thoughts together, let alone strategize for the next pitch, so he didn't. He just put down his index finger.

In came the fastball. It was a few inches closer to the middle of the plate than Casey would have liked, but Vazquez liked it a whole lot. He liked it so much he took a great big swing and drove a low liner into no-man's land in shallow right field. Nuñez swooped in and fired a rocket to home plate.

"Here comes Brown with the slide... and he's safe! Casey quickly throws the ball to second base and... safe. Now the tying run is standing on second."

"And the lead-taking run is in the batter's box. I have to say, that was a heads-up play by Casey to get that ball to second in a hurry."

"Yeah, but I do wonder what went on there with that play. They had a base open at first and Vazquez has been one of the Mammoths' best hitters this series. I'd rather walk him than have him burn me with the bat."

The fans were in hysterics now. Many began tearing up their tickets and programs and tossing them into the air. Paper drifted down onto the field like snow and began accumulating on the turf. The grounds crew ran out to sweep up as much as they could. Meanwhile, a chant started up in the crowd—*"Rear-don."* Clap. Clap. Clap. *"Rear-don."* Clap. Clap. Clap.—and beer cans began to rain down. At first, they were nothing but a few black dots against the white field of the stadium lighting, before float-ing down from the fifth deck and crashing to the turf with sudden and unexpected force. Soon enough they were pummel-ing the ground in a tinny sticatto, sending players, umpires, league officials, police officers and the grounds crew scrambling for the safety of the dugouts.

Once the fans ran out of beverages, they began to throw what remained: hats, jerseys, big foam fingers, towels, and the like. The stadium announcer pleaded with the crowd to stop, then threatenened them with forfeiture of the game. A line of police officers in riot gear filed out of the dugout tunnels and waded into the crowd to apprehend those who had yet to cease their disruption.

Even after the crowd was subdued, it took the grounds crew almost ten minutes to sufficiently clear the field for the resumption of play. During the break, the chant continued uninterrupted.

"Rear-don." Clap. Clap. Clap. "Rear-don." Clap. Clap. Clap.

"It appears Lou has seen enough, as he steps out of the dugout and calls for the southpaw out of the bullpen."

Cheers went up as the bullpen gate opened and out came Reardon, walking toward the mound in giant strides, the blue thirteen glowing on his back.

The noise from where Casey, Lou, and Reardon stood on the mound was deafening, so they had to lean in close to make themselves heard. Lou plopped the ball into Reardon's mitt and yelled, "There you go, you sonofabitch."

"Thought you were done with me, huh?" said Reardon as Lou started walking back to the home dugout.

Lou turned around and approached the rubber.

"You know something, Reardon? I wish there wasn't all these people here so I could knock all those teeth out of your kisser, blend them up into a goddamned milkshake, and feed 'em back to you through a straw, but we ain't that fuckin' fortunate, are we? I don't know if you've gone and made a deal with the devil or what, but for whatever reason the universe seems to be compelling me to put you in this ball game, so here we are. But Reardon, I swear to God, if you blow this for me, I'll make sure you never eat another solid meal again."

"You oughta be thanking me, Lou," said Reardon.

"Yeah? And why's that? You going to share your winnings with me?"

"No," said Reardon, spitting tobacco into the dirt. "You've just won yourself the Globe Series."

Lou shook his head.

"You cocky son of a bitch."

Casey waited until Lou was halfway to the dugout before he turned to Reardon and said, "He's going to be disappointed." He glanced back at home plate. "I guess we ought to get this over with."

Reardon grabbed Casey by the arm, leaned in and said, "You know something? I've been anticipating this moment. I've played it over and over in my mind, and every fucking time I've imagined this scenario, I've come out here and stepped on the mound, fed them one right down the middle, and they've gone and cranked it for a home run. That's how I thought I'd like it to happen: have it ripped off like a bandage and put a quick end to the whole thing. Relatively painless, right? Get the next two batters out and call it a night."

"If you say so," said Casey, yanking his arm away.

"By now you'd think I'd be able to just come on in here and do it."

"What the fuck are you talking about?"

"I'm saying I thought it would be easy, but now that I'm here, with all these people losing their shit, I'm finding it hard not to get a little excited."

Casey leaned in close. "Are you saying you want to win this thing? Quit fucking around, man."

The umpire tapped Casey on the shoulder. Startled, Casey wheeled around, fearing he had given something away, but if the umpire had heard anything he didn't let on. He just stood there with a look on his face that said *let's get this shit show on the road* as he pointed at Baba waiting in the batter's box. "Have you got it figured out yet?" he asked.

Reardon didn't bother throwing any warm-up pitches and his first pitch was a rocket that nailed the target Casey had set up on the inner half. Baba jumped back to avoid getting hit by the pitch, which nipped the corner of the plate. When it smacked the palm of Casey's glove, his hand felt like it had broken in six places, but he held on to it.

"I'll can tell you from experience, when a fireballer knocks it off the palm of your glove like that—it hurts," said Rodriguez.

"Yeah, but back in our day you didn't have anybody throwing one hundred and seven miles per hour," said Sadler.

"That certainly didn't look very good, but Casey's waving the trainers off. He's okay, so play will resume."

Casey sent the ball back to the mound and glanced up at the 200-level ticker. The number he saw explained why his hand hurt so bad. When he returned his attention to the mound, Reardon was standing in the stretch, waiting for Casey to present a target.

The next pitch looked like a fastball when it came out of Reardon's hand, but when it was halfway to home plate Casey picked up the spin and got ready for the break. Baba took a big hack, and missed.

"Stee-rike two."

Now the crowd was on its feet, clapping frantically and rhythmlessly, a buzzing wall of sound. Reardon got set and made his pitch. The ball started off way to the outside corner, but this time Casey picked it up right out of Reardon's hand—the tight rifle-spin—a slider that cut across the strike zone to catch the inside edge of the plate.

"You're out!"

The fans erupted as Baba walked back towards the San Francisco dugout shaking his head. Next up was McTeague, who spat in the dirt and cast an almost frightened glance at the still roaring crowd before stepping into the batter's box.

"In case you're just joining us," said Sadler, "we're in the top of the ninth with one out and a man on second. The Birds entered the inning with a two-run lead, but for some reason opted to send out Bigwood to close out the game. He promptly coughed up a run, which cut the Birds lead down to one."

"You know, he hasn't been on his A-game this playoff series, but I think Reardon's still the guy you want here in these big game situations," said Sadler.

"McTeague steps to the plate. He doesn't have a hit in eight regular season at-bats against the man on the mound, but that record somehow hasn't seemed to matter in these playoffs. He's two-for-two against the closer in this series with a home run—a two-run shot that shut the door on Game Three—and a double. Reardon gets set to pitch, winds up, fires."

This time Reardon threw a changeup that hung in the upper half of the strike zone, begging to be crushed for extra bases. McTeague swung and the ball cracked off his bat so loud that Casey thought for a second that it had left the park, but the ball towered up towards the rafters in a narrow parabola right into Steele's awaiting mitt.

"Not a great looking pitch there, but it got the job done," said Sadler.

"And that brings to the plate what may be the last batter of this Globe Series. Zapatista has been a huge contributor for his team all series long."

"He's been real good with runners in scoring position this postseason, including a two-run triple in game two that gave his team the lead in what would ultimately be a losing effort. He's the type of big, strong batter that leaves most pitchers shaking in their boots."

Vazquez took his lead at second. The Mammoths were probably hoping to get into Reardon's head by taking a few extra meaningless feet, but he didn't even cast Vazquez a glance. Instead, he a spat a brown wad of tobacco to the turf and toed the rubber. He fired a pitch home, a curveball that caromed off the plate and might have got past Casey on the bounce had he not leapt to block it with his chest protector. The runner at second, seeing the ball hit the dirt, had taken off, and now Casey came up with the ball, throwing. Vazquez dove back to second, but Casey had fired a laser right at the bag where Manny was waiting with an open glove. It looked like he had applied the tag before Vazquez had got back to the base, but the umpire called him safe.

The crowd really didn't like that. They were so worked up that Casey was afraid they might start tearing the seats out of the concrete and chucking them onto the field. Bird players came out of the dugout and implored the fans to calm down. Finally, Reardon held a finger to his lips and managed to quell the crowd. Players returned to their positions, the closer got set again, threw a bullet home, and got himself a strike.

Casey called for a time-out and jogged out to meet Reardon on the mound.

"What's the hold up, kid?" said Reardon from behind his glove. "I thought I told you I wanted to get this win."

"I can't let you do this."

"Do what?"

"Don't act stupid. You know what I'm talking about. It ain't worth it. Just give him a pitch to hit."

"Nobody's going to buy that old gag when I've been throwing high heat the last two batters. The way I see it, we gotta make the last out sooner or later. Besides, who's to say yous guys won't take it back in the bottom half, even if I cough up the lead?"

"Well then put it out of reach," said Casey, spitting into the dirt.

"Rear-don! Rear-don! Rear-don!"

"You hear that?" asked Reardon.

"Ya, but—"

"You know something, kid? I've had a good long run, or at least longer'n most, and certainly longer than I really ought to've had," said Reardon, looking down at the ball. "And besides, I can't exactly go down looking like the guy who lost Toronto the Globe Series, now can I?"

"Reardon—"

"So long, brother," said Reardon, shoving Casey off the mound. He stumbled back so hard he might have fallen had the umpire—who had been approaching the mound to tell them time was up—not caught him. When they reached home plate, the man in black turned to Casey and said, "Cut it out with the interruptions. Some of us got families to go home to."

"Don't worry," said Zapatista. "I'll make short work of the rest."

Casey pulled down his mask.

Reardon looked back at second. There was no secondary lead now, so he got set and threw a fastball for a strike. The second pitch: curveball, low, for a ball. Next, he threw another fastball—again for a ball.

"That brings the count full."

In the pitch came, flat as a needle and too tempting for Zapatista to lay off. Casey watched as the bat flew over the suddenly diving ball. He reached down, plucked it of the dirt, and applied the tag.

Epilogue

It wasn't until everyone had gathered for a team photo that they realized Reardon was gone. In all the craziness after the closer had recorded the final out—the families, the fans, the photographs, the interviews—Reardon had somehow managed to slink away unseen. It was strange, to say the least, but the players chalked it up as typical Reardon. Besides, champagne awaited.

It was a while before Casey was able to extract himself from the celebration. His phone said it was 2:47 AM. Cars were arranged for the players to be returned home and security was tight due to the crowds. As his driver approached the Gardiner entrance, Casey saw several overturned cars. A drunk staggered into the street, causing the driver to brake hard, throwing Casey forward against his seatbelt.

"Jesus," said Casey.

"Sorry," said the driver. "It's pretty crazy out here."

It took almost two hours for Casey to get back to the apartment, and when he arrived he found it unlocked. Stepping inside, he was greeted by the wheezing of the balcony door as it flapped in the wind. He turned on the lights, picked up the bat he kept behind the door, and knocked it against the wall. "Anybody in here?" he asked.

No answer. He searched the apartment, but found no one. The place had been gutted, just like the time of Reardon's knife injury, but this time there was no blood, and no Reardon.

Casey weighed whether to call the cops, but ultimately decided against it. Instead, he cleaned the place up, smoked some weed fresh from the freezer, and stayed up most of the night worrying and puzzling over what cruel fate had befallen his roommate.

It was nearly three in the afternoon when Casey finally woke up. There was still no sign of Reardon, so he made himself some breakfast and went downstairs to check the mail. It was the usual garbage that Reardon normally threw straight into the trash—grocery store flyers, glossy cardstock advertizements for high-end real estate. There was, however, one white envelope with no address. It bulged in the middle and Casey could hear the clink of metal as he extracted it from the mailbox.

Once he was back in the safety of the apartment, he tore open the envelope and emptied it onto the kitchen counter: a single key, on a tag branded by a storage facility in Clearwater, Florida.

The parade had been scheduled for the following day, and faced with the impossibility of making up some sort of excuse for Reardon's absence, Casey decided to report his roommate as a missing person. The police came by and asked questions, but Casey didn't mention the break in, or Lyuba, or much of anything, really. He just answered their questions as accurately as possible while denying any knowledge of anyone who might have wished to cause the closer harm. By the time the investigators left, Casey was exhausted, so he crawled back into bed and fell asleep.

Reardon's absence made some waves in sports sections and blogs the next morning, but most of the coverage was focused on the coronation of the new World Champions. It wasn't until the realization that Reardon was still missing a week later that it began making headlines.

A photo began circulating on the internet and in the newspapers: a grainy, low-light cellphone shot taken on the night of Game Seven. It was of a man much taller than the surrounding crowd, holding up the collar on his jacket, trying to mask his face. It had been posted on Sawit shortly after it was taken with the caption, "Look who I saw walking home after the game tonight." It was taken at Yonge and Dundas Square at around 11:57 PM. From there the police had been able to use CCTV footage to track Reardon to a parking garage where he got into the Beast and made his exit.

With no further evidence, the volume of articles dwindled until the media finally lost interest altogether. Lyuba's men, after a few interrogations and some light waterboarding, decided Casey didn't know anything and eventually left him alone. As the heat died down, Casey felt relief. It had been difficult, not to mention frustrating, to have to fraudulantly answer the same questions over and over as if he were holding out hope that Reardon might return imminently, when he knew they would never see Reardon again.

In November, Casey learned from his agent that the Birds had opted to renew his contract and suggested he fly down early take advantage of the team's training facilities. Casey was happy to oblige, having just moved his stuff out of Reardon's apartment and into storage.

The flight to Florida was uneventful, and Casey waited for the other passengers to disembark before exiting the plane. The one good thing about being the last passenger to leave the airport was that the rush had mostly disappated and it was easy to find a cab. The driver popped the trunk and Casey tossed in his suitcase, slamming the lid shut before settling into the back seat.

"Where to?" asked the driver, turning around with a grin.

It was Andres. Casey reached for the door handle and tried to get out, but the door was locked.

"Relax, man. Relax. No funny business this time. I'll just take you where you need to go."

"I think I'd better get out."

"Come on, man. I fuck with you one time and you're going to hold it against me? You can't take a joke or what?"

After some debate, Casey finally relented and told the driver the address of the apartment he was renting for the winter. Andres was true to his word, speeding only slightly in ferrying Casey to his destination.

Upon arrival, Casey squinted at the meter as he took out his credit card.

"Don't worry about it," said Andres, waving the card away. "We're even."

"You sure?"

"Yes. Absolutely."

Casey thanked the driver, then paused as he reached for the door.

"You know, I heard what happened to Reardon," said Andres. "It's too bad."

"I guess," said Casey. "He's probably out there somewhere."

"Yeah? Well, if you see him, tell him to come see Andres," said the driver, spitting out the open window. "Son of a bitch still owes me money."

It took a few minutes for Casey's eyes to adjust to the gloom of the storage locker. Inside were boxes containing books, tools, and some grow equipment. Aside from that there was, of course, the Beast, with its flame decals and stripped-out interior. Everything was dusty, including the air Casey presently coughed into his fist.

He peered into the car, the same black Volkswagen Golf as the one Reardon had disappeared in, with the exception of the Florida plates, the serial number and a stain Casey had made last spring when he dropped an ice cream cone on the seat— Reardon had nearly taken his head off for that. There was also a blue envelope on the driver's seat. The keys were in the ignition.

The door was unlocked, so Casey opened it and picked up the envelope. Inside he found two pieces of paper: the car's title along with a handwritten note. Glancing at the title briefly, he read the note:

hey kid,
bet by now uve probably noticd im gone. i figgerd thoz 2 mob lugs would probably ransack the place b4 comin after me so i left u a lil present where they couldnt find it. not bad, rite? well if ur readin this u kno ive split. figgered id give u this. check out the reg. all u gotta do is sign.
see u on the other side,
-r

And then, scribbled on the bottom of the page:

p.s. burn this shit after u read it

Casey cast a doubtful glance past the open door of the storage locker. That last bit would have to wait. He opened the title again. His name had been written down as the purchaser, the sale made for a mere five hundred dollars. The date of sale was October 1. Further down was Reardon's printed name and his signature. Reardon had marked in red ink where Casey was to sign.

Fishing around in the glove box, Casey located a pen and, with a trembling hand, signed his name.

Acknowledgments

The bulk of this book was written during a period of forced unemployment while I was living in California being a househusband to my wife while she completed her PhD. This, even though I was hearing advertisements for people to join my specialized field on the radio due to a labour shortage and my efforts to jump through their hoops to make it happen. Thus, I would like to thank the US Government for their unnecessarily punitive policies towards the spouses of students, and Brian Mulroney for the shit deal he got us with NAFTA. Without you, I wouldn't have had the time to sit down and teach myself how to write well enough to produce a publishable book.

I would like to thank Bailey Gardner for being an early reader of the book. Also, Anthony Tsikouras, for taking a considerable amount of time from being Dad-squared to provide me with detailed feedback and further thanks for introducing me to the beauty of the game of baseball. Further thanks to Matthew Chong for being a friend when I really needed one, there are few people as kind and generous as this guy, and everyone who's met him knows it.

Thanks to Chris Needham for taking a chance on my book and providing an opportunity to debut novelists with no credentials. If you've read this book, it's probably thanks to the publicity efforts of Nat Moore of moorehype, so thanks to him as well. I'd also like to thank Jason Lapidus for patiently putting up with my indecision while designing the cover.

Most importantly, thank you to Maria Cichosz, my best friend and soulmate, who has stuck with me through the good and the bad and led me on many adventures—sometimes kicking and screaming. Without her constant support, encouragement, and guidance I would not have been able to finish this book. There is no one I would rather share this journey with.